TAKEN BY THE BOSS

NOAH MADDIX

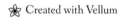 Created with Vellum

PART ONE

ONE

CHAPTER ONE: MAKSIM

In spite of the warm, glowing sun coming up over the horizon, casting a pristine glow into my bedroom, I felt nothing but darkness inside. It'd been three months since my world fell apart around me, and each day was still a new day of mourning for me. I looked at my blond hair and green eyes in the mirror every morning I walked into the bathroom, waiting for my old self to look back at me, but every day he seemed more foreign.

The man in the mirror was not Maksim Pasternak.

Waking up in St. Petersburg without any of the Petrovs in it was something that was incredibly difficult for me. The former head of the Petrov bratva family, Vladimir, was like my father, and his son, Sascha, was like my brother. I was still having nightmares of bullets sinking into their chests one right after the other—Sascha's at my own hands. Sometimes, I would have entire, hour-long dreams of copies of Vladmir and Sascha's bodies just stacked up and up until there was no room left for me to move or breathe. I'd shoot awake gasping for air and flexing my pointer finger like I was still pulling on the trigger.

It was never ending.

And then there was Katya.

The heiress to the Petrov family and Vladimir's long-dismissed daughter was engaged to be married to me. She'd let me put my ring on her finger and move her into a home I'd picked out for the both of us. I told her that I'd raise the baby she was growing in her belly as my own, and had even designed for it a whole bedroom—one that was still arranged and untouched. There were times when she would look at me and I could *almost* see her bending and about to become my wife in earnest and make me the happiest man in the world.

But then Vincent Costello came into my life.

Never had I expected that a man who lived clear across the world from me would become the villain I had to overcome, but when I blinked he was in my backyard and every step closer to me he took, I lost more and more. He took Vladimir from me. He took Sascha from me.

He laid with my fiancée while she still had my ring on and in the end, she'd chosen him over me and left for New York.

Katya Petrova, the woman I'd adored from afar for close to a decade, returned my ring to me, took a million dollars of her family's money to repay the man I hated, and left me a heartbroken, somber mess. At least she allowed me to move up to take Vladmir's seat as the head of the Petrov group, and had even allowed me the honor of changing my name from Maksim Pasternak to Maksim Petrov to maintain the family name, but what was that without any of the rest of the actual family by my side?

The only thing I really had left of the family, the matriarch Annika Petrova, was taken from me a month after Vladimir and Sascha died. Katya wanted to have a relationship with her mother, and had her relocated to New York once they had a home renovated and set up just for her. Though I played the role of the supportive family friend, I was seething inside.

How dare they take everything from me and then just leave like there was nothing else to be said? Had all my years of dedication to this family meant nothing? Did the way I was willing to bend over backwards for Katya and give her my entire life mean nothing?

I was just beginning to think that my stream of misfortune had ended. From the time when I was just a lost ten year old boy all the way up to my twenty-eighth year, it'd been nothing but one bad thing after another for me. It started when my best friend Chloe was snatched away to the United States —my only friend and the person who'd been there for me most when my mom got sick. Then after she left, my father decided he wasn't up to the task of caring for my mother and being a single dad, and he left as well.

There were days I slept on the street and ate out of garbage cans because I didn't have any other option.

And then I met Sascha.

Though I already knew him from when I first started school, we didn't form a friendship until after Chloe left and my mom got sick. Out of everyone, he was the one who noticed when things changed for me, and he was the one who ultimately saved my life.

He dragged me home to his family like a lost puppy and begged his father to help me, and boy did he ever. Vladimir, purely out of the kindness of his heart, decided to move my mom to a high end facility and start taking care of her medical bills without asking for anything in return. He bought a home for me and made sure that there were staff there at all times to care for me and make sure that I wasn't fending for myself anymore. When I wasn't at his home with Sascha, I was at my own being cared for by the staff he hired.

The Petrovs completely turned my life around.

Katya was a bright, shining light in a sea of clouds. While Sascha and Vladimir took care of me physically, Katya made me believe in the world again. Each time she smiled at me or gave me a tight squeeze whenever Sascha would bring me home from school, it made me fall more and more in love with her. She never judged me or pushed me away. She always allowed me in her space. By the time I was in middle school, half the reason I would go to the Petrovs was to see her, and she would always welcome my presence.

But Katya never saw me in a romantic light.

Perhaps I could blame it on the fact that I spent so much time with her father and brother that she started to feel like I was just another brother of hers as well. Even though I tried my very hardest to keep myself out of that specifically familial place with her, and unlike a typical brother, Sascha approved of my crush on her, she simply never got to that place.

That was okay with me though.

I didn't feel *entitled* to Katya. She was an adult who could make her own decisions. If we were to be together, I wanted her to be with me because she *wanted* to be. Vladimir had another thought in his mind though, and when I was sixteen, he invited me into his office for a conversation.

He told me that he needed someone who would follow him blindly and that he wanted me to be that person. He disapproved of how close Sascha and Katya were, and didn't believe that Katya should be involved in the business, at least not on the surface. He force-trained her in stealth and espionage and then made her use those skills to his benefit. In exchange she got no notoriety and no acknowledgement, except from her older brother Sascha.

Due to Sascha's best attempt to keep his sister from breaking, Vladimir wanted another puppet to do his dirty work, and for everything he'd done for me, I was more than willing to agree. Along with continued financial support for both me and my mother, I accepted Vladmir's request to work for him. Right before I left his office, he offered me one final thing as thanks for accepting his offer.

His daughter's hand in eventual marriage.

I really didn't want to start treating Katya like she *belonged* to me, but I'd be lying if I said I didn't start looking at her as a sign of my future. As she got older and even more beautiful, I started to buy into the idea that we would be together one day, which made me fall even more in love.

It was my fault, but I couldn't help it. She was intelligent and stunning. I wanted to marry her one day, so when she came back from New York after being kidnapped, and found herself pregnant by her kidnapper, Sascha asked me to marry her and I rapidly agreed.

Maybe that was a mistake as well.

Katya never wanted to marry me. She saw me as a safe option, and that hurt me more than anything, especially when she openly chose the more dangerous option regardless.

"Mr. Petrov?"

A knock on my office door pulled me out of my lamenting, and I was surprised to discover that I was even sitting in there at all. The last thing I remembered, I was looking at my reflection in my bathroom mirror. I'd been just going through the motions for months now, which was a problem considering the number of things that had to be taken care of in the wake of losing both the head of the family and his heir. I didn't feel like a real Petrov without another Petrov by my side, and therein lied my problem.

I needed a *real* Petrov by my side—a Petrova. I needed Katya.

Even though I was only six at the time, I was already crazy about my best friend, Chloe. We played house because we wanted that future, and when she was taken away from me, I promised myself I would never let that happen again.

Vincent Costello had taken Katya from me, but when he was dead, she'd choose me.

That meant I just had to kill him again, this time, for good.

"Come in," I said to the person who'd knocked on my door.

My office door opened, and Latva walked in, the Petrov family assistant. He'd served the family for many years, and committed himself to continue serving me after all of the rest of the Petrovs had departed Russia. Apart from Vladimir himself, there wasn't anyone living who knew more about the family than Latva, and I wanted to keep him extra close for that reason.

"Good morning, sir," Latva said. "I hope you had a restful night."

He said the same thing to me every morning, and every morning I gave him the same answer. "I didn't, but that's neither here nor there. Did you get that information I asked you for?"

"Yes, sir," Latva replied. "Vladimir had close to $3.7 billion in offshore accounts and in his personal vault, and he has an additional $500 million in properties, assets, and investments."

"Any outstanding loans that need to be paid?" I asked.

Latva nearly laughed in my face at that, but quickly corrected himself and cleared his throat. "No, sir. Vladimir didn't allow loans to get past the pay date."

"People always paid him on time?"

"Paid or lost their lives," Latva said simply. "Vladimir didn't like being owed money."

That didn't surprise me. Vladimir wasn't the kind of guy that anyone wanted to make angry. I knew well, along with his children, that Vladimir was indiscriminate with who he would take his wrath out on. I just assumed that there were still a few lingering idiots who didn't know better, but it seemed Vladimir didn't give anyone a second chance.

"I'll need a full report of all of the properties, prioritizing the things that Vladimir ran personally. Those are likely falling by the wayside in his absence, and since it took us so long to crack his information and gain access, I'm going to need to get bodies in those buildings as soon as possible to make up for the loss."

"Yes, sir."

"Were you able to set up my meeting with the manager of Dacha?" I asked.

At that, Latva reached into his pocket and pulled out a slip of paper. It had appointment information on it for the manager of the bar I owned in NYC, Dacha. It was something of a gift from Vladimir when I turned eighteen, but really, it was his way of ensuring I stayed effectively woven into his business. It wasn't that I minded though. Running Dacha had become something of a passion of mine, and it allowed the Petrov family to have extra ears in the United States at all times, which was a huge boon.

"I was, sir. Dino Sparetta is awaiting your call. I've impressed upon him the importance of being available whenever you are, so you should expect to reach him despite the time of night in New York."

"Thank you. I'll call right now." I opened up my laptop and prepared to make the call, but Latva just stood where he was. I glanced up at him, but when he still didn't move, I asked, "Did you need something else from me?

Latva seemed borderline embarrassed when I asked. "Um, no, sir. Vladimir always liked to keep me in his office so I could get him something at a moment's notice if he needed me to."

"I do not anticipate our relationship to be that formal," I told him. "I have a little more patience than the former pakhan. If I need something, I will call you with the expectation that it will take you a normal, human amount of time to provide me with it."

Taking a shaky breath in, Latva huffed out. "Really?"

This had been the atmosphere I was getting from all of Vladimir's staff, and I wasn't sure how to change it. I didn't want the staff to lack respect for me, but I didn't want them terrified of me. Then again, I'd never seen a leader in an organized crime unit that wasn't feared. Maybe I just needed to get used to it.

"Yes, really." I flicked my hand towards him, coaxing him away. "You can go. I'll let you know if I need something else."

"Understood." Latva offered an obedient bow. "Thank you, sir."

Turning his back to me, he walked out of the office and closed the doors after himself. I stared at the doors after him for a few moments, wondering if it was better for me to try and step into the void Vladimir had left behind or try and change the perception of this empire and mold it in my own image. Would it suffer if I tried to wash away Vladimir's unfettered, murderous shadow, or would I be doing worse to try and pretend I was the same tyrant he was?

Before I could fall too far down that hole, I turned my attention back to my laptop and started a video call to Dino Sparetta at Dacha. I folded my hands on top of my desk while the video call connected, and after about three rings, the feed picked up. Despite the hour in the states, Dino was dressed in a suit and seemed bright eyed and bushy tailed.

"Hello, Maksim!" Dino greeted me in English, in his thick New York accent. "It's been a long time since we've spoken, friend."

"It has. As I'm sure you've heard by now, the dynamic in the family has changed quite a bit, which has filled my plate close to shattering."

Dino's face lost all the color. "Wait. So the rumor is true? Vladimir *and* Sacha Petrov are gone?"

I returned a shallow nod with a somber expression on my face. "I'm afraid so. Vladimir made the wrong enemy and it cost us dearly."

"Is it true it was Vincent Costello?" Dino asked. "Word on the street is he's back here with Vladimir's daughter at his side. She's one of his caporegimes."

I swallowed hard as I digested that information. Katya was about five months pregnant by my calculations. She was a valuable asset to any empire, but while she was carrying their child? Just how stupid was Vincent?

"That is new information to me," I replied. "I'd also heard that she may have ended up there, but I wasn't certain after she disappeared from St. Petersburg."

This was, of course, only half true. I knew that Katya had chosen to go back to New York with Vincent, but we decided that only the three of us would know that. Learning her involvement in Vincent's ranks was new information—and not information that made me very happy.

"Well, he's walking around NYC like he owns the place, and in all honesty, he kind of does. No one can touch him. He's turned out to be even more ruthless than his old man. Everyone's on pins and needles."

"I don't want to talk about that," I barked. Just thinking about Vincent achieving success made me want to spit fire. I wanted him dead so much more than I was willing to admit. "I want to talk about how things are going with the Bonettis."

"Oh!" Dino's mood lightened significantly. "Smooth sailing so far. Stavio Bonetti is grateful for a chance to prove himself to those higher up the ladder, and the biscuits are moving like that stupid, blue anteater thing."

"He's a hedgehog," I replied, "but that's good to hear. I can arrange for another shipment to come in next week. I'll deliver it personally."

"You're coming here?" Dino said. "I don't really think that's necessary. We've got everything under control and—"

"Are you hiding something?" I cut in.

"N-no..."

"Do you have some sort of issue with me coming?"

Immediately, Dino started to sweat. "No, sir. Just don't want you to trouble yourself."

"An owner should trouble themselves every now and again. I've never gotten to see Dacha for myself and I'm interested to meet Stavio and cement our relationship."

Again, I wasn't being fully honest with Dino. Though I was invested in the nightclub and wanted to step foot in it myself, that wasn't my main reason for going to New York. Vincent was there, which meant Katya was there. Hearing that she was actually ranked in his legions meant that he was already making decisions that weren't the best for her or the baby.

I was what was best for Katya and the baby, and I was going to eliminate the problem and bring her back to St. Petersburg where she belonged.

"Prepare for my arrival," I told Dino with resonance. "I'll be arriving in three days' time."

TWO

CHAPTER TWO: CHLOE

I didn't quite understand why I was waking up in my old bedroom back in St. Petersburg. The faded yellow wallpaper and old, wooden bunk bed that my father had built for me never traveled far from my memory, but as far as I knew, they were long gone. The small two bedroom house that was just *barely* enough to fit me, my parents, my sister, and our dog Bosco, was sold along with all the furniture in it when my dad caught his latest get rich quick scheme.

He was going to uproot his family and move them to New York City in search of the "American Dream." A friend of his had *supposedly* made his millions owning a convenience store in a small, NYC neighborhood and my dad was convinced he could do the same.

The money from the sale of the house was used to purchase a small bodega in Brooklyn, New York's Brighton Beach, otherwise known as Little Odessa. It was a concentrated Russian and otherwise Eastern European neighborhood. Here, my dad believed our untapped fortune was waiting for us, so he named his new shop, Nasha Udacha—*Our Fortune*.

But he couldn't have been more wrong.

"Hey!" A tiny head popped down over the divide between the lower bunk I was in and the upper one, and I was surprised to see my baby sister, Chandler, although not the nineteen year old woman I knew her to be, but rather the little four year old that she was right before we left Russia. "Are you awake yet?"

"You're looking into my eyes aren't you?" I replied, and then I touched my hand to my throat. It was my voice in a sense, but it wasn't my *current* voice. It was prepubescent, which I supposed made some sense. If Chandler was still four, then that would make me only ten. "Do you feel weird?"

She tilted her head to the side, looking like a strange little monkey hanging upside down from the top bunk. "Weird? I'm not weird!"

"No, that's not what I mean."

I tossed back the covers and climbed out of bed, running over to stand in front of the little mirror we had with our favorite Russian cartoon character all over it. It didn't give me a full view of my body, but I didn't really need one to see that the curves I sported as an adult were gone in the interest of a perfectly plank preteen form. My lips were back to being thin and flat, as opposed to my dad's plump ones that I developed over time, and my long, dark brown, portuguese hair was gone, and back to the blond Russian locks I'd been born with that grew dark as I got older. I lifted my hand to my cheeks, wide nose, and even poked a few of my freckles, but there was no denying it.

Somehow, I'd reverted back to my ten year old self.

Chandler dropped down from the top bunk, jumping as opposed to taking the ladder like the little daredevil she was, and walked over to me. "Are you okay, Chloe? You're being weird."

"Where are we?" I asked her.

"Um..." She looked around like I was stupid. "In our bedroom."

"No, like where is this place that we are right now?"

"Our house?"

"But where is it?"

Chloe pushed her hands into her blond hair and groaned. "You're not making any sense!"

Before I could clarify my question, the door slammed open, and my mom came storming into the room. "Chandler Nikitina, did you jump off that bed again like I've told you a thousand times not to do?"

"I didn't!" Chandler lied. "Ask Chloe!"

My mom looked at me, and damn was that fierce blue gaze hard to face. My mom was a badass bombshell straight out of Portugal, but she didn't have any trouble finding that Russian grit. I could only hope that my eyes would one day carry her strength, but for now, I just didn't want to fold under pressure.

"She didn't," I lied as well. "Just jumping."

The way my mom wrinkled up her nose, I could tell that she knew I was lying. She looked from me to Chandler before hissing, "Keep your feet on the ground."

"Yes, mama," Chandler hummed back.

After that, she clapped her hands. "Come on, come on. Get dressed you two. Your dad already left and I told him we'd be along in an hour."

Chandler immediately started to jump up and down again despite what she'd just been told, but my mom didn't seem to mind. She smiled along with Chandler, clearly reveling in her excitement. My younger sister was already bolting to our dresser and fighting to pull out the drawers that were still just a *little* too heavy for her, but I was still staring at myself in the mirror. My mom came up behind me and put her hands on my shoulders. It was weird looking at her in the mirror, because she looked so much like me as an adult. It was like I was looking at my younger self *and* my older self. I just didn't know what that meant.

"You alright, Chlocumber?"

I smiled at the warm nickname I hadn't heard from my mom's warm, comforting voice in a long time. She was so excited to give her first born a name that would go along with a food so that she could call me something cutesy. Unfortunately, she ended up loving the name my dad picked out for me, Chloe, and Chloe doesn't go with a lot of foods. My dad tried to sell her on Chlover and Chloke'o Cola, before jokingly suggesting Chloroform and being removed from the nickname finding committee on threat of bodily harm. I'm told my mom tried for weeks and weeks to come up with a cute, foodie nickname for me before randomly blurting out Chloecumber, which stuck purely because of the way it made both her and my dad roar with laughter.

"Yeah, I just think I had a weird dream or something," I said. "Are we in New York?"

My mom snickered. "What? New York in the United States? Of course we aren't. We're in St. Petersburg, Russia, where we've always been."

It wasn't until that moment that my brain processed the fact that me, my sister, my mom—we were all speaking Russian. I occasionally spoke my first language with my dad and sister, but it was something we all did less and less of after moving to New York.

Had I just made all of that up in my mind?

"I think Chloe's sick, mama," Chandler said, then she jumped up, spread her arms wide, and proudly displayed her self-chosen outfit of many colors and patterns. "Tada! All ready for my first day of work."

"Ooh, um..." My mom walked over to her. "You know, layers are fashionable, but I think in this case, less is more."

Chandler pouted as my mom tailored her outfit to something a little more presentable, but she cleared up when my mom let her keep the bright, pink bow she'd affixed to her hair. "Now, you head into the bathroom and wash up. Five minutes only. Chloe's gotta get in there after you."

"Okay!"

She scuttled from the room and then my mom looked at me again. "Your turn."

"I can pick out something less chaotic than Chandler," I said. I walked over to the dresser and pulled out the drawers before stopping and suddenly feeling very lost—I had no idea what I was dressing for. "Um... why am I getting dressed again? School?"

"Well, seeing as it's the middle of the summer, you'd be a little out of place," she replied, walking over. She reached into my drawer and pulled out a comfortable pair of shorts and a t-shirt. "This is good. Nice and comfy for a long day of work."

"Work?" I scrunched up my nose. "I have a job?"

"We all do. Your father bought the bodega, remember?"

"Nasha Udacha?" I murmured.

She gasped. "How did you know that? Your father was going to surprise you girls with the name today."

At that, I just fell silent. There was no explanation for what I was currently experiencing. Even if I could be convinced that I'd somehow gone back in time, or was actually still just eleven and had dreamed up an additional fifteen years of life, that didn't explain how a bodega that had only existed in the New York I remembered was actually a shop in Russia.

Something wasn't right. "Mom, I'm scared," I admitted.

"Aw, baby." She bent down and rubbed the top of my hair. "I'm scared too. We all are. This is a new adventure but—"

"As long as we stick together, we'll make it through?"

She recoiled a bit, but smiled. "Well, you snatched the words right out of my mouth."

Of course I did, because my mom had said the exact same words to me when we opened up Nasha Udacha in NYC. "Great minds."

I was considering telling my mom about the strange experience I was having when the door to my bedroom opened again, and a little boy walked in. He had a calm, barely-there smile that still somehow expressed an exceeding amount of love, and feathery blond hair that I'd long missed. His green eyes locked into mine and then his smile got a little bigger, creating dimples in the sides of his cheeks.

"Maks," I said, almost subconsciously. "I... I can't believe it."

"What do you mean? I promised I'd be there with you for your family's big first day! I wouldn't miss it!"

My whole body was captivated by an emotion that I couldn't quite explain. Or maybe it was a collection of emotions. Relief, happiness, sadness, anger, grief, longing, and a long unfilled void. Maksim was my very best friend in the entire world. He lived just three houses down from me, and our parents were friends even before we were born. My mom and his mom had joked that as soon as one of them heard the other was pregnant, they were going to quickly get pregnant as well so that their children were the same age.

And our birthdays were only three days apart.

All of my best memories of growing up in Russia were filled with Maksim and the time that we'd spent together in that less-than-wealthy neighborhood we grew up in. He taught me how to be happy and how to have fun. He was the one who broke the rules even when I was staunchly fighting to uphold them, but we still always managed to see eye-to-eye at the end of the day.

I missed him so much, and it was so nice to see his shining face again.

Suddenly, I was unable to resist, and I bolted away from my mom and jumped at Maksim. Rather than being afraid, he welcomed me with open arms, spreading them wide. Time seemed to slow as I launched in his direction, and everything else faded from my view. For a brief, yet somehow long moment, it was just Maks and I. Reunited, or maybe we were never torn apart in this world.

I prepared myself to land against him, my heart beating at the thought of getting to hug him once again, and just as I was about to collide with him...

...my alarm went off.

Pillows and blankets fell off my bed, thankfully, because I went shortly after them thumping down to the ground. The immediate pain in my chest told me that my boobs were back and I frowned with unhappiness.

So it *was* a dream after all.

I sat up in place and looked around my small, unsatisfying studio apartment. The bland bed I'd just fallen out of and pale walls were boring compared to the colorful bedroom of my past I was in moments ago, and it made waking up there alone that much more painful. No, I had not returned to St. Petersburg, and no, I had not reunited with my long lost best friend.

And no. My mother was not still alive.

I was very much in New York City, in my too small, too expensive apartment, with very few friends to speak of, and a strain in my family that would not produce the joy and laughter the eleven year old me experienced, if only fabricated and for just a moment.

Figuring I should probably climb off the bed, I started to crawl up off the floor, when my still screaming alarm was interrupted by my equally screaming ringtone. I groaned, knowing that my alarm went off at five in the morning, which meant someone was calling me at five in the morning.

"Hello?" I grumbled out, with my phone in hand, I slumped down onto my bed and did my best to rub the sleep out of my eyes.

"Hey, kid." It was my favorite co-worker, Max Volte, otherwise known as Mitzy. He'd shown me the ropes when I first started at the department, and now he and I were working on the same organized crime task force. "Cox is out here blowing his stack that you're not at the precinct."

"It's like... five," I hummed.

"Sure," Mitzy said. "Plus a few hours."

"What?" I pulled my phone away from my hand and my stomach knotted. It wasn't five in the morning at all—it was a quarter past eight. "Oh shit! I slept through my alarm. Tell him I'm on my way!"

"You got it."

I hung up the phone and jumped up off of my bed, hissing a line of swear words as I went. I was a New York City detective and I was *never* late for work. My job meant way too much to me to be so lackadaisical with it. Being two hours late to work could be the difference between someone living and someone dying.

Some little girl from Russia losing her mom.

Like a machine with eight arms, I started multitasking my morning routine—starting a pot of coffee while brushing my teeth, rushing a shower during the time it took to brew, quickly frying up a couple of eggs and throwing on a light coat of makeup while I was waiting to turn them. I scarfed down breakfast, dumped nearly the entire pot of coffee into a massive mug, scraped a brush through my hair until the waves were at least halfway decent, then grabbed a hair tie and bolted out the door. I put my hair up and affixed my badge at a couple of red lights between me and the precinct, and I was running out of breath off the elevator a mere thirty minutes after Mitzy's call.

"You know, if you come running like that every time he complains, he's going to start to expect it."

I looked over and Mitzy had his feet up on his desk, ankles locked, and was working on a bagel topped with cream cheese. He clearly made no attempt to brush his graying, long blond hair and his blue eyes screamed of a lack of sleep. He always looked so out of place to me as a cop, because he tended to keep a long, knotted beard and his hair was a little ratty. In my personal opinion, he looked more like the men we busted versus the ones we served, which was pretty on brand for Mitzy because he worked under the table behind the scenes.

It made my relationship with him complicated, because though I absolutely adored him, I lost respect for him knowing he worked for the very men we sought to take down.

The ones who took my mom from me.

"I get it," I replied to him. "But I'm the one who's late for work, so I rushed more for me than for him."

He snorted. "Yeah. I'm sure he'll see it that way."

Ignoring Mitzy after that, I walked through the Organized Crime Unit, otherwise known as the OCU, and into the office of Captain Herman Cox, my boss and grade A jackass. He was honestly part of the reason my relationship with Mitzy was so strange. Mitzy was a knockout—a wonderful husband, an excellent dad, a hard worker and an all around great guy—but he continued to make this one bad decision, versus Captain Cox who was one of the worst people I'd ever known in my life, but he was as committed to dismantling organized crime in NYC as anyone.

Who should I hold more respect for?

"Captain," I huffed as I walked in. "I'm so sorry. I slept through my alarm. Weird dreams and I think I—"

He held up his hand. "I don't care."

Though my lips were still open, I closed them and bit the inside of my cheek. Det. Cox looked like the kind of guy you would see slacking off on a construction site instead of heading a unit for New York's finest. He had a pot belly and push broom mustache with a pair of beady, gray eyes. His ruddy cheeks and crow's feet hid what might have been a halfway handsome man at one time, but between his permanent scowl and the passage of time taking its toll, that man was long gone.

"Is there anything you'd like me to get to right away? Otherwise I do have some backlogged cases to complete some paperwork on," I said.

"Paperwork can wait. Close the door." Furrowing my brow, I turned around and closed the door, then sat down in one of the chairs facing his desk. He folded his hands in front of his face and looked at me with an eerily serious expression. "I received a tip last night from a notable source, and if it's true, things are going to start to get crazy for us. I need you on your A-game."

"What tip?" I asked.

"According to my source, there's a crime boss from Russia headed here, potentially to settle a score with Vincent Costello."

"What crime boss?"

He took a sharp breath in and blew it out his nose, rustling his mustache. "Vladimir Petrov."

THREE

CHAPTER THREE: MAKSIM

Even though I was frustrated about it at first, when I heard that the word on the street was that Vladimir Petrov was coming, and not me, I realized it was a blessing in disguise. It meant that, A: most people in NYC didn't know yet that Vladimir Petrov had died and, B: hopefully people would be operating the way that they would be if *he* was coming, and not his no-name predecessor who got his role because he was the only one left.

Of course, there were cons to the pros. The fact that there was already a rumor about Vladimir coming back to New York meant that Vincent and Katya would know I was coming. They, of course, *did* know that Vladimir was dead, and if not Vincent, Katya was definitely smart enough to know that meant I was en route. It took away my element of surprise and put me in a rather precarious position for moving about New York without being noticed at all. The only true hopes I had were that no one outside of Dacha really knew my face, apart from Vincent, Katya, and Mario in the Costello empire, and Katya and Vincent hopefully believed we were still on good terms.

Though I doubted the latter would last for very long.

"Please return to your seats and fasten your seatbelts. We will soon begin our descent into New York City and will have you on the ground in about twenty minutes."

I looked up from my huge sleeper seat where I'd been the entire flight and saw the rest of Vladimir's—my—men skittering around to get back to their seats. I was smart enough not to come to the states on my own, although grabbing the reins of Vladimir's legacy was still proving to be an awkward and difficult task for me. Even though the Petrovs had made sure I wanted for nothing as I was growing up, I personally had no money. I still had to be frugal with how I spent any money I had, and even once Vladimir started paying me for my work, it was meager compared to what the family had.

Most of the money I received, I threw into a savings account in case I ever found myself without the Petrov's help, and used it intermittently to make it seem like I was wealthier than I was. And of course, my savings took a huge hit when I bought Katya a massive engagement ring and a home for her and the baby we were planning to raise together.

Those things weren't losses, though. We would still use them as intended.

Upset that Vladimir and Sascha were gone, though I was, with Katya and Annika moving to New York to live under the Costello's umbrella, it meant that I'd, quite literally, become an overnight billionaire. Not having to only eat at discount, fast food places, or buy the cheapest clothes was still taking some getting used to.

And that was on top of all of the assets of the Petrovs that I'd inherited, including their multi-million dollar home which I was liquidating and selling for an unbelievable profit, as well as the private jet I was on now. The pilot, flight crew, and even the fueling company had all been lifetime paid so that the jet could be used on a moment's notice.

Lifetime paid.

I didn't even know that lifetime payment was a thing that existed.

Vladimir had an airtight contact with each of the properties ensuring that, should any of them come to an expected or untimely demise or are unable to fulfill their duties, there must be a successor in line to continue the job, who would of course inherit the lifetime payments. The text read like a good businessman's playbook, and the subtext read like a pakhan who knew he'd be killing some pilots and flight crew in his lifetime.

"Boss," Brusch, one of the higher men I'd brought with me, said. "Will you be heading straight to the club when we touch down?"

"Yes," I replied. "The penthouse is being prepared for me."

He nodded respectfully. "Of course. I'll prepare transport."

As he was turning to leave, I remembered something else I needed and called out, "Oh, Brusch." I reached out and grabbed his arm and he jumped so hard, he slammed into one of the seats. "Whoa."

"Sorry," he said, ducking his head *very* low. "Did I forget something?"

The way people jumped when I so much as spoke to them bothered me. Maybe I liked the way people respected the Petrov name, but having everyone within arm's reach of me be terrified of me was taxing. I had no plans to kill anyone, at least not anyone on my side of the table. I really just wanted them all to relax a little bit.

"No. You're fine, don't worry. I just remembered that I need to make sure Dino Sparetta is there to meet me when I get to the penthouse. It's very important. Please make sure it gets done," I explained.

"Of course, sir. I'll get on that right away."

"Okay." Then I released his arm and brushed the area where I'd wrinkled his jacket. "And calm down a bit, will ya? You're all doing a great job. I'm not dumping anyone into the ocean."

A little wave of relief crossed Brusch's face before he quickly wiped it back to neutral. "Of course, sir."

I dragged my hands across my eyes in irritation, but dropped the matter for the time being. As much as I hated Vincent Costello, there was something about the relationship that he had with his right hand man that I admired. That was how I wanted to lead. Not through fear, but through loyalty. What I didn't know was if that was beyond me because I was standing in Vladimir's overwhelmingly dark shadow. Was there a way to escape it, or was the only way forward to attempt to fill his shoes exactly as he filled them?

I watched out the window as New York City came into greater view, parting a sea of dark rain clouds with its skyscrapers and bright lights. Cars and people looked like swarms of ants stampeding across the city streets below and I scowled. I'd heard all of these things about New York, but personally, I'd rather get back to Russia as soon as I was able, preferably with Katya in hand. I knew that there were people who desired to escape their hometowns, but I was no such person.

St. Petersburg had always been and would always be my home. New York and the United States in general, simply wasn't for me.

That didn't mean that it wasn't a worthwhile endeavor to take a trip to the city myself. The Petrovs helmed control of a nightclub there after all, Dacha, and thanks to that, we had a budding relationship with the Costello's main rivals, the Bonetti family. Stavio Bonetti was the Bonetti don's youngest son and one of his caporegimes. Trying to prove himself to his family and work his way up the ranks, he took advantage of the void left when Vladimir's double sale was found out. There was an opening left behind by Stavio's older brother, Christian, who was the former underboss and had died to Vincent some time ago.

I'd made the deal assuming Vincent Costello was staring down the barrel of a gun. Now I had to see for myself if the Bonettis were worth working with and what benefits they could bring to my new role as pakhan of the Petrov family.

Exactly as Brusch had said, there was a limo waiting for me to get in when I touched down. I expected that more of the people I brought with me would be riding with me, but a caravan of black SUVs was lined in front of and behind the limo to escort it. I was ushered into the limo alone while the rest of my ranks divided up amongst the SUVs.

Just before shutting the door, Brusch stuck his head in and said, "Dino Sparetta said he is out of town and can't make the meeting."

That didn't make me very happy at all. "Please call Dino Sparetta and tell him that if I get to Dacha and he isn't there or on the way, he isn't going to like what happens to him... or his daughter."

The little bit of relief that had come to Brusch's face on the plane evaporated and he went right back to being terrified. "Yes, boss."

He stepped backwards and shut the door, at which time I let out a frustrated huff. I still had to lead with a reasonably strong fist. Mario knew that Vincent was that way but he wasn't terrified of him. How was I supposed to strike the balance?

Dacha was a nightclub in Little Odessa, which was known for its high concentration of Russian immigrants—both legal and illegal. Part of the reason Vladimir wanted to establish a club there specifically, where the money to be earned wasn't great, was because he was paranoid that there may be other Russian crime bosses with investments in NYC, and that those may be affecting him in St. Petersburg. With dozens of planted staff listening out every night, Vladimir siphoned information from hundreds of people who were working for other, smaller bosses in Russia, and even a few who were attempting to take Vladimir down. It wasn't well known that the Petrovs owned the place, and by the time any rival bratva members found out, it was too late.

Armed Dacha employees met my limo as it pulled up. When I got out, they flanked me on either side to lead him through the back entrance. I would make his official appearance in the club the next day, but for now, I wanted to get settled in the penthouse.

"This way, Mr. Petrov," one of the guards said, holding open the door. He dropped a key in my hand and then said, "Straight back to the elevator and then press the 'P' button for the penthouse."

"Thank you." I nodded to the guard as he passed him by, and made my way back to the elevator.

In the distance, I could hear the music thumping from the club. Multicolored lights were flashing down the hallway and *did* pique my curiosity, but I didn't allow myself to get distracted. I wanted to make my grand appearance when I was bright eyed and bushy tailed.

Besides, I had said some important business to take care of before I could proceed, and that took precedence over everything.

I took the elevator up as the guard instructed and entered the key that the guard had given me into the lock in order to get the elevator to open on the penthouse floor. When the doors slid aside, I was happy to see that the penthouse had been designed to the exact specifications I provided when I had one built above Dacha. Northwest of the elevator was a living room with two perpendicular walls of windows that looked out over the city, and immediately to the left was a kitchen, with an already stocked liquor bar, and a fresh meat and cheese platter waiting.

Down a hallway to the right of the elevator were a bedroom and an office, along with a huge bathroom with a sunken bathtub big enough to fit four people inside of it. I was the kind of guy that liked to kick back after a long day's work and enjoy a glass of whiskey while soaking. It was something I made sure my home had back in St. Petersburg, and I wanted to ensure the same was here as well.

The last room was the first I would be using in the new penthouse. It had solid, steel walls and a flat, iron floor with a grate in the middle. There were no windows and the only door was the one that led in from the hallway. When I stuck my head back out the door and pounded my hand against the steel wall inside, I was pleased to discover that I was unable to hear it from the outside at all.

It was the most important room in the entire home, and I was glad to see it was crafted exactly as I'd asked for it to be.

Just as I was setting my things down and coming back down to the living room, I heard a doorbell go off. An electronic panel that hung on the dividing wall between the living room and kitchen showed me that Dino was right on the other side of the elevator doors, looking to gain entry.

Walking over to the doors, I pressed the button to open them and smiled at my cohort on the other side. "Dino," I said, holding out my hand for a shake. "Thank you for coming."

"Of course," he said, with a notable shake to his voice and sweat already prickling at his brow. "I was on my way out of the city, but the boys called me up and said, 'Dino, you gotta get back. Boss wants you back.' So I gets my ass back, you know?"

I gave him a simple smirk. "I do. Thank you for the sacrifice. Come in. Would you like something to drink? I was going to get a glass of whiskey myself."

"Uh. N-no. I'm okay, boss. Thanks though."

"Very well. Please..." I motioned towards the living room. "Have a seat."

With a bit of hesitation, Dino walked past me and into the living room. I took my time pulling down a glass and pouring myself some whiskey over a spherical ice cube, before returning to the living room with it in hand.

"This place is *real* nice," Dino said. "I remember seeing the plans for it and knowing that it was gonna be swanky. We all been curious, but I said, 'Nah. No one goes in there, but da boss.'"

"I appreciate that. I'd have been quite unhappy if I found out someone was in here without my permission." I took a long sip of my whiskey, staring directly at Dino over the top of the glass, then I pulled it down and crossed my legs. "So tell me, how's business?"

This question seemed to pull some of the tension out of Dino's shoulders. "Business is up. Ever since the Bonettis got in here, things have been running smooth as silk. Couple o'folks claim to have seen some of the Costellos' punks sniffing around here, but we been servin' 'em drinks, makin' 'em pay, and sendin' 'em out. Everyone 'round here knows that if the Costellos get a whiff of what's going on in here, the Petrovs are gonna blow us all sky high."

I nodded at him. "Very true. I'd be quite aggrieved to discover that any of my information was getting out of here to the Costellos, especially after I've gone out of my way to make sure everyone's being treated very well here."

All of the tension shot right back into Dino's shoulders. "Y-yeah..."

"Which leads me to my next question," I said, taking another long drink of my whiskey to grow the intensity of the moment. "How exactly did the word get out that I was coming into town? As far as I knew, no one knew about that but you."

Dino was sweating bullets now. His fear that this topic may come up was evident in the way he tried to avoid meeting me and then got off the elevator looking like he'd just run a marathon, but the light conversation soothed his anxiety. It was now back, doubled, and I had no plans to ease his mind this time around.

I wanted him worried.

"L-l-look, boss, there's a real logical explanation for that," he stuttered out.

"Is there?" I swirled what was left of my whiskey around in its glass. "Tell it to me."

He started to fidget nervously, wringing his hands and darting his eyes all around. "Well, you know, I had to get the place ready for you, so I had to tell a few people that you were coming in order to help get ready. I think that maybe one of them might have spilled the beans."

"You *think* that *maybe* one of them spilled the beans?" I repeated. "Which one?"

"Well..." He swallowed hard. "I'm still trying to figure that out."

I lowered my gaze and pursed my lips. "Hmm."

"B-but I'm gonna! And as soon as I do, there's gonna be hell to pay!"

"You see, here's the problem I'm having, Dino," I started. "Either you're employing incompetent staff who don't understand the importance of keeping my comings and goings covert, or you're lying to my face and you sold off the information that I was coming in order to line your own pockets. Neither of those things are okay with me, so I'm wondering if you can tell me what you think I should do."

Dino started to sit right on the edge of the couch like he was ready to jump up and run if he needed to. "Just gimme some time to figure out who let it slip and I'll write 'em off. Don't worry."

For a long moment, I sat in silence, just watching Dino melt. It was obvious in his eyes that he knew he was staring down the barrel of a gun. The issue for me honestly was that even if it wasn't Dino, it was someone he'd spoken to, which meant he was a liability. I'd been wanting to take more direct leadership in Dacha anyway, and it had always been a problem for me that our representative at the club wasn't *technically* a representative of the Costello family.

So as much as I didn't want to lead with the same heavy hand of fear that Vladimir led with, now was the time to make a statement, so everyone knew the fact that the title of *Pakhan* changing hands had nothing to do with what they could get away with.

"Follow me, Dino. I want to show you something in one of my spare rooms."

As I stood up, Dino looked up at me with a worried gaze. "You know, boss, I really gotta go."

"No," I told him. "You'll stay. Come with me."

With another gulp, Dino stood up off the couch and followed me out of the living room and down the hallway towards the additional rooms. I opened the door to the metal-encased room and then stood back, ushering Dino inside. He wasn't a dumb guy by any means and as soon as he saw the inside of the room, he looked at me, and then looked over his shoulder again, as if he was weighing the possibilities that he could escape successfully.

"I wouldn't," I said calmly. "Dino, there's still a chance we can talk this out. Consider my moving the meeting into this room my way of... raising the stakes." I motioned for Dino to enter again, and though he was obviously reluctant to do so, he chose to trust my words and walked into the room. I entered behind him and shut the door, then I snaked my hand under my suit jacket and to the back of my waistband where I had a gun stashed. I pulled it out and looked at Dino with my eyebrow raised. "Now. Why don't we start speaking to one another a little more honestly. You know more than you've shared, and I want to know everything you know, and I want to know it now."

Even though backing away from me made little difference in the contained space, Dino tried anyway, holding up his hands defensively as he moved. "N-now, Boss. I thought that I had covered my bases using Vladimir's name instead of yours."

"So it was you?"

"A couple o'people pay real nice for information like that, you know? All the money went right back into Dacha. Well... I did take my gal out for a fancy weekend. You know, I been working so much lately... And my mom's house. I needed to pay some back mortgage on it so it didn't go into foreclosure, but everything else—"

"How much?" I asked. "And from whom?"

"Few folks," Dino explained. "One of the Costellos' soldiers, a general street gremlin who just likes to know everything, and..."

"And?"

"And the captain of the OCU, Captain Herman Cox."

"You sold out my information to a police captain?" I asked. "For how much?"

"The Costellos' soldier and the guy on the street paid me a few grand each. Captain Cox gave me about ten."

"About ten?"

"T-Ten," Dino said. "He gave me ten grand."

"So you got just shy of fifteen grand for telling people I was coming when I specifically needed you to do the opposite of that?" I asked. "So, technically, that's my money."

"Like I said, it all went back into the club."

"Except your date night and mom's mortgage," I replied, glaring at him. "Surely you would have a record of pouring the money back into the club."

"W-well no. Gotta keep stuff like that off the books."

I shrugged. "But you had to have bought things, right? A weekend out with your lover and some old mortgage from your mother's home can't have been more than five grand, so you should have ten grand worth of receipts for things you paid for around here."

"I mean... I'm not really the one who handles the books, so..."

"So we'll just go ask the accountant," I said simply. "They should know."

"Well I try to keep other people out of it, you know? More folks that know, more folks that can cause problems."

I frowned. "You certainly have a lot of excuses, Dino."

"You gotta understand, boss, I'm just trying to steer the ship. Ol' Dino's gotta get a piece of the cake too."

"Perhaps," I responded, and then I lifted my gun to point at him. "But not my piece."

Though Dino made a weak attempt to get out of the line of fire, I shot my gun, piercing the bullet straight through his forehead. His head slumped backwards, taking the weight of his body and crumpling him onto the floor. The blood and matter from his brain splattered against the metal wall behind him, and the pool of crimson liquid gathering around his head was already seeping towards the drain—the exact reason I'd had it installed.

With a sigh, I let myself out of the room and closed and locked the door behind me. I wandered back towards the living room and retrieved my phone, picking it up and calling Brusch.

"Hello, boss," Brusch said in Russian with a thick accent. "Are you ready for us to come up now?"

"Yes, it's been handled. Bring my things and supplies to clean up."

"On the way." Then he hung up the phone.

I sat back down on the couch and finished off my glass of whiskey. I was hoping that that'd be the last show of force I'd have to display, and instead I could run my new emptier with a little more finesse. But if the captain of the Organized Crime Unit knew that I was in town, or at least believed that Vladimir Petrov was, then I highly doubted that wish was going to come to fruition.

The doorbell for the elevator rang, and I stood up to let the outside parties in. Brusch and my other men climbed off the elevator, but the last person in the group wasn't someone I recognized.

"Boss," Brusch announced after sending the others off to deal with the mess of Dino. "This is Stavio Bonetti."

I reached out my hand and shook Stavio's. He was a younger looking guy, with greasy, black, slicked back hair, and a villainous goatee. "Mr. Bonetti," I said. "Come in. Let's have a little chat."

CHAPTER FOUR: CHLOE

After briefing me on what was going on, Captain Cox gathered everyone in our squad's meeting room. Mitzy and I, along with the other three members of our unit, all took seats around the table, while Captain Cox went to stand at the front of the room. He had a file in hand that was labeled 'Petrov' and had the huge projector screen down and on. There was a case file image of Vladimir Petrov on the screen, with his son and right-hand man, Sascha Petrov, just behind him.

"Alright, Judge Peci signed our warrant about twenty minutes ago and it's on its way here by way of courier. As soon as we have it in hand, we'll be headed to Dacha. This is a full scale raid. The warrant gets us in, but any wanted party in that club, we can take 'em if we can catch 'em," Cox explained.

Mitzy was sort of half leaning back in his chair, rocking it back and forth like he didn't have a care in the world. "Aren't there diplomatic immunity rules in place with this guy? He's from Russia, right?"

"Diplomatic immunity doesn't apply in this circumstance, since Vladimir Petrov committed crimes on US soil. We could negotiate with Russia for extradition if it was in the best interest of OCU and the NYPD, but we're under no obligation to do that since he broke US laws," I told Mitzy. "Trust me, the tedious relationship between America and Russia is something I've studied very closely."

"As a Russian native, I bet," Mitzy replied. "This doesn't feel like a conflict of interest?"

"Why would it? Just because we're both Russian? Vladimir Petrov is a notorious criminal all over the world. He has one of the largest body counts of any crime boss in his country or any other—he has blood up to his neck," I replied. "Believe me, I want to take down Vladimir as much as anyone else."

"That's good, because this is a once in a lifetime chance to get our hands on someone the entire world would like to see behind bars," Cox said. "I want our unit responsible for bringing in Vladimir Petrov, so please, for the love of fuck, don't screw this up. We're talking better funding, a nicer precinct, some much needed upgrades. If you guys are as ready as I am to stop sixteen or seventeen hour minimum days, then let's bring this guy in."

One of the other unit members, Gauge, raised his hand. "So, what about the fact that there was a rumor Vladimir Petrov had died? Is there any fear that this contact of yours may be luring us into a trap?"

"Trust me. He isn't," Cox responded, and said nothing else. We all waited to see if he would explain further, but he just pointed his remote at the screen and clicked, sending it to the next set of photos. These ones were more familiar to me, The Bonetti family. Right at the front was Stavio Bonetti, surrounded by a handful of his goons. "My contact has also informed me that the Petrovs are developing a relationship with the Bonettis. This warrant isn't just a chance to get our hands on Vladimir, but if we play our cards right, this could be a payload. We could walk away with Stavio Bonetti as well, and figure out exactly what illegal activities are taking place in Dacha. We've been trying to get some covert information on the place for months with no luck. I want this entire building swept from top to bottom. Find me drugs, guns, whores—anything we can stick to Vladimir or Stavio, and I'll be handing out bonuses like they're fucking lollipops."

Before Captain Cox could say anything else, there was a knock at the door, and our precinct's receptionist came walking in. She had a manila envelope in her hand and Cox cast her a huge smile.

"Sir, your—"

He didn't even let her finish. He snatched the envelope right out of her hand and then ripped into it like a kid at Christmas. He pulled out a set of papers that were unmistakable as warrants, then he unfolded them and looked them over.

The receptionist lingered, likely unsure of if she'd been dismissed or not, so I looked up at her and smiled. "Thank you, Amber. You can go."

"Thanks, Chloe," she replied, then she ducked out, ruminating under her breath as she went.

No one in the entire fifteen floor building liked Cox.

"This is it, kids," he said, slapping the pages against his hand. "Head downstairs and get geared up. We're on a truck rolling out in ten minutes."

After Cox dismissed us, the five members of the OCU stood up and walked out of the meeting room. I was the last out and cast a wayward glance at my boss. He seemed a little *too* thrilled to be doing this for my comfort level, but an asshole though he may be, he was also fiercely dedicated.

He must just be excited for the chance at such a huge win.

It wasn't until we were on the elevator on the way down to the warehouse that anyone said something, and it was another member of the unit, Sydney.

"That man is so far off his rocker I'm surprised it still rocks," she said. "Is anyone even marginally concerned that we're all gonna die in this raid?"

"That's what I'm saying!" Gauge yelped. "One second we're hearing that Vladimir Petrov is dead, and the next he's supposedly flying to New York. I mean, didn't they report it on the news that he and his son had died."

The final member, Lucas, spoke up then. "Technically, I think all reports have said that their deaths are unconfirmed. No one knows for sure that they're dead. Everything up to this point has just been a rumor."

I certainly wouldn't have put it past Vladimir to fake his own death in order to keep operating covertly. After the trouble he caused in New York with the Costellos a while back, he might have thought it was the best move to fly under the radar—way under. The thought that he might not only be alive, but be in this club we were about to raid actually scared me a little. When I was a little girl in Russia, people told stories about him like he was the boogeyman.

If Captain Cox's contact was telling the truth, I was about to come face to face with the monster I thought was hiding in my closet.

"Well, listen, I'm a proud boy in blue or whatever, but if it's obvious Cox is walking us into a bear trap, I'm out. I got kids and shit, man. I'm not about to die behind this," Gauge said.

"No one is dying," I said finally. "Even if it is a trap, we're all well trained special operatives. We know what we're doing, and we can keep one another safe. If it's obvious they're turning the tables on us, safety is our priority. We get out and regroup, but if there's a chance at this salvation, then as much as I hate to admit it, Cox is right. We gotta go for it."

"And look at it this way," Mitzy tacked on. "If it *is* a setup, the chief might wanna give Cox the boot. He already hates the program."

Though Gauge, Sydney, and Lucas all laughed at that, I didn't think it was funny. I took my job very seriously. People out there were dying every day behind these amoral people who thought they were above the law, and

Vladimir and the Petrov empire were the worst. I didn't like Cox as much as the next guy, but if this unit folded, I'd feel lost. How else could I work to get these people off the streets?

The elevator opened on the warehouse floor and I led us off. As Cox's sergeant in training, I was the commander when he wasn't around, so I tried to lead the team whenever I could. Even if it was something as simple as overseeing this team get on their bulletproof vests and strap on their guns, it was worth it to show them that I had their backs. Besides, it had been a long time since our unit got to go out and actively hunt any gang members, let alone such notorious ones.

There was no room for error.

"You good?" Mitzy asked me as I pulled on my vest.

"Of course I'm good. Why wouldn't I be?" I replied.

He crossed his arms. "You were super late this morning and now you seem distracted. You know when I asked you if this was a conflict of interest, it wasn't just because you're both Russian. Did you deal with this guy at all as a kid?"

"Not really," I said. "I heard stories, and my parents were always telling me to stay far away from anyone with his emblem on their shirt. In my mind, he was a myth—something parents told their kids to make sure they got home on time, or so they didn't wander off. It wasn't until I was much older that I realized this threat was very real." I folded over the last straps of velcro, then I turned and looked Mitzy straight in the eyes. "I think I'm the one who should be asking if this is a conflict of interest for *you*."

"Nah," he said. "My work is mostly with the Costellos, and the Petrovs and the Bonettis are both Vince's enemies. If anything, if this goes how Cox is thinking it will, this could be a huge benefit to me." He fanned out his hands in front of his face. "I can see Bora Bora already. My wife lying on the sand in some sexy-ass bikini. We'll leave the kids with her mom, but I'll throw 'em some bucks so she can take them to Chuck 'E Cheese or wherever the hell."

I just shook my head at him. "This job doesn't matter to you at all, does it?"

"Sure it does." He wrapped his arm around my shoulders, knowing that I'd long since started looking the other way at his extracurriculars. Mitzy had saved my life once and been nothing but good to me. I couldn't bring myself not to like him. "Look, we're all just pieces on a chess board, you know what I mean? The irritating thing is the board we're on has absolutely no rules at all. It's the wild west. The only way to survive is to move with the ones who make the rules. When I first graduated from the academy, it was the good ol' boys in blue, now, it's the crime syndicates. I do what I gotta do for me and mine. I would think that you of all people would get that."

I didn't like having my dedication to taking crime bosses off the street compared to Mitzy lining his wallet with dirty money. I did my job because I lost my mom to this world, he did his so he could lie on a beach in Bora Bora with his wife.

We weren't the same.

Still, that was an argument I'd had with Mitzy on more than one occasion. He didn't see things the way I did, and I didn't see things the way he did. No matter how hard we tried, we couldn't see eye-to-eye, but that never truly interfered with our relationship. He was like an older brother to me, just one I was maybe a little disappointed in from time to time.

"Well, I hope your head is in the game right now," I told him finally. "I need someone out there that I can trust."

Mitzy frowned. "Chloe, you know that regardless of which side of the fence I'm on, I'm always going to have your back. You're like family to me. That doesn't change just because our thoughts differ on this subject."

I smiled at him. "I know. I've got yours too. Never forget that."

He slapped my vest. "I know. Now, let's go kick some ass!"

Once everyone was dressed and ready to go, we all got the last of the equipment we had to gather and climbed into the van that had arrived to transport us to Dacha. Captain Cox wasn't dressed as protectively, proving that he had absolutely no intention of actually going inside. It wasn't that it surprised me—he wasn't a throw himself before the bullet kind of guy—but for all this glory he was hoping to achieve, I assumed he'd at least take a step in the place. Maybe he was planning to do it after all the bullets had flown and he knew he would be safe.

Unlike what anyone was expecting, when the van pulled up down the street from Dacha, we were surprised to see it didn't have its typical line around the block. It was a Friday night, and Dacha was the go-to club for the Russian and otherwise European community in the area, so it was strange to see it so low key.

"I don't like this, captain," I told Cox. "It feels like they know we're coming."

"I've told you already that it's not a trap. My contact is good for this. Maybe it's just a slow night." Cox turned to address the team then, saying, "Make sure your earpieces are in and on. I want communication out there. Let's not screw this up."

Although everyone was feeling reluctant about doing so, we piled out of the van and out onto the street. I led with my gun up, and crept my team up the darkened street, towards the front of the club. Dacha was a big place with a nightclub on the bottom floor, and several other things on the floors above. It had a huge, glowing, purple neon sign that made it difficult to sneak, but we weren't really trying to.

Raids typically weren't stealthy.

At the front door, there were a couple of security guards who stood up straighter at the sign of police. One of them opened his mouth, but I didn't let him get any word out before handing over a copy of the warrant for them to review.

"Start rounding 'em up," I said. "Every employee goes in cuffs until the raid is over."

"Wait, you can't do that," one of the security guards said.

Mitzy pulled a couple of cuffs from his back pocket and said, "Watch us."

Stepping through the front door of the club, my team and I were immediately assaulted with loud music, flashing lights, and a sea of people. From the outside, it almost appeared as if Dacha wasn't functional, but inside, it was very much alive. It raised the stakes for me an uncomfortable amount. The image of my mom's face popped into my mind as I considered how important it was to make sure no innocents got hurt in this raid. Maybe we wanted to try and keep our presence unknown for as long as possible, but if the Petrovs or any other unsavories were hiding behind the club goers, it put everyone in there at risk.

"What do you want to do, Nikitina?" Mitzy said from behind me, using my last name as opposed to my first. "You must be breaking out into hives with all these people in here."

"I don't want anyone hurt," I responded. "This is probably their plan. Keep the place packed, and we gotta go through these guys to get to them."

"It's not a bad one." Mitzy's voice was just barely carrying over the thump of music. "We've rounded up the guards outside and I have Gauge keeping an eye out. We're damned if we do, and damned if we don't. If we try to rush all these people out, some of the ones we're after could slip into the fray and get right past us. Thanks to our lack of any sort of backup, we're obviously outnumbered."

He wasn't wrong, it was just frustrating. "I can't imagine that, if Vladimir is here, he's out there." I nodded to the morphing waves of dancers. "He's gotta be on one of the upper floors."

"Elevators are over this way," Mitzy pointed down a hallway to the right. "Although the lack of security is certainly suspicious."

"Cover me," I told Mitzy. "Syd, Luc, you two fan out down here. As quietly as you can, start getting civilians out. Let Gauge know so he doesn't start cuffing 'em."

Sydney and Lucas crept past the front entryway and down the stairs into the club, while Mitzy and I proceeded to the right. It was a thin, decrepit looking hallway with peeling paint and a cracked cobblestone floor. Even down here, the music was muffled but loud. It was deafening, save for my own heartbeat which was managing to carry through my ears louder than anything else.

The farther we moved down the hallway, I started to get more and more nervous. Confident, though I was, I didn't think I would ever come face-to-face with Vladimir Petrov, especially not in a situation where it felt like he might have the upperhand.

"You're right about the lack of security," I said. "If this is access to the upper levels, someone would be here. Probably multiple people. Stay close, okay?" I stopped talking and only the bass filled music made its way back to my ears. "Mitz?" I looked over my shoulder and froze.

Mitzy wasn't there.

Suddenly, it was as if everything was miles away. The hallway was so dimly lit that I could no longer see the front entrance, and the music sounded as muffled and distant from me as ever. There were a few different doors down the hallway, two of which were marked as bathrooms.

Did Mitzy just poke into one of the bathrooms to make sure no one was hiding inside?

Carefully, I pressed my hand against both of the bathroom doors and tipped them open, but they were small rooms that were easy to see around just from the door, and it didn't seem Mitzy was in there either. They didn't even look like the main bathrooms that the club goers used, but maybe employees?

Mitzy was nothing if not a man that could take care of himself. Though I doubted he would leave me without telling me, he may have just made a rushed decision to help one of the less seasoned detectives. He trusted me to look after myself the same way I trusted him, so I had to assume that even if he was in a tough spot, he could handle it. If they were already getting the jump on us, then the only way out was through.

Praying my partner and friend was okay, I continued forward, stepping one foot over the other and made no attempt to hide my gun. I kept it up, right in front of my face and ready to shoot if I had to. In a situation like the one I was in, there was only a split second between life and death.

At the end of the long hallway, it opened up into a small back room. A square space had a couple of doors that looked like it led out to the back, and then a set of silver elevator doors that I knew would take me to the higher levels.

But it was concerning that there was no one standing watch.

By now, I was certain we were walking into a trap, and I couldn't put myself or anyone else in any more danger. I decided it was best for me to turn around, locate Mitzy, and get my team out of the club. We could regroup and figure out the best way forward. Cox's attitude I could deal with, but I refused to have anyone's blood on my hands.

"Going somewhere?"

When I flipped around to walk in the other direction, there was a man right behind me. He was twice my size, both in width and height, and even when I pointed my gun up at him, he seemed totally unbothered.

"NYPD! Put your hands in the air!" I thundered at him.

"Ooh, scary," the man replied to me, then with lighting speed he whipped out his arm and knocked the gun straight out of my hand. It clattered off to the side and even though I knew I had another gun in my waistband, I didn't want to tip that it was there before I was going to have a clean shot to pull it free. "You were headed for the elevator, weren't you? You want to see the boss? I can take you up to him."

This man didn't strike me as Russian, but rather seemed like a born and bred New Yorker. When he spoke of a boss, was he talking about Vladimir, or was he referring to someone else?

"If you resist, you'll be under arrest," I warned the man. "Turn around and put your hands behind your back."

He let out a frustrated sigh. "Fine."

As I'd asked him to do, he turned his back to me and brought his wrists together behind him. The fact that I'd asked him to do that and was now shocked that he actually had wasn't missed on me. A lot of these guys thought they were above the law, so I told myself that he just expected that nothing I tried to pin to him would actually stick.

I slipped a pair of handcuffs out of my back pocket, along with the gun I had hidden there. I opened the latching on the cuffs and stepped forward. My hands were actually shaking as I reached forward, and I was right to be nervous. As soon as my hand touched his, he reached around and took my wrist between his sausage fingers. He yanked me around so he could look down at me and shook his head like he was a disappointed dad.

"Are you trusting?" he said. "The boss wants to see you."

My team was so small that I now knew it was a mistake to split up. I thought we could manage if we were catching them by surprise, but the second we suspected it was a setup, we should have stuck together. I felt stupid for making such a mistake. I relied too much on Cox's confidence that it wasn't a trap and had put myself and my team in a bad situation.

"I'll come with you as long as you let the rest of my team be allowed to leave," I replied. "If you have any of them hosed up, let them out."

The guy studied me for a minute then he lifted the lapel of his coat to his mouth and said, "Release the others."

After a few seconds I heard a quiet voice scratch back, "Yes, boss."

"Now, you and I both know that I didn't have to do that," he said. "It's not as if you have any bargaining chips here, but I'm not an unreasonable guy. I suspect that means that we won't get any trouble out of you."

I nodded. "Don't worry about me."

He muscled my second gun out of my hand, then pulled me by the wrist and dragged me over to the elevator. My stomach started to knot up. There wasn't really any indicator that I was going to come out of this situation alive, but if I could at least save my team, it was worth it.

After pressing the button, the elevator responded immediately, the doors sliding open to a totally steel box that looked more industrial than for casual human use. The man stepped in, dragging me with him, and then pressed a button marked 'P.' The doors slammed closed, causing me to jump a little, and then it lurched to life. We rode in total silence as the elevator climbed. I watched as the buttons lit up past the second, third, and fourth floors, wondering what was on them, and then eventually it came to a stop with the P-button lit up.

But the doors didn't open.

"Why don't you do the honors?" my captor said, pointing at a button above the floor numbers that I had clocked, but was unsure of what it was for. "Let's let him know we're here."

Nervously, I reached forward and pressed the button, hearing as it caused a ringing on the other side of the elevator doors. Footsteps followed the ding and I suddenly felt like I was going to be sick. A man who'd haunted my nightmares since I was a little girl was right on the other side of that door, and for all the times I thought he might be the one to kill me as a child, as an adult, I'd convinced myself it was just a silly, childhood fear.

Maybe he would be the one who killed me.

Finally, the doors opened and a man appeared on the other side—but it wasn't Vladimir. This man was much younger, much better looking, and had a hint of familiarity that I couldn't shake off. He had blond hair that was shaven down on the sides and feathery and swept back on the top, with a five o'clock shadow, and bright green eyes. The way he looked at me covered me with a layer of chills, like I'd looked into the eyes recently.

Then it hit me—I had looked into those eyes recently... in my dream.

"Oh my god," I whispered. "Maks?"

The cocky smile that he had when the doors slid open, almost immediately faded out. He looked me up and down, and when his eyes came back to my face, it was with a light of recognition.

"Chloe?" he said softly. "Is that you?"

FIVE

CHAPTER FIVE: MAKSIM

"Leave her and everyone get out," I thundered at all of my men.

They exchanged curious looks, and the Dacha employee that had Chloe kept a firm grip on her as he took a couple of steps into the penthouse. He looked at Brusch, who walked over to me and leaned in. "Uh, is everything okay, boss?"

I turned and glared at him. "Did I say something in a language you didn't understand?"

He seemed taken aback by the harshness in my voice, but gave me an obedient nod. "No, sir." He looked to the guy who had Chloe snatched up and said, "Release her."

The man gave both Brusch and I a strange look, which pissed me off. I had my gun in my hand, though down at my side, so I walked up to the guy and lifted it, pointing it at his head. "You've got only about ten more seconds of not responding to my commands before I start to get really angry." It was clear from the look on his face that he was irritated, but he swallowed hard and eventually let Chloe go. All of the men I'd brought with me and a handful of those who worked in Dacha under the late Dino, were scattered around the penthouse. I held my gun up and repeated again, "Everyone get out."

If I wasn't so thrown off by the circumstance I'd found myself in suddenly, I'd be amused by all the stacked men cramming themselves into the elevator. Brusch was the final one in and had to back himself flush against the nearest person to him and still barely fit. Still, they stood there as the door closed and eventually whirred to life to carry them back down to the lower floors.

Then I turned and looked at the woman they'd dropped at my feet. A cop, yes, but it was the person under the uniform that I was far more interested in. Her long brown hair was pulled up into a ponytail and she had sky blue eyes that rocked me with recognition. Her lips were full, they always had been, but she certainly didn't have the curves she was sporting the last time I saw her. She was blond as a little girl, but the smattering of freckles across her nose and cheeks were proof positive that I was looking at who I thought I was.

It was Chloe Nikitina, my first friend ever, and definitely my first crush.

How in the hell did the daughter of a small-minded Russian man end up heading a unit for the NYPD?

"Chloe?" I said again. "I... I don't believe it's you."

She looked back at me with a defensiveness about her, though the same level of disbelief. "I don't understand," she said. "What are you doing here? Where is Vladimir Petrov?"

I crossed my arms, torn between what I would tell Chloe as a long-lost friend, and what I would hold back from a police officer, whether they were Russian or American.

"Vladimir Petrov is dead," I responded coolly. "I am his replacement. I've even taken on his last name. I'm now Maksim Petrov."

All of the natural color drained from Chloe's face, leaving her wide-eyed and pale-skinned. Her lips carved a hard line across her face and her eyes narrowed at me as if she didn't believe the words that had just come out of my mouth.

"That sounds like a lie. All of it," she said. "You were a good person. You'd never work for someone murderous like that."

"While I understand your disbelief, I have nothing to soothe your shock," I retorted. "Not long after you left, Vladimir took me under his wing and cared for me as if I was his own. When he and his son both died, not too long ago, I was given the honor of taking on his family's name and carrying on his legacy. That is why I'm here."

Chloe took a step back from me, giving me an even better view of her full form. Even with most of what she had hidden within her police uniform, it was clear that she'd grown into a modelesque figure. She had thick thighs that lent themselves well to her round hips and full backside, and a slim, though not overly so, waist that pinched in before swooping out to her full c-cup or possibly d-cup sized breasts. Her neck was long and I could imagine myself sinking my teeth into it.

Time had been good to my old friend.

In different circumstances, it might have been nice to get a drink or maybe even some dinner and catch up properly. I'd like to hear about how her family is doing, or how she found her way to her current job. We wouldn't be given such a blessing. The way we'd crossed paths was poisoned and much worse.

"I don't understand how you could do something so heinous," Chloe whined. "Men like Vladimir have killed hundreds of people. Have... You haven't... right?"

In the back of my mind, I considered my most recent kill, whose blood was still splattered on the walls of a room not twenty feet from us until just a couple of hours ago. "Of course not. I'm not a monster."

She seemed to register a little bit of relief, but stayed high on alert. "My team is outside," she said quietly. "Once they realize I'm gone, they're not going to stop until they get in here."

I crossed my arms, intrigued by the statement—almost a warning versus a threat. "Are you that concerned about me?"

"As much as I don't agree with your choices, I'd like not to be the reason you go to prison here," she replied. "If you let me go and leave the country, we can avoid further issues."

Chloe may have been my oldest friend, sure, but she was most importantly a cop—one I was probably destined to cross paths with more than once while I was in the states. Part of me wondered if I could be successful in steering her off that path. I could keep her in my back pocket as a contact within the force and maybe the two of us could even do some "reconnecting" in the process, but then Katya's smile flashed across my brain. She was the one I was there to get. We had a whole life we needed to get back to, and I wasn't settling for anything other than that. Maybe if Chloe and I hadn't been snatched apart, things could have been different, but Katya Petrova was the only woman I was interested in. I couldn't let myself get distracted by a passing interest.

So where did that put me with the woman standing in front of me?

I couldn't just let her go. It was clear by her reactions that she took her job very seriously, and whether or not she still considered me a friend, that job was going to cause problems between us. She wanted me to leave, but there were things I had to take care of before I could go, and I had no idea how long those things were going to take. If I let Chloe leave, my plans would be interfered with by the NYPD at every turn and that simply wouldn't work.

Still, I couldn't kill her. Well... I could, but I didn't want to. Just like she was willing to turn a blind eye to me to keep from having to arrest me, I wanted to do the same to keep from having to kill her. If I didn't kill her, though, and I couldn't just let her walk out of there, what other option was there?

"I'm afraid we have a bit of a problem," I said simply. "You see, I'm in

New York for a very specific reason. Vladimir's daughter, Katya, has been taken by Vincent Costello. After a series of unfortunate circumstances, she found herself in his clutches and I'm here to retrieve her and bring her back to St. Petersburg where she belongs."

"Katya Petrov?" I could see Chloe searching her brain, when she looked at me with a now suspicious gaze. "There has been a Katya in Vincent's ranks recently as one of his caporegimes. I had no idea that she was Katya Petrova. It doesn't seem like she's serving him unwillingly."

"That's the ploy," I told her. "He's threatening her and her unborn child to convince her to serve him without question. She's in danger and needs help, Chloe. Vincent is the man responsible for killing Vladimir and Sascha Petrov. If I don't do something, she's going to live the rest of her life in fear."

My story seemed to be tugging on Chloe's heartstrings in the right way. Her eyes were wide and saddened, and she was fidgeting nervously. "If that's true, I'll look into it. We don't deal in street justice here. I can't allow that."

I frowned. For obvious reasons, I wanted things to go well between Chloe and I, but it seemed we were going to have more issues than I was hoping for. "Unfortunately, old friend, you aren't really in a position to do anything about it."

"I'm a detective with the NYPD, and a special operative in the Organized Crime Unit."

"You," I said, "are an unarmed woman standing in the secured penthouse of a Russian pakhan who isn't entirely interested in having his plans disrupted by a crusading cop with a hero complex." What little bit of warmth had found its way to Chloe's face drained out of it at the distinct change in my tone. "What do you suppose the chances are that you could get a pair of cuffs around my wrists before I could put a bullet from this gun..." I held up my magnum. "...into that pretty little head of yours?"

"I thought you said you hadn't killed before," Chloe said. "You're not a monster."

"I may have bent the truth a little."

"How little?" Chloe asked.

With long, ominous strides, I closed the distance between Chloe and I. She backed away from me until she was pressed against the closed elevator doors behind her. In the time we'd been apart, Chloe had grown to about five and a half feet, maybe a little more, but I still towered over her easily at six-foot-two. She had one hand fumbling behind her for the elevator buttons, so I reached down with my free hand and grabbed her wrist and held it in place against the wall, and used the other to lift the barrel of my gun under her chin.

"Let's just say, had you shown up a couple of hours sooner, you would have crossed paths with another deceased who made the mistake of ratting out my visit. The man who told your captain that I'd be coming? He's now in several pieces being driven to the far reaches of New York and beyond." A few nervous tears started to fill Chloe's eyes, but I could see her clenching her jaw and trying to remain strong. "I don't want to have to kill you. I believe in a world where we can work together. You help me deal with Vincent Costello and save Katya Petrova, and I will leave the country quietly."

"That sounds a lot like you having your cake and eating it too," Katya grumbled.

"Perhaps. I suppose we could work out an additional benefit for you. Maybe there's a way we can make you the hero who took down Vincent Costello. That sort of thing is sure to garner you many rewards."

"*Additional?*" she huffed. "I don't think this current plan benefits me at all."

"Sure it does. You get to leave here with your life, for one, but there's something else you shouldn't forget." I leaned my head even closer to her, until her cocoa butter lotion drifted around me, making me wish our interactions didn't have to be so hostile. I'd have loved to restrain her in other ways, but in that fantasy, she'd be more than willing to oblige. "I know you, Chloe Nikitina. I know your family. How difficult do you think it would be for me to locate your parents, or your little sister? You're here in New York, they must be too, no? Maybe we should continue the reunion?"

"Stay away from my family," Chloe hissed.

"I will. As long as you help me. Information, the ability to move around without additional eyes on me, and oh... I'd quite like it if the rumor that it's Vladimir in town and not me could continue. That makes things much easier for me while I'm here."

"You *are* a monster." A tear broke loose of Chloe's eye, but it was uncertain if it was from fear or from disappointment. Either way, I couldn't be bothered. "I'll do it."

"Very well." I backed away from her, releasing her from her grip, and when she reached for the elevator buttons, I didn't stop her. She kept her back to the elevator and her eyes on me, narrowed and angry. The doors squeaked open behind her and she backed onto them, rapidly then pressing the button to shut the doors. I wasn't concerned though, I just threw on an evil smirk and as the doors slid closed, I lifted my hand to wave. "Bye, Chloe. We'll be in touch."

CHAPTER SIX: CHLOE

I actually had to sit down while the elevator traveled to try and center myself. My body was torn between being relieved that Maksim was actually alive and in the United States, sadness that he would threaten me, and fear that something was going to happen to my family.

Knowing that I had just had a gun to my face held by the most dangerous man in Russia, and arguably one of the most dangerous in NYC.

And my very first friend ever.

When the elevator doors opened on the main floor, some of the same men I'd seen up in Maksim's penthouse were waiting to receive me. They'd clearly been informed that I was meant to be let go based on the way they stood to the side so I could get to the back door, but I knew I couldn't just walk out.

"I need you to make an exchange," I told the one who looked most like a leader to me. "I'm going to protect your boss, but if I just walk out there, they'll know something is up." I took a calculated risk and pulled my spare handcuffs out of my pocket and slapped them on my wrists. "Take me out there and negotiate my life for the unit to leave anyone we've arrested up to this point. I'll take it from there." The guy I was talking to exchanged looks with some of the others standing around, and I could see them trying to decide if they should take an order from me or not. "It's not a demand, it's a request," I said. "To help your boss. I'm going to work with him, but there won't be much I can do if I get ousted."

That seemed to convince the main guy, who stepped forward and wrapped a hand around my arm. "Just so we're clear," he said. "I'm doing this because it will benefit the boss. Don't run around thinking we take any sort of orders from you."

"Of course," I replied, rolling my eyes. "I wouldn't dream of it."

With his arm on mine, the man led me out the back door with a few additional men arming him on either side. One of them, either to create a convincing illusion or simply to prove a point, pulled out a gun and pointed it straight at my head. To my surprise, many more cops appeared to have gathered, but I quickly deduced that was likely due to the fact that I and other officers had been captured. Even though the other departments were not keen to give us any aid with the raid to begin with, a cop getting captured or possibly killed made national news. If people didn't see the full support of the boys in blue, there would be a riot.

The kind that prevented police chiefs and governors from being re-elected.

Not far from the back door, I could see the van that my unit had traveled in, but none of my team was visible. It made me temporarily nervous that my group hadn't been released as Maskim said he would do, but once the other officers had eyes on me, they pulled up their guns, and a few moments later, Mitzy and Captain Cox came rushing around from the front of the building.

"Don't shoot!" I screamed. "Stand down!"

The other cops didn't seem like they were going to listen to my order, but then Mitzy stuck out his hand and barked, "You heard the woman! Stand down!"

Captain Cox nodded to signify that they could listen, and the pack of police officers slowly lowered their guns. After that, Mitzy removed his gun from his person and handed it to Cox, then with his hands up in the air, approached where I was being held.

"You alright there, Chlo?"

"I'm okay," I said, trying to make my breathing seem ragged to really sell it.

He shook his head. "I'm so sorry. They snatched me right out of the hallway." He seemed legitimately frustrated with himself. "I really fucked up."

"It's okay," I said to him. "How many of theirs do we have?"

"About fifteen," he said, and when I opened my mouth to respond, he cut me off to say, "Cox already said he's not handing over any Bonettis. We've got some of the Russians though." Mitzy rolled his eyes. "Says it's not worth the paperwork if we don't have the big gun."

I looked up at the man who had his hand on my arm. "If we can release any Petrovs, will that suffice?"

The man looked up, and I followed his gaze to where a dark figure was just barely visible in the windows above. He waved his hand and the man turned his attention back to me. "That's fine."

Mitzy backed away then, walking over to Captain Cox to quietly negotiate.

"Do you have prior experience with our boss?" the man hanging onto me asked at nearly a whisper's tone. "I've never seen him behave that way before. I can tell by your accent that you're Russian."

"If there is information your boss wishes to share with you, then I'm sure he will," I replied simply. "I'm not going to put either of our lives in danger by sharing more than I should."

In response, the man let out a strained huff, but at least seemed to accept that, and didn't ask again. We stood in silence while Mitzy and Cox spoke, then after about fifteen minutes, the rest of my team appeared from around the corner with about five men in tow. I was relieved to see that everyone at least seemed okay, but made sure not to show too much ease or comfort in my current situation.

Finally, Mitzy lined the men up, undid their handcuffs, and then he and Gauge held their guns up and pointed them forward.

"A clean exchange now," Mitzy said. "Even if you were to take down a few of ours, we've got you outnumbered four to one."

The man held up his hand and then pushed me forward, and I started out. It was so silent you could hear a pin drop as I approached my cohorts while the Petrovs returned to Dacha. They sort of parted awkwardly like I carried a disease or something so I could pass between them, then finally, we'd made it to our respective sides, earning a collective sigh of relief at the general lack of bloodshed.

"Let's do this again soon, Captain Cox," the man who'd held onto me called out.

Cox just guffawed, and the Petrovs retreated inside of Dacha. Once they were inside, the sea of law enforcement outside started to carefully but rapidly retreat.

"Come on," Mitzy said, wrapping an arm around me. "There's a bus around the corner."

"I don't need it," I demanded. "I just want to leave."

"Nikitina," Cox thundered. "Go to the ambulance. I won't tell you twice."

Frustrated, but understanding the threat in Cox's voice, I let Mitzy lead me around the corner towards the now darkened front of Dacha. Both ends of the street had been blocked off by barricades, and officers with shields were holding back curious crowds. As people started to notice the police leaving, so too did they start to dissipate, with only a few hanging around to try and fight the views of their camera phones around the barricade cops to get a shot or two of me.

"Were you hurt?" one of the EMTs at the ambulance asked.

"No," I replied. "No one even touched me."

"Okay. We'll just give you a quick check up then," he replied, then he started into his normal routine, checking my vitals, taking my blood pressure, giving me the once over for scratches—basically whatever he had to do to make it seem like he gave the police officer he was handling a thorough once over.

"What happened?" Mitzy asked.

I waited until the EMT was distracted in the ambulance to lean in and say, "It wasn't Vladimir."

"What?" Mitzy whispered. "What do you mean?"

I looked over my shoulder, and ensured that the EMT wasn't returning yet. "It was his third in command. His son's best friend... My former best friend."

Mitzy's eyes widened. "You know the guy?" I nodded weakly. "Is that why he released you?"

"I'm honestly not sure why he did," I said, and it wasn't all a lie. Even with the *deal* that Maksim and I feigned to have made, it was obviously in his best interest to kill me, but he didn't. "Maybe he felt sympathy, or maybe he truly just wanted his men free. I couldn't tell you."

"So what are you gonna do?" Mitzy asked.

I looked up at him like he'd lost his mind. "What do you mean?"

"Well, he's an old friend. He just saved your life—"

"He endangered my life and then chose not to kill me. That's notably different," I snipped back.

"Still, I know you well, and I can see the conflict in your eyes," he said. "You don't want to arrest him."

"That's where you're wrong," I contested.

"You're all set," the paramedic said, and I stood up so he could go about packing up and setting off.

"Thanks," I told him before walking side-by-side with Mitzy back towards the van and the rest of our team. "I want to take him down regardless of our past. I owe it to my mom and literally *millions* of innocent people. Does it make me happy that I have to go head up with a former friend? No. But he chose his path in life and I chose mine. If this is the way we're meant to cross paths again, then so be it."

"I wonder..."

I looked at him. "You wonder what?"

"Do you really feel like you chose this path?" Mitzy asked. "When you were a little girl, this is what you dreamed of? Do you think it's what he dreamed of?"

I opened my mouth to shoot out a response, but stopped. In all honesty, I wasn't sure how to answer that. On one hand, no, I knew that it hadn't been my nor Maks' plans to end up in the places where we were currently. When we were kids, we delighted in playing things like house, pirates, and superheroes. Maksim always wanted to play the strong protector in anything that we did. When we played house he had to be the strong dad, when we played pirates he was always the resilient pirate captain, when we were superheroes he was the leader of the gang. I didn't really mind letting him play those roles, because we didn't live in the best neighborhood and it felt good to be protected.

Maybe that was why it haunted me so much to have him threaten me the way he did.

"It's been so long since I dreamed of anything that I don't know what I wanted to be before this," I responded.

"Hmm." Mitzy furrowed his brow. "I think that's sad. You haven't dreamed of *anything?*"

"Only of ridding this city of the vicious murderers," I responded.

All Mitzy could do was shake his head. "Whoo, girl. I want more for you. You're still young. This world has so much more in it, you know? I mean what if tomorrow all the mafiosos in the world decided to just hang it up? You'd find yourself without purpose?"

"I'd be glad, because my goal would be accomplished."

"Yeah, but what would you do next?" he asked. "I've always dreamed of moving down to some warm, tropical place and owning a house on the water. Not *near* the water, but one of those house boats that floats right on top. My youngest is getting up there. My wife and I could see the kids into college then go for like Florida or Georgia or somewhere like that. She's always wanted to write her own novel, and I could start a little support group for idiot kids like I was and tell them all about how the world isn't as black and white as it seems when you're a snot nosed teenager." Then he side-eyed me. "Or apparently a mid-twenties adult woman."

I glared at him. "I know the world isn't black and white."

"I'm not sure ya do, kid." But he wrapped his arm around my shoulder and pulled me into a side hug. "But maybe this is a conversation for another day. Or one you need to have between yourself and your reflection. I'm just glad you're okay. I'll never put you in a spot like that again."

"I'll never put *you* in a spot like that again," I said. "I'm glad you're okay too." I was excited to drop the subject as we reached the rest of our team, all of whom quickly came forward to check on me. I put my hand up to reassure them that I was okay and said, "I'm so sorry. I never should have let us walk into that situation. The second we thought something fishy might be up, we should have backed out." Captain Cox was about five feet away, leaning against the van and just watching with a look of frustration on his face. "Captain, your contact set you up."

"I see that," he replied. "Don't worry, I'm planning to deal with him. He was my inside guy in exchange for my looking the other way on some charges he has. He's going to have a bad day tomorrow."

"Uh, it can't be any worse than the night he had tonight," I replied. "He's dead."

Captain Cox stood up straight. "What do you mean?"

There was only so much I could tell Captain Cox without it becoming an issue. I couldn't pretend that it actually was Vladimir because he was bound to find out that wasn't the case, and then he would immediately question why I didn't tell him that. However, I also didn't want him to know about mine and Maksim's history, not simply because I had no idea how this deal Maksim and I had made was going to pan out, but because I had virtually no idea what a man like Cox was going to do with that information.

"Vladimir Petrov is dead as rumored, as is his son, Sascha," I explained.

"Then who was inside?" Sydney asked.

"It was a man named Makism," I replied. "He says he was the next in command to take over the family after Vladimir and Sascha. He said his last name is Petrov as well, but I'm unsure of his actual relationship to them."

"I've never heard of a Maksim Petrov," Captain Cox said. "I've looked into this bratva, and no such relative has ever come up."

"I don't know what to tell you," I said. "That's who he said he was, and he also told me that he chopped your guy up into pieces and was shipping him across the country, so I doubt you violating him on tax evasion is going to hurt him much at this point."

Cox's cheek folded in as he bit it, something he frequently did when he was angry. "Get in the van. We're headed back."

My poor, battered and bruised team climbed into the van we'd taken to get to Dacha and made our way back to the precinct. The only words were the few spared to tell me how Mitzy was actually the only one of my crew snatched, and that he almost immediately regained the upper hand. Maybe if

I'd known that, I could have leveraged myself better with Maksim, but then again, maybe not. He was right when he said I wasn't in a negotiating position. But that didn't mean I was above saying whatever I had to in order to spare my life. The thing that continued to tickle my brain was the strong belief that Maksim had to know that. We'd been kids together once, weaving tall tales to get out of trouble when my ball flew through his dad's car window, or when a hole ended up in my bedroom wall from his superhero antics.

Maksim and I had one very important thing in common—we were survivors.

For that reason, I had to believe that Maksim knew the risks involved in letting me leave, but he did it anyway. Was it because he was that certain he could find and hurt my family if he wanted to? Either way, I couldn't let him get away with what he'd said or done. I told him I would work with him, but I had no intentions to do so. I'd throw him as far as I had to in order to cast a net that would snag him and possibly Vincent Costello as well. If what he said about Katya Petrova was true, I wanted to help her.

That was going to be my main reason for stringing Maksim along, no matter how dangerous that might be.

When we got back to the precinct, Cox looked at me only long enough to say, "Leave your badge and gun on my desk. You're off for three days, and you had damn well better see a counselor."

My jaw dropped. "But, captain, that's not—"

"I'm not asking, Nikitina," he barked. "If your gun and badge aren't on my desk in five minutes, you can consider yourself referred for traffic duty."

I deflated quickly as he walked away, but Mitzy saddled up next to me and slapped his hand on my back. "Consider it a paid vacation," he said. "Get some rest, figure out your next moves, and you know I'm not one to agree with the cap, but I think the counseling could be good. Think about it, huh? If you're really opposed to it, I've got a guy who'll sign off on a fake thirty minutes."

"You really don't care that you're shady as sin, do you?" I said.

He flashed me a bright smile. "Nope!" Then he reached down to my waist, snagged my gun and badge and pulled them out of reach before I could snatch them back. "Go home, Chloe. I'll check on you tomorrow."

Though I was reluctant to leave after what honestly felt like a fail of a day to me, I had no choice, and after unloading the rest of my gear, I got in my car and went home. I white-knuckled the whole way, frustrated that things had gone so poorly—on top of not getting our quarry at all, I found out my former best friend was now my enemy. It was almost like the dream I had that morning was giving me a few last warm memories of Maks before my image of him was tarnished forever.

I'd give anything to go back to that morning before I knew what I knew now.

Walking into my house, I tossed my keys to the side and only got a few feet into the door before my phone rang.

I assumed it was Mitzy already checking on me, so I answered. "Mitz, I'm home, I'm fine."

But instead, a voice both new and familiar said back, "Ah, Chloe, I'm glad I could reach you. You left in such a hurry that I didn't get a chance to get your phone number or anything. I would have even taken an email address."

"Maksim," I huffed. "How did you get my phone number?" It wasn't even my work phone, but my personal one. I glanced at the screen to see if there was a number, but it simply said, 'Private Caller.'

"I told you, Chloe, I have my ways of getting the information I need. Now that I know you're here, you're never far from me," he explained.

The feeling that left in my stomach was unsatisfying. There was a time in my life where hearing those words from him would have given me comfort, not the intense fear I was feeling now. "What do you want?"

"To catch up," he replied simply as if it should have been obvious. "I hear you've been placed on leave for a few days. Let's use one of them to go out on a little date. My treat."

I frowned. "How did you hear that I was placed on leave?"

"Some of my staff have recommended a bistro in the village. They say if I'm looking for good, home cooked food, that's the place to go. I'll send a car for you at noon. Let's spend some time catching up."

"So I'm assuming you know where I live then?" I said.

Maksim simply responded with a dark chuckle and then said, "I'll see you tomorrow, old friend," before ending the call.

SEVEN

CHAPTER SEVEN: MAKSIM

Though I was very much looking forward to my lunch with Chloe, my trip to New York was far from a leisurely vacation. I still had Vincent to deal with, and now that I'd gotten things under control both with the former rat in my ranks, and now having the police at bay, I wanted to lay eyes on Vincent, and if I was lucky, Katya as well.

Due to the fact that Vladimir had Vincent's old home blown up from the inside out, he no longer lived in the place that was known to the Petrov family. However, I wasn't totally without resources of my own to locate his new premises. I didn't want to alert Katya to my arrival in case she'd heard the rumor that her dead father was coming to town and had figured out that it was me, but there was someone else who knew that address that I could reasonably trust to keep any probing under wraps.

Annika Petrova.

I'd thought ahead and contacted the former Petrov Matriarch for Vincent's address so that I could send Katya and the baby some gifts, but unfortunately, she only had a P.O. Box. Either Vincent had thought really far ahead, or Annika still didn't understand United States addresses, maybe both. Still, what she was able to provide was enough for me to lay eyes on *someone* who knew the Costellos' current address.

Packages had to get from the P.O. Box to the house somehow. All I had to do was wait for someone to come and check that P.O. Box and then follow them back to their boss's home.

I got an early start, making sure I was at the post office well before it was scheduled to open. If Vincent was anything like Vladimir, he wasn't above paying off people for early or late access to places like that to keep them from falling into the exact trap I was setting. The problem for them, however, was that I was in the same line of work as him and had the ability to think along the same lines.

It was for that exact reason that I knew immediately when I saw an unmarked black truck with personalized plates and tinted windows outside the post office two hours before it was scheduled to open, I had a pretty good idea of where that truck may be headed.

From across the street, I watched as a postal worker wheeled a mail cart from the front door of the post office to the truck, and then the driver climbed out and started loading mail and other packages into the trunk. The driver slipped the person who'd wheeled out the cart a white envelope, and then did a scan around the area before climbing back in the truck. I waited until he was about half a mile off, and then I started to carefully follow after them.

They actually drove fairly far outside the central metropolis of NYC and out into a secluded, forested area. I was unaware that such a natural looking place existed so near one of the largest, most densely populated cities in the world, but it looked like we'd left New York all together for something more scenic and remote.

Eventually, however, I reached the point past which I could tell that if I proceeded, my presence would be questioned. The winding road was clearly the only one leading in or out of the massive estate I could see cropping up out of the trees in the distance. If I had to imagine, Vincent had the place well surveilled, and if I tried to turn off the main road someone would quickly notice that I was there.

So instead, the only thing I could think to do was pick a spot on the shoulder of the main road and pull over. It was about fifteen feet away from the turn onto the road that would lead up to the estate, though I still felt pretty noticeable. In order to try and make it convincing that I wasn't sitting there spying on the estate, I threw on my hazards and called a mechanic who was more than happy to accept a few thousand dollars to come lay under my rental and pretend he was fixing it. I sat on the side of the road with a zip-up hooded sweatshirt and the hood pulled over to hide my face.

Over the course of the next couple of hours, I watched as several people came and went from the estate, none of them with a clear purpose. I did recognize Mario leaving at one point, and thank god he didn't seem to notice me, and a couple of additional people left that looked like they were of higher importance.

My lunch date was fast approaching in just about an hour and I was beginning to think I was going to have to give up, when I finally caught a break. A four-door, Ford pickup that looked brand new came rolling out from the estate. I nearly missed it, thinking it was just another staff member leaving, when I noticed that Vincent was driving, and he had a passenger with him.

My beautiful Katya.

I paid and ran off the mechanic, nearly losing track of Vincent in how long it took to do so, but then I noticed the truck a ways down the interstate. I was grateful for the lack of a massive population in the area that made it easier to catch up. There were a few other cars on the road that I kept between us to not get caught, and I followed them back into the hub of NYC.

Eventually, they parked and got out in front of a Mexican restaurant. Vincent got out and walked around to open Katya's door, and when she got out, I actually let out a little gasp. Whereas she wasn't showing the last time I saw her, her belly was now at a full bulge in front of her. She was beyond the six month mark now and was glowing brighter than the sun. She'd cut her hair, so instead of the long waves, she had short ones that barely made it to chin length. The little bit of weight she'd put on during the pregnancy only added to her beauty, and she was wearing a maternity sundress and a pair of roman sandals like she was about to strut out onto the catwalk.

Both she and Vincent chuckled as he took her hand and they walked into the restaurant. There were clear windows in the front, and I was able to keep a close enough watch on them as they found a table and sat down. The one thing I could give Vincent was that he *did* seem to have fallen head over heels for Katya's grace, and who could blame him? The way she looked back at him though...

...that was a little more difficult to stomach.

What did he have that I didn't have? What was he offering that I couldn't offer?

That could have been us. Smiling over the table at one another like we didn't have a care in the world. Didn't she realize that I would do anything for her? She was going to marry me. She'd even followed me to my bed once. If we hadn't been interrupted by Vincent's arrival, I was certain she would have eventually come to see that we were supposed to be together. We would have found love and had the baby and been one big happy family. Her brother and father would still be alive. How did she not realize that Vincent was the reason half of her immediate family was gone? How could she smile at him like that with love, knowing the darkness he'd brought?

But then I stopped myself—this wasn't her fault.

She'd been pushed into a bad situation by her father, and then at the very edge of her sanity, Vincent took advantage of her need for love and stability. Things she never should have had to fight for, she suddenly found herself severely lacking, and in that Vincent provided it, Katya was tricked into thinking he was good for her when he wasn't.

But it was okay. That was a problem I was going to rectify. In my entire life, everything I'd ever had and cared about had been taken away from me. My parents, Vladimir, Sascha.

Chloe and my childhood.

I wouldn't allow Katya to be taken from me as well. I knew that she had the key to healing my perpetually broken spirit, and I wouldn't stop until I had it.

Having seen where Vincent lived and gotten a sense for how easily he left his home, allowing his unearned arrogance to convince him that he was always safe, I'd gathered the information I needed for now. Continuing to sit there and watch Katya bat heart eyes at Vincent was only making me progressively more angry.

And I still had a lunch date of my own to woo.

So I left the Mexican restaurant behind and set a course for the bistro where I was meeting Chloe. I took some deep even breaths and tried to put Vincent and Katya out of my mind, purely because having them on the brain would do me no good for now. I swapped out the sweater I was wearing for a nicer suit coat and tie, then I swept my fingers back through my hair and entered the bistro.

Sitting at one of the tables, with her phone in her hand despite the fact that she wasn't looking at it at all and was instead checking her surroundings nervously, was Chloe.

She was wearing a pair of tight-fitting jeans and a black blouse, and she had her hair down as opposed to up in a ponytail like it was the night before. She wasn't wearing much makeup at all, allowing me to really see the fact that she didn't need it. Chloe had a very naturally beautiful face that made her look like a model all the time. Having just come from looking at Katya, even though the Petrova princess was the only one I was interested in being with, I had to admit that, objectively, Chloe was more attractive. Maybe it was just because she was, for all intents and purposes, the first girl I ever thought was cute when I was a kid, thus defining my type, but there was something about her that made my whole body buzz with electricity.

"Good afternoon," I said as I approached the table.

She actually jumped a little, which bothered me more than I wanted to admit, but I understood, so I put it out of my mind.

Chloe didn't stand to greet me at all, which I supposed I was a little delusional to think that she would, so I sat down across from her and folded my hands on top of the table.

"Why are you doing this?" Chloe asked with a notable shake to her voice.

I frowned. "I told you. I want to catch up."

"You don't want to catch up, you want to exploit me," she spat back. "If it's all the same to you, I actually have things I *want* to do with my day, so if you could please tell me what you want, and I can be on my way."

I'd be lying if I said I never dreamed of Chloe and I reuniting after all this time. I hadn't really considered what I actually wanted from the experience, but I never imagined it would be this hostile. Of course, our chosen career paths put us in this predicament, but I didn't quite like the fact that there was such a bad feeling between me and my old friend.

"I don't want anything from you. Not at this time," I replied. "I realized that the way things went between us yesterday was a little nasty and I was legitimately hoping to smooth things over."

"Smooth things over?" Chloe said. "How? By telling me that you're no longer going to run the Petrov bratva family and are going to leave the United States and head back to Russia before it costs us both our lives?"

I tilted my head at her. "You really take this cop thing seriously? I remember when we were kids, we hated the cops."

"That's because all the cops in our neighborhood were only looking out for themselves. They were taking bribes to look the other way instead of dealing with all of those issues that made where we lived so dangerous. I don't want to be that kind of cop. I actually want to do my job. I want to protect people. You used to want that too."

I was quiet for a few moments as I considered that. When I was a kid, I used to make a big deal out of being the one to protect Chloe from all of the danger in our run-down old neighborhood. "I realized the world is too cruel for people like me to be effective in protecting," I said honestly. "I've fared much better being someone one needs to be protected from."

"The world is never so cruel that someone who truly wants to protect can't protect," she responded with a look of desperate sadness on her face.

I just shook my head. "You speak with the confidence of someone who hasn't had to deal with a whole lot of pain," I said. "I guess things have gone for you pretty well here. Climbing the ladder at the department. Your family owns a relatively successful business from what I could see. You live in a nice apartment in Manhattan. It's pretty easy to preach about how the world is good when it has always been good to you."

Chloe gave me a deep, loathing glare. "You think because you knew me fifteen years ago that you've got me all figured out?" she scoffed. "You don't actually know anything about me. You're basing all of your opinions off of, what? The little girl you used to run around with back in Russia? I'm not that girl anymore, just like you're not that boy."

"So, I'm wrong?" I asked.

She scoffed. "More than. This world has been plenty cruel to me. My father uprooted my entire family chasing some fake dream he had to own the first ever million-dollar bodega? I suppose one could say the business has had relative success, but that's only because it's the only place in all of Little Odessa that no mafioso will touch because it belongs to the father of a cop. Every other place for miles is either crooked or had their owners beat half to death and went bankrupt from medical bills. When I was sixteen years old, my drunk of a father left my sister, my mother and I to run his dumpster fire so he could shut a bar down with his stupid friends, and some no name don shot my mom in cold blood while I watched. My sister's a drug addict now and I still jump every time I hear the click of a gun. Before you go judging someone blindly, maybe don't assume that you're the only person the world has been bad to. Your life hasn't been easy, but tough, neither has anyone else's. That's no excuse for you to be a piece of shit."

That rendered me absolutely speechless. It wasn't just because, as far as I could remember, no one had spoken to me like that before, but also because I remembered how close Chloe and her mom were and it actually did break my heart to hear that the woman had died. Quinn Nikitina was a kind woman who always took care of me and treated me like her own. It was sad, unexpected news to receive.

"I had no idea your mom was killed, Chloe, I'm so sorry," I said. "Did they catch the guy?"

"No one even made a valid effort," she said. "That was why I decided to become a cop. I wanted to help at least one person not feel the way I felt. Just abandoned. And now, that guy is dead. Some larger group swallowed his up and chopped him off so he wasn't an issue. I can't even fight for her. The guy who killed her made off with our shop's two hundred dollars, and for that, she died. And then here you are, and you're one of them. The same one of those people that ruined my life, here with the nerve to tell me that I've never suffered in my life."

"I think you're probably right, but what was I supposed to do? It's not like I knew that I was going to run into you all these years later. Not that it would have made much difference. I didn't have a choice."

"You always have a choice."

"I didn't," I responded. "After you left, my mom got sicker and my dad broke down entirely. He wasn't ready to be a single father, he said, so he just left. My mom was barely catatonic on a good day. Our bills were piling up, our home was in trouble, and I was just a kid. If it hadn't been for Sascha, I wouldn't be alive right now, and neither would my mom. Vladimir paid for my mom's medical care. He put her in a private facility and hired the best doctors for her. There are days when I can actually *talk* to my mom because of him. How could I do anything other than serve in his wake after he and his son died? After all they did for me." I just shook my head. "We didn't really do much different. The world spat on you and you chose to persecute the spitter, I just decided to spit back. We both just made the choices that were best for our lives. Neither of us is doing what we would be doing if we hadn't both been fucked over."

Chloe sat back in her chair a little bit and sighed. "I hate admitting that you're right."

"I swear, Chloe, I invited you here because I don't want us to be enemies. Not after our history. There are people who would kill for the opportunity to be reunited with someone from their past. After the shit we've both been through, this has gotta be a sign, right?"

She lifted her eyebrow. "A sign of what?"

"Maybe we're supposed to get through all this pain together." I laughed. "Could you see us putting our differences aside?"

"And dating?" she said.

I shrugged a shoulder. "It's really good to see you."

Though she tried really hard not to, she cracked a smile. "You're insane."

"A little." I smiled at her. "Let's ignore what we do for a little bit, and just focus on who we are. Two people who were torn apart long before we were supposed to be. Do you think we'd be high school sweethearts or something?"

She actually seemed to be getting a little coy all of a sudden. "What? Why do you think that?"

"Because you very *obviously* had a crush on me."

Her eyes widened. "Boy. Humility is not your key personality trait, is it?"

"I had one on you too," I said. "You were the cutest girl in our whole neighborhood. Now, it seems you're the cutest girl in this neighborhood."

"Changing from threatening me with a gun to shameless flattery is a pretty good tactic, I'll admit."

"Well, good then." I flagged down a waiter after specifically asking that no wait staff visit our table until I asked them to. "Then let's enjoy some good food and talk about nicer things. Pretend as if there isn't a huge barrier between us for now."

For the next few hours, Chloe and I did just that. Though neither of us had many happy stories to tell about our families, I did get to hear about how she came to join the police academy and become a cop, and I was candid with her about my very strange and at times tenuous relationship with Vladimir and his family. I left Katya out of a majority of my story telling, because I didn't need Chloe understanding the nature of that relationship when I was trying to flirt my way into her good graces, but I did take some time to talk about how she ended up with Vincent in the first place.

"Both she and Sascha believed that Vladimir never intended to save her, but I believe he would have. However, because she honestly believed no one was ever going to save her, Vincent had the leverage he needed to convince her that he was her only real option in the world," I said. "Then, when she became pregnant by him, even after Sascha managed to take her and escape, she didn't think she had a choice but to be with him. She claims she loves him, but I know she just feels afraid of what will happen to her or her baby if she tells him no at this point."

"That's so horrible," Chloe said. "I don't approve of any of this. Not your world or Vincent's, but if there is an innocent woman *and* baby caught in the middle, I want to help."

"All I want is to bring Katya back to Russia where she belongs. After everything her family has done for me, I owe her that much. The problem is, I too fear what Vincent may do if he's left alive when I try to take Katya away from him. The only way I can think to deal with that problem is to kill him."

"I can't condone that," Chloe said. "But, if it would help Katya and keep you from falling into the United State's horrible criminal justice system, then I would be willing to do whatever it takes to arrest him and make sure he can't hurt her anymore."

"I'd prefer him dead, but if that's something you can pull off," I started and then smiled, "then I'm okay making that compromise. In the name of justice or whatever." I rolled my eyes and Chloe laughed.

"Then you'll leave the states and not come back?" she almost said it with a hint of sadness.

"You wouldn't like that?"

A little bit of color actually rose to her cheeks. "I didn't say that. I was just curious."

I didn't tease her anymore, though I could see the disappointment. It was at that exact moment that I knew, in the case of convincing Chloe that I was interested in her, and allowing that to make her more agreeable in my plans to take down Vincent, I'd been successful.

Once the meal was over, I offered to give Chloe a ride home and was thrilled when she agreed. It felt like some of the tension between us had broken, and I was actually enjoying the time we were spending together. It made me sad that more couldn't come of our reconnection, but I couldn't afford to let myself get off track.

But then I pulled up in front of Chloe's and stopped and she looked over and said, "Do you wanna come up for a cup of coffee?"

What was I going to do, say no?

"This is a great place," I told her as we walked in.

She laughed. "Yeah. Not as good as your city penthouse."

"Well..." I snorted. "Yeah, it's not that good."

Thankfully, Chloe just chuckled. "How do you prefer your coffee?"

I decided to take a calculated risk and say, "With a kiss."

She turned and looked back at me and I saw her gaze turn a little sultry. I expected her to flat out ignore me or give me a snarky response, but instead, she crossed the room up to me. It was almost like she was calling my bluff, moving slowly to see if I would stop her at any point, but I just remained quiet. Finally, she got up to where I was standing, getting even closer then until there was only a few centimeters of space between us.

And then she pressed her lips to mine.

CHAPTER EIGHT: CHLOE

About two hours before my date with Maksim, my panic got the best of me, and I found myself calling Mitzy for help. I'd never been in a situation before where I was fraternizing, willingly or unwillingly, with someone in Maks' position, but Mitzy had more than his fair share of experiences with it.

"I'm not convincing Cox to let you come back early," Mitzy said as soon as he picked up the phone. "You could use the time off."

"That's not why I'm calling," I said. "Are you somewhere where our conversation can't be overheard?"

"Uh, no, but I can take a smoke break, hang on."

I listened, slightly jealously, as Mitzy chatted with people around the precinct and discussed upcoming cases. When the OCU wasn't actively pursuing one of our targets, we could lend ourselves to other cases. Even though organized crime was why I became a cop, being able to do anything at all made me feel useful. I was annoyed that he got to do work when he didn't really care about the job, while someone with all the passion in the world like me was stuck on leave for the dumbest reason.

"Okay," Mitzy said. "I'm in the clear. What's going on?"

"Not long after I got home last night, Maksim called me and set up a date for us," I said. "He didn't really give me a choice in the matter of whether or not I wanted to go."

"A date?" Mitzy said. "You didn't tell me this thing between you two was romantic?"

"It's not," I said. "I mean... Yeah, I guess I probably liked him a little when I was a little girl, but that was then and this is now."

"So you aren't attracted to him?"

"N—" I went to speak but stopped myself. "I mean, objectively, yes. He's very attractive, but that's not the point."

"But it could be," Mitzy said. "If he has the hots for you and you have the hots for him, what's stopping you two from bumping uglies."

"The fact that he's a bratva pakhan and I'm an organized crime unit detective?" I spat back, but then I realized who I was talking to. "Yeah. I guess that doesn't make a huge difference to you, does it?"

"Look, let's not beat around the bush. Did you call for advice, or do you just want me to make you feel better? Because I can do both, but which one you're looking for is drastically going to change what I say to you."

"I need advice," I replied reluctantly. "As much blatant hypocrisy you can avoid, the better."

"You've got yourself a great opportunity here if you actually want to do your job," he said. "Cops go undercover all the time, and damn near every single one of them ends up meeting someone while they're under and having a little fun. How do you think cops end up with kids by criminals? The lines are much blurrier than you think."

"So you think I should exist in the blurred lines," I concluded.

I heard him snap his fingers on the other line. "Exactly. You find this guy attractive, and you have history. It probably wouldn't be the worst thing in the world for you to have someone to spend a little time with, and if he ends up developing a little thing for you in the interim even better. Who knows what you'll learn if you give a little. People do the most talking when they're drunk or in the afterglow of sex—that's always been my experience."

Something about *pretending* to be attracted to Maksim or sleeping with him just to extract information from him felt inherently wrong. Still, I had to imagine he'd do the same thing if he thought that he'd be successful. We were two ends of a game of chess at the moment.

"That feels so gross to me," I admitted.

"Well, it's kind of gross," Mitzy said. "But maybe he'll be good in bed."

"At the Christmas party last year, your wife told me you were a romantic, and I just don't know that I'll ever believe her," I said.

He snorted. "Look. I'm a romantic when it counts, and that same tactic could help you out right here, right now. When you go to that date, instead of being all cop, just be Chloe. His old friend. His really hot current friend. Let him flirt with you and make him think he's wooing you right into a trap, when really, you're opening the door for yourself. Invite him up for a drink. Turn on the charm. I'm telling you, Chlo, these guys are all about thinking they have the power. Let him think he's got you eating out of the palm of *his* hand, and he'll be eating out of the palm of yours. You could have him behind bars within a few months. If that's really what you want, that is..."

Against my better judgement, I ended up taking Mitzy's advice. I might have backed down if it didn't seem like it was going so well, but from the date to inviting Maksim up to my apartment, everything was going exactly how Mitzy said it would, which meant I could keep going and probably get what I really wanted out of it, or stop now and ruin the best chance I'd ever gotten to weasel my way into the mind of a organized crime boss.

"How do you prefer your coffee?"

"With a kiss."

In that moment, I had a split-second to make a decision that would change the scope of my entire relationship with Maksim, not to mention my job. All up to the moment that Maksim walked into the bistro, I'd been planning to ignore Mitzy's advice because it just sounded like a bad idea, but the "date" changed things for me a little bit. Once we dropped the cop vs. criminal act, it felt like I was with my old friend again. Catching up with him and getting to know him again, it wasn't hard to see that if we'd stuck together, we probably would have found love after some time. It was frustrating, because it had been a long time since I'd had a date that went that smoothly. All of the perfectly eligible guys in the world, and the first one I connected with in a long time was an international criminal and the sole target of an open investigation that I was working on.

Life was nothing if not cruel.

But there I was, standing in front of Maksim, still half-lingering on the way I actually enjoyed the time I spent with him, and following Mitzy's advice suddenly didn't seem so difficult.

So I kissed him.

It was a test at first, tentative and slow, letting my lips just cast across his. I wanted to know how it would feel, and I was curious to see how he would react. Maybe he thought I wouldn't follow through, because he seized up at first, but then he melted into it. His hands folded around my sides and slid down my back to rest just on top of my ass. I slid my hands up his chest and wrapped them behind his neck. In a weird way, it felt like we just fit together. It was so easy to wrap around each other and fall even deeper into the kiss.

Maks was the first one to push us even closer, letting his tongue slip out to lace between my lips and request entry into my mouth. I parted and allowed him to come in, swirling my tongue with his.

My living room couch wasn't far from where we were standing, so I pressed my body closer to his and he relented to my push, stepping backwards until we were falling down onto the couch. He easily shouldered my weight as we fell, and then it felt like he was a ship I was cradling in as we landed.

Something about Maksim just felt *good*.

After a few minutes of continued makeout, Maksim left my lips behind in the interest of running his mouth across my jawline and down my neck. My hands almost moved on their own to the buttons of my blouse to start undoing them. Maksim seemed to delight in this, running his hands under the open flaps and pulling it over my shoulders to drag it off. I dropped to the base of his shirt then and pulled the t-shirt up and over his torso.

And then I actually let a little gasp embarrassingly escape my lips.

"Is that a good thing?" Maksim asked.

Looking down at him, I was blown away. He looked like he had good fitness when he was dressed, but I had no idea what was waiting just underneath. Maksim wasn't just fit, he was *ripped*. He had clearly defined abs that poured down between his hip bones and were a red carpet to an unbelievable bulge now pressing against the fabric of his pants. He looked like a god.

"Yeah," I replied breathlessly. "You must live in a gym."

He laughed. "I have a lot of pent up frustrations. Sometimes working out is the only way I can get it out." One of his hands came up and curved into the bend of my neck. I actually closed my eyes and leaned into his touch. "To be in the presence of someone so beautiful, the last thing I expected was for you to compliment me."

Clearly, Maksim was going to be an issue.

I fell back down to kiss Maks again and his hands traveled farther down my back and slipped under the hem of my pants. Everywhere he touched seemed to tingle and made me catch my breath in new ways.

When I sat back, Maksim sat up with me and buried his head against my chest. He dotted kisses everywhere he could reach, simultaneously, undoing the clasp on my bra to drop it from my body. My heart started to beat a little faster, but when he closed his mouth over one of my breasts and began to suck, it felt like it stopped for a moment. The wetness and heat of his tongue, and the firm way he sucked sent a chill down my spine.

We weren't even doing much yet, and it still felt better than anyone I'd ever been with.

Suddenly, I found myself insatiable for more. Whereas he was the one steering before, I quickly helmed control and took over. I undid his pants with the quick flip of his button and yanked the zipper downwards, then I drove my hand between the fabric of his pants and boxers. His cock, though still sheathed, was the largest I'd ever experienced, and goosebumps rose to my skin as I palmed my hand over it.

Maksim stopped moving and I watched as he leaned back a little and closed his eyes. His mouth fell slightly open and he seemed to just breathe into the feeling of my hand massaging him below. His face of ecstasy was so sexy and I wanted to see more, so I reached in and pulled him out of his pants fully. I latched one hand to the side of his neck and used the other to slowly start working up and down his hard length. He was rock hard and twitching, dribbling beads of his essence out of the top, and he locked his eyes into mine with a darkened, hungry gaze.

"Oh, you're a problem," he said.

I smiled at him. "It's funny. I was just thinking the same thing about you."

His breathing got a little more ragged and hot, so I increased the pressure and speed. He craned up to latch onto the side of my neck, and I moaned along with him as I continued to give him a hand job.

Finally, it seemed Maksim wanted more, so he grabbed my wrist to stop me from pulling. He took my other wrist and pushed me backwards, flipping us so that I was under him now. He grabbed the edges of my pants and underwear and dragged them off in one fell swoop, then kicked his own off. I half expected him to go straight for gold, but he pulled back and laid on his stomach in front of me, he hooked his arms around my thighs and pulled me closer to him. He let his head fall between my legs, and a few seconds later, I felt his tongue against my center. I let out a moan and my head dropped back to the arm of the couch.

Maksim quickly worked himself into a rapid pace, slurping between my hole and the sensitive bundle of nerves at my crest. It seemed giving head was something Maksim enjoyed, because he was doing it like I was a full course meal. He was eager and had a perfect rotation of hitting all my best spots. Before I knew it, I was a mess, moaning and curling my hands into Maks' hair.

"Don't stop," I whimpered. "I'm gonna come."

He seemed to be inspired by that, and started to swirl his tongue even faster. To help, he poked a finger into my hole and crooked it upwards. He hit a delightful spot with precision and it yanked me over in an instant. I came, spasming and clenching around his hand, before falling a little limp.

"Hopefully that's not all you have," Maksim joked, looking up at me and kissing the inside of my thighs.

I sat up and looked down at him. "Not even close."

I stood up off the couch and dragged him with me, leading him down to my bedroom. As soon as Maksim saw the bed, he bent me over it. I braced myself up on my hands and Maksim lined up behind me. He lifted his massive length between my legs and just slipped it up and down for a few seconds. It felt even bigger than it looked, and thick.

How was he not married yet?

Finally, he tipped the head of himself into my entrance. It applied a fair amount of pressure for how big he was, but my walls didn't seem to mind, giving to him perfectly and letting him slide in. The fullness of him had me screaming out and throwing back subconsciously. It pulled him inside of me faster than he was moving, and his hands on my hips tightened.

"Shit," he huffed at me. "You're going to bring this to a rapid end like that."

"Sorry," I whined. "It feels so good. I want more."

Maksim let out a sigh. "You are unnaturally sexy."

With his hands on my hips, he started to thrust in and out, molding my insides to his huge size. He had no problem reaching the spots deep inside of me that were lighting me on fire, and despite his warning, I couldn't help but start to seesaw with him, pushing backwards as he thrusted forward. My legs shook and everything inside me burned.

"Fuck," I hummed.

Maksim pushed me down onto my stomach and grabbed my arm to twist me back to look at him. His blue eyes, wide and hungry, found mine, and the new position had him burying so deep into me that I couldn't think straight.

"I'm gonna come again," I moaned.

"Me too," Maks said. "You've brought out the worst in me."

This was his worst?

Eventually, both Maksim and I started to pant harder. The center of my gut started to sear as I came, finding myself totally without the ability to even make any noise at all. All I was able to do was hold my mouth open and squeeze my eyes shut as the powerful orgasm came over me, before it finally released me. Just as I started to register that I hadn't even considered having Maksim put on a condom, he pulled out of me and I opened my eyes just to see him stroke his seed out and onto my skin.

He let out a deep breath and smiled down at me. "How long do you need to bounce back? I'm definitely going to need more."

I gave him a darkened smile as I flipped around and curled my legs around his hips. "I'm already ready."

The rest of the night was a blur of both devouring and being devoured by Maks. It seemed there was no end to how much we could take from each other, but eventually in the early hours of the morning, we'd exhausted ourselves. The last thing I had a cognisant memory of, was Maksim rolling off to my side and folding a hand over his stomach, before I passed out on the pillow next to him.

When I finally woke up with the early morning, I looked to my left and was surprised to find that Maksim was still in my bed. I had him pegged as a gone before sunlight kind of guy, but if he wasn't, I supposed that was good for me as we got closer.

Then I remembered what was going on.

It wasn't good. I didn't want Maksim to be in my bed still. I didn't want to create any falsehood that this was anything more than a sexual relationship.

"Maks," I huffed, shaking him awake. "Hey."

He stirred, groaning at the sudden interruption to his sleep. "Hm?"

"You have to go," I said. "It's morning."

He stretched his arms out, circling one behind my back. "Does your bed catch fire in the morning or something?"

"No," I said, a little annoyed. "I have things to do today. You have to go."

"You're still on leave for a couple of days," he retorted. "Let's go get breakfast."

"No," I said defiantly. "This isn't a breakfast sort of thing." What was with the wave of regret I was feeling all of a sudden? "I need to go and see my dad and sister at the bodega today anyway. I neglect it, but since I'm off, I should go." I slid myself out of Maksim's hold, which felt just a little too intimate to me. "This was fun, but I need you to go now."

Maksim seemed put off, but thankfully he said, "Very well. I'll go."

He stood up and walked out of my bedroom, not making any attempt to hide his nakedness, and my face burned a little at the sight. Memories of our night together flashed across my brain, but I hit my head a few times to knock them out and then got up myself. I grabbed my bathrobe and wrapped it around myself before going to oversee Maksim's departure. He'd gotten dressed only as much as he needed to, and was already heading towards the door.

I wasn't sure what I should say or do, so I offered a weak, "Talk soon," as I opened the door for him.

"Yes, very soon," he replied, then he left without another word.

After shutting the door, I slammed my head against it.

This had been a mistake.

In order to not be a total liar, I did get dressed, and after grabbing a protein shake for breakfast, I left to go to my father's bodega. I needed something to distract my mind from the whirlwind of the past forty-eight hours anyway, and my dad and sister were always looking to dump the work on me when they could.

My car was a newer model and attracted the wrong kind of attention in Little Odessa, so I left it at home and took public transportation to the bodega instead. When the bus turned the corner onto the block where my dad's bodega was located, I smiled a little. The "Nasha Udacha" sign was tattered and fading, and one of the front windows was still busted from a break-in a handful of months back, but my recent dream made me think of my mom when I saw it. It was going to be nice to let my brain fade away and just have a few hours with my family.

Unfortunately, Maksim had other plans for me.

"Hello again," he said with a smile when I walked in. He was standing at the checkout counter, sharing a beer with my dad, and being ogled by my sister.

"Why are you here?" I said.

He tilted his head and looked at me with faux-innocence. "Was what you said earlier not an invitation?" But I knew what it really was. It was a silent threat, that just like he was able to get all of my information, he was able to get my family's as well. "I was catching up with your father."

"You didn't tell me you'd reconnected with Maksim," my dad said. He had his gray hair pulled back into a stringy ponytail, and his slender form was swimming in both a t-shirt and pants that were too big. "It's so good to see him."

Chandler, my sister, was surprisingly sober that morning, and had her face balanced in her hand and was batting her eyes at Maks like she was some sort of princess. "I can't believe I don't remember you."

"I remember you," Maksim said with a warm smile. "You were always running around after your sister and me. She always wanted you to leave us alone, but I didn't mind."

Chandler giggled. "Chloe's always been mean to me."

I rolled my eyes at the younger visage of myself. She had my same long brown hair and bright blue eyes, though she'd gotten my father's slender lips as opposed to the full ones I'd gotten from my mom. She was more sallow than me as her addictions had left her mostly skin and bone, but she didn't look half bad this morning in a pair of harem pants and an ombre t-shirt.

"Well, we have to get to work," I said. "Maks, I'll walk you out."

He sighed at me but said, "Very well," and finished his morning beer before leaving the counter behind.

I walked him out to the front of the bodega and tried to keep my voice low as I said, "You've made your point."

"I just wanted to cover my bases. After you hurried me out this morning, I wasn't sure what to expect. I was hoping we could continue our time together.

Maybe even go for another round, of course doing things how *I* like to do them, this time."

I furrowed my brow. "How *you* like to do them? What does that mean?" It was probably a bad idea to ask, but I couldn't help myself.

He stuck a finger out and curled it under my chin, tilting my head up. "I'll let your curiosity wander, but I'll give you a little hint. I have a particular kink." He flashed me a toothy, hungry grin. "I wonder what a woman who feasts off of control would do when she suddenly has none?" The way he said it made me shiver. He'd said that last night was his worst. Was his best related to his mysterious anecdote? "Anyway. I'll leave you to your family. Thank your father for the beer." And then he left without another word.

Maksim Pasternak, or rather Maksim Petrov now, just what long game was he really playing at?

CHAPTER NINE: MAKSIM

I believed I'd left Chloe in enough suspense that she'd be calling me for a more in depth tutorial on my preferred kinks. It truly had not been my plan to sleep with anyone else, least of all Chloe, while I was fighting to get Katya back, but creative problems required creative solutions.

Running into someone who not only knew and had background information on me, but was also a police officer, was not good for business. It was a risk being involved with a detective at all, let alone someone that I could actually see myself developing a thing for, if even just on a physical level. Chloe was obviously beautiful, and the way we connected was really nice. Katya was certainly having her fun while we were finding our way back to each other, why couldn't I?

However, if I was being totally honest, I'd have to admit that I wished I didn't have to be so manipulative with someone I legitimately cared about. Chloe was pretty much all I had left of my childhood and the people I considered family. As we were getting to know each other again, it was plain to see that we would have maintained our connection if fate hadn't pulled us apart. I would kill for an opportunity to just get to know Chloe again legitimately and maintain our friendship afterwards, but deep in my gut, I knew this was going to end badly.

But she was still a detective and one that probably wouldn't hesitate to cuff me if she got the chance to. She had a vendetta against people in organized crime units as much as I had a vendetta against Vincent Costello, and just like I would do anything to put him in the ground, she'd do anything to stop me.

And so, I'd use our history and obvious attraction to one another to make sure she was never one step ahead of me, and now that she knew I could find her father and sister when I needed to, I had a little extra padding to ensure that was the case. Between her interest and fear, I should be able to keep her right where I needed her.

With that phase of my work done for the time being, it was time to head back to Dacha and change gears to the club and the problems that were budding there. With Dino gone, the club had no management for when I did eventually go back to St. Petersburg, and the Bonettis were down a handful of men thanks to the raid, which was not only less people in my pocket, but also was bound to have rubbed Stavio the wrong way. There was some damage control I had to do with him, and I needed to figure out who would continue running the place once I'd gathered Katya and we had gone back home.

"Boss." Brusch seemed concerned, if not a bit irritated when I walked through the back door of the club. "I was unaware you'd be away last night."

"Some unexpected things came up," I responded to him. "Don't worry. Everything is fine. Have you done what I asked you to do?"

"Yes, sir," he said. "I've sent the link to your email."

"Very good. I'm heading up to do some work. Please gather all of the Dacha employees, the Bonettis, and any of our men in the main bar for a meeting at two before we open."

He nodded his head obediently. "Yes, sir."

Leaving him behind, I took the elevator up to the penthouse and made sure to lock it at the top so that no one could get in. Images of Chloe's naked body raced across my brain each time I allowed my brain to wander and left me wondering how long it would be before she'd call, looking to step through the door I'd opened. Imagining getting to have even more fun with her had the crotch of my pants tightening a bit, but I shook it off. I had to at least get *something* done, because if she did come through wanting more, I doubted I'd be able to focus on anything else for a while.

Exactly as Brusch had said, when I checked my email, I had an unchecked message in my inbox from him that had nothing but a link attached to it. When I clicked it, it brought up an encrypted webpage that asked me to download a program client. I did so quickly, anxious to see if Brusch had really done as good a job at the latest task I'd given him as he swore he could.

After a little bit of loading, the client I'd downloaded opened, showing me a camera feed of the front of Vincent's estate. Not long from where I'd parked my rental and pretended it was broken down, a camera providing surprisingly high grade footage had been placed and was live streaming Vincent's estate directly to my computer. I smiled as I watched it, able to see the comings and goings of every person traveling throughout the estate. It wasn't a perfect view, but at least I'd be able to know when Vincent was leaving, and in one of those trips away, was my opportunity to strike.

To my surprise, as I watched, I did see Katya leaving at one point in a sleek-looking, two door, silver Maserati. I honestly wasn't expecting to see Katya leaving the estate on her own. I imagined her existence in the Costello household being totally hingent upon her being with Vincent or in his home at all times. As confusing as it was, however, it was enlightening and told me that there would potentially be an opportunity to take my strike against Vincent when Katya was away as well. That would make it even easier to pass his death off as something that had nothing to do with me.

Two in the afternoon approached faster than I was planning on as I lost track of time taking mental notes on the activity at Vincent's estate. I just barely noticed the clock with enough time left to shower and change, then I went downstairs to where Brusch had gathered everyone I asked for in the main bar area. Wait staff, bartenders, barbacks, and chefs weren't as much of a concern to me, but I wanted all eyes and ears related to Dacha in the meeting. A small group of people was sitting in one corner surrounding Stavio and I held a groan in.

There were even less surviving Bonettis than I realized.

"Thank you all for meeting," I said. "As I'm sure you all can see, our little visit from the police left us in quite the predicament. Your fearless leader, Dino, is no longer with us, and it seems the Bonettis are a handful of men short as well."

"More than a handful," Stavio spat out.

"So we need to do some restructuring, don't we?" I said. "The police are clearly on our case now, and eventually, I'll leave to return to Russia and someone will need to steer the ship here, so I guess you could say I'm looking for suggestions."

Over in the corner, Stavio Bonetti raised his hand with an arrogant snarl on his face. "I've got an idea." He stood up and started to saunter in my direction. Immediately, Brusch and my other bratva members started to get defensive, but I held a hand up for them to stand down. "How about next time the police come sniffing around, you don't sell out my men for your own?"

"No one sold your men out," I replied quickly. "Your men got caught, and where something akin to diplomatic immunity saved my crew, yours were already wanted men in this jurisdiction. There was nothing I could do for them."

"Bullshit," Stavio snapped. "We all saw that pretty little cop walk in here and walk out like you two were best friends. What, are y'all fucking? Got you a little honey dew on the unit to watch your own skin?" He got so close to me I could smell his stench. "The least you could do is spread the wealth. What do you think? Maybe she'll take a double team for letting my guys go, huh?"

Without thinking, I threw my head forward, colliding it with Stavio's in a painful headbutt. Even though waves of pain started to sear across my skull, I was far more concerned with the man in front of me. He fell backwards down onto the ground and immediately his crew jumped up, mine were faster and already on guard however, and guns came up in a second. The club's lower staff yelped and hid, but it was one to one with the handful of guys I'd brought with me from Russia and the Bonetti's remaining grunts. It really just evened the playing field again so I could continue dealing with Stavio.

A stream of blood was trickling down his head, and I could feel a wet spot on my own from where we'd connected. Stavio had gotten his bell rung, though, and seemed to be struggling to get himself oriented. In his distraction, I pulled a foot back and kicked it firmly into his ribcage. He doubled over even further and coughed, spitting out a spatter of blood.

"You and I don't know each other very well, so I suppose I can forgive your misdirection," I said. "Unless I invite your presence, you should refrain from getting close to me."

Stavio stood up off the ground and wiped his mouth, then I saw his hand dive for his waistband. In that flash, I jumped forward, caught the gun as he was pulling it out and slid it across the room, then I cocked my fist back and smashed it across his cheek, hearing the crunch of bones as I did so. He went down again, dropping to the floor with a grunt.

"Fuck you," he hissed.

"I don't want to fight with you," I said simply. "If you would just calm down, we could discuss this like adults. If you're looking to fight like children, I'm here to tell you that you will most certainly lose. I may look put together, but I promise you a rougher world raised me than raised you."

"You think you're tough?" Stavio staggered back to his feet. "If you didn't keep throwing sucker punches, this would be a totally different fight."

"You think so?" I said, then held my arms out to my sides. "I'll give you one then, but I'm warning you, I'm coming dangerously close to losing my temper."

Taking the opportunity I'd presented him, Stavio flung himself forward and tossed his fist out at me. In his rush to do so without really thinking about it, he tripped and barely cut across my cheek. It felt more like someone had swatted me with a pillow rather than had hit me with a fist.

No wonder this guy struggled to get anywhere in his family.

As he toppled over, I brought my fist up and shoved it into his stomach. He folded around it, groaning, but clawed his hands up onto me to try and gain some leverage. To his credit, he got a couple of scratches in, but those few slashes I felt of his fingers raking against my skin only made me angrier. I uppercut my elbow under his chin, sending his head backwards and his whole body unfolding in that direction, then I slammed the same elbow against his cheek like a wrecking ball, and ended with a swing from my other hand. His head bobbled between my elbow and fist before he dropped to the ground in a useless heap.

Annoyed beyond my limits, I crouched down in front of the broken Stavio and muttered, "I thought you to be a smarter man than this, Stavio. I now see why no one in your family respects you."

He lifted his head and puffed his cheeks like he was going to spit at me, but I punched him again, knocking him out cold.

The room was so quiet you could hear a pin drop in the wake of the fight, and though I had intended to get more done with the meeting, I was now so angry I couldn't think straight. Nothing productive would come from me working under these circumstances. I'd have to calm down and try again later.

So, instead, I looked over at Stavio's crew and simply said, "When your boss stops swallowing his own spit, let him know the relationship between the Bonettis and the Petrovs is over. You should only show your faces around here if you want to meet the bad end of my gun." Then I sneered. "Get him out of here."

Though the Bonettis were still half in a stand-off with my men, they could see they lacked the upper hand. Each of them slowly lowered their guns, and then a couple of them came forward to pick Stavio up off the ground and drag him towards the front door. One of the staff scuttled over quickly to unlock it, and the Bonettis hauled themselves out before the door was shut and locked behind them.

"Boss," Brusch said. "The Bonettis are important partners. They're the ones moving our products through here."

I ran a hand through my hair and said, "I'll figure something else out. A hot head like that is no use to us. It wouldn't have taken much to turn him against us." Then I looked out at the Dacha staff. "But let this be a warning to all of you. The Petrov family doesn't do well with betrayal or insurrection. This was the least I could do, but your old boss Dino met a worse fate. If you aren't prepared to remain loyal to the Petrovs, then when I turn my back, I suggest you leave. I'm not going to settle for any additional problems. I've only got one or two inconveniences left in me before I really start to get pissed off." I looked at Brusch and demanded, "Clean up this mess."

"Yes, boss," he replied, then looked over to address the other men. "You heard him. Let's get this cleaned up, and the rest of you, get ready for the bar to open. We still have a business to run."

Frustrated, I stormed away from the scene and made my way back to the elevator to head up to the penthouse. My fist and head hurt from where I'd made contact with Stavio, but those weren't the biggest of my problems at the moment. Brusch was right, the Bonettis were a key part of Dacha's underground success, and with them gone, I now needed to also find a new group of people to move Dacha's supply. I already hated being in the United States so much.

Every time I took a step forward, it felt like I was taking two more back.

CHAPTER TEN: CHLOE

After spending the prior day at my father's bodega, I was glad that Maksim had left me alone for my final day on leave. I still had to see a therapist before Cox would let me back in the office, which annoyed me because I didn't think I needed it, but I decided to take Mitzy up on his offer to see his crack guy that would just sign the paperwork without any of the hard stuff. Maybe there was a lot in me that needed to be unpacked, and maybe it would even be best unpacked by a trained professional, but I wasn't ready for any of that. Not at this time.

"Just ask for Dr. Angiulo Corsatta and tell them I sent you," Mitzy told me. "I'll call ahead to let him know you're coming."

For whatever reason, I'd convinced myself that Mitzy was sending me to some back alley side-door that I was going to need to enter with some tough-guy code, and trudge through a dive bar to get to a man whose glasses were purchased from a dollar store. I'd brought my personal gun with me, the one I was licensed to carry, and took public transportation again to prevent putting my car in a position to potentially be broken into, but it was all for nothing because the address led me to a high rise in Manhattan. It had a gorgeous, glinting golden plate on the front clearly stating that it was a clinical building that contained several different facilities.

Walking inside, I saw a rotating directory stand and walked over to it, quickly finding the name of the place that Mitzy had told me to go to. Of course, when he told me that I would find his contact at a clinic called "Mind Reader," I assumed it was a fake name, but it seemed it was very real. It even had a beautiful logo of a brain with a band-aid on top of a book. It was very cute.

Maybe not all of Mitzy's contacts were shifty—although this guy *was* going to sign off on a psych evaluation, even though I wasn't going to be evaluated at all.

After seeing that the place I was looking for was on the fifteenth floor, I walked over to the gold-plated elevators where a man was waiting to operate it on my behalf. "Which floor, ma'am?"

"Um, the fifteenth, please," I replied.

He nodded. "Great." He pressed the button to call the elevator and then the doors opened almost immediately. After I walked on, he reached around to press the fifteenth floor button for me, then offered me a friendly smile and wave and said, "Have a wonderful afternoon."

"Thank you. You as well."

The doors closed and the elevator moved so smoothly, I almost didn't think I was moving at first. If I didn't see the light on the elevator buttons gradually moving up the floors, I wouldn't have believed I was actually going up.

Once I reached the fifteenth floor, the elevator announced—"Floor Fifteen. Mind Reader in room 1501. Placement Placemat in room 1502. Jumbleree in room 1503,"—then the doors opened, letting me out into a stunning lobby with a fountain.

This place felt way too fancy for me.

Nonetheless, I turned to the left out of the elevator, following signs for room 1501. I found it, just a little down the hallway and entered to a fairly normal looking doctor's office. There were a few people sitting, keeping to themselves and waiting for appointments, and I wasn't sure where the people here for fake psych sign-offs were supposed to go.

"Good afternoon," the receptionist said. "Can I help you?"

I crossed the room to the desk and kept my voice low like we were both in on some hidden conspiracy. "Uh... Yes. I'm here to see Dr. Angiulo Corsatta."

"Did you receive a referral?" she asked.

"Yes?" I said. "Maximilian Volte."

"Oh, of course!" she responded cheerily, not making any attempt to keep her voice low. "Dr. Volte sends us patients all the time." She typed a few things on her computer and then looked back at me. "Chloe Nikitina?"

"Yeah." It was difficult not to break out with how impressed I was with what was clearly a multi-person operation.

"Great." She typed again and then said, "Okay. I've got you all checked in. If you'll just take a seat, we'll call you when he's ready."

"Perfect. Thanks." I went and sat down in one of the chairs, letting my anxiety decide that I needed to sit as far as possible from the next person over. When I felt comfortable enough that my shoulder wasn't being looked over, I sent Mitzy a text that simply said, "Dr. Volte?"

A few minutes later I got a response. "LOL! I thought you'd enjoy that."

After about ten minutes of waiting, someone opened a door next to the main reception desk and said, "Miss Nikitina?"

I stood up and walked over and she offered me a bright smile. "Welcome. Dr. Corsatta is ready to see you."

"Thank you," I replied.

She led me back to a room where a young, handsome enough man with dark ginger hair and glasses was sitting behind a desk. He stood to greet me, holding out his hand to shake and said, "Good afternoon, Miss Nikitina. Or should I call you Chloe?"

"Chloe's fine," I said.

"Well come in, sit down," he said, motioning over to the couch.

"Oh, um, okay." Mitzy had said that it wasn't a real session. Maybe he just needed to sell it for the sake of his employees? I walked over and sat down and the woman who walked me back left. Dr. Corsatta picked up a notebook and pen from his desk and walked over and sat in a chair perpendicular to where I was sitting. "Okay. Shall we get started?"

My eyes shifted from side-to-side like I was being pranked. "Um... My friend Max sent me."

"Yes! Mitzy and I are good friends," he replied. "He told me you'd need a signature on a psych eval."

I let out a sigh of relief. For a second, I was afraid I'd have to do more than I was planning on. "Yes, please."

"He also told me that you could probably benefit from an *actual* therapy session," he said. "He asked me, as a friend, not to sign an eval unless we at least, as he put it, chatted."

My jaw dropped. That was *not* what Mitzy told me. "Oh, um, no thank you."

Dr. Corsatta sat back, crossing one leg over the other. "Can I ask why not?"

"It's nothing against your profession or anything, but I'm not a therapy person. I prefer to keep my personal information to myself."

"Well, then don't share any personal information," he said. "What happened that made your boss put you on leave?"

"I really don't want to do this," I groaned.

"Come on. You've gotta do it anyway to go back to work tomorrow, right?

So humor me. Here." He reached to a table behind him and grabbed an hour-glass and tipped it up on the coffee table between us. "This is five minutes long. We can take five minutes now, or you can go suffer through an entire hour with someone who won't sign off until they're convinced you're fine."

I let out a deep sigh. "I'm gonna kill Mitzy."

"Please don't. That wouldn't be good for my pocketbook or client base," Dr. Corsatta joked. "So, what happened?" He set down his book and pen as if to say he was just listening, not being a clinician.

"It wasn't really that big of a deal. We went on a raid and it turned out it was a setup. A member of my team got snatched away from me, and then I got captured by the boss. He held a gun to my head, but it was clear he didn't really want to kill me. It didn't have that big of an impact on me. I made it out unscathed."

"Ah, I see. So simply because you had awesome negative interactions and were in a life-threatening situation, your boss thought that you should see a therapist?"

"Exactly," I replied.

He nodded. "Got it. Have you ever been in a life-threatening situation before?" My mind immediately flashed to the day my mom died. I must have shown it on my face because then Dr. Corsatta said, "You have."

"I have," I said. "I don't really want to talk about it."

"That's fine," he said. "You don't have to talk about anything personal. That was the deal. If you don't mind my asking though, do you think that your prior near-death experience warped the way you responded to this current one, or do you think they were totally unrelated?"

"That's kind of a tricky question to answer," I said. "My first near-death experience changed my whole world view, so in that regard, it had an effect on the second one, but I don't know that I think they were directly correlated."

"You seem somewhat deafened to this one," he said. "Would you say you've spent any time at length attempting to deaden your senses to that first experience?"

My stomach twisted into a knot. Of course I'd spent time trying to block that memory out. It was the day my mom died—the day I watched her die. But I didn't think that changed what I did when Maksim had a gun to my face...

Did it?

"You know," I said. "This is getting a little too much for me." I glanced down at the hour glass and the last of the sand was dropping into the lower basin. "And our five minutes is up."

"So it is," he said. "Well, a deal's a deal." He stood up and walked over to his desk and pulled out a pad. He scribbled some things down on it and then ripped the top page off and brought it over to me. It had my name on it, along with a thirty minute time slot and then at the bottom in the notes section, he'd written that I was cleared to return to work. "Here you go."

"Thank you. Have a nice day." I slipped it into my purse and then quickly started for the door.

"Miss Nikitina." I stopped and turned around. "I'm sure you think that I'm an under-the-table kind of guy who just signs fake evals for money, but that's not it at all. I met Mitzy about ten years ago when he was in a situation not all that different from yours. He was required to have an evaluation to return to work and had been referred to me. I find people in positions like yours often don't seek the help they need unless they're required to do so. You shoulder a lot of burden, but sometimes you shouldn't be afraid to let others carry some of it. Just like Mitzy, I opened the door for him to return and didn't pressure him, and I'll do the same for you." He walked over and handed me a business card. "If you ever just want to talk, about anything at all, I'm here."

I swallowed hard as I pulled the card from his hand. "Thank you."

"Of course. Have a wonderful rest of your day."

He opened the door for me and I walked out, feeling very different about the situation than I felt going in. He was a doctor who dealt in shady sign-offs in order to screen for cops who needed more help than they were admitting to?

If that was true, he was a next-level guardian angel.

I considered just chucking his card in the first garbage can I saw, but when I was about to toss it, I couldn't bring myself to do it. If anything, he was a good contact to have in case I ever needed someone to sign off on a psych eval again, so I slipped the card into my wallet and made my way back outside to catch the bus back home.

Of course, I was at the precinct bright and early the next morning with my signed off evaluation in hand. Captain Cox never came in that early, but I thought there was a slight possibility that he might find another reason to force me out for a couple of days, and I wanted to get a little bit of work done before he arrived, just in case. None of my cohorts were there yet, and only a handful of people in the entire building.

I made my way up to my desk and sat down at my computer. There was some work that needed to be filled out and followed regarding the raid, but I'd get to that after I'd been cleared to stay at work. What I wanted to do to begin with was use my resources here to gather some more background information on Maksim. Maybe he had a way to find out everything about me, but he wasn't the only one.

I had my ways too.

Checking international databases, I was able to see that his name had, in fact, been legally changed to Maksim Petrov about six months prior. Oddly enough, he had a mostly clear rap sheet, save for a couple of fights when he was still a teenager. Whatever Vladimir must have had him doing, it kept him out of the spotlight. He was listed as the legal owner of Dacha in NYC, which led me to wonder how I never came to at least see his name before.

Then I found some pictures of him. He hadn't been arrested on Vladimir's behalf at all, but he'd been pictured in both he and Sacha Petrov's presence on more than one occasion. It seemed he was at the very least known as one of their associates, but without a criminal record of any kind, no police officer, international or otherwise, had been able to use that information to their benefit.

Seeing his face in the photos brought on a new wave of issues for me though.

Suddenly, my body was heating up.

I pulled at the collar of my shirt, wondering if I should have left the top button off, but I knew that wasn't the problem. Seeing Maksim's face and remembering what we did the night he came over was actually getting me a little hot and bothered. That sort of thing had never happened to me before.

"You know," a voice broke into the empty unit room and I slammed my laptop shut out of fear. "If I ever lose this job, I could certainly earn a *killing* knowing you better than my own wife and kids. I knew you'd be here bright and early on your first day back." I looked up and Mitzy was walking up behind me with a cup of coffee in each hand. He handed one to me and then said, "Why'd you slam it shut. You watching porn?"

"No!" I yelped. "I'm at work and that's inappropriate."

"Calm down, we've all done it," he retorted.

I looked up at him. "You've watched porn at work?"

"Last year when my wife's mom was sick. She went up to Maine to stay with her for like six weeks. It was brutal," he replied. "I damn near went to the doctor. I swear to god, it wouldn't go down."

"Max," I hissed. "That is just... *way* too much information."

He shrugged. "Whatever. Besides, I can see your cheeks are all red."

"No." I picked up my phone and opened it to look at my reflection, but was disappointed to see there was a bit of color there. "Anyway, I wasn't watching porn, I was just doing some research on Maksim."

"Ahhh," Mitzy replied, leaning against my desk next to me. "So pretty much the same thing?"

"It's not," I grumbled.

"Did you guys, you know…" He leaned down with a fake look of intrigue on his face. "Do it?"

"I don't know why I put up with you."

"Because you love me," he replied. "And don't avoid the question." I side-eyed him and that was all that he needed to know the answer. "Oh snap! But… aw, getting laid is supposed to make you less of a tight ass."

I swatted at him, but he backed up so I couldn't make contact. "It was a mistake. I never should have listened to you."

"Why, was it bad?"

"No it wasn't bad!" I snapped and then realized what I'd just said, "Er…"

Mitzy just started laughing. "You know what? I'm gonna leave you to sort all this out on your own. You know my stance on it, and I have too much paperwork to do to sit here and listen to you chase your own tail."

He started to stand up, but I grabbed his arm and pulled him back. "Wait, I have a question for you."

"Chlo, really, I don't think I can give you any additional advice on this matter."

"No, no, no. This question is about the Costellos," I said, and Mitzy leaned back against my desk. "Well, more specifically, it's about Katya Petrova. Have you ever met her?"

"Yeah. Great woman," he said. "My wife and I went on a double date with her and Vincent a few weeks ago. It was lovely."

"Really?" I said. "Part of the reason Maksim is here is because he says she's not here of her own free will. He says she's only humoring Vincent because he took advantage of her when she was kidnapped and is just afraid of him, so Maks is here to take her back."

Mitzy recoiled harshly. "What? No way. Katya and Vincent are the most sickening lovebirds I've ever seen. Vincent Costello was a grade A player. Half the women in New York hate his guts, but when he snatched Katya, from what I heard from his dad and other Costellos, she turned his whole life upside down. If anyone was tricked, it was him." Then he laughed. "Not that I think he minds at this point. Who knew there was a woman out there who could turn him."

I crossed my arms and spun my chair around a bit as I processed that. "He seemed pretty convinced."

"Sorry, kid. Either he's lying to you, or he's wrong. I'm not sure which."

"Why would he be so intent on taking Katya back if she's actually happy there. He owes everything to their family," I said.

Mitzy just shrugged. "Maybe he has a thing for her?"

I hadn't considered that possibility, but it gave me an unwelcome feeling in the pit of my stomach. If it *was* that Maksim had a thing for Katya, then what was he doing messing around with me?

Frustrated, I cracked my neck. That wasn't the point. It wasn't whether or not he had a thing for her or me, it was whether or not she was safe or in danger. Mitzy had promising insight on the Costello family because he worked for them, so I was inclined to believe his take on things, but then that meant that, like Mitzy had said, Maksim was either lying or mistaken, and I couldn't take a single step further with him personally or in my investigation until I found out which.

CHAPTER ELEVEN: MAKSIM

It had been a couple of days since I'd heard from Chloe and I was beginning to wonder if I hadn't enticed her enough with my hint at a kink. Chloe shared a lot of my same personality traits, which led me to believe that she probably shared my hidden wild side in the bedroom. After that first night we'd spent together, I saw first hand how dominant she could be and how her eyes flared with excitement every time things got a little rough. It'd convinced me that I was right to assume she'd take some dropped bait if I hinted at an even wilder time, but two days worried me that I'd made a bad judgement call.

Fortunately, before I had to make a decision about how best to rope Chloe back in if she was already trying to cut herself loose, I received a text message from her. It was simple, if even a little cryptic, and simply read:

I have a question about...
    something you said...

Typically when one has a question, they proceed to ask it immediately, but I could see that Chloe was starting and stopping her text several times. I was sitting on the couch in my penthouse, overseeing the camera I had propped at the Costello's and watching the sunset fade into night outside the window when she reached out. I leaned back, bemused by her apparent struggle to frame the question she had to ask, and could only assume she was trying to find the best way to initiate a conversation about my kink.

So I decided to help her out.

> *Are you wondering about my kink?*
> *All you have to do is ask and I'll*
> *tell you...*
> *If you're lucky, I'll show you.*

The dots had been going steady when my message went through, but then they came to a stop and stayed stopped for a while. Maybe I'd made another mistake in assuming, I thought, but then a new message came in.

Are you one of those BDSM guys?

A new smile found my face as I read the message.

> *No, not at all. My interests lie a*
> *little West of there, I would say.*

What does that mean?

> *Are you sure you want to know?*

I wouldn't have asked.

> *It seemed you were struggling to*
> *ask.*

Fine, don't tell me.

> *Haha. Have you ever heard of*
> *sensory deprivation?*

...No.

There's a concept that says that people who have deprived senses in one area will heighten them in another. It's the reason that some blind people can hear way better than the average person, or why people who are deaf can read lips so well.

That's your kink?

You'd be surprised what a little deprivation will do to the rest of you. Don't knock it, until you try it.

Oh, and are you going to show me?

If you'd let me.

Then we'd have done sex the good way?

Ah. You seem to have mistaken my words. I never meant to imply that the way we did it the first night wasn't good. In fact, it's been a long time since I've felt so satisfied. I simply meant that I can get a little particular when it comes to the bedroom. I made an exception for you, and I was glad I did. You were so sexy.

You sure seemed to like it. That face you made when I was

*rubbing your cock... I never
would have guessed you had an
alternative, preferred method.*

I lifted an eyebrow at the phone at the sudden change in tone and realized Chloe was trying to goad me into a bit of sexting. She was going to be successful, because just seeing those few words already had the lower half of my body waking up.

*Well, when I have a beautiful
woman on top of me, how
could I resist? Though I must
admit, I was hoping you'd take
a little taste. If you were here
now, that's where we'd start.*

*Oh yeah? How? Would you
have me get down on my knees
in front of you, or are you more
of a lay me backwards over the
bed and take my throat like a
hole kind of guy?*

I let out a dark gasp. My initial thought was right, Chloe was a closeted freak.

*When you put it like that, I'd
go for both, or is there a
mysterious third option?*

*It just so happens, there is.
One where I sit on your face
and we feast at the same time.*

Seeing where this was heading, I let a hand drop to my waist and undo the button and zipper of my pants. My dick was rapidly hardening in the wake of

Chloe's naughty turn, and I had to wrap a hand around it and take a few strokes.

That's getting me hard just thinking about it.

Getting? Your dick is already out, I imagine.

Caught red handed. What about you? Are you using your hand, or helping yourself with a toy?

I have a purple, plug-in one. I ditched battery operated ones a long time ago.

The image of Chloe, naked on her bed, with her legs splayed open, pleasuring herself with a purple vibrator was one I would pay to see. I started to fist myself faster just thinking about it.

Put it inside you and pretend it's me.

Already way ahead of you. I bet your hand doesn't feel as good as I do, though.

You've got me there, but I'm a slave to what I've got to work with.

I wish you were here

*to suck my breasts the
way you did before.*

*You and I both. I don't
feel I got enough the
first time.*

*Make sure you take
your fill next time then.*

A heat began building in my thighs the faster I pumped myself. Sweat started to accumulate on my brow and I could tell I'd be hitting my limit soon.

*No response for a while
there. You must be
getting close*

I am.

*It really is a shame I'm
not there. I'd drink it all
down if I was.*

*I'd give you some to
drink and paint your face
with the rest.*

*You'd have to get it out
of my mouth first. My
throat can be pretty
punishing.*

With a grunt, I came, erupting my milky substance all over my hand, and even squirting some onto the computer in front of me. To be cheeky, I took a picture of my dirtied laptop and sent it to her.

You made a mess.

She delighted me when she sent one back almost immediately of a darkened spot on her bed sheets, with her bare legs and the infamous purple toy on the edges of the screen.

You made a bigger one.

Before I knew it, I was laughing out loud in my penthouse.

I've never done anything like that before. I feel like a goddamn high schooler.

Lol. I'm just looking at my sheets so sad that I have to change them now.

I caught a glimpse of my reflection in the mirror across from me and took note of the genuine smile on my face. I tried to think of how long it had been since I'd seen a smile like that on my face or even felt one. Chloe had managed to get something out of me that I'd long thought dead.

Genuine happiness.

I have to go to work now, and I have no idea how I'm going to focus now.

Sucks to be you. I get to go to sleep.

.   .   .

She tagged her last message with a little smiley face with its tongue sticking out and I just snickered. It really was like we were kids with a crush.

Sleep well then.

Thanks to you, I'm
  certain to.

That was the last message exchanged between us for the night. I sat in a bit of a stupor in the wake of it, wondering how I managed to get so turned on from just words on a screen, but even re-reading them, I started to feel my length twitch a little. The fact that I felt so satisfied, like I'd just been with her, when all we did was exchange a few messages was foreign to me, and even a little scary. And it wasn't just a physical satisfaction, but something else too. Like emotional satisfaction. Suddenly, I felt like I could take on the world and I had no idea why.

Smiling at the thought of Chloe nuzzling into her bed and falling asleep after pleasuring herself to the thought of me, I changed my clothes and then went downstairs to see Dacha in action for the first time since I'd arrived. I had to try and identify someone amongst the staff who could potentially manage when I'd left, and with the Bonettis gone, it was up to me and my crew to run our product through the club while we were here.

And I had no idea what we were going to do when it was time for me to leave.

"Brusch," I said, greeting him in the VIP area of the club. "Do we have any customers yet?"

"Several," he said. "Everyone wants more of the new drug. It seems the Bonettis were slinging it pretty hard."

The crux of Dacha's success was that it was an epicenter for drugs that could typically only be found overseas, including a drug of Vladimir's own design after he got an idea from me, or so he claimed. It deadened the senses when one was under the influence and gave them crazy trips. They would go wild to their heart's content and never feel the effects of it until the drug wore off.

What happened to them when the drug *did* wear off was their business.

"So, we definitely won't be able to rely on the staff here to do it?" I said.

"Absolutely not. Whoever is running these drugs needs to have a reputation and be able to protect themselves and the club if someone gets uppity." He crossed his arms. "Are none of your contacts panning out?"

"Not so far. The ones who Stavio hasn't already run his mouth to are reluctant to work with the Petrovs in the wake of their simultaneous losses. They think the loss of Vladimir as pakhan means the Petrovs will lose their standing. I'm not counting them out yet," I said. "If I can deal with Vincent, then they'll see the Petrovs haven't lost any power."

"Have you exhausted all of your options?" Brusch asked. "Nothing your cop can do to help you?"

I went quiet for a minute as I thought it over and realized that thought hadn't even crossed my mind. Chloe was an organized crime detective. She had to know who the best suppliers were in the city. It'd be nice if there was an option for me that didn't mean getting involved with another arrogant crime boss who thought the world began and ended at their feet.

"That's not a bad idea," I said. "I'll give her a call in the morning. For now, let's move some product. I don't want my stint as pakhan to start with me losing money."

"Yes, boss."

I was a little too eager to call Chloe the next day. I tried to ignore the way my heart started to beat faster and my stomach did a little flutter when the line picked up, mostly because I didn't know why my body was reacting that way at all.

"Hey there," Chloe said in a warm tone. "How was your night?"

"Productive," I told her. "Then I slept like a baby. Don't know who's to blame for that."

"I wonder..." Chloe replied.

"How would you be up for another date today?" I asked. "Surely you must know some really good, hidden gem in NYC."

"I know a few..." Her tone changed, like she was reluctant to go. "I have to work today though."

"We'll go after," I said. "I'll pick you up."

Chloe was quiet for a long time and I couldn't quite figure it out. It felt like last night had gone so well that I couldn't even wager a guess at why it suddenly seemed like she wanted nothing to do with me. I really wanted the relationship between us to be workable as opposed to contentious. I didn't want to make her do anything if I didn't have to. I'd rather her choose to help me.

"Is there a problem?" I asked finally, putting a little heat into my tone and hoping it was enough.

"No," she said. "We can go out after I'm off. I should be done by five."

"Excellent. I'll see you shortly after that, then."

"Okay. Goodbye."

"Bye."

The dissonance in that conversation left me a little worse for wear. As high as I felt from talking to her the night before, I now felt that low knowing that things had gone back to being strained between us. I went into my room so I could get ready for my date, hoping that I'd not only be able to smooth things over with Chloe yet again, but hopefully I'd be able to sweeten the deal by convincing her to let me show her my kink up close.

CHAPTER TWELVE: CHLOE

After hanging up the phone with Maksim, I was concerned that I was letting too much happen without knowing the answer to whether or not Maksim was mistaken or lying about Katya being with Vincent against her will. He'd been so adamant when we spoke that I was inclined to believe what he said, but after doing some research of my own, I wasn't able to determine the answer. I knew the only way to know for sure was going to be to present him with the information I had and ask him flat out, but I feared what may happen if I did.

It was hard to focus on the rest of my day knowing I had that date coming up, and I was kind of hoping that I'd be able to slip out a little early and get home with plenty of time to center myself and put on my best eating-out-of-the-palm-of-his-hand act before he picked me up.

Thankfully, it wouldn't be too hard to act like he had me in his palm after the night we'd had. I text him looking for more answers about Katya, but when he brought up his kink again, I let my curiosity get the best of me. Once my brain remembered the incredible time we'd had in bed, I found myself initiating sexting, and the rest was history. Not only did I not get any answers, but I fell prey to his whims yet again. I'd be lying if I said I wasn't curious for more, and if I wasn't careful, he'd distract me with his temptations once more.

Just as I was packing up for the day and preparing to let Cox know that I was gonna head out a little early, I heard a commotion.

"Holy shit," I heard Mitzy say behind me. "That's fucking ballsy."

I turned around and my jaw dropped when I saw Maksim striding into the Organized Crime Unit squad room like he belonged there. All of my unit members were watching him with wide eyes and fallen jaws, and apart from Mitzy laughing his ass off, it was totally quiet.

"Good afternoon," Maksim said to me, approaching me at my desk. "I hope it's okay, but I figured I'd come and check out your workplace."

"It absolutely is *not* okay. You're going to cost me my job," I hissed quietly at him. "Get out now! I'll meet you downstairs."

"Don't worry. Everything will be fine," he replied.

I was so furious I could spit fire. "If my boss sees you—"

"If?" Maksim said. "I intend on it."

Then he turned around and started striding towards Cox's office. My heart was beating so hard it felt like it was going to blow a hole in my chest. "Don't!"

"What's going on?" Sydney asked, watching him. "Do you know him?"

"We got well acquainted when I shoved my gun down her throat. That sort of thing bonds people, you know?" Maksim replied, not even looking back at her.

"This is my greatest nightmare come true," I huffed.

"Really?" Mitzy put his feet up on his desk and folded his hands behind the back of his head. "I'm having a great time!"

"Fuck you," I barked at him.

"Knock, knock," Maksim announced as he tapped one of his knuckles against the door to Cox's office. The door opened and Cox appeared on the other side, his face going white as a ghost when he saw Maksim. His sunken brown eyes started to twitch a little bit and he slowly lowered his hand towards his gun. "That's not necessary," Maksim said. "I'm not here to cause any trouble. I just wanted to come by and formally introduce myself." He held out a hand like he was a business person, not the target of the highest profile case our unit had ever taken on. "My name is Maksim Petrov."

"Is this a joke?" Cox asked. "I mean, am I being punked here or something?" He looked past Maksim to me. "What the hell is going on?"

I just shook my head. "Uh, remains to be seen there, captain."

"Your unit hasn't been very welcoming," Maksim said. "I know you're looking into me, so I merely wanted to come by and give you the opportunity to ask me any questions you have. Better to hear it from the horse's mouth as they say."

I glanced sideways at Mitzy who looked up at me with a blown away, agape, half-smile. He was clearly having more fun with this than I was.

I was mortified.

"You think because you're safe now that you can come into my squad room and mock me? Do you have any idea how quickly I'll put you behind bars?"

Maksim tilted his head. "But I haven't done anything wrong."

"You snatched members of my squad," Cox growled back. "Nearly killed one of them?"

"Me?" He scanned the squad room, locking eyes with me for an extra moment, and then looked back at Cox. "I don't believe *I* took any of your staff. And your second-in-command here," he motioned to me, "drew guns in my establishment first. I hadn't seen a warrant, I didn't know why anyone was there. As a visiting foreigner, I barely knew what was going on."

Cox's jaw was flexing and releasing in a constant pattern. "You think you're pretty cute?"

"Objectively? I think I'm quite handsome." Mitzy doubled over in his chair and wheeled around to keep from bursting out laughing in Cox's line of view.

"You," I barked at him and Maksim looked back at me. "Get out."

Our eyes locked into one another and I forced forward as much ire as I could. I wanted him to know I wasn't playing around anymore, that if he lingered here any longer, things were going to get nasty between us. He held my gaze for a while, the smile slowly dropping from his face, but then he finally shrugged.

"Fine. So much for American hospitality," he huffed. He strode back across the squad room with a permeating arrogance that nearly blew out the windows. As he passed me, he very quietly whispered, "I'll be downstairs," and then left without another word.

The squad room was totally silent for a moment as everyone just breathed in the wake of what had just happened. There were additional connotations for me, but everyone else had just watched as the target of our investigation walked in and out of our precinct like he was stopping by for an afternoon tea. Cox looked so gobsmacked that I was almost convinced he was actually just a glitched out projection, until he suddenly turned and threw his fist at the wall, piercing straight through the drywall, and sending crumbles of it down onto the ground.

"Are we fucking kidding with that?!" he bellowed. "That's how much of a joke our unit is, that a notorious serial killer can just walk in and out without any of you even getting up out of your goddamn chairs? Am I a fucking joke to you? What am I doing this for?!" Mitzy was still snickering at his desk until Cox picked up the nearest file box and chucked it across the room. It didn't even make it close to Mitzy, but the scattering of files and papers everywhere was enough to get his attention and make him stop laughing. "You think this is fucking funny?"

"I was amused by the audacity," Mitzy replied simply. "What the fuck did you want us to do? It was like he'd said, he hasn't done anything wrong. We can't arrest him just for walking in here."

"Like fuck you can't!" Cox screamed. "Next time any of you fucks lets a bratva boss walk up to my goddamn door and knock on it like he's delivering the mail—making an absolute mockery of our unit—*everyone* is in the unemployment line the next day! Fuck!" He retreated back into his office, slamming the door behind him and sending even more of the broken drywall sprinkling to the floor.

"Well, if he was looking to get under Cox's skin, I'd say he succeeded," Gauge grumbled.

My head started to pound with a terrible headache. I looked down at Mitzy with a sympathetic look, and he just nodded and waved his hand at me. "Go. I'll cover."

"Sorry to ditch after that, you guys, but I promised my dad I'd pick him up for this appointment," I lied. "Thanks to that, I'm already late."

"We'll keep Cox occupied," Lucas said. "See you tomorrow."

After gathering up all of my things, I took my leave. Each additional step I took had my blood boiling more and more. I couldn't believe that Maksim had the gall to walk into my job like he owned the place and enrage my boss. If Cox had come out and seen us talking, I could have been fired, or worse, arrested. On top of all of that, when I finally got downstairs and outside, Maks was *still* just sitting right in front of the precinct without a care in the world. When he saw me approaching, he smiled—even dared to chuckle as if his little stunt should be funny to me.

Without even looking in his direction I barked, "I'll meet you around the corner."

He let out a sigh like he was terribly put out by the request. "Fine."

I stormed around the corner, surprised I wasn't leaving footprints in the cement I was stomping so hard, and came to a halt behind a building where I was fairly certain no one walking in or out of the precinct could see me before I saw them. Maksim backed his car out of the parking lot and rounded the corner, parking then across the street from where I was and getting out. He walked across to me, still with a casual gait, and actually leaned in for a kiss.

Rearing my head back violently, I hissed, "Have you lost your mind? Do you have any idea the kind of trouble I could have gotten in?"

"I told you I had it under control," Maksim said. "I even had a cover story for your squad members."

"*If* they even believe you," I spat back. "My boss put his fist through a wall. Are you trying to make my life more difficult? Is that your actual goal here?"

He crossed his arms. "You know my goal here. It's to save Katya."

"Is it?" He furrowed his brow and recoiled a bit. I'd planned to discuss things more reasonably with him, but I was so angry that the words just flew out, "I have reason to believe that Katya is here voluntarily and of her own free will. You're either mistaken when you say she's a prisoner or you're lying to me, which is it?"

A look of fury came across Maksim's face, the likes of which I'd never seen before. "You think I'm a liar or a fool?"

"I think it's one or the other," I said. "I have it on very good authority that Katya very much *wants* to be in New York with Vincent."

"She *wants* it?" he repeated quietly. His eyes got a manic appearance to them and when he took a step closer to me, it was ominous and radiated darkness. "Katya doesn't know what she wants. She's confused. When her spirit and will were most broken, she turned to the only living, breathing person that was interacting with her and that was Vincent." He continued to close the distance to me, and I backed up, suddenly fearful of what he was going to do. "You think you know? Why? Because you asked your friend *Mitzy*?" My eyes widened a little bit and Maks said, "That's right, I know about his relationship with the Costellos. I know *everything*, Chloe."

"Back away from me," I warned.

He didn't listen, continuing to close in on me until I was pressed against the brick wall behind me. Like a huge claw coming up to threaten me, Maksim lifted one of his hands and perched it next to my head against the wall. He loomed over me, all of a sudden unrecognizable from the man I'd seen so far.

"You don't know anything about this situation. You're a mouse in a lion's den. You think that *you* or some cocky cop can tell me more about this than what I've seen with my own eyes? What I've experienced with my own body?" His words were uttered with such thunder that I began to wonder if maybe Mitzy actually *was* mistaken. "Katya went from wearing my engagement ring and living in my home, to suddenly choosing to come back to New York with Vincent. One of his men snatched her right off the street when she was shopping with her mother. The woman is still haunted by the vision of coming back to see her pregnant daughter's bags skelter in the street with her child nowhere to be seen."

"You were engaged to her?" I asked quietly, hating that a pang of jealousy still coursed through me.

"Katya was meant to be *mine*," he hissed. "We had a home. We broke bread with her family and celebrated. Now, you tell me, how does a woman go from that to suddenly wishing to fly back across the country with a man she'd met and known only in his capture of her?"

Frustrations with Maksim's connection to Katya aside, I was back to thinking that maybe the woman really *did* need help. If everything Maks said was true, I would certainly think the same way he did—Katya was just acting out of fear for herself and for her child.

Hearing this story and seeing the way Maksim turned into someone unhinged at the mention of it, I realized that I'd fucked up and walked into a far more complicated situation than I first realized. I wanted to help Katya if she needed help, but I now had to help myself. The person I was dealing with had two sides that were polar from one another and both equally frightening. I had no idea how I was going to unravel the truth for myself and even less idea how I was going to escape Maksim's clutches, or at least this dark Maksim, with my life.

"I don't think it's a good idea for us to go out tonight," I said.

To my surprise, Maksim responded, "I think you're right."

He pulled back from me and I watched as he skulked back across the street, suddenly keeping his head on a swivel, and got into his car. His fists throttled the steering wheel, and for a moment it was like there was nothing he could do to calm himself down. He took deep, even breaths and then ran a hand through his hair, before starting his car and zooming off.

It was only once the car was so far down the street that I could no longer hear it, that I released the tension in my body and collapsed backwards onto the wall. My heart was slamming so hard I could feel it in every corner of my body, and the headache that I'd developed while still in the precinct had doubled in pain. A few tears actually came to my eyes, but I was uncertain if they were of fear, frustration, defeat, or a combination of all three. Even having seen what I'd seen, there was still a part of me that was jealous of the dedication Maksim seemed to have to Katya. It wasn't like I would be with him—or could—even if I wanted to, but a very tiny piece of me wished his feelings were for me instead, if for no other reason, so that he wouldn't continue flipping to that dark person I just saw.

One thing was for absolute certain, Maksim's dedication to Katya was turning him into a monster, and if I didn't sort it out, I was going to get gobbled up in his warpath, along with half of the state of New York.

CHAPTER THIRTEEN: MAKSIM

Regret over the way I let my anger issues erupt with Chloe didn't come until well after I'd gotten back to my penthouse. My frustration persisted during my drive, but once I got back home and realized my mistake, it rapidly started to eat me alive. Not only had I shown Chloe a very unsightly side of myself, but I'd also tipped my hand about Katya, both of which were very bad things.

On top of all of that, I also let my pride get the best of me and keep me from following through with our dinner plans. Aside from just wanting to spend more time with her, a huge part of the reason I'd made those dinner plans to begin with was so that I could pick her brain for possible suppliers.

If I was going to rate this mission on a scale of one to complete success, I was coming in at around a negative one hundred. I'd given up too much of my own information, failed to get any helpful information for Dacha, and isolated Chloe all in one fell swoop.

Well done, me.

"Boss?" Brusch questioned when I walked through Dacha's back door. "I thought you were gone for the night?"

"My plans changed," I growled back.

Brusch seemed to understand that he shouldn't push the limits with me, and simply pressed the button to call the elevator. "Do you need me to stay on watch?"

"Do whatever you want," I hissed as I climbed on.

He seemed a little put off by the harsh response, but nodded his head nonetheless and said, "Yes, boss."

Once I got upstairs, there wasn't much else I could think to do except open up my laptop and spy on the Costello estate a little more. I'd noticed that early in the evening was when things seemed to get the most quiet around there. A few cars of staff would leave around six or seven in the evening and not return until well after three in the morning, and by my best guess, these cars were either staff on their leisurely time, staff going to move product during the busy bar and club hours, or both.

Neither Katya nor Vincent seemed to leave the estate after about five in the evening. None of the vehicles I'd come to know as theirs would be caught on camera after this time, and I wouldn't see them moving about again until early the next morning. I'd only been surveilling the property for a few days, but things seemed oddly routine. Vincent, Katya, Mario, and a few other higher up looking individuals came and went almost on a perfect schedule, with Katya being the outlier oddly enough. She seemed to be defining her own schedule and doing what she wanted.

Which of course brought my earlier conversation with Chloe back to my brain.

Who did she think she was trying to tell *me* about Katya? She thought because she had a cohort who was in the Costello's back pocket that she suddenly knew the whole story better than me? No one knew the Petrov family better than me. Not Chloe, or Mitzy, or anyone. Katya was supposed to be with me. We were happy together.

We were...

I glanced up and looked at my face in the mirror across from the couch I was sitting on. It was the same one where, just last night, I saw the first honest smile I'd seen or felt on my face in longer than I could remember. It wasn't Katya on the other end of that smile, it was Chloe. Had I ever smiled like that when Katya and I were together. Even if we were feigning a relationship, I believed that having her around me made me happy, but nothing ever made me smile the way I had last night...

"No," I said out loud.

I slammed the laptop shut and slid it onto the coffee table, frustrated beyond measure. Why was I doubting myself all of a sudden? I could blame it on the fact that Chloe and I had history and I was predisposed to listen to her because I did respect her, even if our paths were ill-fated. Sure, there was a part of me that realized that Katya truly believed she wanted to be here with Vincent, but the circumstances that bred their love weren't healthy. If Katya hadn't been kidnapped—if she hadn't been forced to stay with Vincent because of her father's long game plans—she never would have allowed someone like that into her bed. I was certain of that. I saw first hand how terrified she was for her baby and how much she wanted her child to have a father in its life.

If all of it was stripped away—if Katya didn't have to be worried about the relationship she formed with Vincent while she was his captive, or his baby that she was carrying in her belly, or the fact that her father and brother died as a result of Vincent's presence in Russia—would she *still* choose to be with him? If she had the choice between being here in New York, or moving back to her hometown with her mother, and raising her baby in the same city she grew up in with a man who would do anything to keep her and that baby safe, wouldn't she choose the latter?

I had to believe that she would.

And it was exactly for that reason that I needed to help Katya make the decision she most wanted to make. I needed to eliminate any threats from her life, and then I intended to follow through on my promise to be there for her and her child. We were going to be a family.

That was what was best for all of us.

So I couldn't allow myself to start getting caught in Chloe's web now. She was still a useful asset to me, given that she was a New York City detective, and that was the angle I needed to keep working with her. I had my options to keep her working with me as opposed to against me, but I was hoping that an apology might help keep things amicable between us. I gave it the night and then I called her in the morning, not getting angry when she didn't answer, but rather just chose to leave a voicemail.

"Chloe, it's Maks. I wanted to apologize for yesterday. I blew up about the situation with Katya and Vincent, but that's just because it hits very close to home for me. Vladimir, Sascha, and yes, even Katya, have been huge parts of my life. If there's any possibility at all that Katya isn't happy here, I need to rectify that, because it's what I owe to her and it's what I owe to her late father and brother. I'd love to be a little more candid about this and offer you the in-person apology you deserve, so please call me back so we can talk this out. Thanks."

I'd never left such an honest and vulnerable message before, but I figured it'd be worth it if Chloe saw reason and returned my call. Unfortunately, the entire day elapsed and I didn't so much as receive a text message from her. I tried calling a couple of additional times, but never got an answer.

Thanks to my tendency to explode, I wanted to get angry, but I did my best to exercise patience. I'd shown Chloe a pretty scary side of myself after all, and it would be perfectly normal for a person to want to keep their distance after that. We had an agreement, and I planned on making sure she followed through with it, but I could give her a few days' space if that was what she needed.

Chloe —I texted her around the end of the third day since we'd last spoken — *I know you're probably frustrated with me, but I thought we were together on this. Please give me a chance to explain myself. I'd like to hear from you tomorrow. Thanks—Maks.*

I could see on the phone that she read the message, but again, I received no response. Still, I gave her until the next day, so I didn't blow my stack just yet. I worked Dacha that night, meeting some of the New York clientele and realizing that what Brusch had told me was correct—we needed some people with experience to handle the pushing here. There was money to be made, but not if I didn't have someone who knew what they were doing heading up the operation on this end.

It wasn't long after Dacha closed for the night that I rolled myself into bed, maybe around four in the morning, and I woke up about six hours later. I took my time going through my morning, showering, eating breakfast, and doing a little bit of work—really giving Chloe those last few hours to make a decision.

But by the time three in the afternoon rolled around and I still hadn't heard from her, I let out a deep sigh. I didn't want to have to get rough with her, but she was giving me no choice.

I had to remind her what was at stake if she didn't cooperate.

Dacha was located in Little Odessa, which was where the largest population of Russian people in New York City lived. Because it was a bratva owned and run club, it only made sense to put it near the community that was its target demographic. I remembered when we first conceptualized the place, Vladimir wanted to put it closer to other high-end clubs and bars in NYC, but I told him we'd make our money off of creating a place that felt exclusive to the Russian community, and I was right. A majority of our customers were Russian immigrants or first generation, and those who desperately wanted access to our products didn't mind coming out to Little Odessa to get it. It kept our business as close to home as it could be in New York, and gave our community a feeling of superiority whenever people from outside the community had to come in to get what they wanted.

If you pissed off the people of Little Odessa, you weren't allowed in.

Not far from Dacha, located right in the heart of this area, was Chloe's family bodega, Nasha Udacha. I'd gone there once on friendly terms when Chloe and I first reconnected. I thought the one time was all it would take to show Chloe exactly how important it was for her to maintain the deal we'd made, this recent hiccup proved that wasn't at all the case.

So unfortunately, my second trip would not be as pleasant.

It was a short walk from Dacha to the bodega, and when I entered, I saw that Chloe's father wasn't there, but her sister, Chandler, was. She was standing behind the checkout counter, flicking through her phone because there weren't any customers inside, but she stopped and stood at attention once she saw me enter.

"Oh. Hi, Maksim!" She was a bit jittery, and by my best guess that was a result of the drug addiction Chloe mentioned her having. "Chloe's not here right now, but you can hang out if you want to. I'm pretty bored."

Skipping right past pleasantries, I hissed at Chandler, "Call your sister and tell her that I'm here."

Chandler frowned. "Huh? If you want to talk to her, call her yourself."

I rested my hands on the countertop and leaned a little over, towering over Chandler with a dark and ominous presence. "Call your sister and tell her that I'm here."

Though Chandler seemed a bit put off by my tone, she was also two sheets to the wind, and hadn't yet seemed to grasp the seriousness of the situation. "Can't you hear? If you want to talk to her, go call her yourself. I'm not her errand girl, and I'm not yours either."

I twisted my head to the side, cracking it as I did so, then I reached into my waistband and pulled out my gun. Chandler yelped, falling backwards onto her butt before cowering backwards into the corner. Her phone fell and clattered to the ground a few feet away from her, but she suddenly had tears in her eyes and was holding up a hand in defense of herself.

"I'm really not in the mood to play games with you, little girl," I growled at her. "I realize I have an accent, but I believe I'm speaking perfect English. Is there any part of what I said that you don't understand?"

She shook her head, shaking. "N-no."

I stepped on her phone and kicked it over to her and then repeated, "Then call your sister and tell her that I'm here."

Chandler nervously reached out and grabbed her phone, though her shakes were violent as she tried to dial. She was twitching and could barely control herself enough to make accurate taps on her phone, but she was forcing herself through it due to the gun pointed at her. I remembered Chloe telling me the way her mom died and that it was the result of her sister's drug use. Knowing this experience was probably triggering Chandler pretty badly, I actually felt bad, but Chloe left me without options. I needed to show her I was serious.

Why did I come all this way to New York if I was just going to get side-tracked and not finish what I came here to do? Failure wasn't an option.

"C-Chloe?" Chandler said weakly. "I n-ne-ed you to c-c-come to the..." She let out a pitiful little whine that nearly made me back off. "The bodega. It's serious." She nodded, likely in response to something her sister said, then she replied. "I'm o-k-kay. Please, just hu-hurry." She set down her phone and looked up at me teary eyed. "She's c-o..." She was shivering wildly. "She's—"

"Just stop," I said. "Don't speak."

As I stood there pointing my gun down at Chandler, I started to feel some regret. In the far, far back of my mind, I considered whatever possibility there was that Chloe and I would be able to continue our physical relationship and figured that this was pretty much going to kill it. Not only that, but the Nikitina family and my family were close once. Threatening Chandler didn't make me happy.

In fact, the more I thought about it, the more horrible I felt. I tried to think backwards to whatever turning point led me to this moment, but I was unable to pinpoint it. By now, though, it didn't make sense to waver. I'd already gotten here, I already had a gun pointed at the girl's face and she was already having a panic attack in front of me. It'd almost be worse, after forcing her here now, to then try and go easy on her.

This had officially turned into a lose-lose situation.

"Chandler?" Chloe's voice called out. "Are you o—" Chloe rounded the corner and saw me standing over her sister, pointing a gun down at her. I glared over at her and the look on her face shattered me internally. She looked a combination of betrayed and heartbroken, and I knew in an instant that I'd made an irreversible mistake. "Maksim." She held up her hands. "Just calm down, okay? I'm sorry I didn't call you back." Her voice was quiet and begging. "Please, just don't hurt my sister."

"Chloe?" Chandler squeaked.

"It's okay," Chloe called out. "Just don't move, okay? Everything's gonna be okay."

Chandler tucked her head between her legs and whimpered out, "Mama," and it made me want to turn the gun on myself.

All of a sudden, I had no idea why I was doing this.

"Maksim please," Chloe begged. "I'm sorry. I'll do whatever you want, just please..." Tears filled her eyes. "Please don't hurt her."

I pulled my hand back and walked around the counter. Chloe let out a ragged breath, fighting hard to hold back her emotions as I approached her. Even she had a small shake to her. As much as I wanted to break down and start apologizing and begging for forgiveness of my own, I didn't know where that would get me either. At least this way I could accomplish what I came here to do.

"You brought this on yourself," I told her. "You can't ignore me. The only reason you're living—the only reason your family is living—is because I've deemed it so. Do you understand?"

Chloe nodded. "Yes."

"Good. Let this be my final warning to you," I threatened, leaning in closer to her. "I will not be so forgiving the next time."

Then without any additional words, and wishing terribly that I could turn back time, I left the bodega, listening to the sounds of both women's sobs as they relived the most traumatic day of their lives because of me.

CHAPTER FOURTEEN: CHLOE

When my alarm went off for work, I groaned. I was going on day six of next to no sleep. It was a lot of just tossing and turning, and the few times I did fall asleep, I'd start having some nightmare about my mom or Chandler being killed by Maksim, and I'd shoot awake only an hour or two later. Things at work had been particularly stressful because Cox was still up in arms about Maksim coming by nearly a week later and had the entire squad on pins and needles. Mitzy did his best to keep things light, as he tended to, but with the stress from dealing with Maksim weighing down on me as well, I wasn't in the best place to be moved to humor.

To make matters worse, while part of me was reacting to this issue with Maksim like the horrifying situation it was, there was a part of me that was treating it more like a bad breakup. There were times I just found myself thinking about him or longing for lighter days when we successfully managed to put our crossroads behind us and just enjoy one another's company. I would randomly remember that night we spent together or our heated sexting session and wish we could do it again.

I wished I knew how much of that was fake and how much wasn't.

When I finally convinced myself to get out of bed, I saw that my dad had called me, which he did very rarely. It was usually for help evading a speeding ticket or DUI, but it was a bit early in the day for either of those things, so I called him back just in case. With Maksim on the loose, I couldn't be too careful.

"Hey, Daddy," I said when he answered the phone. "Sorry I missed your call. I'm not sure how I missed my phone ringing."

"Is your sister there?" he asked.

I froze halfway between my bedroom and the bathroom. "No. Is she not at home with you?"

My sister, though twenty now, still lived with my father, really because they were both incredibly co-dependent. It made me feel better knowing they were together—but only to the end that one of them called me and asked where the other was when they should be together.

"No. I haven't seen her in three days."

"What?" I yelped. "Dad! How could you not tell me that sooner?"

"Don't yell at me, Chloe!" he barked. "Your sister goes missing from time to time. It's normal at this point."

"It's not normal! She's probably on a bender!" I palmed the sleep out of my eyes, trying to adjust to this sudden wake up call. I'd been keeping in close contact with my sister because I expected something like this might happen after her experience with Maksim. I'd texted with her last night and she said she was fine and at home. She must have lied. "Have you checked around for her?"

"Some of her usual spots, but she's not there," he replied. "I need you to find her. Call your network or whatever you normally do to fish her out."

I let out a long sigh. "I've got it. Just keep an eye out for her and let me know if she comes home."

"Fine. Love you. Bye."

"Love you too, bye." I ended the call and stood in my hallway in an exhausted stupor for a few moments. Plain and simple, I did not have enough energy for all of this. After taking a few minutes, I brought the phone up to my ear and called a friend of mine from the academy who worked in narcotics now. "Ace?"

"Hey, Chloe. Long time, no chat," he replied. "Is this a good call or a bad call?"

"A bad one, unfortunately," I replied. "My sister is missing again. My dad's checked out some of her usual haunts, but hasn't been able to track her down. Do you think you can spread the word and see if you can track her down and get her back home? I'd really appreciate it. I'm trying to keep her from going back to jail."

"Yeah, of course, I'll get right on it," he responded. "Actually, can we trade favors? I need some info that I think you might have."

"Sure," I said. "What's up?"

"I'd planted a UC in the Bonetti family to try and get a handle on what drugs are running in and out of that Russian club in Little Odessa, Dacha, but it seems like things have gone bad between the Petrovs and the Bonettis."

"Yeah," I said. "The pakhan and Stavio clashed and they gave the Bonettis the boot."

"Fuck," he said. "You wouldn't happen to know anything about the new pakhan would you? Some other way I can get my UC in there?"

"He's in a particularly untrustworthy place right now, so you're gonna want to tread lightly. He's not hesitating to shoot right now. Is your UC Russian?" I asked.

"No."

"You might want to switch up," I told him. "Based on the way things have gone, first with the Costellos, and now with the Bonettis, the Petrovs are not going to be prone to trusting anyone who isn't Russian at the moment. If you want my honest opinion, you should put that investigation on ice, at least for now. The pakhan will be going back to Russia at some point, and then you'll be in a better spot to get someone new in there. Spend the time between now and then to train a Russian UC."

He sighed. "I was afraid you might say that, but I appreciate the honesty."

"Of course," I replied, feeling icky that part of why I told him to lay off was actually for Maksim's protection. "You can always call if you need anything. We're happy to share any info we have."

"Thanks, Chloe. I'll get the feelers out for Chandler right away. Don't worry, we'll find her."

I let out a little sigh of relief. "Thanks, Ace. Talk to you soon."

"Yeah. Bye."

Officially, I hated what I'd become. I'd just intentionally interfered with an investigation into Maksim and Dacha because of the deal he and I had made to keep him safe. Even though I no longer saw him as a friend, only an enemy, he'd made it clear he wasn't above hurting me or my family, so to protect us, I had to protect him. Internally, I made a silent promise to myself to undo that mistake as soon as I could. If I could just get Maksim out of the US, then I would help narcotics get into Dacha and hopefully bust them from inside out. Maybe even take down Maksim in the process. I was hoping things could end more peacefully between me and my old friend, but he'd proven I couldn't trust him to treat me as an equal. I was a tool to him only, and if I ever let that slip from my mind again, it was going to cost me or one of my family members our lives.

I trudged into work not feeling much better than I did when I woke up for the day, and Mitzy was quick to notice. Despite my best attempts to just ignore him and sit down at my desk, he tapped me on the shoulder and simply said, "Come on. Let's go get a coffee."

Part of me wanted to argue. I knew things were going to get more personal than I wanted them to if I went with him, but I was without the ability to argue with him too much. Besides, I cared about Mitzy and knew he was just worried, so I reluctantly stood up and followed him back out of the precinct and to the elevator doors.

"You look like death, Chloe," he said when we were on the elevator headed down.

"Thank you," I said. "Always nice to hear first thing in the morning."

"You know what I mean," he said. "What's going on? Is it Maksim?"

I nodded, knowing it was pointless to hold anything back. "I learned that he was engaged to Katya briefly before she left him for Vincent. He's here to try and take her back, but he's pretty convinced she's not here of her own free will," I explained. "When that conversation sort of erupted between us, I stopped talking to him out of frustration, and he flipped out and threatened Chandler. Went to the bodega and held a gun to her face."

"That was why you left in such a hurry last week," he said. "I was wondering when you were going to tell me why." We stepped off the elevator, but before we could get too far, he pulled me into a hug. "I'm so sorry. I can't imagine how horrifying that must have been for you two after what happened with your mom." It was oddly welcome after the week I'd had, and I sort of melted into it. I was glad I had Mitzy. He was like an older brother or crazy uncle that I could always count on. I had no idea where I'd be without him.

Well I did, I'd be dead. Twice.

"Chandler went off the deep end and my dad just called me this morning to tell me he hasn't seen her in days."

Mitzy leaned back from me and was already going for his phone. "I'll call Ace."

"I did already," I said. "He's already trying to hunt her down, but then..." I let out a strained grunt of frustration. "Ace wanted some info on Dacha and Maksim to try and get a UC in there and bust the new drug they're running, but I lied to convince him not to."

"Because Maksim threatened your family, so now you're trying not to piss him off more," Mitzy filled in.

"Yeah. So now I'm just this..." I threw my hands in the air. "Hypocrite! I'm protecting someone I'm supposed to be fighting. I'm doing the thing I hate most. And I'm terrified for my family and I haven't gotten more than like two hours of sleep a night for the last week and—"

"Whoa..." Mitzy pulled me back into a hug. "Okay, just calm down."

"And I don't know what to do about Katya. Because if she's really in trouble, I want to help her, even if that *isn't* to send her with Maksim, but I also don't want to rip her from a situation she wants to be in..." A tear broke loose and dripped down my cheek. "I don't know what to do."

Mitzy stepped back again, but set his hands on my shoulders. "Okay, well let's just take things one step at a time. Maksim's in an okay place now, right? No fear he's going to fly off and do something at this point."

"I don't think so," I said.

"Okay, so that's dealt with for the moment. Ace is already looking for your sister, so we're good there. I'm gonna buy you some melatonin and warm milk so you can try and get the sleep you desperately need, so that just leaves the thing with Katya, and I think I know the best way to deal with that," he said.

I furrowed my brow. "How?"

"You need to just talk to her yourself," he said. "Ask her all the questions you have and then judge for yourself if you think she's here of her own volition or not. Then you can decide the best way to help her or if you need to just leave her alone."

"Okay, but how am I going to talk to her?" I said. "I'd be willing to bet if I went anywhere near the Costello's estate, Maksim would know in a heartbeat."

"So you won't meet with her there," Mitzy said. "I'm in contact with them. I'm certain that I can set up a meeting between the two of you. She's a really wonderful woman, honestly. I'm sure she'll answer any questions you have about Vince or the Petrovs. She'd probably tell you her life story if you asked. You've been getting all your information second-hand, and that's put you in this spot. Don't let me tell you or Maksim tell you anymore. Go right to the source."

I wiped my cheeks free of the tears that had fallen and nodded. "Okay. I like that idea. If she's willing to talk to me, then I'd love to talk to her."

"Good. Wait right here. I'll be right back."

Once Mitzy had walked away, I found the nearest bench and sat down to try and collect myself. I was embarrassed that I let my emotions get a hold of me that way, but in truth, I was so tired that everything felt magnified. I redid my ponytail and tried to wipe my face down with my hands a little bit. I needed to pull it together. I was a New York City detective. My behavior was unbecoming and an embarrassment to the other brave men and women who wore the same badge I did.

In my pocket, my phone started to buzz and I pulled it out. I saw it was my dad, so I quickly answered, "Hello?"

"Hey," he said. "Your sister is home. Some cop named Ace brought her a few hours ago. She's messed up, but it's nothing I can't handle."

Relief was only half as potent because I knew it was going to be an uphill battle fighting to keep Chandler from running back out to the streets. "Okay. I'm glad she's home. Keep me posted and I'll come by after work tonight and check on you guys."

"Alright. Love ya."

My dad, as shiesty as he might be, never ended a call without saying he loved me. Not since my mom died. "I love you too, Dad. Bye."

Once I hung up with my dad, I shot Ace a quick text thanking him for his help—even though it left a pit of guilt in my gut—and just as I was firing that off, Mitzy was walking back over to me.

"Hey," he said. "You good?"

"Yeah, that was my dad," I replied. "Chandler's back home."

"Whoo," he breathed out. "Ace works fast, doesn't he?"

"Thank god," I said.

"Alright. Well, let's go so we don't waste anymore time," he said. "We gotta hurry so we aren't late."

"To... coffee?" I said.

He chuckled at me. "No. To see Katya." My jaw dropped. When Mitzy said he was going to set up a meeting, I thought he meant for sometime in the future. "We're meeting her at a cafe in ten minutes."

CHAPTER FIFTEEN: MAKSIM

I could admit it, I was a little drunk.

Drinking to the point of being inebriated wasn't something I liked to do very often. People made dumb decisions and got loose-lipped when they were drunk, and neither of those things served me very well. The thing was, right now I was making dumb decisions and getting loose-lipped while perfectly sober, so I might as well be drunk.

Brusch had collected me early that morning to bring me down and listen to a few options he'd identified as possible managers for when I left to return to Russia. We'd decided that he would work on trying to find a manager for Dacha while I focused on finding a replacement distributor for our drug through the club.

And he was obviously doing much better than I was.

The second-in-command to the pakhan was the sovietnik—they advised the pakhan. In the old regime when Vladimir was pakhan, he technically had two. Visually, Sascha was his sovietnik and served as his second-in-command and would become pakhan if anything ever happened to Vladimir. Everyone knew that Sascha was sovietnik and treated him with that level of respect.

Behind the scenes, however, Vladimir had a second sovietnik—me. Not even Sascha knew that Vladimir had me in this role, but he had me in his back pocket as an option with a little less familial responsibility. Because he'd helped out so much with my family, when he asked me to step into this role, I of course accepted—I wanted to do anything I could to repay him for all of his kindness. When he was concerned that Sascha would be too closely related to something to make an optimal decision, he would defer to me. He used to tell me often that my vision aligned more with his own, and at some point, he began to plan as if I would take over as pakhan rather than Sascha. Of course, Sascha was the one who'd brought me to his father to begin with, so I never would have taken that role from him if he wanted it, but it ended up being cruelly poetic that Vladimir and his son died at the same time, leaving me in charge anyway.

It didn't really occur to me until I was sitting there that I needed to start building new ranks of my own. I would need my own sovietnik eventually. The issue was that a pakhan's sovietnik was traditionally someone they trusted, and I didn't really trust many people outside of my barely living mother. Brusch was proving himself to be useful, but I could tell that he was still passively judging every decision I made.

In short, he didn't trust me either.

There was probably a part of me that was hoping I could make Katya my sovietnik if I could get her back to Russia with me. Her father never trusted her enough to involve her in the business, though his mistrust was misplaced. Katya respected her family and her father's empire to the edges of her existence. If he'd just accepted her into his ranks, it was entirely possible that he'd still be alive right now.

And not just because it was Katya herself who shot the gun that killed him.

Every single day, it felt like I found something new that I was going to have to deal with. I'd been stuck in a funk in the wake of Vladimir and Sascha's deaths and just sort of towing the line, but being in New York seemed to have erected a new need to start doing more than just going into auto-pilot. Regardless of how, things were going to come to a conclusion with Katya soon, and when they did, it would be time for me to turn my head towards taking over as pakhan fully, which meant more than just figuring out how things were going to go at Dacha.

Huh... maybe drinking was making me more introspective...

"Boss?"

I snapped out of my thoughts and looked up to see everyone in the meeting looking back at me. "I'm sorry, what'd I miss?"

"I really think that Tonia could be a good option for us," he said, motioning to the tall, slender, redhead woman looking back at me. "She's been at Dacha for a while now and has always had a lot of respect for Vladimir."

"He saved my family during one of his trips here," she said in a thick, Russian accent. "I have always considered myself indebted to the Petrov family, and I would of course extend that respect to you as the new pakhan. I never cared much for the way Dino tried to juggle multiple lucrative opportunities. I'm nothing if not an appreciator of an entrepreneur, but there's an etiquette to that sort of thing. One he frequently disobeyed."

"What do you think? Do you have any questions for her?" Brusch asked.

I shook my head, working on the glass of whiskey I had in my hand. " Not at this time. Thank you for coming in, Tonia. I'll have a decision for you soon."

She nodded her head. "Thank you, boss."

Then she left the VIP booth we'd communed in. The other Dacha employees that had gathered, I believed to back up Tonia's bid for manager, also left to allow Brusch and I to convene about the meeting alone.

"She seems promising," I told Brusch.

He snorted. "I'm surprised you captured a whole lot."

I leered over at him. "Something you want to say?"

"Just that this is important," Brusch replied, "and you seem very distracted. Did something happen that you want to discuss?"

"No," I said. "If something happened that I wanted to discuss, I would have discussed it."

Brusch cleared his throat and then looked at me nervously. "Sir, I don't mean to overstep, but you *do* realize I'm here to help you, right? You seem to be committed to doing all of this on your own, but I want to help you achieve success. Whenever I ask questions or try to implore you to see reason, it's only because I want to help lead your empire to even more success."

"I understand," I said. "You'll have to forgive me. I'm not quick to trust. I haven't had much luck doing that. I realize you're just trying to be an aid to me, for which I'm grateful. I'll work on being more honest, but I also need you to continue respecting my desire not to share too much about my personal life at this point."

"Of course," he said. "So long as you know that I'm here for whatever you need, then I'll follow your lead on what you choose to share and what you choose to keep to yourself."

"Thank you," I said. "I will say, an issue between myself and the detective I've been working with had a bit of a falling out, so getting information on a possible new distributor has been going much slower than I was hoping for. I will get to something eventually, but I'm afraid it isn't happening at the pace I was planning on."

"I see. I'll keep my ear out for something as well, but in the meantime, you may want to consider making nice with your detective. The last thing you would want is for her to strike out against you by attacking Dacha."

"I don't think that she would. I have her pretty well contained. There's too much at stake for her to act against me," I said. "I've made it very clear to her the consequences of her lack of cooperation."

"You haven't left her without hope though, have you?" he said. "Everyone has an instinct to survive, but those backed into a corner will lash out in ways you aren't expecting."

Rather than responding, I finished the rest of my whiskey while taking in his words. I was living proof of that concept. When my only friend was taken away, my mother fell so ill that she couldn't even take care of herself anymore, let alone a child, and my father decided to leave me, it left me with little option but to accept help from Russia's most dangerous and notorious man. It was something that came up between Chloe and I not long after we reconnected. She felt as pushed into her choice as I felt pushed into mine. Brusch was right. If I pushed against Chloe too much, she had the power to push back and take me down, even if she took herself down with it.

"I'll keep that advice in mind," I replied after a moment of reflective silence. "Thank you." I stood up and started out of the VIP booth. "Can you get a car for me? I need to do a couple of things, but I probably shouldn't drive in my state."

"Of course," Brusch replied. "I'll call for it now and let you know when it has arrived."

"Thank you."

It was the middle of the day, and I knew that Katya tended to leave Vincent's estate on her own for lunch. I honestly wasn't planning on connecting with Katya at all until I was ready to take Vincent out and return to Russia with Katya in tow, but recent events had me questioning, well, everything...

For whatever reason, I felt like if I could just speak with Katya, maybe she would help me see the path forward. I still firmly believed that Katya's future was not with Vincent and was in fact back in Russia, but thanks to Chloe's presence in my life, I was beginning to wonder how big my role in her future should be. I had feelings for her—I imagined I always would—but was there an alternative route out there for me that didn't involve the two of us ending up together? If I could at least give her the option to return to Russia if she wanted, then could the outcome for us be different?

After having the driver that Brusch had orchestrated for me go and sit outside the Costello's estate, I saw Katya's Maserati leave and asked my driver to follow behind it, of course keeping a safe distance. Though I'd done this a couple of times before, something about this time felt oddly unsatisfying to me. It even felt a little creepy. When I popped up at whatever restaurant Katya decided to dine at for the day, she was going to wonder how I knew where to find her, and I did not relish the idea of telling her that I had her current home bugged or had been stalking her from a distance. When I first placed the camera and started to gather the gist of Vincent and Katya's routine, it felt like it had a purpose.

Now I wasn't entirely sure what that was.

I knew I'd have to come to blows with Vincent at some point and convinced myself that this was the best way to know when I could get him alone for a strike at him. Eventually, I'd make use of this system that I'd set up, but for some reason, for no discernable reason, it felt really out of place to me.

Putting it out of my mind, Katya eventually led us to a cafe about halfway between the Costello's estate and the heart of NYC. It was bustling enough, but far away from the main metropolis that we were able to avoid traffic. I asked my driver to park and wait for me about half a mile away so that I could walk off my buzz and figure out exactly what I wanted to say to Katya. I was going to have to offer an explanation for sure, but I wasn't sure if it was a good or bad idea to be open with her about Chloe. I'd never even discussed my life before the Petrovs other than my mother.

I was just reaching out for the door handle when I caught a glimpse of someone out of the corner of my eye and was certain I was mistaken. I slunk backwards from the door—graciously there was a large planter and shrubbery to hide me—and waited until I was able to ensure it was just my mind showing me what I most wanted to see at the moment. A woman approached the door with a man at her side, and I could have sworn it was Chloe. It was difficult to pull her all the way out of the rotating crowd of people in the area, but I was certain that the fact that I had Chloe on the brain was simply making me see things.

And I was wrong.

As the door to the cafe swung open and the woman stepped in, I was able to see her a bit clearer and was surprised to see that it was, in fact, Chloe. The man next to her was her coworker Mitzy, and not long after they entered, they both started scanning the place like they were looking for someone.

What were the chances that Chloe would be at the same restaurant Katya was at?

Suddenly more interested in Chloe than Katya, I watched as Chloe watched Mitzy, who was looking around the cafe. He gave the area a good scan before pointing and ushering Chloe forward. She walked forward with Mitzy behind her, and eventually made her way to a table with a single person sitting at it.

Katya.

"No," I murmured out loud.

Katya stood up from the table and gave Mitzy a hug, then held out her hand for Chloe. Chloe gave it a firm shake, offering a friendly smile, then Katya motioned to a chair and both she and Chloe sat down. Mitzy put a hand on Chloe's back and said a few words before walking off, eventually sitting himself down at a table a few away from where Katya and Chloe were sitting. Once he was gone, the two of them began to speak and my stomach started to churn.

What were they meeting for? Had Chloe gone behind my back after what I'd told her about Katya and was revealing what I'd said? I could think of no other reason for Chloe to be speaking with Katya and didn't see any outcome where her speaking with Chloe had any outcome other than her revealing to Katya that I was here and maybe even that I was trying to take her away from Vincent.

Chloe was betraying me. Brusch's warning came to fruition much sooner than I was anticipating.

Infuriated, I stood up and walked away from the cafe before I lost my cool and did something I would regret. Chloe would need to be dealt with for her insurrection, but I couldn't do it in such a public place. I thought I'd made myself clear to Chloe, but she seemed to be defying me at every turn.

But that was going to end.

I got in the car and instructed the driver to take me back to Dacha, immediately thereafter pulling out my phone and calling Brusch.

"Boss," he said immediately. "Is everything alright?"

"No," I retorted. "You said you were around to help me with anything I needed, right?"

"Yes, boss," he said.

"Good. I'm about to send you a picture. There's someone I need you to snatch for me."

CHAPTER SIXTEEN: CHLOE

Katya took a sip of her tea before frowning at the cup. "I miss caffeine."

"I can only imagine," I said. "I survive on the stuff. I have no idea what I'd do if I couldn't drink it."

"I know it'll be worth it when I have my baby girl in my arms, but..." She sighed. "It'll be even more worth it when I have my baby girl in one arm and my cup of coffee in the other."

I laughed. "I bet." Looking over my shoulder at Mitzy, I said. "Do you want me to drink something else in solidarity, because I will absolutely do that for you."

"God no! Someone has to drink my share of coffee! If anything, I want you to drink more of it so I don't feel so bad," she said.

"Somehow, I think I can manage drinking your share of the world's coffee," I joked. "In all honesty, I may have been doing that already."

"Good. Then it wasn't feeling neglected," Katya said. After a fading chuckle, she lifted an eyebrow at me. "So... You're sure this isn't a setup? I trust Mitzy, he's a good man, so I believed him when he said I'd be safe here."

"You absolutely will, I promise," I said. "I have a bit of a problem. I've been getting some crazy, conflicting information about your being here and Mitzy gave me the idea of coming straight to the source. I'd never really thought about just coming to you directly, obviously because I'm a detective and you're a capo, but I think I'm learning lately that the lines are that clear cut."

"I learned that myself," she said. "The hard way, but I learned it eventually." She took another sip of her tea and then said, "Well, if there's any way I can help, I will."

Not only was Katya the exact sweetheart that Mitzy said she was, but she was beautiful and didn't look afraid or worried about her life in the slightest. Just during our introductions, she spoke about her life and her baby with a smile on her face, not at all like someone who was afraid or being forced to do something she didn't want to.

"Thanks," I replied. "Really, this whole thing is kind of about you."

"Me?" she yelped. "What did I do? I mean... apart from the obvious."

"It's nothing you did, more like your presence here gives someone in a position like mine a bit of concern." I wanted to be very careful not to tell Katya that Maksim was in New York City, or that he believed she may be in danger. I knew that Maksim legitimately believed that Katya was unsafe, but with his drastic turn in behavior lately, I also didn't entirely think she was safe with him either. If possible, I wanted to keep them totally separated from one another, especially if Katya really *was* happy with her current arrangements. "I'm a detective for the organized crime unit, so naturally, we follow all sorts of events related to any organized crime groups, whether they be mafioso, bratva, or otherwise. I'm sure it doesn't surprise you to know that your father and brother have come up in our investigations before, though we were never able to charge them with anything."

"My father was devilishly good at keeping all signs of his presence out of the spotlight. It's a trait I'm glad I inherited and can bring to my current role. He knew how to protect himself, that was for sure," she explained.

"We hadn't ever heard of you, in fact we didn't even know that Vladmir had a daughter until you came with him on his last trip to New York City and things ended up going haywire with your family and the Costellos and Bonettis. You were kidnapped as a result of that mess, correct?"

"Yes," she said. "In order to recoup the money my father stole from him, Vincent captured me. He gave my father a two week time period to pay up or he was going to kill me, but as you can see," she tapped her belly, "he ended up going a different route."

"Right... That's kind of where my concern is," I said. "From an outside perspective, after knowing that you were kidnapped and that was how you came to be in Vincent's life, the fact that you're *still* in his life, even left America and returned with him... It makes someone like me wonder if you're truly here by choice."

Katya's eyes widened and her jaw dropped. "Oh my god. You think I'm in trouble!" She reached across the table and set her hand on top of mine. "I already thought you were adorable, but my god." She shook her head and laughed. "No, no, no. Trust me when I say, no one can force me to do *anything* I don't want to do." The confidence in her voice made me believe her instantly. "I mean, it's true that Vincent and I came into one another's lives in a very atypical way, but Vincent wasn't really ever cruel to me. Even when he saw me more as a captive, he put me up in a nice room and made sure everyone in his estate treated me well. He wanted to be certain not to punish me for my father's fuck up."

"Really?" I said. "You were never forced or hurt there?"

"No. Vincent isn't the kind of guy who would hurt someone needlessly. Don't get me wrong, he can be ruthless, and if you cross him or hurt someone he cares about, bad day for you, but Vincent knew I wasn't his enemy. We got involved pretty quickly after he brought me there, and our feelings just continued to increase until we couldn't live without each other. When I thought my father had killed Vincent, it was the darkest time in my life. Learning he was alive was like I'd been given a second chance at happiness. I love Vincent from the bottom of my heart. No force involved. Just two people very much in love."

I couldn't help but smile as Katya spoke. She was radiating as she talked about how much she loved Vincent and it eliminated any doubt that she was telling the absolute truth. From talking to her, I knew she was absolutely here in New York City because the man she loved and the father of her baby was here.

I was actually a little jealous of her happiness.

"Are you gonna make him put a ring on it then?" I asked.

Apart from those I worked with, I didn't really have any girl friends, or many friends at all. What time I wasn't spending at work, I was spending with my family at their bodega. Like most people I had some leftover friends from high school and college, and even a few from the academy, but they were closer to being general acquaintances for how often I kept in touch with them. Mitzy was the closest thing to a real friend I had, but sitting and gabbing with Katya kind of felt good. I was having fun.

"I made him put a ring on it right away!" she barked. "I'm just not wearing it because my fingers are so swollen, but look." She reached into her purse and pulled out an absolutely blinding, white diamond ring, the main rock of which was probably more expensive than my entire car. "Isn't it stunning? I mean, in all honesty, he could have proposed with a ring pop and I would have said yes, but this'll do."

"It's seriously beautiful," I said. "So you're engaged. You're having a baby. You're happy?"

"The happiest I've ever been in my entire life," Katya said. "My mom moved here to be close to me, and sometimes I think she and Vincent love each other more than they love me." She rolled her eyes. "So much for the cliche that husbands and mothers-in-law don't get along. Mine make me sick."

"That's adorable." I let out a sigh of relief and relaxed in my chair. "I'm so happy for you. I've been worried that maybe you'd been forced to be here, but I'm so glad that you're just happy and living a nice life. That's all I really want for people at the end of the day."

She snorted. "I've never had a cop tell me that she wants me to live a happy life, but I'll take it."

The smile faded from my face a little. I guess I *was* still talking to a criminal, even if she was one who was satisfied with where she was in life. It registered such a conflict deep inside of me. There were people like Katya, who was legitimately one of the most wonderful people I'd ever met, who also claim that Vincent can be ruthless but doesn't indiscriminately harm innocent people. But then there were people like Vladimir and Maksim who fell into the same same category as them and hurt innocent people without thinking twice.

There were police officers like Ace, who dropped what he was doing to look for my sister and had her returned home within a couple of hours, or even Sydney, Gauge, and Lucas who were good, solid cops, but then there were cops like Captain Cox, who despite being a cop, were cruel and uncaring about those around them—Cox sent us into the lion's den without thinking twice.

And then of course, there were people like Mitzy, who sort of towed the line. A good cop, who did less than reputable things. He looked out for people like me and like Vincent Costello. How was I ever supposed to know which side of this war I should be fighting on if there were good and bad people on both sides and in the middle?

"Did I lose ya?" Katya asked.

Shaking my head free of my thoughts, I smiled. "No. I was just trying to decide how to know the difference between good and bad people."

"That's a tough one isn't it?" she replied, setting her head in her hands. "My own father left me to die, but the man who kidnapped me flew across the world to save my life. The world is strange and messy and undefined. It's nearly impossible to find a truly perfect place in it."

"You seem to have found something close to perfect," I said. "How did you do it?"

She took a deep breath and thought about it for a long time. I took the time to study how absolutely beautiful she was. She could have been a model or an actress easily with her wavy brown hair, slim features, and bright eyes. I got why Maksim had a thing for her with how gorgeous and kind she was, and comparing her to myself, it seemed he definitely had a type.

"I don't really think I found perfection, I think I stopped looking for it. Don't get me wrong, I'm so happy in my life. I really don't think there's a more perfect man out there for me besides Vince, and once we have our baby, I have confidence that she's going to be perfect too. I guess what I mean is I stopped looking for the definition of *perfect*, you know what I mean? Instead, I came to realize that as long as I was happy and the people around me were happy, that was as close to perfect as I was probably gonna get, but that for me... that's perfect." The shook her head and chuckled. "I'm sorry, I don't think that made any sense."

"It made a lot more sense than you think," I replied. "Thanks."

"Of course." She reached into her purse and pulled out a business card with her name—Katya Costello—and her number, and the card said she was a beauty consultant, which was a perfect cover story for her. "Hang onto this. If you ever need anything, you can call or text me directly. We don't need that old *fart* in between us," she said, nodding to Mitzy.

Mitzy didn't even look up from his coffee, but grumbled. "I heard that."

"I gotta get going. The baby's been nice, but pretty soon, she's going to make me have to pee every five minutes."

I laughed. "Sounds like fun."

"It's a riot," she responded, standing up from the table. "It was really nice to meet you, Chloe."

"It was really nice to meet you too." Instead of a handshake, Katya said goodbye with a warm hug, then she walked over and gave Mitzy one as well, before walking out. As she went I noticed the very subtle outline of a gun in the back of her maternity shirt, and gasped. "She's packing," I whispered to Mitzy.

"Of course, she's a capo," he replied.

It was clear that Katya was a woman that could take care of herself. I wasn't sure why Maksim developed such a knight in shining armor complex with her, but she far from needed it. Katya was happy with her life and I was happy for her, but it didn't entirely eliminate my inner conflict. Technically, my job was to charge and arrest her, or at the very least her husband, but she was such a wonderful woman, that the idea of uprooting her life felt wrong to me. Whether it was by helping Maksim steal her back or by doing my job, I'd end up hurting her, which bothered me deeply after finding that she was actually very kind hearted.

"What you got going on in that noggin?" Mitzy asked.

"I'm just confused," I moaned. "What do I do? If I keep doing my job, eventually I'm gonna come toe to toe with the Costellos, right? I'd have to arrest her or Vincent. I'd be tearing up their family. But if I don't, they'll continue to circumvent the law for their own gain. What's the right answer?"

"I'd love to give you the out, but this is something you have to decide for yourself," Mitzy said. "There comes a time in all of our lives where we have to decide what's important and what isn't. Sometimes what we thought might be important turned out not to be such a big deal, and the things we damn near ignore, turn out to be the most important. It all depends on what you value."

"I just want good people to be happy and live without fear," I said.

"Then it sounds like you have a few words to define," he replied.

"Define?" I said.

He nodded. "Yep. What does it mean to you to be good, and what does it mean to you to be happy?"

The question blanketed over me with a heavy weight, and I knew searching for the answer wasn't going to improve my sleep at all. Still, I had no choice but to forge ahead. Until I knew more about what I really valued, I simply didn't have the tools to get myself out of the predicament I was in, nor protect anyone else from Maksim's wrath.

Outside the cafe, Mitzy walked over to his car and unlocked it before opening the door for me. "Come on. We're stopping by a drug store for melatonin, then I'm taking you home. I'll cover for you with Cox."

"It's okay," I said. "I need some time to clear my head and I think some walking and fresh air will do the trick. There's a drug store a couple blocks from me. I'll catch the bus there, get some melatonin, and then walk home."

"You sure?" he asked.

I nodded. "Yeah. Thanks for this though. It was nice to meet her in person and see what she's all about. You're right, she's pretty great."

"You two were getting on like old friends," he said. "I'm just saying, if part of your soul-searching results in you realizing you don't mind blurring the lines a bit, the Costellos are great, and there's big bucks in being a dirty cop."

"Do you even *hear* yourself?" I asked.

Rather than responding, he wrapped around me and gave me a big hug, then climbed in his car and started it up. I stood and waved after him as he pulled away, then took out my phone and earbuds. I navigated home, letting the app tell me the best bus or subway stops to use, and then popped my headphones in and started for home.

While I walked, I let the entire day wash over me. My sister's relapse, my dad's irresponsibility, Mitzy's support, Katya's revelation and advice. I didn't know what to do with all of it. The one thing I knew for sure was that I'd suddenly found myself at a crossroads, only instead of feeling like there were too many paths and I didn't know which one to take, each path was coaxing me forward, but none of them felt right for me. I didn't want to be a dirty cop, but I also didn't want to be someone who busted up happy homes. I wanted to protect people and prevent as many of my future selves from happening as possible, but with a unit or people like Maksim hellbent on just doing what they want regardless of the impact, then what was the point?

I had no way forward and I had no way back. I didn't know what to do.

As I got to the less busier parts of the area, I pulled one of my earbuds out for safety, but it wasn't my ears that alerted me to trouble, but my eyes. When I looked over my shoulder to tuck my earbud away, I noticed that there was a black unmarked car driving rather slowly down the road. I had a gun on me, but I didn't want to pull it around civilians without being certain that I needed to. Instead, I tried to duck into the darkness of an alleyway to see if the car would stop or keep going.

But I ran into a tree trunk body instead.

I looked up and my heart sank as I recognized the same man who I'd made negotiate for me the night of the raid, Maksim's right-hand, Brusch.

"Hello, Miss Nikitina," he said. "Mr. Petrov has requested your presence."

Before I could do anything else, he socked me across the face, knocking me out cold.

CHAPTER SEVENTEEN: MAKSIM

"We got her, boss," Brusch said on the other side of the phone. "Had to get a little rough because she was going for her gun, but I didn't hurt her too bad."

"It's fine," I told him. "You were acting on my orders, so anything you did within those bounds to get the task done is acceptable. How far away are you?"

"About twenty minutes."

"Very well. Get her here as quickly as possible, and make sure she's been stripped of any weapons and her cell phone and that her hands and wrists are tied. There'll be no more wiggling out of trouble for her. I want her powerless."

"You got it, boss. See you soon."

I ended the call with Brusch and sat down on the couch in my living room, trying to breathe in and out to dissipate my fury. Yes, Chloe and I hadn't exactly seen eye-to-eye lately, but the last thing I expected her to do was turn around and rat me out to Katya and Vincent. Here she was, claiming that she was this major police detective who wanted to protect people and make sure that she was helping the innocent, then she runs off and gets in bed with the worst of them all. For that, she could have stuck with me—anything was better than Vincent Costello.

The thing that frustrated me the most was how betrayed I really felt. Our differences aside, I thought that we'd bounce back just like we had in the past. I knew that I'd crossed a line threatening her sister. Putting the two of them in that situation was something I would probably regret for the rest of my life, but that didn't give Chloe free reign to just turn on me to my greatest enemy. Did she warn them that I was gunning for Vincent? Did she tell Katya that I was planning on bringing her back to Russia? Did she give them every single little detail of the past two weeks?

How much did they know now?

All at once, I realized just how much I'd trusted Chloe with that I shouldn't have. She knew where I was staying while she was in New York. She had my phone number. She knew what kind of rental car I'd been driving and what all of my men looked like. She knew that things had gone south with Stavio and the rest of the Bonettis.

The truth was, I'd let my guard down.

Was part of me hoping that I could convince Chloe to bend in my favor? Absolutely. I couldn't say that I had feelings for her, per se, but I was beginning to feel like I had my old friend back. Those times when he laughed and the little bit of time we'd spent together intimately made me yearn for more of both. It was why such deep regret came over me when I knew I'd pushed the envelope too far. I was trying to tread the line between Chloe the cop and Chloe my friend, but I leaned too far towards her position as a detective.

Maybe this was all my fault.

Either way, Chloe had turned on me, and I couldn't just let that go. The very thought of hurting her made me sick to my stomach, but what choice did I have? This was about so much more than paying her back for her betrayal, this was about proving a point to anyone who was watching. I didn't want to lead as viciously as Vladimir, nor did I want people to think I was soft and could be taken advantage of.

So let this act be a warning to the world: Maksim Petrov isn't above killing anyone. Even New York City's finest. Even his former best friend.

I threw back the glass of whiskey I was working on, and then filled the glass up again. Any minute, Brusch was going to cart Chloe through those doors, and I was going to have to take her into the soundproof, metal plated room and end her life. It actually carried a swill of emotion up to burn my nose and knot my throat.

I didn't want to do it, but Chloe was dangerous to me now. It was like Brusch had said—I'd pushed her past hope, and now she was baring her teeth.

Just as I was getting near the bottom of my second glass of whiskey, the doorbell for the elevator went off. Chloe was just on the other side, unaware that she was enjoying her last few moments alive. Even as I stood up and walked across the room to open the elevators, I wondered if there was an alternative option. Was there any way I could release her into the world again and trust that she wasn't going to turn on me again or work with Vincent to take *me* out as opposed to the other way around?

But there wasn't.

Tomorrow, I was going to wake up in a world without Chloe in it, and that actually shattered a much larger part of me than I was ready to come to terms with. I'd have to live for the rest of my life knowing that the two true friends I'd ever really had in my life, Chloe and Sascha, had both died by my hand.

I'd never be the same after this. Chloe's death was going to cement a new, much darker version of myself. Maybe even a man crueler than Vincent. I was rapidly learning that I wasn't meant to have happiness. It didn't matter what I had, big or small, eventually the world would come and take it away from me. So maybe it was time to just become that man fully. Let the darkness that had been trying so hard to consume me ever since I was a little boy finally get in. It would be bad for many that I'd cross paths with.

But at least it would stop the pain for me.

I pressed the button to open the elevator doors, and saw Brusch standing on the other side with Chloe thrown over his shoulder. Her ankles and wrists were bound exactly as I'd asked, and when he glanced at me as a silent way of asking where to put her, I reluctantly nodded towards the kill room.

When he turned to pass me, I could see that Chloe was knocked out and hanging limp over Brusch's back. There was a small bruise staining her beautiful face, but it would take a lot more than that to tarnish her splendor. At least I'd get to have one final good look at her before she met her end.

I'd get to say goodbye.

"Thank you," I said to Brusch after he set Chloe down in the armchair I'd placed inside the room. "Be on standby for cleanup, please."

"Yes, boss."

He walked out of the room and I shut the door after him, leaning back against it then, and just waiting. I owed Chloe final words, and I wanted answers of my own anyway, so I'd wait for her to come around.

While I waited, I thought back over the couple of weeks since Chloe and I had reconnected and wondered if there was a different way things could have gone, or if we were always doomed to end up this way? Was there a Maksim and Chloe in a different universe happily enjoying one another's presence? Where Chloe comes to see that Maksim was right to distrust Vincent, and after ending him and giving Katya her freedom, they find a way to remain in one another's lives?

As friends or maybe more?

It confused me when I let my mind wander to being with Chloe as more than just a friend. Katya was the one I wanted to be with. I told myself that over and over, but lately, it'd been becoming less of something that was, and more just something I said. I used to think about Katya all the time, but lately, it was Chloe who was on my mind more. All of the regret and frustration of knowing I didn't try harder to keep things smooth sailing between us. Every morning when I looked into the mirror, I was searching for that smile that only she had managed to bring to my face. I was a happier man when Chloe was involved.

Why did it have to end up like this?

"Mm," Chloe started to stir with a grumble, first trying to regain control over her head. It flopped off to one side, then she lifted it before losing it and dropping it down. When she hit her chest, she popped up, and her eyes shot open. She looked around the room, getting her bearings, and then she finally looked up at me. "Maks."

"You finally woke up," I said softly. "I was beginning to worry."

She realized her wrists and ankles were tied and immediately started to wriggle and panic. "What's going on? Let me out."

"No. I'm afraid I can't do that," I said. "You see, I know what you did."

Her brows knitted deep on her forehead. "What?"

"I know that you went and saw Katya, Chloe, and I know that you betrayed me," I said. "I know that we haven't been getting along lately, but..." My frown worsened. "I really didn't think you'd do that to me."

"What are you talking about?" she yelped. "I didn't betray you!"

"You did!" I screamed. "I saw it! With my own eyes! You met with Katya, Chloe! You sat across from her at a table and you told her everything!"

"I met with her, but I didn't tell her about you!" she screamed. "I swear!"

"You're lying!"

"I'm not!" She was fighting against her binds to get free, but they were too restrictive. "Maksim, I took your last threat seriously! I knew that you meant it when you said I didn't have any chances left! I wouldn't turn on you after that! I just had to find out for myself if Katya was here by choice or force. I needed to hear directly from her what she really wanted."

"And she just told you because you asked nicely?" I scoffed. "Do you think I'm an idiot?" I pulled my gun out and pointed it at her. "Do you think I won't do this? Do you think that just because the thought of killing you hurts me that I won't do it to save what the Petrov family has built? This empire keeps my mom alive. This empire saved my life. This empire is all I have left of the man who was more like a father to me than my own dad, and the man who was like a brother, who saw someone who needed help and took me in. I can't let you ruin it!"

"I don't want to ruin it!" Chloe screeched. "Maksim I swear to god, I didn't tell Katya about you! I told her that my unit had been following the Costello-Petrov dispute since its inception when Vladimir stole from Nick Costello. I told her that we knew she'd been here and been kidnapped, but that she went home to Russia after that, so when we suddenly noticed her turn back up, we feared it was because she was being forced! I lied to her to protect you, because I knew if she knew you were here, it would create problems with Vincent! Don't you get that? After all this, I'm still protecting you!"

I took a step back, but kept my gun trained on Chloe. There were tears in her eyes and her cheeks were slightly red with frustration. She'd stopped trying to get out of her ties and was instead just looking at me with an expression of desperation on her face. Maybe it was stupid of me, but seeing that expression on her face, I was actually inclined to believe her.

It was yet another new experience for me. Whether she was doing it because she was afraid for her family or for some other reason, if Chloe was telling the truth, she had been loyal to me despite the tension between us lately, and that was something unique for me.

"You didn't tell her anything?" I asked.

"Not about you," she replied. "I didn't even tell her that we knew one another. I didn't want her path to cross with yours. At least not before you were ready for it to."

Slowly and somewhat reluctantly, I lowered my gun. Chloe was taking hard breaths and was sweating a little around the top of her forehead. Nothing about her demeanor read as disingenuous to me, but if that was the case, I'd made another snap judgement that had only pushed me further from an amicable place with the woman in front of me. While what she was doing was causing me to trust her more, what I was doing was no doubt causing her to trust me less.

"Okay," I said finally. "I believe you. I'm sorry."

She shook her head. "Have you never heard of talking things out? A final warning before you fly off the handle?"

"Honestly? No." I shoved my gun away. "Vladimir taught me that there's no time for second guessing. If you're going to do it, then do it, and do it fast." I frowned. "Although, in my defense, I tried to contact you before going to your family's bodega."

She looked up at me, surprisingly, with guilt behind her eyes. "Yeah... I was struggling with finding out that you were actually engaged to Katya and were here because you wanted to take her back. I didn't know what that meant for..." Then she stopped.

"For?" I pressed. "For us?"

She averted her gaze and seemed a little embarrassed. "I'm an idiot.

You've literally threatened to kill my family, and my brain has the audacity to dedicate some of its focus to being jealous."

Jealous?

"I'd be lying if I said my mind hadn't wandered in that direction," I said. "I assumed I'd pretty much killed all chances of that with my actions."

"If I were normal, you would have," she spat back.

"So I haven't?" I asked.

She pulled her eyes up to meet mine. "I don't get it," she said. "I know that I shouldn't want you, but..."

My body covered with chills at her honesty. "I know what you mean."

Holding up her wrists, she looked at me and said, "So can you untie me? I'm not going to do anything."

"I will," I said, approaching her. "Although, it's a shame. You look so good all tied up."

Chloe's eyes flickered with interest and she said, "What do you mean?"

I undid the binds around her ankles first, then looked up at her over her legs. "I won't tell you. I can only show you."

When I reached up to grab her wrist binds to undo them as well, Chloe pulled them away from me. "Okay then," she said, now giving me a minx-like look. "Show me."

CHAPTER EIGHTEEN: MAKSIM

Chloe's sudden change in demeanor was surprising, and slightly confusing, but the temptation was too much to resist. I was still crouched in front of her and she was looking down at me with a darkened, curious gaze that let me know she'd let me have my way with her.

Considering the fact that I'd pretty much written off any hope of getting to be with Chloe this way, having it right in front of me let me without the ability to say no. However ill-advised it might be, Chloe with her wrists tied, asking for a demonstration on sensory deprivation was a bag full of candy, and I was a kid with a devilish sweet tooth.

First things first was getting Chloe out of this room only meant for death and into my bedroom where we could really unfold and get down to business. I had untied her ankles, so she technically could have walked.

But where was the fun in that?

Instead, I bent down and picked her up, lifting her over my shoulder. She let out a yelp of surprise, but didn't fight at all. With her ass right next to my head, I couldn't help but turn and take a bite.

Chloe squeaked, although happily, and said, "That was unexpected."

I laughed. "That's your first lesson."

I carried her out of the metal room and down the hallway to my bedroom. It was delightful to see that her cheeks were already splashed red when I dropped her onto the bed. She seemed eager to experience something new, and I was more than eager to show her.

Because we weren't back in St. Petersburg, I didn't have all of the materials with me that I would normally have for a sensory deprivation session. I'd been considering investing in some to keep in my penthouse in the states, but once things sort of fell apart between Chloe and I, I didn't think there was a point. She was an exception, but I knew if I couldn't be with Chloe, then I wouldn't really want to be with anyone until I'd sorted things out with Katya, so there was no real reason to be prepared. Chloe caught me off guard, however, so we would just have to make do with what we had.

I loosened the tie around my neck and leaned down over Chloe. Her eyes flared with a little bit of excitement, and I rewarded her interest with a kiss on the lips before trailing a few down the side of her neck. One of my knees, I lifted and placed between her legs, giving her center something to press against and get teased a little while she waited. As she bucked her hips forward, I dragged my tie from around my neck and looped it over her face.

"See you afterwards," I hummed. She let out a little gasp, but once again didn't argue, and I tied the blindfold behind her head. "You can't see, and you can't feel for things with your hands... I wonder how that will change the way you experience me."

Chloe didn't respond. She was still massaging herself against my leg, but I pulled away from her, leaving her totally without stimulation. Her head turned from side to side, and I could tell she was trying to gather where she thought I was. I sat perfectly still and tried to remain as quiet as I could, giving her a moment to feel totally isolated.

"Maks?" she called out quietly.

With a smile, I leaned over and slid my hands up her thighs. She jumped a little and tensed for a moment, before relaxing. "Oh... I get it."

While simultaneously kissing her stomach, I undid the button to her pants and hooked my hands into the waistband. I dragged them down slowly enough that she could feel every centimeter as it moved. A couple of my fingers I held out, nails pressed into her skin, dragging down with ever so much force as I moved. She wriggled a little bit and I knew the sensory deprivation was already taking hold. She was feeling each movement so much more now that she could focus on them.

Throwing her pants aside, I was torn between untying her enough to get her shirt off, or just pulling them up over her neck. Chloe's impressive bust was one of the most enticing things about her and I'd be lying if I said I wasn't a boobs guy.

But then a third thought occurred to me. Once that was probably going to get me in trouble, but I'd rather ask for forgiveness than for permission.

In my pocket, I always kept a switchblade for the number of occasions that the need for one came up. This was one such occasion. I knelt on the side of the bed, immediately pulling Chloe's attention over to me, and I flicked out my blade. She must have heard it, because she recoiled a bit, but I dropped my hand between her legs and started to massage her pussy gently.

"Relax," I whispered into her ear. "I won't hurt you."

Cute, starved moans came from between Chloe's lips as I ran my hand up and down her center below, and with the other hand, I poked my switchblade under the collar of her shirt and dragged it down. The fabric tore, filling the room with the sound of it ripping, before it finally got near the end of the sleeve, and I stopped. I then swapped hands, this time using my free hand to massage one of Chloe's breasts, while I used the other to rip her other sleeve.

Once both sleeves were cut down to the end, I folded the switchblade up and set it aside, then I used my hands to rip her shirt the final way off. She jumped each time, and seemed to want to complain, but before she could, I set my mouth on hers. She lifted her body, subconsciously I imagined, to meet mine and melted herself into the kiss. While my tongue wrestled with hers, I pulled the ripped remains of her shirt away and dropped them to the floor, then after making short work of her front-clasping, strapless bra, she was finally bare before me.

"Beautiful," I hummed.

Chloe twisted, trying to cover herself up, but I grabbed her knees with both of my hands and wrenched her legs apart. She followed my silent command, leaving them open, and I pulled back from her once again, letting her take in a moment of silence and isolation. A few whimpers came out of her mouth, but she was waiting so patiently for me to return that I had to reward her.

Without putting my weight on the bed at all, I leaned down and propped my head between Chloe's legs. I didn't touch her at first, only waited for a moment and enjoyed the perfect sight of her eager vagina, before blowing a little air over the top of it. Chloe let out a quick moan, but breathed it off, so I blew again. That time, her lips parted slightly and she leaned her head back.

She was really starting to feel it.

Taking her by surprise, I suddenly leaned in and gave her a hard lick, from her hole up to her clit. A moan jumped out of her and her hands clenched on top of her where they were still tied together. I pulled back, gave her a few seconds, and then did it again. Each time, I left an inconsistent amount of time in between licks, some short and some long, really waking her up to the concept of not knowing what was coming next, or when.

In my pants, my dick was starting to beg me to be released. I was having fun with Chloe, and wanted to continue to do so, but my body was begging for reprieve. I hadn't been with anyone since that last time I'd been with Chloe, and I'd even been too distracted to help myself along. This first run out was going to be a little rushed.

Because I needed to be inside her as soon as possible.

Stepping back and letting her soak in an elongated moment alone, I started to disrobe myself. Immediately upon pulling myself out, I wrapped a hand around my length and started to stroke it. There was just something about Chloe, as stunning as she was, on *my* bed, totally naked, with my tie around her eyes and her wrists bound on top of her. It was like I'd died and gone to heaven.

"I'm stroking my big cock for you, Chloe," I told her. "You look so good, I don't know what to do."

Then I watched in absolute, gobsmacked shock, as Chloe didn't respond, but rather opened her mouth and stuck out her tongue. My jaw dropped. It was a good thing she was blindfolded so she couldn't see my physical response. My cock twitched in my hand and tried to drag me over to her mouth like a goddamn homing beacon.

What? Was she a porn star in her former life?

Still, who was I to say no to such a delectable invitation. I walked over to her and pet the top of her head, loving the way she responded to it immediately by turning towards me.

"If you want it so badly, I'll give it to you," I growled at her.

I pushed up to the edge of the bed and guided her head towards me, then slipped the tip of myself into her mouth. Despite my size, her lips folded around me perfectly, and then she seemed committed to trying to take me down whole. Her throat clenched around me and her tongue formed a basin, like it was trying to give me a nice little slide to move further down. It was unbearably hot and wet inside, and with her eagerness to take me in, I found myself resting a hand against the back of her head and thrusting in gently.

Maybe the woman didn't have a gag reflex, but no amount of moving farther into her mouth seemed to bother her. She swallowed me up, continuing to coax me with her tongue attempting to coat my entire shaft. I closed my eyes and my hips started to twitch and buck.

It felt so good I could die happy right at that moment.

"Oh shit," I said, suddenly pulling back and popping out of her mouth. "Note to self, don't start that unless I want to end there." Sexily enough, Chloe's hands moved for a moment, almost like if she had free reign of her hands, she'd grab me and stop me from leaving. "Such a greedy woman," I said. "Don't worry, I'll give you your fill later. For now, I need to be inside of you."

"Yes please," Chloe replied breathlessly.

I just shook my head. She was already so sexy. How was she getting more so by the minute?

Causing her to let out a small scream, I grabbed Chloe's leg suddenly and twisted her around, then I rolled her onto her stomach. She moved exactly as I was instructing her to, and even lifted her ass a little for me like she was a dog in heat. Somewhere, *way* in the back of my mind, there was a tiny voice telling me I shouldn't trust this, but there were a million much larger voices beating the shit out of that one and telling it to keep quiet.

If Chloe Nikitina wanted to stick her ass up at me and give it a little shake to entice me to stick my cock inside her, I was going to listen, plain and simple.

I came up behind her and started by just letting my rock hard length lace between her cheeks. The beads of my seed that were already dribbling out were leaving spots on her perfect, tan skin like artwork. I nuzzled the head of myself into them, not only painting them more around her body, but using them to slick myself, then I brought myself down to her entrance, poked my head there, and then popped myself in.

Chloe let out a sharp gasp—something I was used to with my lovers. Thanks to my size, which was a blessing and a curse, I always caused my partners a little bit of pain, but I knew how to navigate carefully and protect them, and soon, we'd both be swimming in pleasure.

Due to the fact that Chloe must have been really receptive to the sensory deprivation, she was particularly wet and ready to take me in. Part of me wanted to teasingly poke my tip in and out, but once I was in, out wasn't an option. I could only move forward, persuaded by her walls which were squeezing tightly around me and trying to take me down, until I was buried all the way inside of her. We let out conjoining grunts of pleasure, and I pressed my hands against her back, setting my thumbs directly into the dimples right at the bend of her back to her ass, and started to pump in and out of her.

Thank god I had the restraint to move slowly at first, because the inside of Chloe was so heavenly that if I moved too much faster, this would be a short run. Something about the way she seemed to form around me almost perfectly, made it feel like she was made for me to slot into her. I rolled back and forth, rowing in and out at a considerate pace, desperate to make this first round last as long as I could.

Chloe had other plans though, as she rocked backwards and tried to increase the pace between us. I pressed on her body with my hands and then gave her ass a quick slap and said, "Ah, ah, ah. You're not in control here. I am." She stopped trying to control the speed then, but that slap made her squeeze even tighter. I did it again, just for experiment's sake, and she spasmed around me quickly. "Oh, you like it rough."

"Yeah," she half-moaned, half-breathed back at me.

I gave her another slap, but then she clenched so hard, I had to stop moving to prevent myself from releasing right there. It was borderline unacceptable how good she felt.

It was probably just in my best interest to get the first one beyond me, otherwise I'd constantly be trying to stop it from happening.

So I buckled in, leaned even further up Chloe's body and buried myself even deeper inside of her. She let out a loud scream and clenched me, and I started to thrust in and out of her at a faster, harder speed.

"Yes!" Chloe screamed. "Harder, Maks!"

I answered her request, slamming into her until the sound of my skin smacking against hers was filling the whole room. Each time I hit her deepest spot, she let out a louder yelp, until she finally went silent. She began to stutter and shake, clenching and releasing me in a rhythm like she was giving my dick a massage. I stopped moving and let her continue to squeeze around me, until I couldn't take it anymore. I slammed stacco humps into her until I exploded, burying my seed deep inside of her. It made her even slicker and easier to navigate, and my hips continued moving on their own, long after I came.

"I can't stop," I huffed.

"Don't stop!" she screamed.

Even long after I didn't have anything else to give, my dick stayed hard, and I continued to push. I couldn't pull too far out without her body trying to snatch my length right off my body, so I was condemned to pushing in and out of her deepest parts, seemingly striking a good spot inside of her. She screamed repeatedly, a mix of my name and swear words and incoherent noises that only turned me on more. I couldn't stop thrusting, until finally both Chloe and I went silent and perfectly still.

I couldn't feel anything else but Chloe's insides milking a second orgasm out of me, while she contracted and released rapidly, no doubt coming herself as well. There was a white whine in my ear for a moment, and when I closed my eyes I nearly passed out, then all at once all of my senses came back like my spirit had temporarily been pulled from my body and then slammed back into me.

My whole body went weak and I fell forward onto the bed next to Chloe. I landed half on and half off the bed, but I was too weak to move or care.

"My god," I hummed. "So I'm guessing that was okay for you?" But she didn't respond. I gently pulled the blindfold from around her head and smiled when I saw her eyes closed. She was breathing deeply and looked totally at peace, and I just laughed. "Yeah. It looks like it was okay for you."

CHAPTER NINETEEN: CHLOE

Maksim and I were still helter-skelter on his bed when I woke up some undefined amount of time later. He was lying half on the bed and half off, with one leg kind of tossed over mine, and the other hanging off the edge. He hadn't even made any attempt to clean himself up. It actually brought a little bit of a smile to my face. With him asleep and totally wrecked like that, he didn't look nearly as dangerous as he was. His sleeping face was so peaceful and calm—it reminded me more of the little boy I used to know. It made me miss that little boy and wonder how much of him was still inside this terrifying, intriguing, all-consuming man.

Sleeping with Maksim had been a huge risk for me. When I came to, tied up in that chair, in a room that had clearly been designed for killing without being heard or seen, I knew I was on a countdown to the end of my life. Whatever had set Maksim off—what I learned was that he'd somehow seen Katya and I meeting—had upset him so much that he was going to kill me. Even still, I could see the anguish in his eyes as he looked down at me and knew that he didn't actually *want* to kill me. How much desperation had to live inside of a person for them to kill even if they didn't want to?

How big were the demons inside of Maksim, and was it possible to get them out?

Ultimately, I knew that if I wanted to spare my own life, it was going to be with some creative conversation, and a little bit of scary honesty. If even a bit embellished, nothing that I said to Maksim while begging for my life was untrue. I very intentionally *hadn't* sold him out to Katya, and it was true that part of me was jealous of his affinity for her. I'd thought about it more than once, Maksim and I continuing whatever relationship we'd begun forming. That was part of the reason I felt so conflicted—because how could I feel that way about someone who existed as everything I was against?

But there was a draw I had to Maks, a pull that consisted of our history as kids, and how well we got along now, when we weren't a cop and criminal, but rather just ourselves. If I was being honest with myself, I *did* like Maksim. Not the manic man he was when it came to Katya, or the dangerous one he was when he was being a Petrov, but just the honest man he was at his core.

Maksim Pasternak—the boy I knew then, and the man I knew now.

"Mmmmm," Maksim grumbled out next to me. "I'm not in a comfortable position."

I giggled. "No, I can't imagine you are." He sat up and his hair stuck straight up off his head and flew in all directions. I snorted and said, "That's a good look."

He glanced at me and then up, then ran his hands through his hair, desperately trying to lay the wild, blond feathers back down. "Yeah. I tend to get bad bed head." Then he looked over at me. "Interesting to see that you wake up just as beautiful as you go to sleep."

"I think you're still in a sex daze, but I'll take it," I replied.

"It's possible. That was unbelievable."

I nodded at him, a little starry-eyed. "It really was."

And I wasn't lying. My first tour through Maksim's world of sensory deprivation had resulted in the best sex I'd ever had, and I knew we couldn't have pulled it off if I didn't trust Maksim to take care of me, so even in spite of everything that had transpired between us, there was a part of me that still wanted to trust him. Thinking back, every chance that Maksim had been given where he *could* have hurt me, he didn't. He'd threatened me, and my family, but he hadn't hurt me. As a cop, I knew that sometimes that was how it started, but I didn't think Maksim had any desire to hurt me. Any time he did, or even threatened me, he did it because he truly thought he didn't have another choice.

Was there a world in which I could show him that he did?

"I'll go get you something to clean up," I told him, starting to get out of bed. The binds on my wrists had been loosened, but were still hanging limply from me. I pulled them off and set them aside, but before I could get out of bed, Maksim's strong arms wrapped around my torso and held me in place. "Did you want me to drag you with me?"

"No," he grumbled into my thigh, then he lifted his head and looked up at me. "I just didn't want you to go."

"I'm coming right back," I said.

"Still..."

He crawled up a little bit so that he could press his lips against mine. I rapidly got lost in it, wrapping my arms around his neck and pulling him down against me. We fell backwards onto the bed, our mouths and tongues battling with one another for dominance, and before long, Maksim kicked one of his legs between my thighs to part my legs. I didn't stop him, loving the feeling of his huge length poking against me. I could probably say I was insatiable for it from a purely objective place.

Who didn't want to experience the best sex they'd ever had over and over.

Smoothing his lips down the side of my neck, Maksim fished a hand between his legs to help guide the tip of him into my entrance. I let out a choked moan and lifted my legs to clasp behind Maksim's back and pull him farther into me. He slid in and started to thrust, this time lazy and slow. It kind of made me tired, in a good way. It was relaxing almost, feeling him fill me up and slowly churn in a rhythmic pattern. He still hit the best parts deep in me, and even at this slower pace, I started to feel my insides tingle.

"Maks," I hummed out. "Right there. Don't stop."

And he didn't, hitting the spot with continued precision, rocking backwards and forwards against me. He let his mouth take in one of my breasts while his hand massaged the other. His suckling mixed with the pinching of my nipple between his fingers, and his rowing between my legs made me feel like I was actually in heaven.

And when I came, it consumed me from tip to tail, washing over me in warm waves like I was swimming in a sea of ecstacy.

"Fuck," Maksim said. He rocked forward a few more times, and then I felt him twitch inside of me. His lower half started to spasm and a second later, I could feel him emptying into me, pouring so much out in spite of our earlier dalliances that it overflowed and spilled out. He pulled out and then fell flat against my stomach. "I swear I did not mean to do that."

"You accidentally put your dick in me?" I replied.

He started to laugh. "Maybe I chose the wrong words. I had no *intentions* of doing that, but you..." He lifted his head so he could look up at me. "You bring it out of me. You're too sexy, I just want to be inside of you all the time."

I sat up so I could place my hands on either side of his head and give him a kiss. "I get it."

"Okay. Now *I'll* go find something to clean us up," he said.

After placing a quick peck on my stomach, Maksim hoisted himself up on his arms and climbed off the bed. His cock still had some hardness to it, but it was fading, which was good, because I didn't have anything else left in me for the night. Somewhere in the back of my mind, I registered that I probably should get dressed and go home, if for no other reason than to make sure that Maksim would actually let me leave, but I didn't really want to. As soon as I got dressed, in the only clothes I had with me which were my uniform, I was going to go back to being a cop and Maksim was going to go back to being a criminal, and who knew what was going to happen next.

I wanted to enjoy this world where neither of us felt obligated to our responsibilities for just a *little* bit longer.

Besides, if Maksim and I were in a good place, my family and I were safe, and that was all the more reason to do it. Was I leaning more on that so that I could enjoy spending more time with Maks? Probably. But my life was totally up in the air at this point. All I could do was go with the flow and hope that things panned out okay.

When Maksim finally came back into the bedroom, it was with both a cloth to clean us up, as well as with a small plate of meats, cheeses, and fruits.

"I realized I hadn't eaten," he said, putting the plate on the bed in front of me, then he sweetly wiped between my legs and his own stomach, before climbing back into bed. He lifted the plate so that he could pull the blanket over us and then he pulled me against him and set the plate in my lap for us to enjoy.

It was sinful how delightful it felt.

I popped a piece of cheese into my mouth and hummed with happiness. Rich people could afford the best tasting stuff.

Maksim snickered at me and said, "I assume you hadn't eaten either?"

"No. Being snatched right off the street didn't give me much time to catch dinner," I said.

Maksim huffed a little and then said, "Yeah. Sorry about that."

"Can we at least agree that you'll just try visiting me in person first next time? Give me a chance to explain myself before you go insane?"

"Next time?" he said. "Are you planning on meeting with Katya again?"

I shrugged. "I don't know. She's really nice."

"She's incredible," he said quickly and it left a deposit in my stomach that I didn't like. "But she's working for Vincent as much as she's with him. Can you be friends with someone like that?"

That was the million dollar question. "I don't know. I'm not really sure of anything anymore." I picked up a piece of the salami off the plate and ate it to distract my mind for a moment. "Sometimes I feel like I'm in a crazy dream. Other times like I'm in a nightmare." I frowned. "I have no clue what's going on anymore."

"Part of that is my fault," Maksim said. "Do you ever find yourself wishing that the circumstances we reconnected under were different?"

"All the time," I said. "It's a little scary to think about."

"Scary? How do you mean?"

"You know..." I leaned my head against him and breathed in the beating of his heart against my ear. "I wonder where we'd be. If we'd just bumped into each other randomly. If I weren't a cop or if you weren't bratva. It feels like those are the only real barriers between us right now. I just wonder if it's one of those cruel fate things where..." Then I stopped. It was getting to be a little too close to honest.

"Continue," Maksim said.

I shook my head. "I don't want to."

He kissed the side of my head. "Fine, then I'll say it." He grabbed the side of my face and tilted it so I was looking up at him. "You wonder if we're supposed to be together, but these barriers are in the way. Living with a fear that you'll never be truly happy because we can't be with the one we're meant for?"

It gave me chills how exactly correct that was. "Can I take that to mean you feel the same?"

He knit his brows together and seemed a touch conflicted. "If I'm being totally honest with you, Chloe, not many days have gone by that I haven't thought about you. Even when I was engaged, there were days I thought about you and wondered where you might be, or if I'd actually be with you if you hadn't been taken away from me. I regret that we found each other again this way. It's not at all how I would have done things if I had the choice."

I smiled at him and asked. "How would you have done things?"

"I loved spending time with you so much that I probably never would have grown out of it. As we got older, and you continued to get more and more beautiful despite what should be possible, I definitely would have developed a crush on you."

"You said that before," I reminded him.

"And I probably would have been a little possessive. If you had decided that you wanted to date other people or experience someone else before you and I finally got together, I would have been open to it, but I would have been an asshole to all of your boyfriends for sure," he said.

"What about your girlfriends?" I said. "What if *you* were the one dating other people. Would you have settled for me running them all off?"

He gave it a moment's thought, but then shook his head. "No. I don't think I would have dated anyone else. Maybe I'm just a romantic or it's wishful thinking, but I doubt I would have been able to find anyone who excited me the way you did. I would have just been waiting for you."

"No matter how long it took?" I asked. "What if it took me *forever* to come around."

"It wouldn't have," he said confidently. "Because I can see it in your eyes, you know that it would have been the same for you too. In truth, we probably would have been that sickening couple who made everyone around us irritated with how lovey-dovey we were."

A smile came to my face as I thought about it. If we'd never left Russia, my mom would probably still be alive. I imagined this life where I had both of my parents, my sister didn't have the issues she did, and I was with Maksim, so grossly in love that everyone around us was annoyed with us.

That would have been a pretty good life.

"Oh the things that could have been," I said, resting my head against his body again and laying back.

"Yeah," he replied.

Things had gotten so honest and intimate there, that I almost felt overexposed. If I wasn't so against ruining this moment we'd found, I'd get up and leave before either of us got anymore attached. Because the reality was, that *wasn't* our life. We were two teens who could be together and sickening to everyone around us. Our being together would be problematic and doomed from the start. As my eyes started to get heavy, I made a quiet promise to myself to be careful with how much I let Maksim in from that moment on. Not just because he was dangerous and I needed to keep my guard up.

But because if I wasn't careful, I'd forget about the circumstances between us, and easily start to fall for my old childhood friend.

CHAPTER TWENTY: MAKSIM

At first, when I woke up and felt a body next to mine, I thought that maybe I was dreaming. It wasn't something I was used to, in fact, I hadn't really experienced it much at all. I'd been with women throughout my life, and even had a few of them stay the night after a long session, but waking up the next day after that was more just about getting her out the door and on her way. This time, the other body was snuggled up against me, breathing in and out deeply, and when I looked down and saw Chloe's face, I couldn't help but smile.

I was happy that she was there.

In the back of my mind, I tried to remember that I had to be on my guard when it came to her. Her demeanor changed *very* suddenly after I'd had her snatched and tied up last night, and she was smart enough to know that before she managed to talk me out of killing her, I was well on my way to do it. That sort of thing didn't typically turn women on, so I knew that, at least in some part, Chloe's code switch was just about protecting herself.

That considered, our night last night felt very genuine to me. She seemed to enjoy the sensory deprivation, and then just sitting up and talking with her after that was really delightful. I thought about being able to wake up like that all the time. To just look over and see an image of perfection next to me. Some lazy, sudden sex before snuggling up and talking over a plate of meat and cheese. It felt like something that only happened to people in romance novels, but it had happened to me for real.

And I'd be lying if I said that I didn't want more of it.

My whole life, this was something I'd always wanted. Deep in my core, I was a man who had a lot of love to give someone. I just wanted someone to protect and love and share my life with. For a really long time, I'd always drawn Katya into that picture, but did that mean it *had* to be her? When push came to shove, Chloe was definitely more my speed. After talking last night, it was clear that we were both harboring feelings that we simply refused to bring out only because we both knew it was dangerous to do so.

I wondered if there was any possibility of finding a way to give into those feelings without committing ourselves to certain doom.

Either way, she was here right now, and I didn't want to waste the time we had together, so I pulled her closer against me, snuggled back down into bed and closed my eyes again. I didn't know if I'd fall back asleep, but at least I could enjoy a few more moments of this quiet peace that I hadn't really earned but was grateful to have. Once Chloe left, we'd be back to navigating the harsh waters of her world versus mine, and how that affected how much we were able to feel for each other before it started to become a problem.

And I feared it was only a matter of time before I did something else stupid that dragged us apart again.

Just as the silence was settling over the room, an ear splitting horn of some kind cut the room in half, and Chloe lifted her head with a grunt.

"Oh, shit, my alarm," she hummed. She let her head fall back down against my chest for a moment before she pulled away from me and climbed out of bed. I was dissatisfied with our morning being interrupted, but at least I got to watch her beautiful body as she wandered around the room looking for her phone. Finally, she found it, turned it off, and then crawled back into bed next to me. "Let them fire me, I don't care."

I laughed and rubbed her back as she laid her head back down on my chest. I wondered if that was true, if she really didn't care if they fired her. If she wasn't committed to her job, then what was stopping her from just quitting so that we didn't have this huge wall between us. Chloe would probably never accept my lifestyle fully, but at least if she wasn't a cop, it would feel like we had more options.

My head fell down to hers as I closed my eyes, and I was just about to drift off again when Chloe's phone started to ring again. The tone was different from the alarm, and she let out a much longer groan that time.

Without really moving too much, she answered her phone, lifted it to her ear and said, "Hello?" I could hear a voice muttering quickly at her from the other side. "Yeah. I was trying to catch up on sleep though..." The voice said another string of things and then Chloe let out a long sigh. "Okay. Give me a chance to shower and then I'll be there. Bye."

She slapped her phone down on the bed and buried her head further against me. "I was going to call in today, but Mitzy says Cox wants me in right away."

"Sounds like you'd better go then," I told her. She looked up at me and her beautiful eyes gave me butterflies for a moment. I bent down to kiss her and was relieved when she let me, then I pulled back and asked, "Can we do this again soon?"

"Yeah," she said. "Things are going to keep being weird, I know that, but maybe we just make a deal for now that as long as we're in your house or mine, we just leave everything else out there."

"I like that deal," I said.

"And maybe you don't have me snatched off the street and tied up," she said.

I nodded. "I can do that."

"And maybe you don't go to my family's bodega and threaten my sister."

I nodded even heavier. "I can do that too."

"I really don't feel comfortable weighing my job against you, but I don't want to see you get hurt or caught up in this mess. As long as we can keep it from getting *too* bad, I'll do what I can to keep you out of trouble."

"Okay," I said with a smile. "Thank you."

She left my arms then, leaving me unsatisfied with her departure, but then she bent down and picked up the ripped halves of her shirt. "Right."

"Oh yeah," I said with a laugh. "I'll get you a shirt. Do you want me to drive you home?"

"No, it's okay. I have a spare work shirt at the precinct, so I can change when I get there," she replied, pulling on her pants.

All I really had were me-sized shirts, but I handed one to her and she pulled it on. It looked unbelievably cute, drowning out her form, but she rolled it and tied it back until it fit her a little better, then she walked up to me and gave me a quick kiss.

"I'll call you later?" she said.

"Yeah. I'm looking forward to it."

Scratching the side of my face with her fingers as her final departure, she collected her phone, badge, keys, wallet, and gun, and left my bedroom finally. The room felt much larger and colder when she was gone from it, and I dropped back to sit on my bed and really think about what just happened. I didn't know how we managed to come out the other side of me very much planning to kill her, but I was glad we had. I now just had to deal with the fact that the dynamic between Chloe and I had changed yet again, and what that meant for what I came to New York to do. For the first time ever, I was feeling like I didn't *need* Katya for myself. Chloe was better for me anyway, but that didn't change the fact that I had an issue with Vincent.

It didn't change the fact that he still needed to pay for what he did to the Petrov family.

Because I was paranoid, I *did* do a sweep of my penthouse once Chloe was gone to make sure she hadn't lifted anything. I didn't think she was a thief, but I did know she was a detective, and all of that could have been a front to get me not to kill her and leave my place with some juicy information. I'd definitely been asleep multiple times while she could have been awake and roaming. Most of my stuff I kept locked up in a safe, but the few things I didn't were all where I left them. Nothing seemed to have been touched or moved, which really meant that Chloe didn't have any interest in gathering any dirt on me.

We really did just have a wonderful night together, and that made me very happy.

Not long after I finished washing up, did Brusch come upstairs looking for an update. I supposed he was probably pretty confused, given last he heard he was supposed to be on standby to dump Chloe's body, but he just watched her walk out wearing one of my shirts.

"Is everything okay?" he asked.

"More than," I replied. "It turns out, Chloe didn't tell Katya or Vincent anything about me. She was doing her own footwork, but she had a cover story prepared to make sure she didn't sell me out."

"That's good," Brusch said. "So you made nice with her?"

I smiled, remembering our night together. "I'd say so."

"Were you able to ask about new distributors?" he asked.

"Not yet, but I didn't want to do too much all at once. She did assure me before she left that, as long as I wasn't putting her in too bad of a spot, she'd do what she could to help me. So I think she'll be willing to help once I ask."

"Good," he said. "What about Katya and Vincent?"

I sat down on the couch in the living room and rested my head in my hands. "That is a question I don't quite have the answer to. Ultimately, I don't think my plans have changed. Vincent is still responsible for Vladimir and Sascha's deaths. Even if he didn't pull the triggers, it was because of him that things came to a head the way they did. He destroyed the Petrov family, and I can't let him slide for that. He needs to pay for what he did. Now, I just have another issue to solve—what happens with Chloe at the end of all of this?"

"Can we bring her back to Russia with us?" Brusch said. "She could become a cop there and you could keep her in your pocket. It would probably be very helpful for your empire."

"It's not a terrible idea, but there is a chance she won't want to go," I replied.

"If she doesn't, then what happens?" Brusch asked. "You can't leave her here knowing everything she knows, can you? She'd be too great a risk."

That was the exact fear that had been working its way into my mind over the course of the past couple of hours since Chloe and I woke up. If I didn't find a way to keep the balance between us, or maybe even some sort of relationship, then eventually, Chloe was going to be a huge risk to my livelihood, and there was really only one option when it came to something like that.

"If it comes to that, do you think you'll be able to do it?" Brusch asked.

"I won't have a choice," I replied. "If Chloe won't come back to Russia with me and wants to remain a police officer, then it's very likely that before I go back to Russia, I will have to take her life."

CHAPTER TWENTY-ONE: CHLOE

Thankfully, I was able to get to my locker and change before anyone saw me. I still couldn't believe that I'd let Maksim *cut* my shirt off my body without complaining at all, but by the time we'd gotten that far, my brain was far from having an intact shirt. The way that man worked his hands and his mouth and his...

...other parts.

It can be very distracting from something as simple as whether or not I'd have a shirt to put on the next morning. It wasn't even until I picked up my shirt that I remembered he'd cut it in half. I was grateful for the wisdom to keep some spare clothes in my locker at work, and for the fact that I was able to get to the lockers without having to pass my unit.

For sure if Mitzy saw me in the shirt Maksim gave me, he'd turn into an annoying asshole of questions.

The fact that I'd spent the entire night with Maksim and woke up in his arms the next day was still swirling around my brain when I got up to the squad room. Everyone was working, a couple of them together and laughing quietly, but Mitzy noticed me immediately when I walked in. He stood up and walked over to me, opening his mouth to say something, but then he stopped and stepped back from me. He looked me up and down, studying me like I was some sort of science experiment.

"What?" I huffed at him.

He leaned a little closer to me and took a big whiff, then a smile cracked across his face. "So. I'm guessing the two of you made up?"

Instantly, my cheeks burned with embarrassment. "Shut up," I barked, walking around him and over to my desk.

"I'm happy for you," Mitzy said. "This Chloe is much better than the normal one."

"What do you mean *this* Chloe?" I snapped.

"You know, normally you're all brooding and serious. A tight ass about work. A little high strung. Too complicat—"

"Are you finished?" I asked. "Or did you have a few more insults?"

"Come on, you know I'm crazy about ya, kid, but you were always so tightly wound. Maybe you feel like you're being a hypocrite or whatever, but you're happy, and you deserve to be happy. If he makes you happy, then you should just be okay with it. Don't worry so much about the fine details."

That was easy for him to say. Mitzy didn't take his job seriously regardless, but I actually cared about what I did. It wasn't like I was seeing just *any* criminal, I was seeing an organized crime boss specifically. The exact kind of person that I was supposed to be hunting down and getting off the streets—I'd slept with him in his bed last night. He held a gun to my head, and that still somehow translated to me letting him tie me up and have his way with me.

Maybe I was losing my mind.

"Chloe..." Mitzy sighed. "Come with me." I looked at him, but he seemed pretty committed, so I stood up and walked after him. He stopped by Cox's door and knocked, pointing me out. "Hey. Chloe's here, so we're gonna head downtown and talk to those people who called in."

"Good. Keep me posted, and neither of you make a move if it comes to that. I want *my* face at the front of this thing if this lead goes somewhere. You hear me? Don't go seeking any glory. Don't forget, I'm the captain."

Mitzy held up a thumbs up. "You got it, cap," then he pulled me away from the office grumbling. "That guy is an ass."

"He'd let us get shot and then tell the world he took the bullet," I replied.

Mitzy and I took the elevator down to the garage and got into his car. "Cox wants us to follow up on this lead, but I thought I'd tell you a story before we left. Something I've never told anyone here, because I think it's time you heard it, and I really think it would help you."

"Okay?" I said.

"Not long after I joined the force, about fifteen years ago, I had the opportunity to work with a different budding organized crime unit. It was right when this new family was trying to ride up, out of Little Odessa in fact, and was turning the whole area upside down. I was eager, really wanted to stop guys like these, so I ended up being assigned to doing a lot of the foot traffic in Little Odessa. I was more trustworthy than the average cop for whatever reason, and eventually I ended up meeting a woman who turned out to be the daughter of the crime boss of that family. She was just as involved in the family business, but she wasn't a bad woman. She was just doing what she'd always been taught to do, and her family had been persecuted by the police since long before her father decided to try his hand at being a pakhan of his own group."

"I never knew that," I said.

"Yep. She and I got on pretty well, so even though she was kind of betraying her family, she helped me out by selling out her dad, and even though it was kind of betraying the force, I helped her out by looking the other way when she decided to dismantle the group and just run the product on her own. She was beautiful, intelligent, kind, funny—it wasn't long before I'd fallen head over heels for her."

"You fell in love with her?" I asked. "What happened?"

He shrugged his shoulders and smiled. "I married her and we have three beautiful children together."

A smile came to my face. It was his wife. I had no idea. "Wow. That's kind of an incredible story. How come you never told me that?"

The grin walked away from Mitzy's face then. "Because her father was Matteo Tshovsky."

My stomach knotted up in an instant. A memory flashed across my brain of a tall, dark haired man storming into my family's bodega in Little Odessa. The man was trying to extort my mom, but she refused, so he chose to kill her in front of me and rob us instead. We had less than a hundred dollars in the shop when it happened.

That man was Matteo Tshovsky.

"Your father-in-law is the man who killed my mother?" I asked weakly.

"Was, until he died," Mitzy said. "I never knew how to tell you. You'd met my wife before and you guys seemed to get along really well. I didn't want you to hate her for something I don't even think she realizes happened." I was speechless. How could I not have known? "Knowing that she's the descendant of the man who killed your mother, would you kill her? You could finally get your revenge for your mom?"

I shook my head. "No, of course not. I adore your wife. She didn't carry on her family's legacy, even if she is working in tandem with you and your shady dealings," I said. "I don't get it. Why are you telling me this?"

"Because my wife taught me something *super* important," he said. "No matter where you go. No matter what you do. There are always going to be good people and bad people. Sometimes you'll meet good people who do bad things, and other times you'll meet bad people who do good things. It's just part of being human and living in this fucked up world. My wife taught me that the best way forward is to look out for yourself and the people who mean most to you. I learned that I was better off making whatever decisions benefitted *me* the most, and it has never steered me wrong. I just try to be as good a person as I can, take care of my family, being a good husband. The rest of this shit I leave to just work itself out and it has never steered me wrong, not once."

It made me think back to what Mitzy had told me the day before after I finished meeting with Katya. He said that it sounded like I needed to define a couple of words like what 'good' meant and what 'happy,' meant. If someone had asked me a couple of weeks ago, 'good' meant someone who obeyed the law and didn't hurt other people, and 'happy' would have been something close to being physically, emotionally, and mentally healthy along with financially sound.

Now I know those things are not what define those words for me anymore. The biggest problem for me was, I still didn't quite know what *did* define those words for me. It was like I'd told Maksim before, I didn't really know *what* was going on anymore. I was supposed to be moving forward, but while it didn't feel like I was moving backwards, it also just didn't really feel like I was moving. I had no idea *what* to make of my life right now, I just knew that I cared about people on both sides of the fence, and where that left me was scared and confused.

"Sorry," Mitzy said. "I didn't mean to overload your brain."

"It's okay. I appreciate you telling me that story. I get what you're trying to say," I told him. "I guess, for me, I just don't know what happens for me now. I'm supposed to be finding the answer, but I don't even know where to fucking look."

"So stop looking," Mitzy said, tapping me on the head. "Searching for this answer is your problem. Don't look for it, just let life show you what it all means."

For whatever reason, I smiled when Mitzy said that. "Katya said something similar to me. I asked her how she found perfection in her life, and she said she didn't, she just stopped looking for perfect."

"You know that old phrase, 'A watched pot never boils'?" Mitzy asked.

I nodded my head. "Yeah."

"Stop watching the pot," he said. "You'd be surprised how quickly it boils."

"I'm not a 'not watch the pot' kind of lady, but I think I'll try and take this advice," I said. "It's gotta be better than nothing."

"Definitely, and in the meantime, getting laid has made you a *much* better person."

"Why do you have to ruin the moment? It was sweet. We were bonding."

Mitzy laughed. "Sorry. You know I make jokes when things get uncomfortably real." He started up his car and put on his seatbelt. "Now, let's go. We have actual work to do."

"Where are we going again?" I asked.

"All the way out to Long Island," he replied. "Some new group making waves out there. Could be a new mafioso group. They call themselves 'The Wreckers.' At first, the police out there just thought they were a group of dumb kids causing problems, but lately their crimes have been increasing in consistency and seem to be connected. Apparently, in one of the most recent calls, the lead that we're going to interview said that it sounded like they had some sort of hierarchy, like a deck of cards. King, Queen, Joker, Ace... No idea what that's about, but if they have a hierarchy and are committing organized crimes. Sounds like a job for us."

"Take one out, pick up two more, huh?" I said, putting on my seatbelt.

Mitzy nodded his head as we pulled out of the precinct parking lot. "Ninety-nine bottles of milk on the wall."

CHAPTER TWENTY-TWO: MAKSIM

Blessedly, the next few weeks proved to be better as opposed to worse for Chloe and I. We both worked hard to hold up our end of the bargain to leave our work lives outside when we were together, which meant we were not only allowed to continue seeing one another, but to continue sleeping together as well. Chloe's trust in me grew, and it meant we were able to experiment more and more with sensory deprivation. Chloe even came to me with some new stuff she wanted to try one time. I'd been able to introduce other people to my kink in the past, but I'd never had someone share that kink with me and want to do more and grow in it together.

It was very exciting.

On top of that, Chloe took everything in her stride. Things that other women had shied away from, she was excited to try and it created a challenge for me. I wanted to find all the best ways to make the both of us feel good when we were together. Not that I had to try very hard in that area. I pretty much always felt good when I was with Chloe.

After an additional two weeks, something weird happened that I wasn't expecting at all.

"I'm hungry," Chloe said when she walked into my penthouse after work.

Of course, I'd been planning on doing what we always did when she came over. Having fun, sleeping together, talking and then eventually falling asleep. Nothing *outside* of our homes was part of this undefined relationship we had, because we'd agreed to shut everything out so that we didn't have to face the barriers that existed for us in the outside world. But Chloe was hungry and she looked like she'd had a long day. Some new case had cropped up for her out on Long Island that was taking up a lot of her time, and I didn't feel right just throwing her into sex.

"Should we go get something to eat?" I asked after a long period of thinking it over.

She looked back at me with a curious expression on her face. "Outside?"

"Yeah," I replied. "I don't really have much in here, I'm afraid, and if you're hungry, you should eat."

"So..." Chloe looked at the elevator doors like they were magically going to open and give her the answers she was looking for. "You and I will go out to eat... outside... together?"

"That's pretty much what I had in mind," I responded. "As long as that's okay with you."

"It's okay with me," she said. "I'd maybe want to travel out a ways so that I'm not seen by anyone who would recognize me."

I nodded, understanding that. "Okay. You know the best places in New York I'm sure. Do you know a place that's a good distance from here?"

"Well, Mitzy and I have been spending a lot of time on Long Island and we've passed a few places that look good," she said. "It's about an hour away. We could go there and pick one of those places?"

"Long Island?" I repeated. "Okay. We can go out to Long Island and eat there."

Chloe looked back at me and a cute smile came across her face. "Okay."

It was the first time that we'd done anything other than just meet up and have sex. Our nights together usually involved a fair amount of talking, catching up, and reminiscing, but this was the first time we were going out on something like a *date* without me having to force her to come along.

Chloe went home and got dressed into something a little nicer and did herself up, I put on one of my suits and picked her up, complete with flowers, and we drove out to a delicious Asian restaurant out on Long Island and shut the place down. We laughed and talked all night until the staff had to come and reluctantly tell us that we had to leave. I gave a huge tip, which endeared Chloe to me more, then we went back to her place and...

...well then things got a little more typical.

After that, it felt like things had turned a corner for us. We started texting each other, flirting and sexting throughout the day. Whenever we met up after Chloe got off of work, we found ourselves making plans to eat something first, whether it be delivered or we went out, and then we'd cap the night off with sex. Suddenly, the physical part of our relationship wasn't the main course anymore, it was the cherry on top of the dessert. Chloe started to stay over most nights, and I got used to having her around whenever she wasn't at work.

It was like we were actually dating—like she was a real girlfriend.

I'd never really had a true blue girlfriend before. I'd dated women in the past, and I'd had lovers before, but between my work with the Petrovs and the fact that I'd always been infatuated with Katya, I just never really found anyone who seemed worth it enough to forge an actual relationship with. When it came to Chloe, that infatuation with Katya didn't really exist, and my work with the Petrovs was something I agreed to keep *out* of my life with her, so there weren't really any barriers.

And it made me incredibly happy.

But just when I was beginning to really settle into my happy new life, I got a call I wasn't expecting.

"Latva," I said as I answered the phone. "Is everything okay? You don't usually contact me outside of email."

Latva, the Petrov's long-standing family assistant, was back in Russia taking care of things on that side of the world. He'd been running the Petrovs' affairs for a long time and knew what he was doing, so I didn't have any fear he couldn't keep things afloat while I was gone. He usually just sent me emails when he needed me to make a decision or to update me on something he was doing, so receiving an actual call was concerning.

"Pakhan. We're starting to battle a new issue back here in St. Petersburg," he said in hurried Russian. "It seems word has gotten around that Vladimir and Sascha are no longer living, and rival bratva believe our family is without a head. We've already had one attempted attack and are hearing whispers of another. I've managed to keep things stifled up to this point, but lately there are talks on the wind of the other groups forming a temporary alliance to dismantle and distribute the Petrov empire. We're going to need you home to prepare for this new threat."

I could already feel my anger starting to rise up. I'd tried my hardest to keep the deaths of Vladimir and Sascha under wraps at least for a while. I knew word would get out to the other groups at some point, but I was hoping by then to have already returned with Katya and be making plans to restart the regime with the pair of us at the top. Hearing that things were already moving was a problem for me, especially because I didn't have all of my ducks in row here in NYC.

In fact, I'd been kind of neglecting my ducks altogether.

"I understand. Do you know how much time I have left before I need to come back?" I asked.

"I would imagine a few weeks would be the absolute maximum," Latva replied. "If I know anything about these groups, it's that it's going to take them a while to rally themselves, but once they get there, they'll charge full steam ahead."

"Okay. Let me expedite getting things sorted out here and I'll be back to Russia soon. Please keep me posted on everything that's going on."

"I will, pakhan," he replied. "Goodbye."

I ended the call and immediately developed a headache. Chloe and I had made a deal that we would keep our outside lives out of our relationship, but I had no choice but to bring it up now. When we first reconnected, I imagined I would only be involved with her so long as I was in New York, but I no longer wanted that to be the case. It also just *couldn't* be the case. I would never be able to kill Chloe at this point, but I had no idea what I'd do if she didn't want to return to Russia with me.

Maybe I'd have to pass that unpleasant task off to Brsuch and just become that dark man I'd been afraid of.

Immediately after I got off the call with Brusch, I called him up to the penthouse to talk. I filled him in on what Latva had told me so that we could bounce some ideas off of one another of the best way to handle things. I didn't want to leave the group back home totally without leadership. Some of the higher ranking members were there, but I didn't know them as well as Brusch, or how capable they were of handling this in my stead.

"I could go back," Brusch offered. "I'll make sure things stay above the board until you get back."

"I thought about that, but I'd really prefer to have you here," I said. "I really just need to fast-track getting back there, which means we're out of time to find a distributor and to deal with Vincent. Those things just move to the top of our priority list."

"And what about Chloe?" Brusch asked. "Have you asked her about returning to Russia with us?"

"No."

The truth was that, not only were Chloe and I just sticking to our rule to keep our outside lives out of our relationship, I think both of us were actively avoiding thinking about it. We knew that eventually, holding up that rule wasn't going to work anymore and we'd have to face what was next for us. It was difficult to think about, especially when considering the fact that there was an outcome where Chloe and I weren't together, or worse...

"I think you need to deal with that first," Brusch advised. "She's going to be our biggest aid in finding a distributor and our biggest barrier in taking out Vincent Costello. We need to know where she's at before we can take any steps forward."

"Yeah," I said. "I know." My phone buzzed, and based on the time, I knew that it was probably her getting ready to arrive after work. "She'll be here soon and I'll ask her about it. Then we can go from there."

"Yes, boss." Brusch stood up and walked back to the elevator doors, but then he stopped and turned around. "You aren't having second thoughts, are you?"

I tilted my head. "Second thoughts?"

"About being pakhan," he said. "You seem so happy like this. In the penthouse above Dacha, being with Chloe. Is going back to Russia and ruling the Petrov empire what you want?"

That question had never been posed to me before and I had never considered anything other than it. "Of course I do," I said. "It's what is expected of me."

"But if it wasn't?" he said. "Would you stay here, with Chloe?" I opened my mouth to respond, but he held a hand up. "Don't. Just think about it. I spent many years serving Vladimir, doing the nasty stuff. This isn't a life for the faint of heart. Consider that for a while and let me know what you come up with."

"Okay," I said, but there wasn't much to consider. I *was* the Petrov pakhan. There was no second-guessing that for me. It was what I was born to do.

Brusch and Chloe must have crossed paths, because I listened as the elevator went down and then came right back up. The doorbell rang and I walked over to it and let Chloe in. She offered me a huge smile before stepping forward to wrap around me for a kiss. For a moment, all of the stress that was just weighing on me went away, but as soon as we parted it was back, because I knew it was time for us to face some difficult truths.

"Can we eat in tonight?" Chloe asked as she walked into the living room. "I'm exhausted."

"Sure, but first... I need to discuss something with you," I said.

She sat up a little straighter on the couch and gave me a concerned look. "Okay..."

I sat down next to her, not entirely sure how to discuss things, especially when we'd both been pretending for three weeks now that these things didn't exist.

"I got a call from back in Russia today," I started. "It seems my empire is in danger there and I have to go back soon, otherwise all of my group are going to be attacked, and I'm unsure what could happen after that. I need to finish up doing the things here that I said I was going to do, so that I can get back home and take care of things."

"Oh," Chloe said, with notable sadness in her voice. "Well, I get that. I've been trying not to think about it, but I knew you didn't live here permanently. I figured you'd be going back to Russia soon, I just didn't think it'd be *this* soon."

"Yeah. So, unfortunately, I have to break our rule and discuss outside things with you," I said.

Chloe shook her head. "Why? You're going back to Russia, that's all I need to know. You don't need to tell me why or what's going to happen when you get there."

"No, Chloe, I need to discuss what's left to happen here in New York."

She furrowed her brow. "What do you have left to do here in New York?"

Now I was just as confused as she seemed. "What are you talking about? I told you when we first reconnected what I'm here for."

"What?" she said.

"Chloe, I still need to kill Vincent Costello and take Katya with me back to Russia."

CHAPTER TWENTY-THREE: CHLOE

I sat staring at Maksim in total silence. The last three weeks that we'd spent together felt like a dream. We didn't discuss any of his criminal activity and I was able to forget the fact that he was anything other than the wonderful guy I was dating. We'd gotten past our differences, and with us getting closer and closer, I honestly thought he'd put Vincent and Katya out of his mind. Why did he need to kill Vincent if he no longer felt like he had to get Katya back somehow?

"I don't understand," I said. "I thought you were done with Katya. I mean... I thought we were... us?" I shook my head. "Katya told me she's happy and she's here by choice. You don't need revenge against Vincent anymore. You don't have to start a war here, you might never escape the United States if you do. Why do you have to do that?"

"Chloe, Katya aside, Vincent still killed the man who was like a father to me and the man who was like a brother," Maksim explained. "He crippled the Petrov empire with his actions. I can't just let that slide."

"But what about the baby?" I said. "You're going to tear up a happy family, for what? Your pride? Katya needs the father for her child."

Maksim stood up. "Katya will be fine. She'll have her mother, and besides, she'll have more than that. She belongs back in Russia with..." Then he stopped.

"With you," I finished for him. "After all this time, your mind never left Katya. She's always been your ultimate goal?"

"Chloe..."

"I don't want to hear it," I said. "You know what? Do what you want. I'm exhausted with this. You don't have to worry about me selling you out or interfering. I don't want any part of this anymore. Any part of *you* anymore."

Maksim seemed hurt by that and tried to reach down to touch my face. "Chloe..."

But I slapped his hand away. "Don't! I don't want to be thrown around anymore. I just want it over. Whatever you're going to do, just do it and leave me out of it."

I stood up and stormed past him, headed for the door. He followed after me and continued reaching out to try and grab my arm, but I pulled away from him each time. When I finally reached the elevator door and stabbed the button, I turned around and Maksim was just looking at me sadly.

"We agreed to talk things out," he said.

"There's nothing to talk about," I said. "Unless you're going to tell me that you're going to drop this whole Vincent and Katya thing?"

His frown deepened. "I can't."

"Then we're done here."

The elevator doors opened and I backed up onto them and watched Maksim broken hearted until the doors shut and closed him off from me. I blew right past Brusch keeping watch at the bottom and ran outside to hop in my car. I felt so stupid that tears were actually coming to my eyes and that I had the audacity to feel more broken up about the fact that it seemed like Maksim and I were over than that I'd actually allowed myself to get involved with a criminal like him. I'd made many mistakes in my life, but letting myself develop actual feelings for Maksim was by far the worst.

By the time I got home, I was feeling so lonely that I wanted to call someone, but was unsure of who. Katya and I had actually been in loose contact since she and I first met, but this was a problem I could specifically not tell her. And it wasn't like this was something I could share with my dad or sister. I didn't have many friends...

So I called the only person I could think of.

"Chloe?" Mitzy said when he answered the phone. "What's going on? Is everything okay?"

"No..." I whimpered.

"Are you hurt?"

"I'm not hurt. Not physically anyway."

"Oh boy..." he said. "Maksim?"

Suddenly, I felt very stupid. :You know what? Nevermind. I'm sorry I bothered you."

"Wait. Chlo—" but before he could finish, I hung up the phone. Mitzy was like ten years older than me, and a man with a family. He didn't have the time to be worried about my stupid love life.

I wandered around my apartment for a little bit, unsure of what to do with myself next. I told Maksim to do whatever he was planning on, but I couldn't really let that happen. Not just for my job, but because I actually believed that Katya and Vincent were good people who didn't deserve Maksim's wrath. There had been such a back and forth between the Costellos and the Petrovs, in what sounded like an international conflict, that more reasonable people would call a truce and just let it go.

But Maksim wasn't a reasonable person.

It was like there were two sides to him. The one I knew intimately and the one who was most like the child who I was friends with as a kid. A man who was caring, romantic, and honestly kind of a hero. He was the man that I'd foolishly started developing feelings for, and losing sleep over wondering how I could live a life that allowed me to keep him close without sacrificing my morals.

His other side, however, was dark and horrifying. He was quick to anger and slow to soothe, which was strange because he was also steeped in regret. He was a man who made choices he didn't believe in and lived a life that never really belonged to him in the first place.

One was Maksim Pasternak and one was Maksim Petrov. The former was a better man, but the latter was stronger, and a world at Maksim Petrov's feet was something I couldn't stand for. I'd stop him even if I had to lose myself doing it.

The very thought of going toe-to-toe with a Petrov scared me so much that it made me dizzy.

No wait...

I was *actually* dizzy.

I'd only just barely managed to make my way to a chair in the dining room before I completely lost my footing. I fell forward a little, landing in the chair, but knocking things off the table in the process. They clattered to the ground and when I looked down to see what I'd dropped, I was confused to find my vision warping. Multiple copies of the things that had fallen were swirling in and out of the prime object and it took all the force in my body not to fall out of the chair.

I was so disoriented that when I heard a knock on my door, I was almost convinced it was all in my mind. I hadn't arranged for anyone to come by, and there wasn't a person I could think of who'd just drop in.

But then I heard, "Chloe? It's Mitzy! I heard some banging. Are you okay?" I opened my mouth to reply, but it was like no words would come out.

My throat was tightening and the room was getting hotter and hotter by the second. "Chloe?"

Then my phone started to ring. I could see it on the floor—one of the dizzying objects that had fallen—so I leaned over to try and get it. Of course, it threw me off balance and I dropped to the floor in a slump. I clawed out, just hoping to hit the button to answer it, when finally, I saw the call pick up.

"Mitz," I said quietly. "Break... the door."

Immediately, I heard thundering against the door before it eventually slammed inwards. Mitzy saw me on the floor and came rushing over. "Chloe! What's wrong?"

"I don't know," I whined. "I'm scared."

CHAPTER TWENTY-FOUR: MAKSIM

I felt absolutely destroyed by the way things had gone with Chloe. When she brought up Vincent or the idea of me letting it go, I immediately went into my default defense of why I was in the United States to begin with. When I got on a plane, nearly two months ago now, to fly out to America, it was with vengeance in mind. Vincent had taken everything from me, and I wanted to pay him back for the crimes he'd committed both against me and against the Petrov family. I believed that *I* should be with Katya and that I was what was best for her and her baby.

But I could admit that my perspective had changed.

There was still a very large part of me that hated Vincent for what he'd done, and an equally large part that believed Vincent might not have been Katya's choice had she not been put in the situation she was in. I truly did wonder if Katya had met Vincent in circumstances outside of the ones she'd met him in, if she would have fallen for him the same way. Would she be carrying his baby? Would she be engaged to be married to him? Would she be working underneath him as one of his high-ranking officers?

In truth, I didn't really picture Katya going the mom and wife road at all.

I'd always had a thing for her, but even in my wildest fantasies, I only ever saw us as taking up a physical relationship. I thought I could probably convince her to form a union with me at some point, but only for the purposes of getting her closer to the top of her father's empire where she belonged. I respected Katya, and there was no denying the attraction I had to her at one point.

Love, however, it was not.

When I thought of Chloe and compared the time we'd spent together to the time I spent with Katya, hand over fist it made me way happier. Chloe was willing to meet me halfway, even in situations where that was detrimental to her. She'd sacrificed so much of what she believed in simply to pursue the chemistry that neither of us could deny we had. She forgave me for my actions long past when I deserved forgiveness, and she helped me see that there was a different, much happier man inside of me waiting to be released. I'd shut out so much of the world because of everything I'd lost. I was afraid to truly care for something because I feared it being ripped from me like everything had in the past.

From the moment I reconnected with Chloe, though, things slowly started to change.

I was fighting for something again, and regretting my actions. I was questioning my purpose in the United States, and in my life in general. I'd been telling myself over and over that Katya was the one I wanted to be with, but that was just the default setting my stock-self came with. If I was going to be totally honest with myself, there was no question in my mind.

Chloe was the one I wanted.

So why in the heat of the moment did I falter? I had a chance to clearly state how I was feeling and ask Chloe to meet me halfway again, and all I did was give her a reason to pull away from me. How many mistakes could I make before she couldn't forgive me anymore? How many before I had to stop viewing her as Chloe my girlfriend, and start looking at her as Chloe the cop again?

The doorbell rang at the elevator and I jumped up from the couch. I was hopeful that maybe Chloe had come back looking to talk things out with me, but when I pressed the button to open the elevator doors, it was Brusch on the other side.

"Boss, we have a problem," he said, sliding into the penthouse before quickly closing the elevator doors and shutting the additional, metal door that permanently separated the elevators from the rest of the penthouse. "Did things go bad between you and Chloe again? I saw her storm out of here."

"We had a bit of a..." I searched my brain for the word. "Disagreement, but I'm going to give her some time to cool off and then call her back and clear it up."

"I think you may be too late for that," Brusch said. "The cops are outside."

"What?" I rushed over to my computer and threw it open, navigating through my security app until I could see the security camera's view of the outside. Both ends of the street had been barricaded, any customers that were trying to get in had been cleared away, and I could see that a few police offi-cers in tactical gear were ushering additional customers out of the club. "What the hell is going on?"

"They just showed up out of the blue with a warrant for your arrest. Said you've levied a verifiable threat against multiple U.S. citizens which is consid-ered an act of terrorism," he explained.

"Terrorism?" I barked. "I didn't terrorize anyone. Well... I haven't in a few weeks."

"Did you say something to Chloe about threatening someone?" he asked.

I went silent in the wake of that question. Even if I set aside her sister, whom I'd very blatantly threatened, more recently I threatened the lives of Vincent Costello, the soon-to-be Katya Costello—whose marriage would make her a U.S. citizen—and the yet-to-be-born baby Costello. I wanted to believe that Chloe didn't rat me out that quickly—I'd jumped to conclusions before and had been totally wrong—but when I thought about any verifiable threat, the only thing I could think of were the threats I'd made to and around Chloe. Nothing else had happened that someone would be able to prove.

"Was she naked in here?" he asked.

"Do you want me to kill you?" I asked.

He was standing guard by the door, but looked over at me. "Boss, I don't care about her. I'm asking for a logistical reason, was she naked in here today?"

"Today? No," I replied. "Why?"

"What if she was wired?" he said. "She *just* left. It would have been pretty difficult for her to tell anyone this information and get SWAT outside that quickly, but if she was wired..."

"...Then they could have been preparing the entire time she was here, and planned to show up as soon as she left."

This time, I didn't think I was jumping to conclusions. Nothing else made sense. The police showed up immediately after Chloe left, they had a warrant for a threat they could verify, the only people I'd threatened, at least around someone who would tell the police something like that, was Chloe. All signs pointed to her as much as I hated to admit it, and it made me want to put a hole through the wall.

No wonder her demeanor changed so severely. She was already in the midst of setting me up.

"I'm so sorry," I said. "I believed her. I let my guard down."

"Well, now you know at least," Brusch said. "What do you want to do? They have the place surrounded. I asked for the courtesy to come and get you to try and reduce any casualties, but I don't know that there's a way out of this without a blood bath, and if you get caught after that, you'll never leave the United States again."

"So what are you saying?" I said.

He frowned. "I'm saying... I think we might need to play their game on this one. I'll contact a lawyer and get your bail posted right away, but the best way to play this is—"

"For me to go to jail here in the United States?" I finished.

"And hope for extradition."

"Extradition? So I can be in jail in Russia?" I retorted.

"We have more pull in Russia." He frowned. "I can't tell you what to do on this one, and I get it if you think your best move is to try and fight your way out, and I'll fight right along with you, but then we've got to get the hell out of the United States before they get their hands on us, and then even when we do, we can never come back here."

I weighed the pros against the cons. I thought about Dacha, and how lucrative the produce we were moving here was, and knew that I didn't want to take the club down with me. If I could get out of the U.S. without going to jail, obviously that would be preferred, but to never even be able to come back. Everything I started here would come to a screeching halt. The club could maybe run itself, but I would never get to free Katya, I would never get to kill Vincent.

And I would never get to make things right with Chloe.

"Boss..." Brusch broke into my thoughts. "I'm sorry, but we have to make a decision. If we wait any longer, they're going to come in, and they're going to tear everything up on their way in here to you. Everyone will go down."

I stood up off the couch and walked over to Brusch. I pulled out my keys, wallet and phone and handed them over to him. He seemed surprised, but took the items from me and nodded with understanding.

"I need you to call Latva and update him. Make sure he's prepared to wire any money you think you may need to obtain the best legal representation in this entire country," I said.

He nodded. "Yes, boss."

"Keep my phone charged and on you. I'll call you on my phone as soon as I have the chance, since I have the number memorized."

Brusch gave me another obedient nod. "Yes, boss."

"From this moment forward, you are my sovietnik and I expect you to behave as such. If anyone questions you, tell them they'll have to deal with me when I get out."

Brusch puffed up his chest a bit more and gave me a determined nod. "Yes, boss, I understand."

"Let's go then," I said. "The sooner we get this over with, the better."

Brusch and I rode the elevator down to the main floor in silence, and then rather than going out the back door, we walked around to the front. Brusch went out first, holding up his hand, and then I stepped out into the bright lights the police had aimed at the front door.

"Get down on the ground!" someone screamed. "Put your hands behind your back! Do it now, or we'll shoot!"

I stuck my hands in the air to show them I wasn't fighting, then I did as told, lowering myself down onto the pavement on my stomach and folded my hands behind my back. I watched as a swarm of police in swat gear rushed forward with their guns out, all of them trained on me, save for one who dropped his so he could cuff me. When my hands were secured behind my back, I was lifted off the ground and walked over to the nearest police car.

"Head," the police officer said who was helping me duck in, and she was about to shut the door, when someone grabbed it and wrenched it back open.

I looked over to see Captain Cox leaning into the doorway with a sick smile on his face. "It's nice to see you again, Maksim Petrov. I see you don't have that cocky smile on that dumb mug of yours now." I didn't respond, only glared at him with all of the loathing in my body. "It was smart of you to come with no issues. You think you can just walk into my house and make a fool of me with no consequences? Come into my house and try to stir up trouble, and I'll do the same to you, only successfully." He narrowed his gaze and smiled even broader. "Enjoy the ride."

He shut the door and banged on the top and the red and blue lights flashed to attention. A siren cracked out from the car and the sea of people and vehicles parted to let us out.

I looked to my left as the car drove off and saw Brusch standing in front of Dacha looking at me. I believed in him to do everything he could, but the look of concern on his face didn't inspire confidence.

After all this time, trusting Chloe Nikitina was going to ruin my life.

CHAPTER TWENTY-FIVE: CHLOE

I lay flat on the uncomfortable hospital bed, freezing thanks to the amount of air the weak gown let in. I'd been through about a thousand tests, had my blood drawn, been given intravenous fluids, had spoken to three different doctors about my symptoms, and still, no one seemed to be able to tell me what was wrong with me. One doctor had tried to say that I just had a panic attack, based on the fact that I'd told them I was under a lot of stress and thinking about it when the symptoms came on, but a fellow doctor quickly discredited it for how debilitating it was. Because I'd never had one before, they didn't think it should have the effect on me that it did.

On top of no longer feeling any of the effects of what had happened, I was exhausted, I was hungry, I was still sad about Maksim—all I really wanted to do was go home, stuff my face with whatever my hand hit first in my fridge, and then go to bed.

"Are you seriously going to throw a mystery diagnosis on top of all of this?" Mitzy asked. "You stress me out, girl. *I'm* gonna be the one being wheeled into the hospital next."

"I'm not doing any of this on purpose, contrary to how it might seem," I said. "I'm just glad you showed up, or who knows *what* would have happened."

"Really, you can thank yourself for that," Mitzy said. "When you called me and then suddenly hung up, I got really worried. You've been so up and down lately that it made me nervous your next down would be *really, really* down. I explained the situation to my wife and she told me to come and check on you. I was actually planning on dragging you back to my house to stay with me, the wife, and the kids for a few days. I didn't want you to be alone."

It made me feel good that Mitzy cared about me so much. He'd saved my life more than once in actual, life-threatening situations, but really I think he kept me afloat every single day.

"You know, you're my best friend..." I said.

Mitzy looked up at me with a concerned gaze. "This isn't the start of something bad, is it?"

"No," I said. "I'm always beating up on myself for not really having any friends. When things went to hell with me and Maks, I was thinking, 'this is why I should have friends, so that someone can be there for me in situations like this.' When I needed to call someone, you were the only person I could think of."

"I'm your only friend? Whoo, that's rough. I am *not* a good choice," he joked, but I wasn't laughing.

"You are absolutely the greatest person I have ever known—next to my mom. You've cared for me so much more than anyone else has in my life, and when I called you, it was because I really wanted you there. Then I felt dumb, because you're so much older than me—"

"Not *so* much," he cut in.

"And you have a family. I was like, there's no *way* he wants to sit on the phone with me while I cry about some guy. So I hung up," I explained.

"Chloe..." He reached out and set his hand on mine. "I've said it a million times, haven't I? I'm always there for you. You're like one of my favorite people. Sure, maybe our friendship is a little unorthodox, but aren't those the best ones?"

"They are," I replied.

"So next time, don't even hesitate. If you need me to drop what I'm doing, even if it's to just listen to you whine about some guy, I'll do it." His smile grew then. "You're my best friend too."

For some reason, the conversation made me unexpectedly emotional. Maybe it was just because things with Maksim ended so badly, or all of my stress was coming to a head, but tears started to fill my eyes. I swiped them away while Mitzy was looking down at his phone, but I stayed smiling at the back of his head. I was lucky to have him. I'd always struggled with the decisions he made and judged him for them, but the last two months I'd been making one sketchy decision right after the other and he'd stuck by me every step of the way. I was beginning to see what he meant when he said it was just important to make sure yourself and the people you loved were happy. Mitzy didn't do life the way I would, but as long as he was happy and safe, then I was happy for him.

"Miss Nikitina?" We both looked up and a fourth doctor was striding into the room. This doctor in particular was a woman, whereas the other three had been men, and she had a higher atmosphere of confidence about her. "Hi. I'm Doctor Courtney Tyrne, an OBGYN."

She stuck out her hand for me to shake, and though I did shake it, I did so loosely and with confusion all about me. "Oh, um. I think you have the wrong room... or patient?"

"Do you think something is wrong with Chloe... down there?" Mitzy asked.

Dr. Courtney looked over at Mitzy with an annoyed look on her face. "I'm sorry, what is your relationship to the patient?"

"Best friend," Mitzy said.

"Well, I think this might be a conversation best had with just her. If you'd like, you can wait outside, and I'll call you back in when we're done."

Mitzy looked at me, but I could tell from the expression on the doctor's face that she believed it was best he left, so I nodded. He stood up and said, "I'll be right outside. Holler if you need me."

"I will. Thanks," I replied.

Grumbling as he went, Mitzy walked out of the room, and the doctor made sure to close the door after him. "I'm sorry about that, I just wanted to make sure you had privacy for this."

"That's okay. Are you going to examine me... you know...?"

She laughed. "No, at least not at the moment. Your symptoms made their way to me through the daisy chain and I wanted to discuss the possibility that you may be pregnant," she said. "Though uncommon, there is a condition in the early stages of pregnancy, especially for women in high stress, high activity jobs such as yourself that results in things like, random bouts of dizziness, immobility, sickness, and anxiety to name a few of the symptoms."

"Well... that does sound exactly like what happened to me, but I don't think I'm pregnant," I replied.

"Could you be?" she said. "Any sexual partners right now?"

Of course, my mind immediately went to Maksim, and thinking back over some of our sessions, we definitely slipped up and he finished inside of me. But I had an implant to keep my particularly horrible periods at bay. "I mean... yes, but I have an implant."

"Yes, well unfortunately, much like any other contraceptive, they aren't one-hundred-percent effective. Have you and any recent partner had sex without a condom?"

I swallowed hard and nodded. "Yeah."

"Then once again, I really think you should take a pregnancy test," she said. "We can do it right here right now, it's quick and painless, and we can have the results back within a handful of minutes."

Though the thought of finding out I was pregnant on top of everything else made me want to vomit, I nodded my head in agreement. "Okay. I'll do it."

"Great," she said. "I'll go get the test and I'll be right back. Do you want me to send your friend back in?"

"Yes please. I am bound to pass out if it comes back positive."

She snickered, but I hardly found it funny, then she stood up and walked out of the room. A few moments later, Mitzy came walking back in, looking as white as a ghost—even more so than he did on a regular day.

"So she told you, huh?" I asked.

"Huh?" Mitzy looked up at me. "Told me what?"

"That I might be pregnant?"

Mitzy's jaw dropped. "You might be pregnant? Would it be Maksim's?"

"Yeah," I snapped back, almost annoyed with the question. "Why?"

"Because I have got some really bad news for you then," he said, and my heart solidified in my chest.

"What?"

"Cox and a bunch of SWAT just finished raiding Dacha," he said timidly. "They arrested Maksim."

My jaw fell to the floor and all I could do was sit there in total silence for a few minutes. I was just there. Not more than an hour and a half ago, I was sitting in Maksim's living room, talking to him about how he wanted to kill Vincent Costello and spend his life with a different woman.

"I knew nothing about a raid, did you?" I asked.

Mitzy shook his head. "No. When I left the precinct today, everyone was complaining about how boring it was there right now."

"What did they arrest him for?" I said. "As far as I know, he hasn't done anything wrong since he's been here." Then I thought of the man he told me he had chopped up and driven to the far edges of the country. "Well... not anything that Cox would know about."

"Apparently they arrested him on a verifiable threat to U.S. civilians," Mitzy explained. "They're trying to slap him with terrorism."

"Terrorism?!" I screeched. "Maksim may be a little shady, but he's not a terrorist!"

"Cox got a tip that says otherwise," Mitzy said. "They drove him off in a squad car, thirty minutes ago." Without really thinking, I set my hand on my stomach and closed my eyes to try and still the sudden churning there. "And you might be pregnant with his kid." He sighed. "I gotta tell ya, Chloe, when I told you the story about me and my wife, I didn't think you'd replicate it exactly."

"This isn't a joke!" I snapped at him. "If I'm pregnant by a bratva pakhan, I can pretty much kiss my job and my family goodbye."

"Well, we're going to figure it out, Chloe, so just relax, okay? You may not even be pregnant, so let's just take it one step at a time." It felt like it was getting harder to breathe again, but Mitzy rubbed my back gently. "Just breathe."

The doctor came back a few minutes later with a pregnancy test, and ushered me into the attached bathroom to take it. I shook the entire time I did it, trying to imagine what I would do if it turned out I *was* pregnant. How was I ever going to explain this to my dad or to my sister? What was I going to do for work? Being a cop was the only thing I knew how to do, and I had to imagine no place would employ a woman who got knocked up by the criminals.

But I tried to do as Mitzy said and just breathed it out. I let my mind drift to a slightly happier thought that I actually *did* care about Maksim, and dream of a life where we could be a family. Even as impossible as that seemed, the fantasy was nice enough that I could calm down enough to take the test. I popped the cap back on and walked back into the room where Dr. Courtney and Mitzy were making idle chat.

I handed the test over to her and said, "Okay. Now what?"

"Now we wait," she said. "We should know if you're pregnant or not in about three minutes."

To be continued...

PART ONE

CHAPTER ONE: MAKSIM

I sat staring at the cement walls around me, uncertain if the bugs I saw crawling across them were real or just hallucinations. I'd been trying my best to keep track of the days that had passed by listening to the guards outside my isolation cell, but it wasn't the easiest thing to do with no context. Once, I heard one of them greet another with "good morning," and I tried to keep a count of the hours passing by in my head, but somewhere in the middle, I fell asleep and had no idea how long I was out. The only real concept of time I had since there were no windows in my cell and the guards hadn't been by once, even to feed me, was my growing facial hair. Based on the fact that I could now actually pinch the hairs between my fingers, it had to have been five days, maybe six.

No food. No water. No contact.

Now, I'd never been mixed up in the United States criminal justice system before, but I was fairly certain that locking someone up with no food, water, or even a phone call was illegal. The issue was, I had a very legitimate fear that they were trying to kill me by starving me to death and passing it off as a suicide. If I went any longer without at least some hydration, I was going to start to go under.

And I had no idea if I'd come back up again.

To entertain myself, if it could be called that, I thought about the events that led me here and tried to figure out how I landed myself in this predicament. Was it trusting one too many people? Was it coming to America in the first place? Or did my misfortune date all the way back to when I first met

Vladimir Petrov and told him I'd do whatever he asked. I'd always just been a man trying to survive, yet no matter how hard I tried, I always seemed to end up falling further down than I thought possible. I just wanted happiness. I just wanted love and peace. Success and not tarnishing the name of the family that gave me new life. I didn't think those things were too much to ask for, but maybe I was wrong.

"Petrov." The voice slightly preceded a series of loud bangs against my thick, cell door. "Get up. You're being moved."

Before I could even get my bearings, the door opened, sending a wash of bright, painful light spilling into my room. I squinted into it, putting up an arm to shield my face, but not managing to escape the splitting pain against my head. It temporarily blinded me, it'd been so long since I'd been exposed to light. The man who had just opened my door was nothing more than a blurry silhouette.

"What's going on?" I grunted.

"Hold out your hands," he responded.

I did as I was told, still half unsure of what was actually going on, and a pair of icy cuffs were slapped on my wrists. After that, the guard took me by the bicep and dragged me out of the isolation room and into the hallway. It was eerily silent, probably a result of the soundproof cells and everyone inside of them losing their goddamn minds. A couple of guards were patrolling the hallway, one of them on his phone like this job didn't matter to him at all.

It was hard not to kick it out of his hand as we passed him, but I honestly didn't think I had the strength. If I lifted up one foot right now, I'd probably fall right over.

"Where are you taking me?" I asked weakly.

"Good news. You're being moved to gen pop," he replied. "Some god took grace on you, I guess. If it was up to me, you'd rot in that goddamn cell."

"Gen pop?" I muttered.

He snorted. "Did your brain turn to mush in just eight days? Gen pop. General population. You're gonna be slumming it with the commoners, big wig. Lucky you."

Though he made it sound like a bad thing, nothing could be worse than being locked up and starved in that isolation cell all by myself. I imagined the prisoners in general population at least got to eat, and I was hopeful there would be a phone I could use as well. I knew as soon as I could get a hold of Brusch and a lawyer, they could have me out relatively quickly--that was probably why I was put in isolation to begin with.

After being led through a twist and turn of hallways, I was eventually taken to a block where prisoners were roaming freely about an open courtyard surrounded by cells. I was still uncertain of what time of day it was, but the light seemed to be getting low outside, so it was getting close to night time. As expected, I got a fury of strange and nasty looks as I was walked in, flanked in the front and back by prison guards, as they led me to a cell on the upper floor. The top bunk had a man laying on top, reading a book, and he didn't even spare a glance as the guard in front of me hit his billy club against the open bar doors.

"Got you a new bunkie, Schmidt," he announced gruffly.

The man didn't respond. In fact, he slowly and somehow loudly turned the page of his book, as if announcing he was ignoring us.

"Schmidty here shouldn't cause you any problems," the front guard said to me. "I expect you not to cause him any either."

Sharing my new roommate's apparent vow of silence, I only looked at the guard before he huffed, took the handcuffs off of me, and said, "Lights out at 8 o'clock sharp. Dinner's in about an hour. If you're late getting to your cell, if you cause any problems, if a guard gives you a warning and you don't listen, if you so much as--"

"Piss, shit, or puke without permission, you're heading right back to solitary." The man on the top bunk, Schmidt, lifted his head from his book. He was bald on one side of his head, and right down his scalp, gray hair started to waterfall down the other side. His face was marred with what looked like burn marks, and he had tattoos that started right at the top of his neck and continued down under his shirt, I assumed, all the way down his torso. "You really gotta get some new material, Delta."

"Fuck off," the guard Schmidt called 'Delta' barked back. "Do I look like I need advice from some degenerate like you?"

Delta and the female guard who had followed behind me let out gravelly laughs and walked away, and I just lingered in the opening to the cell, honestly looking forward to dinner, however disgusting it may be.

"They didn't feed you?" Schmit was looking down at me and I was almost confused, because he was speaking in perfect Russian. He wasn't an American who knew the language, it was his native tongue. "You don't speak the language?" he asked in Russian after I didn't respond for a moment.

"I do," I replied in our home language. "I was confused, I suppose. I haven't crossed paths with anyone who speaks it here."

"Well, none of the guards, and not many of the prisoners, but there's a small group of us. They tend to shove us together, so I just took a wild guess." He folded his book shut, set it next to him on the bunk and then threw his legs over and hopped down. "What are you in for?"

"I'm not sure," I said. "I'm told I made terrorist threats against U.S. civilians. I've yet to see any evidence of it."

"Let me guess: Detective Cox?" he asked.

I furrowed my brow a little. "He got you too?"

"Not me. I stabbed a guy right between the eyes three times and was caught on a security camera. They had me dead to rights. I'm eight years into a thirty-five bid," he explained, "but I know a few guys. You must be bratva then. What's your name?

Part of me was unsure if I should share my real name or not, but I imagined it would come out at some point, so there wasn't much reason to hide it. "Maksim Petrov."

"Petrov?" Schmidt responded. He looked me up and down as if he was trying to decide if he should believe me or not, then she smiled and said. "I'm Colburn Schmidt. You can call me Schmidt. Don't call me Schmidty. I'll kill you if you call me Schmidty."

I held up my hands. "You need not worry." I looked behind me at the people roaming back and forth and asked, "Is there a phone here I can use?"

Schmidt pushed me out of the cell and over to the railing separating the upper floor walkway from the courtyard between the cells. He pointed down, and slightly to the right of the doors I'd been led in through, where there was a small alcove that a couple of people were walking in and out of. "Phones and toilets that way, but be mindful, there's no cameras around that corner, and you're fresh meat."

"I'm perfectly capable of taking care of myself," I responded.

Schmidt chuckled and then switched back to English to say, "Well then handle your business, Mr. Petrov. I'll see you at dinner."

With that, he walked back into our cell, hoisted himself up onto the top bunk, lifted his book, and resumed reading as if he hadn't climbed down at all. He was an interesting character to be sure, but far from the top of my priority list. I needed to call Brusch and get a lawyer out to me as soon as possible, and then I needed to eat before I wasted away.

Walking down to the alcove, there was someone on one of the phones, but the other was free, so I helped myself. No one seemed to be in line or waiting, so I picked up the receiver to call, but no sooner than I did, did a handful of men close in on me quickly, forming a small semi-circle around me. The person using the other phone rapidly hung up and scuttled away, leaving me and this group of men alone.

"Sorry, did I jump?" I asked in English.

"Are you Maksim Petrov?" one of them asked. He had a huge scar down the side of his face and his teeth looked as if he'd never brushed them a day in his life.

"I might be," I returned. "Why? Do I have a fan club already?"

Rather than responding, the man shoved his hand into my gut, crumpling me over his arm. Without thinking, I rammed my head upwards, jabbing it into his chin, then when I was upright, I threw my head against his again in a painful headbutt. Though he fell to the ground bleeding, his cohorts jumped to his aid, and there was no getting around the fact that I was outnumbered. Even though Schmidt had just warned me to be careful, I let my arrogance cause me to lower my guard and I paid dearly for it.

Within seconds, I was on the ground with them punching and kicking the ever loving shit out of me. I could feel the sting of pain against my head, ribs, stomach, and legs. I wasn't helpless, and I got my jabs in, but there wasn't much I could do when there were five of them on one of me.

Suddenly, they started getting ripped out of my line of view one-by-one. I groaned, certain that I was already being saved by the guards, which was not the reputation I was hoping for coming in the door, but when I finally had a chance to look up through a blood-stained gaze, there was a man standing there in a tan prisoner's uniform. He had graying black hair greased back and smoothing down his head into a slight curl at his neck, and a stubble goatee. His eyes, shocking at first, were gray on the left and brown on the right, and he was more rotund, though he still seemed to be relatively fit based on what I could see from his arms and stature.

"Maksim?" He stuck out his hand for me, and in my stupor, I took it and let him pull me to my feet. "Petrov, right?"

I wiped some of the blood off of me and grunted, "Last time I answered that question, I got my ass kicked."

The man let out a barking laugh. "Yeah. We all saw." It was only as he motioned to the men behind him that I saw he was flanked on either side by four men--one of whom was Schmidt. "I'm Borya," he introduced himself.

"Borya?" I replied, then in Russian asked. "Are you bratva as well?"

"Used to be," he responded in the same language.

"To what do I owe this heroic rescue?" I asked.

Borya crossed his arms and a cocky grin crossed his face. "Consider it a gift from Vladimir."

CHAPTER TWO: CHLOE

Mitzy and I had been standing outside of Captain Cox's office for close to an hour waiting for him to show up for the meeting we scheduled with him. He promised to *finally* fill us in on Maksim's arrest after days of not telling us what the hell was going on. It'd been a pain in the ass trying to get information out of anyone. Even Gauge, Lucas, and Sydney were being tight-lipped about it. Mitzy believed that there was a specific reason the raid happened when neither he nor I were working, but everyone claimed it was purely coincidence.

And the fact that we weren't told the raid was even happening.

And the fact that we didn't even know Cox was still looking at Maksim for the time being.

And the fact that Cox had gotten a warrant for Maks' arrest.

All purely coincidence... and I was the goddamn pope.

"You didn't tell Cox anything about what Maksim said to you, right?" he said. "It says on his public record that he was arrested for terrorist threats against U.S. citizens."

"What?"

Mitzy was scrolling through his phone with a frustrated frown on his face. "Yeah. That's pretty much it, though. His facility and sentence are listed as unspecified."

I crossed my arms and glanced sideways at him. "You know that all of this is shady, right?" I said to him quietly. "I mean, I know that Maks is who he is, but he hadn't done anything warranting being raided and arrested--at least not that Cox knew. Whatever arrest he pulled, he pulled it out of the darkest part of his ass."

"Well, it's not like Cox isn't known for that," Mitzy replied, tucking his phone away. "Are you certain you weren't bugged or anything? I mean, I hate to get personal, but did he take off *all* your clothes last time you saw each other?"

"Last time?" I remembered the fight Maksim and I got into when I realized that he was still into Katya and still planning to take her back to Russia with him and be with her. "No. Last time we didn't get far at all, but I took a shower that night. I took everything off. There was no bug. Even if there was, I didn't agree to that."

"Well, you're a cop, he's a criminal. I think you'll find that the ol' court system will be more than willing to look the other way," Mitzy explained. He looked around and I followed his lead, seeing that the rest of our cohorts were keeping a close eye on us, but looked away from us whenever we started to look around. "There definitely is *some* conspiracy going on around here. What that is, though, I'm not sure."

I saw the way that Sydney, Gauge and Lucas were looking at me, almost like they'd been betrayed. My coworkers and I weren't *best* friends by any means, but we were close enough, I thought. What reason they had to suddenly take Cox's side and keep information from me when the main thing we'd bonded over was how much we all hated the guy, I wasn't sure.

But then it hit me.

"They know," I said.

Mitzy turned around and looked back at me. "What?"

Figuring that Detective Cox wasn't coming, I waved Mitzy to follow me and led him out of the precinct and into the break room that everyone working on that floor shared. There was no one in it, so I pulled Mitzy into a corner and leaned in.

"They know about me and Maks," I said. "They're looking at me like I'm a monster. Somehow, Cox must have figured out that I was sleeping with Maks and told them and that's why they're siding with him instead of filling me in. I don't remember him bugging me, but I suppose that doesn't mean he didn't. What I don't understand is, Maks and I have been involved for a couple of months now. He shared concerning information with me all along the way. Why would he wait until *right* now?"

"You two fought, right?" Mitzy said.

I nodded. "Yeah."

"That's why. He was waiting for the two of you to hit a rough patch."

I closed my eyes and groaned. "So that it seemed like it was me who did it."

"He wanted to take you out of Maksim's back pocket. He wanted him not to trust you anymore."

It made the pit of my stomach churn. Yes, Maksim and I had hit what seemed like our end, but I specifically wanted him to leave the United States *before* he got mixed up with Cox and our criminal justice system. This wasn't what I wanted for him. "What do I do? I need to find out what's going on with him, and if Cox's methods for detaining him were as shifty and shady as I'm guessing it was, then I need to get him *out* of prison." Suddenly, that churning in my stomach got a little heavier. I put my hand up to my mouth and tried to swallow it down, but it was clear that wasn't going to work out the way I wanted it to. "Oh god, not now."

"Now?" Mitzy said.

I nodded, and he leapt away from me, grabbing the nearest trash can. Thankfully, it had been changed recently and was a fresh bag, but not for long. I upheaved into it, hating the taste of sour swill spewing from me. Mitzy groaned and turned his head away, gagging himself, but I appreciated that he stayed supportive and kept the can under my head.

"If we weren't best friends before," he joked, albeit queasily, "we are now." Leaning back from the garbage can, I sank down into the nearest chair and wiped my mouth. Mitzy set the can off to the side and then got a bottle of water from one of the vending machines, which he then brought over to me. "You probably should go home for right now, Chloe." Mitzy spoke almost exclusively in a light, humorous tone, but this time, he was nothing but business. "You should get some rest. Let me try and figure out where Maksim is holed up. If our theory is right, having you next to me at all times is probably doing our info hunting mission more harm than good."

As much as I didn't want to agree with him, I did. Everyone seemed determined to keep me out of the loop, which meant Mitzy probably would do better hunting for Maksim's location on his own. I'd also been so caught up trying to learn *anything* about the raid for the last several days, that I hadn't really been sleeping or eating well.

Which given the situation... I imagined wasn't good.

"It's positive?" I said.

Dr. Courtney showed me the test, allowing me to see for myself. Sure enough, the test had two bright pink, vertical stripes on it. "If you'd like to take another one to be certain, we can certainly do that, but based on what you described, and this positive test, I don't have an inkling of doubt that you are pregnant, Miss Nikitina."

"Holy shit." *Mitzy huffed, looking down over my shoulder at the test.* "Well you've found yourself in quite the pickle, haven't you?"

Reading my shocked expression and Mitzy's statement, Dr. Courtney said, "I'm gathering this isn't the news you were hoping for."

I responded with a ghostly shake of my head. "No. This is not good news."

"Well, you have options. All of which I'd be happy to discuss with you. I do think that those conversations are best had when I'm in my own space with all of my own equipment and have literature to provide you and the whole nine. Trust me, this isn't a conversation you want to have in an emergency room."

For some reason, there was only one question on my mind, and no matter how hard I tried to resist the urge to ask it, it finally came out of my mouth without my say so. "Is the baby okay?"

She tilted her head at me and a small smile came across her face. "Well, I can't confirm without doing an ultrasound, but if you're asking regarding the early pregnancy condition that caused you distress earlier, I can say most likely. That's a result of your growing baby taking more from your body than you have to give it. That's why we already impress upon new moms the importance of eating for two. Your baby will make sure it gets what it needs, even if it has to kill you to do it."

Mitzy snickered. "Sounds like its dad." *I turned a slow glare in his direction and he pointed towards the door.* "I'll meet you outside."

Once Mitzy was gone, Dr. Courtney said. "You seem to be concerned about your baby. I imagine you will need time to decide whether or not you want to keep it or if you'd like to look into other options, but I will say if your concern is over the child's father, there are options for that too. You shouldn't feel unsafe, and neither should your baby."

"Chlo?" I took a deep breath as Mitzy's voice pulled me from my trance of memory. "You're home."

"Oh..." I looked over at my apartment complex. "Thank you."

"You sure you're gonna be okay?" he said. "The wife said you can stay at our place if you need to."

Though I appreciated the kindness, the thought of being with anyone other than myself for the time being started to make me sick again. "Thanks, but what I really want to do right now is just climb in my own bed and go to sleep."

He nodded. "I get it. Just... take care of yourself, okay? Call me if you need anything."

"I will."

Climbing out of Mitzy's car, I waved goodbye to him and then took my things and went up to my apartment. Remembering the fact that I hadn't eaten, I *did* do the responsible thing and made myself a significant amount of my mom's fried rice. What I couldn't stuff myself with I shoved into a tupperware container and stuck it in the fridge for later, promising both myself and my baby that I would eat more later.

After that, I went and laid in bed, desperate to get sleep but without the ability to do so. Every time I tried to close my eyes, I thought about Maksim being locked in a cell, thinking that I set him up to get arrested, not knowing that I was pregnant with his baby. Any attempt to force my mind away from *that* topic, only pushed it towards the fact that I was eventually going to have to tell my father and sister that I was pregnant, and I honestly didn't know if telling them it was by Maksim or lying and saying I had no idea who the father was, was worse.

Because it wasn't like my baby's father was actually going to be in its life... right?

Once Maksim found out that he was going to be a dad, was he going to want to be involved? It wasn't like he could stay in the US, but I also couldn't just pack up my life and move back to Russia.

Could I?

That night, my dreams were plagued with fantasies of moving back to my home country and living like a normal, happy family with Maksim. We had a sweet little boy that looked just like him, but had my freckles and his mom's eyes.

Something else interesting happened in the dream that I wasn't anticipating. After waking up next to Maksim and making breakfast for him and our son, Maksim kissed me goodbye and went off to work, and I went up to a studio. There was an easel set up against one wall and several canvases scattered around the room, both blank and painted.

"You gonna paint today too, mama?" my son said to me.

"Yep," I replied. "What should I paint today?"

He stuck his hands straight in the air. "The mountains!"

I watched, like in an out of body experience, as the dream version of myself looked out the window at the mountains in the distance in St. Petersburg and started to paint the beautiful vista. I couldn't remember the last time I painted, but I remembered loving it when I was much younger. Mitzy had once asked me what I would be doing if I wasn't a cop and I woke up the next morning with the answer burning across my brain.

"Painting," I said out loud. "I'd be painting.

Stretching my arms above my head and yawning in the morning, I checked my phone to see if there had been any updates, and my heart dropped like lead into my stomach when I saw that I had a text and a few missed calls from Mitzy. Quickly I dialed his number and called him back, hoping for the best.

"Hey!" he said, answering the phone after one ring. "I want to be mad at you that you weren't responding, but I'll forgive you if it's because you were resting."

"I was, and I ate too."

"Whooo," Mitzy sang. "For being a responsible expectant mother, I have some good news. I know where Maksim is."

"You do?" I yelped.

"Yep," he replied, "and I already got you on tomorrow's visitor's list."

My heart started to beat a little faster. Thinking about seeing Maskim with what must have been going on in his head made me a little queasy. I knew I was going to have to see him, but I didn't think it would happen so quickly. I still had absolutely no idea what I was going to say to him, neither to explain to him what happened with his raid, nor about the predicament we were in with our unborn child. There was so much that had to be said, and it had to be said in the exact right way, which was bizarre considering the fact that when I left him last, I told him I never wanted anything to do with him again.

In such little time, everything changed.

"Chloe, you still there?"

"Yeah," I said. "I'm here. Sorry, I just got really scared thinking about what I have to say to Maks when I see him."

"What do you mean?" Mitzy said. "Isn't it obvious? There's only one thing that you two need to talk about tomorrow. You've gotta tell him that you're pregnant."

CHAPTER THREE: MAKSIM

The food that they served at the prison certainly wasn't five-star cuisine, but after the days I'd spent with no food at all, it was certainly better than nothing. The man who'd saved me, a lifer named Borya, along with Schmidt, and a handful of other men, made sure I was able to get to a table to eat without any issues, and then they all kindly shared their portions of food with me, along with some of the prison's luxury food items, like candy bars and chips. All hope that I wouldn't totally embarrass myself went straight out the window when I got my first taste of sustenance. I knew I was starving, but I didn't realize how much, until something other than stale, isolation cell air hit my throat.

"Slow down," Borya told me, guffawing at the way I was scarfing. "You'll make yourself sick if you eat too much too fast."

"Happened to me when I first came outta Iso," Schmidt said. "Eleven days they'd had me in there, I think? Gave me a couple of glasses of water, but that was it. Just enough that they didn't have to shovel my corpse out of the room."

"That was more than I got," I managed between bites.

"We keep a pretty good eye on the schedule around here, and I think they had you locked up for about five days. At least that's when I started hearing rumors of a Petrov in the house. I can't imagine it would have taken longer than a day for that shit to get to me," Borya explained.

I looked up at the man with a frown on my face, not even bothering to swallow my bite before asking, "Isn't that illegal? To keep a prisoner and not feed them?"

The entire table erupted into laughter at my question. I realized that I wasn't American, and as such didn't know all that much about the American prison system, but I imagined that kind of thing wasn't okay. These guys' reactions seemed to say otherwise.

"Listen," Borya said. "There are two sets of laws in America, the ones they tell you that you have to follow, and the real ones. Those real ones are dictated by what's most beneficial to a decision-maker at any given time. Every rule can be bent if the one doing the bending has something to gain." He took a large gulp of water before continuing. "For people like you and me, we can exist on both sides of these rules. In some cases, we can be the ones giving the rule-benders a benefit. I'm sure you've experienced it. Paying off a cop. Threatening a judge. Supplying a politician. None of that is *legal* if you're following the written rules, but we're all playing by a different code at that point."

"Then we end up here," Schmidt said.

Borya wiggled a finger at him. "Exactly. When that paid-off cop, threatened judge, or corrupt politician no longer see the use in bending rules for us, then it becomes more beneficial for them to put us behind bars. Clean up the streets--especially around election year, which this just so happens to be."

"So everything is dealer's choice here?" I concluded.

Borya stroked his beard. "Pretty much. And if you landed in hot water with Cox, you've pissed off the worst dealer of them all. On top of having made enemies with the Bonettis, you've been dealt a pretty shitty hand I would say."

"The Bonettis?" I repeated. "The men who jumped me?"

"Their brood behind bars," Borya said. "The Petrovs are doing a very good job making friends with New York's elite right now. First Vladimir and the Constellos and now you with the Bonettis and Cox. Throw the Takahashi yakuza and those Red Head Bikers and you've got yourself a royal flush."

"Red *Eye* Bikers, boss," one of the other men who I'd learned was named 'Coleman' corrected.

"Oh, right, right. Red Eye. Whatever."

"You mentioned Vladimir earlier," I said. "That you saving me was a gift from him. I don't understand."

Borya leaned across the table a little bit. "You aren't the only bratva behind these bars, boy. I been in the states since I was a tyke, but both of my folks were born and bred bratva. When they came here, they got a little operation going in Little Odessa that grew and grew. Nothing like those rag-tag wannabes running around stealing and killing indiscriminately. My parents moved billions in and out of New York. Drugs, guns, girls, hell, my mom even got into exotic animals near the end. When they passed on, a man named Alexei Lachinov took over, and when I was old enough, he did right by my parents and made me his sovietnik. I took a pretty big fall for him and landed myself here, but he makes sure my wife and kids on the outside want for nothing."

Now *that* name was one I'd heard before. In Vladimir's many conversations with his contacts in New York, Alexei's name regularly came up. When I first established Dacha, it was Alexei who aided us on this side of the ocean, but I never spoke or dealt with him personally. Vladimir didn't trust many people, in fact, I'd say he probably didn't fully trust anyone, but his working relationship with Alexei was something he held in particularly high regard.

"Alexei is still operating?" I asked.

Borya huffed. "Of course. He runs the streets of Little Odessa now. You're lucky for that, too. He'd heard tell from a convenience store clerk that Vladimir's successor was in New York City and looked you up to keep an eye on you just in case. He heard that you ran into some bad luck with Detective Cox and let me know you'd probably be headed my way soon."

"So this isn't an unusual circumstance?"

"Cox using less than reputable tactics to arrest? It's like asking if bees pollinate flowers to get honey. To say the guy is bad news would be an understatement, but he's also mostly left the Petrovs alone in the past because of the complications of dealing with someone from overseas. What the hell did you do to piss him off so bad?"

Flashes of memories cut across my brain in response to that question. Working with Dino who turned out to be Detective Cox's resident snitch. Letting myself get caught in bed with Chloe, his right-hand girl. Storming into his squad room and letting my arrogance get the best of me, rubbing the fact that he couldn't touch me in his face. In truth, everything I'd done since I first stepped foot in the United States was something that would put me on Cox's bad side. It was probably a miracle that this didn't hit me sooner.

"Let's just say that I may have inadvertently gotten snared in a trap that I don't even think Cox realized he set," I replied.

Borya lifted an eyebrow. "Did it have money, drugs, or breasts?"

I shrugged. "A little of this, a little of that."

"Whoo," Borya howled. "You're cutthroat for such a young'n. I like that. I'm glad Alexei chose to get involved. I think that there's a working relationship here just waiting to blossom."

I furrowed my brow. "What do you mean?"

Suddenly, one of the other guys at the table with us, Zachari, sneezed. The entire table went silent and Borya lifted his glass to his lips and took a big sip. "Who is it?"

"Delta," Zachari responded quietly as he stuffed a bite of what food he hadn't given me in his mouth. "Beelinin'."

The guard who'd brought me to my cell earlier, Delta, had strolled his way over with an arrogant smirk on his face. He looked down at me and then over at Borya. "Well, looks like you all made fast friends."

Borya didn't even look up at him to respond, "How am I ever going to win the popularity contest if I don't keep increasing my word count."

Delta frowned at the snarky response. "Well, I just hope you all ain't causing any trouble."

Motioning to the food on my plate, Borya said, "We are just enjoying this hamburger-like substance with a side of carrot-like substance, and finished off with whatever this hunk of brown, crumbly stuff is. The only trouble we're having is with our teeth."

"Oh? Are you unsatisfied with your provisions? Perhaps you should just take a trip down to McDonalds and get yourself something good to eat." He let out a barking laugh before doing a total 180 into a serious, if not a bit threatening, face. "I've told you a million times not to do that bratva Russian shit in here."

Once again, Borya didn't address Delta directly, but said. "I'm not even sure what those words mean." Then he finally turned and looked up at Delta with fake-innocent eyes and said, "What is this 'McDonald's?'"

I had to bite the inside of my cheek to keep from laughing, but the others at the table weren't as reserved. They snickered quietly to themselves and I could see Delta's blood starting to boil just beneath his skin. "You may think you're smarter than me, Borya, but I'll have you in sol-con so quick, you'll get whiplash from moving out of your cell."

"I could use some time alone with my thoughts," Borya responded. "Although, I highly doubt my friends down at the IPP would like to hear that I've been thrown into solitary confinement because you can't beat me in a battle of wits."

"Delta!"

The guard looked over and the female guard who had been with him earlier was eyeing him. "Quit messin' with the Russians. We got work to do."

"Quittin' time," Borya said quietly.

Delta gave Borya a long, hard glare before reaching down and grabbing my tray of food. He flipped it, sending what was left of my dinner scattering across the table, and then stood there daring someone to do something. Part of me wanted to, as I was still pretty hungry from being starved, but Borya and his guys all seemed to be reserving their anger, and I didn't want to waste their kindness by not doing the same, so I swallowed my temper and sat quietly.

When it was clear he wasn't going to get the rise out of us that he was looking for Delta turned his back to us and walked off.

"Prick," Schmidt hissed in his wake.

"He's fun," I said.

"A riot," Borya replied. "Colors himself a patriot, even down to the people who are allowed to commit crimes here. Mafiosos are apparently as American as baseball and apple pie, but bratva might as well be terrorists."

A light bulb went off in my head. "Terrorists? That's what Cox hemmed me up for."

"Not surprised in the slightest. That probably means that he and Delta are working in tandem, which is *not* good for you." He stood up from the table and motioned to the mess. "You guys clean this up so that the guards don't have any reason to come around and bother us." Then he looked down at me. "You follow me. I've got some more food, and we'll chat somewhere that Delta's dick can't reach us."

I actually did feel a little bad leaving Borya's men to clean up the mess, but none of them seemed to be too bothered by it and quietly started picking things up, so I stood up from the table and followed after Borya, who was already stalking away. A couple of guards were standing outside the dining hall doors, and Borya nodded very subtly at the one on the left.

"Patty," he said quietly.

"Hey Borya," she replied. "Sorry about Delta, but there's not much we can do about him."

"It's not a problem. Seeing him turn bright as a tomato makes my day."

He kept walking past her and I followed, but when we were about ten feet beyond them, I heard Patty in the distance saying, "Keep an eye out, will ya? I'll be right back."

As Borya and I walked down the hallway, I heard Patty's footsteps keeping close to ours. She appeared to be following us, though I was uncertain why. Borya either didn't notice or didn't care, so I just kept walking behind him, hoping that we weren't about to find ourselves on the end of trouble with a second guard in ten minutes.

At the end of the hallway, right where we'd turned to go back into our cell block, Borya stopped. He didn't go in, so I froze and stood back a little, not saying anything, and just waiting. Eventually, Patty caught up to us and walked into the control room, where she leaned down and muttered something unintelligible to the guy behind the control center, and then she stood back up again. There was a loud buzzing from the door directly next to Borya and I, past the cellblock room. Patty then walked back out of the control room and over to the door, which she then pulled open and motioned for us to go through.

"You're a peach, Patricia," Borya said.

"Just be quick," she responded. "I'll be back in five minutes."

"Give us ten," Borya quipped back.

Patty looked at him for a long moment before finally sighing, and nodded. "Fine, but ten's all you're getting."

"Thanks."

Borya stepped through the door and I followed after him. We entered a small, square containment room with only the door we'd come through and another opposite it that was shut and the door behind us shut. A few seconds later, there was another loud buzzing and Borya reached out to pull open the door in front of us.

This door opened to what appeared to be a small, but oddly beautiful chapel. Unlike the gray and white steel walls that the rest of the prison boasted, there was cherrywood paneling in here, and at the front of the room was a pulpit sitting in front of an arched, stained glass window. A colorful mosaic depicted the image of Jesus on the cross, and what was left of the room was about six pews that could hold four people each--five if you crammed in.

"You a religious person, Maks?" Borya asked.

I shook my head. "Not in the slightest. If there was a god, he left me to hell a long time ago."

Borya nodded and picked a pew and slid in, and then tapped the pew in front of him. I followed the instruction and sat in the pew in front of him, and then he interlocked his fingers and folded his hands together, leaning forward then to set his head on his hands.

"You don't have to pray, but close your eyes at least," he said quietly. "If someone comes in, we wanna at least look like we're supposed to be here."

"Did you come in here to pray?" I asked.

He snickered behind me. "Of course not. If any god wanted to help me, they're about twenty years too late. No, because of religious rights and all that, they aren't allowed to have cameras in here. There are supposed to be guards whenever there are inmates in here, but Patty and I have an understanding. Remember when I said everyone follows the rules that benefit them most?"

"Yeah, but... What's Patty's benefit?"

Borya snorted. "Being able to sleep at night."

That rendered me totally speechless. It made me think of people like Chloe, who honestly believed they could make a difference in this fucked up system. Patty was just another Chloe who became a guard to make a differ-ence but quickly found she worked amongst people like Detective Cox and Delta. I suppose this was how she made amends for standing idly by.

Rather than think on that too much because I'd start to feel sympathy towards Chloe, who was the reason I was in here to begin with. I closed my eyes and lowered my head. The eerie silence was calming and stressful at the same time.

"What I started to say when we were interrupted before was that I think there's a partnership to be had here. I may be in here for the rest of my life, but I'll always serve Alexei because he carried on my parents' legacy and brought me into the fold when it was time. You, though, we can get you out and then you can work with Alexei on the outside. Give him some of that Petrov clout and help keep his men out of Cox's crosshairs."

"I want to help you," I replied, "but I couldn't even keep *myself* out of Detective Cox's crosshairs. I don't know that I'm the guy to keep Alexei's men out."

"You're a smart guy," Borya said. "You've got Vladimir's intelligence, but not his insufferable arrogance. If you just assure me that you'll work with Alexei and do what you can, then that works for me."

Thinking back, I did still have a problem at Dacha with the absence of the Bonettis, and now that I knew they were actively trying to kill me, they would have to be dealt with as well. Perhaps there *was* an opportunity to fill the void at Dacha with Alexei's crew and get myself some backup to deal with the Bonettis and Vincent on top of it all. How I would keep Detective Cox off of our backs would be its own challenge, but it wasn't one I didn't think I could solve.

"You're already running the numbers," Borya said. "I knew it was right to trust you."

"Yes," I said. "I do think I have some options. I can assure you, if you can help me get out of here, then I'll meet up with Alexei and work something out."

"Then getting you out of here isn't going to be an issue. Do you have someone on the outs who can help?" he asked.

"Yes, my sovietnik, Brusch. He was the one I was attempting to call when the Bonettis showed up."

"Good," Borya said. "I can get you a phone call and a few people for your guy to reach out to. I mentioned the IPP earlier--it's the Inmate Protection Program. A group of real do-gooders who hate to see inmates being treated unlawfully. They haven't exacted any real change per se, but they know how to make a lot of noise and have gotten at least a few people fired. The boys in blue will do just about anything to stay out of their mouths, because they know a tarnished reputation can do a lot of damage. If it's fairly easy for them to prove that your arrest was sketchy, they'll have you outta here in no time, just to make sure they don't get dinged."

I nodded. "Okay. If you get me the information and a call that doesn't result in me having the shit kicked out of me before I even dial the number, I'll get the information to my sovietnik."

Behind us, the door to the chapel buzzed and then clanged as it was slid open. I opened one eye enough to see that Borya was keeping his head down, so I did the same, until someone cleared their throat.

"Borya." I recognized the voice as belonging to Patty. "Sorry, it hasn't quite been ten minutes, but Delta's snooping. We should get you back."

Delta lifted his head and let out a huge sigh. "It's fine. We're done here anyway."

He stood up and I followed, standing up behind him and following him over to the door. Just as we were about to pass through the door, Patty looked me up and down and said, "Are you Maksim Petrov?"

"Yes," I replied.

She nodded. "Yeah, we just got word from the front. The visitation list for tomorrow has been released, and you're on it. Looks like you're getting a visitor."

CHAPTER FOUR: CHLOE

As if my life didn't have much *larger* things to be worried about, I'd spent my entire morning trying to decide if Maksim and I were in a real relationship, and thus, was my storm out and declaration that we were done considered a breakup? I'd gotten out of the shower a whole thirty minutes ago, and had just been standing in my closet wrapped in a towel, staring at all of my clothes, trying to decide what I should wear by whether or not I was visiting Maksim as a police officer or as his ex.

Each time I caught a glimpse of my sleep-deprived blue eyes and weary expression, I gave myself my own disappointed dad nod. If I kept on like this, I was going to stress me and my poor unborn child to death before we even got to its father this afternoon.

I was glad that Mitzy managed to suss out where Maksim was being held, and even more that he was able to secure a visit because it meant Maksim was okay, but I wasn't quite ready for what the conversation was going to entail. I'd stayed up all night thinking about it, trying to decide if I should just go in guns blazing and say I was pregnant, or smooth into it with some small talk.

I still didn't know when the sun began to peek through my windows, and it was only then that I realized I'd given up the only chance I had to get some reasonable sleep just to get absolutely nowhere--classic "me" move.

Finally, I got so irritated with myself for all this back and forth that I closed my eyes and just reached out my hand. It took some flailing, but I eventually caught hold of a piece of fabric, and when I opened my eyes, it was one of my favorite, rose pink blazers. It'd garnered me some good luck in the past, as I'd received my acceptance letter to the police academy while wearing it, and wore it to the party Chandler threw for me after I was officially sworn in. I had even worn it on a few dates and had success, so if it had brought me luck in both my professional and personal lives, then by my best guess, this was the perfect situation to wear it in.

I looked into the mirror one more time and shook my head at that last thought, then put it all out of my mind.

Knowing that I'd be searched before entering the prison, I didn't want to layer myself too much, or wear anything with too many pockets, so I partnered the blazer with a heather gray tank-top underneath and a pair of black slacks. I started to slide on the pair of blush, platform pumps that I usually wore with the blazer, but realized where I was going and picked out some tan flats instead. I gave my hair a slight curl and applied a thin coat of makeup, then looked myself over in the wall to wall mirror in my bathroom.

"Yeah," I said out loud. "This isn't bad. I could hear both legal information and 'I'm pregnant' coming from this look." Then I groaned. "What has my life become?"

Ultimately, I decided that road wasn't one I wanted to travel down, so I instead went into my living room and carefully prepared myself a bagel and cream cheese along with a cold brew coffee. Visiting hours didn't start until noon and it was only about half past eight. The prison where Maskim was being held was in Beacon, New York, about an hour and a half from my apartment, so I figured if I left by about ten, I'd give myself time for the unexpected and still get there a little early. With my bagel and coffee in hand, I sat down in the living room and passed the time by bouncing my leg for about five minutes before ultimately deciding to just take my food on the road and leave immediately.

Showing up to a place two hours early wasn't desperate, it was responsible--at least that was what I told myself.

Just in case Cox was actually working directly with anyone at the prison, I didn't want to use my badge or mention my job at all when checking in for my visit. Instead, I presented my civilian ID and hoped that no one recognized me or my name. It was nearly two hours from my jurisdiction, but distance didn't really stop those in the criminal justice system from recognizing one another, especially not when one was *not* approving of the other's presence.

Fortunately, I thought I did a pretty good job of playing the confused citizen as I was searched and passed through the metal detector and when I supplied my ID at check-in, no one reacted as if they knew me.

"Here to see Maksim Petrov?" a guard asked me.

"Yes," I replied.

"Relationship to the inmate?"

I didn't know why I wasn't expecting that question. I'd been to prisons more times than I could count over the course of my career. On more than one occasion had I been asked to visit a known associate of a suspect to try and suss out more information, or talk deals with someone we'd recently locked up to try and take down a bigger foe. Maybe because I was a detective, the response was always second nature, but now I found myself embarrassingly tongue-tied.

"Ex-Girlfriend?" I said.

The guard looked up from his clipboard at me. "Are you asking me?"

"N-no," I said. "Sorry. It was recent, and then he got arrested, it was just weird to say, and I think--"

"Ex-Girlfriend," he cut me off. "Take a seat at one of the tables and your inmate will be brought out shortly."

I swallowed hard, nodded and managed to murmur out, "Thanks," before walking away to take a seat at one of the round tables that littered the space. Looking around, there were half a dozen other people there for visiting hours, and once again, I found myself keeping a low-profile, not making eye contact, and hardly moving. There were definitely people in this prison and many others who I'd played a part in putting behind bars. I was hoping none of them were granted visiting hours today, or I might find myself in a particularly bad situation.

After about twenty minutes, the guard who'd checked me in stood up from his desk and addressed the room. "Alright. Visiting hours are now open. You may stay for as much or as little of the following two hours as you'd like." He was delivering his speech in a monotone manner--probably had said it a million times before. "Please keep in mind there is no touching; no hugging, no kissing, no hand-holding, no handshakes or high-fives. There is no disrobing of either your or your inmate's clothes. You must remain seated from the moment your inmate arrives to the moment they leave. If you want to end your visit before the end of visiting hours, please motion to a guard to come and usher your inmate away. Violation of these rules or any other behavior that a guard may find unsuitable will result in the immediate termination of the visit, and may result in loss of visitation privileges for either you or your inmate. Additionally, violation of these rules or any other behavior that a guard may find unsuitable may result in consequences for your inmate, including loss of commissary privileges, loss of outdoors time, loss of freedom of movement, loss of life in general population, and/or additions to their sentences. If you have any questions, you may ask the nearest guard." He then sat back down at his desk and there was a loud buzzing that made me jump, which made me feel stupid because again. I'd done this hundreds of times before.

A door across the room from the one visitor's entrance slid open and a guard led in a line of prisoners, with another guard bringing up the rear. One by one, the front guard undid their handcuffs and asked them if they saw their visitor. They'd point their table out and then the other guard came over to escort the prisoner to their table. One of the inmates went to a table with a woman and a child, and the child desperately tried to claw out of her mother's arms to get to the man. He nearly came to tears as the mother held the child back, trying her best to explain why she couldn't hug daddy. It broke my heart to see.

But he deserved it, right? He broke the law. If you wanted to be able to hug your children freely, you should have behaved.

Still, I looked away from the heartbreaking scene, and turned my attention back to the line, where as the second-to-last prisoner was moved, I finally laid my eyes on Maksim. He must have seen me while I was distracted, because he was already staring straight at me, and he did *not* look happy.

"Do you see your visitor?" the front guard asked Maks.

Part of me expected him to say no and let himself be led back into the cells without me even getting to say a single thing, but I gave him my most pleading expression and he silently pointed at me. The rear guard escorted Maksim over to my table and he sat down across from me, looking worse for wear.

"My god," I said as soon as the guard walked away from us. "What happened to you?" He had small cuts and bruises all over his face, and I could even see a larger, darker one just barely peeking out over the top of his jumpsuit. "Did Cox do this?" Maksim just glared at me. It was obvious that he believed I had something to do with his arrest, and I wasn't entirely sure that anything I said was going to convince him otherwise. "Maks, I swear to god, I did not know this was going to happen. I wasn't even at work at the time. After I left you I went straight home. I didn't hear that you'd been arrested until later that evening."

"Is that right?" he asked in a flat tone.

"I promise you."

"What does it matter to you anyway?" he said. "You said you were done with me. So what happens to me shouldn't matter."

Before I really thought it through I snapped out, "I said I was done because you have feelings for someone else, not because I don't have feelings for you."

Maksim recoiled a bit at that and asked, "Do you?"

My cheeks were burning and I was certain I was blushing. "Do I what?"

"Have feelings for me?"

I looked around, astounded that *that* was what he wanted to discuss at a time like this. "I mean... I wouldn't have been with you all those times if I didn't. I mean we... We went out and stuff, we were dating. This departure has felt like a breakup to me."

He stared at me for a long moment, slowly lowering his gaze before he finally asked. "What's different about you?"

My heart immediately started to beat faster. "What do you mean?"

"There's something different about you," he replied. "Your affect is all off."

"No," I said. "This is just a bizarre situation for me, that's all." Surely, he couldn't tell that I was pregnant, right? He continued to watch me for a moment until I said, "Stop that. Stop leering at me."

"I'm just looking," he responded. "I'm trying to sort it out."

"There's nothing to sort out," I barked. "I don't want to talk about that. I want to talk about what happened to you and how you got here."

"You know how I got here."

"Not really," I replied. "Cox won't tell me anything. Mitzy had to find out where you were being held and get me on the visitor's list."

"Chloe," Maks said in a stern voice.

I widened my eyes. "What?"

"Don't lie to me anymore. Please. Just do me the common courtesy of telling me the truth."

"I'm telling you the truth!"

"You're not!" Maksim thundered.

"Hey!" the front guard yelled from near the inmates' entrance. "Keep it down over there Petrov, or I'm taking you back to your cell."

I took the initiative to wave at the guard. "Sorry! Intense conversation. We'll keep it down." I looked back at Maksim and at nearly a whisper's tone said, "I am not lying to you."

"It wasn't long after you left that Cox showed up with a warrant for my arrest. The time that elapsed would have made it impossible for him to just go and get it that quickly."

"Exactly! So how could it have been me! I didn't do it because I was pissed about you and Katya if that's what you're thinking. I barely knew *what* to do when I left," I argued.

"No," Maksim said. "He already knew that you were coming in to get valuable information and had a judge on standby, or maybe he had the warrant already and you were just keeping him at bay while you continued toying with me. Either way, you had to have something to do with it. Cox said he had a reliable source, and you're the only one I gave any sensitive information to that would have shared it with a police captain. I've spoken to some guys in here, and this isn't far from the course for Cox and your unit I hear."

I furrowed my brow. "What?"

"Don't act dumb with me, Chloe. I know better than anyone how intelligent you are. You're Cox's right-hand. I won't believe for a second that you didn't know what he was up to," Maksim sneered. "And now, here you sit, with this overly apologetic, overly sweet demeanor about you. Why, after the way we ended, would you be behaving like this if not for guilt?"

Little did he know, I *did* feel guilt, but not because I put him behind bars. "This is your problem," I told him. "You are so *unbelievably* arrogant. If I had anything to do with you being arrested, why would I come here and talk to you about it?"

"Because you know the harm I can cause your family," he spat.

I sat back in my seat bewildered. *This* man was the father of my child. This one, who would threaten my family so carelessly. "So much for never threatening them again."

"Your paranoia is not a threat," he responded. "If it's not that, then what is it? Give me one good reason why you'd be here now if you weren't here for that?"

Nervously, I nibbled on the inside of my cheek. Mitzy's voice echoed in my mind, telling me that I had to tell Maksim that I was pregnant, but this conversation was going so poorly that I didn't know if it was best to share right now. What's more, Maksim didn't believe much that was coming out of my mouth at the moment, who was to say that he would think I was lying about the baby as well? It wasn't like I could bring a pregnancy test in here and show him.

I went rogue on the plan and decided now wasn't the time or place to discuss my pregnancy.

"There's a lot we need to talk about, but I don't want to do it here, and you don't know it yet, but neither do you," I explained.

He snorted. "That sounds like a deflection."

"Think what you want. I know the truth. I'm going to get you out of here, and then once you've calmed down and I can actually speak to you on a plane of logic, we'll have an adult conversation."

Maksim gave me a smile, albeit a nasty one. "What page of the police detective handbook has the protocol about flipping the story on the prisoner? Page three? Or is it four?"

I was trying not to blow my stack, but it was difficult, with how intentionally evil Maksim was behaving. It wasn't as if I didn't know that this side of him existed, but that didn't make it any easier to deal with. This horrible side to him was a defensive mechanism--a hardened shell that he'd been forging ever since he was a little boy. When we were dating, if it could even be called that, he never once got this way with me. When Maksim let his guard down, he was far and away one of the best people I knew. Yes, I developed feelings for him while we were fraternizing, how could I not? I convinced myself I was doing it out of fear, but the reality was, I was desperate for the excuse to be around *that* Maksim, and not the steely, cold one that was sitting in front of me.

"I'm not responding to that behavior," I said. "I know there's a good man inside of you."

"Oh, that's right," he said. "Flipping is on page three, using psychology 101 is on page four." His vile smile lowered into a deep frown. "Here's one of my own. Every single time I've asked you a direct question, you've diverted and looked away from me. If you were interrogating someone you believed to be lying to you and they acted like that, what would you think?"

"Maks," I said. "I'm. Not. Lying."

He shot up from his seat, attracting the attention of everyone around, including all three guards whose hands flew to their guns. "Sit down, Petrov! Or I'm gonna have to take you outta here!" the front guard said.

"Take me," Maksim replied, holding his hands up. "I'm done here."

"Don't," I begged. "I want to know exactly what happened with your arrest!"

"Just check your report," he replied.

I opened my mouth to reply, but the guard got to us, and I didn't want to say anything that would give my position away, so I shut up. He attached the handcuffs to Maksim's wrists in front of his body and led him over to the inmates' door. There was a loud buzzing and the guard led Maksim out of the room, with the door shutting behind him.

"Miss," the check-in guard called out to me. "This way, please."

Begrudgingly, I stood up from the table and walked over to the desk to be checked out so I could leave. My blood was boiling with frustration, but it was more at the situation than at Maks. Setting a hand on my belly, I knew the only way forward was to get Maksim out of here, and I had to do it as soon as possible.

CHAPTER FIVE: MAKSIM

It only took a couple of days for me to get used to the routine of prison, but I had to say, it wasn't my favorite place to be in the world. Borya had pull, and thanks to that, it wasn't *as* miserable of an experience as it might have been otherwise, but I was very much looking forward to getting out as soon as possible.

I'd slept very little in the past forty-eight hours, which I blamed on Chloe's surprise visit. Maybe it was the fact that she was committed to lying to my face even though it was obvious the cat was out of the bag, or the fact that even after everything she'd done, I still found myself yearning for her when I saw her, but I couldn't get that conversation out of my head. I was still livid at the fact that she obviously sold me out, but I would have at least thought that she respected me enough to be honest. Yes, I'd threatened her family in the past, but I thought I made it very clear to her that I wouldn't do anything to hurt them. It didn't take me long to figure out that the person who told Alexei on the outside that a Petrov was in town had to be her dad.

In a roundabout way, it was thanks to him that Borya saved me from the Bonettis and took me under his sphere of influence while I was locked up.

There wasn't really an opportunity to say any of that to Chloe, however, as that conversation only really went from bad to worse. We'd both done things to hurt the other, so I was hoping that we might be able to be real about those things with one another and maybe even get past them, but if Chloe was going to continue to lie to my face, then there was no future for us. Keeping someone around who was self-preserving, I could do. Keeping someone around who I couldn't trust? Not in a million years would that work.

Unfortunately for me, though I might have liked to keep my relationship with Chloe totally under wraps in case anyone recognized her as a cop, one of Borya's other men was on the visitation list and saw me with her. He was quick to bring her up at dinner that night, though thankfully, he didn't seem to know who she was.

"Come on," Borya goaded. "I knew you had a skirt out there. What's her name?"

"Nikki," I lied, pulling the fake moniker from Chloe's last name.

"Uh huh..." Schmidt waved his hand in circles to try and get more out of me. "And, is she your baby mama, or just someone you hook up with? Or, ooh! Is she one of those ride-or-die chicks who will do *anything* for you?" He leaned his head back with a dreamy look. "I've always wanted one of those."

"For sure not that," I said, although there was a part of my brain that knew that wasn't true. Chloe had plenty of opportunities between when I showed up and when I got arrested to turn me in. I'd managed to convince myself that she wasn't doing it because she was afraid of me, but even when we first crossed paths again, she didn't speak in terms of arresting me, she spoke in terms of getting me out of the states. It legitimately seemed like she didn't want me to get arrested or worse. "We've had our problems, but I guess the fact that she came to visit me says something."

"You seemed pretty steamed though," the one who'd seen us, Olly, said. "You stood up and screamed and everything."

"Ah, do you think she's sleeping around?" Schmidt asked.

I didn't think that either. It was difficult to explain, but from the moment that Chloe and I started... fraternizing, I was never concerned that I may not be the only man in her life. It was really like we were dating for a while there, and when she said she felt our separation like a breakup... it felt that way to me too.

"No. I don't think that." I frowned. "I guess there's a possibility that she may have had something to do with my arrest. That's the issue."

Borya looked at me for a long moment. It felt much longer than it probably was, because he stared directly into my eyes and didn't let up even when I made eye contact or the overbearing nature of it had brought the entire table to silence.

Finally, I couldn't take it anymore and said, "What?"

"You don't actually believe that."

"Yes I do," I said quickly. "She's pretty much the only person it could be."

Borya just shook his head at me like he was some sort of wise, all-knowing sage. "No. You aren't considering something more obvious to give yourself an excuse to say it's her."

I just furrowed my brow at him. "She's the most obvious option."

But again, Borya just shook at me. "No, it's not." He stabbed a fork into his questionable meat and popped it into his mouth. "You need to think about it more. There's another answer. Part of you knows it, that subconscious brain, but the rest of you won't accept it."

"What kind of seeing-the-future bullshit is that?" Schmidt said. "You know his life or something?"

Borya shrugged. "Maybe not his, but my own. There was a time where I cast off some people close to me because I assumed that they were at fault for something and it turned out that it was someone that I would have never expected. Once everything shook out, it was painfully obvious who I should have actually been blaming the whole time, but it was easier to blame the ones closer to me because part of me feared letting anyone in close." He looked up at me over his tray of food. "This girl... She your first love or something?"

The entire table had gone quiet in the wake of Borya's story, maybe because no one expected it to take such a deep and meaningful turn. I thought of the question that he'd asked me and wasn't quite sure how to answer. Chloe was the first important girl in my life other than my mom. If I was thinking about it honestly, she was definitely my first crush, and when she came back into my life, I was immediately attracted to her. The time that we'd spent together over the course of the last couple of months had been, in a way, more meaningful to me than anything that had happened to me in the past. I'd convinced myself that I was in love with Katya, but when I compared the way I felt about Chloe compared to the way I felt about Katya, I didn't think that was true anymore. The question was, did that mean I *was* in love with Chloe?

Was she my first love?

"It's difficult to say," I finally settled for. "She... she means something to me."

"Do you think she would do something like that to you, in all honesty?" Schmidt asked. "She came to visit you. Would she get you locked up and then come by?"

"No," I said. "That's not really her personality. She's one of those what-you-see-is-what-you-get kinds of people." I looked at Borya with a frown. "But I've thought of everyone else who could be responsible and no one else could have known what Cox knew."

"Someone could have," Borya said, then he waved his hand at me. "Don't think about it for a couple of days. I'm sure the answer will come to ya."

In a really bizarre way, it sounds like Borya knew more than he was saying, but I really did think it was just his experience talking. The only people that I shared the information with that Cox eventually used to get me locked up were Chloe and my guys from Russia. There was really no reason for Brusch or any of the men I'd brought with me from St. Petersburg to suddenly start working with an American detective, especially and organized crime one at that, but if it wasn't Brusch and it wasn't Chloe, then I wasn't sure who else it could be.

I decided to take Borya's advice and put it out of my mind for now. I needed to worry about talking to Brusch and getting the hell out of this place. Chloe said she was going to get me out, and if she was actually working on it, then that would only make things easier for Brusch, but I had to proceed as if that was a lie, because I couldn't be certain what Chloe's true motive was at the moment. I could only rely on Brusch for now.

The issue with the phone call was, the Bonettis had quickly figured out that I needed to use the phone and had been camping it out trying to get another shot at me. Due to the fact that the Bonettis were sticking so closely to the phones, so too were any guards on shift, so we couldn't even just battle with the Bonettis and get them out of the way. Borya had been working his resources trying to find another way, but had been hitting some unexpected walls, which I imagined was probably Cox continuing to work with someone on the inside to keep me from finding an easy way out.

"I don't want to think about Chl--Nikki right now," I said, nearly forgetting to use the fake name I'd given her. "I need to figure out how to call my sovietnik."

"With those damn Bonettis camping the phones, it's hard," Schmidt said. "I wish we could just fuck 'em up."

Borya took a particularly loud bite of his food before grunting, "That's precisely what we're going to do."

I furrowed my brow. "How with the guards sticking around."

"Have patience," he said. "You'll know."

I looked Borya straight in the eyes and said, "If you're getting me an opportunity to strike, I won't waste it."

"That's good, but you'll have to be fast," he said. "If any of those guards see you causing trouble, you aren't getting out of here as easily as you're hoping for."

A small smile came to my face. "Don't you worry about that. Not being seen is my specialty."

"That's good, because the show is just about to start."

I lifted an eyebrow. "The show?"

As if on cue, someone across the dining hall stood up and flipped his tray. "What the fuck, bro?! You trying to piss me off?!"

"Hey!" a guard screamed. "Calm down."

The guy across from the one who had yelled stood up as well. He immediately splashed whatever was in his cup onto the other man, and the yeller launched himself across the table and all hell broke loose. Like a weird wave rolling through the prison, people started to stand up, some of them cheering on the fight, some of them trying to get involved. Others were just swiping food or taking advantage of the chaos to just run wild themselves.

Guards started to blow whistles as they bolted over to the scene of the crime, and those who weren't screeching whistles were demanding for everyone to get down on the floor. We didn't, though. Borya and his men stood up and started to slowly slink backwards out of the dining hall, and I knew why they opted to sit at a table so close to the entrance. There were no guards paying attention, so we slipped out and into the main block where a couple of guards were on alert after hearing the commotion.

One of the guards was unfortunately Delta, and he was standing right by the door so it was impossible to get in without him seeing us. "Stop!" he barked. "What are you doing?"

Borya held up his hands. "Just avoiding the mess," he said. "Big brawl going down in there. We were already on the way out, thank god."

"Just get to your cells and don't move," he barked.

Suddenly, an alarm started to blare and Delta shouted out, "We're locking cells! Everyone get in!" He turned and looked at the other guard and said, "Go help. I've got this."

She took off immediately, running out of the main block, and the scattered prisoners still in the block started begrudgingly making their way back to their cells. To the right, however, it was clear from a collection of shadows that a group of people were still standing near the phones and not moving.

"Delta'll get 'em," Borya said. "After something like this, people are let out in shifts. We'll have an opportunity at the phones. Even if it drops to one or two of the Bonettis at a time, that should eliminate the guards hanging out."

"That doesn't work for me," I said, looking over at the shadows.

Without really thinking about it, I turned and started to head in the direction of the phones. "Hey!" Delta barked. "No phones right now. You need to get to your cell."

But I ignored him. I rounded the corner where the phone and bathrooms were, and as they had been all week, the Bonettis were camping out.

"Oh hey," one of them said. "Foolish of you to come back here all alone when you know the boss wants you dead. We'll take the gimme though. We can quit standing back here by these nasty ass bathrooms."

They started to close in on me and I said, "You got the jump on me before. That was the only reason you survived our first interaction. Getting caught without a guard to protect you is more of a gimme for me."

The one who seemed to be the ringleader stood back and let his guys come at me first. None of them was significantly larger than me, so I didn't have a doubt in my mind that I could take them. One of the three made the mistake of just going for a straight up punch. I waited for a last minute dodge, and when he came towards me, I clutched my hand around his throat, lifted him up off his feet, and power slammed him into the ground. He landed on his back with a loud groan, and the other two hesitated. They clearly weren't prepared for that amount of power, but after a quick moment, they continued at me.

From the ground, the one I'd slammed got a hand around my ankle and tried to hold me so that his two cohorts could get their licks in on me, but when the first one came at me to try and wrap around me I ducked, kicked my free foot down at the face of the one on the ground, which caused him to let go of my ankle. Since the other one was over me at that point, I threw my head directly upwards, headbutting him under his chin, and in his daze, I hit him with a one-two punch and knocked him out cold.

Now sufficiently angry and worked up, I turned and looked at the third guy, who studied me for a long moment before suddenly turning and running off.

The last one standing there was the ringleader, and given that Delta hadn't come after me yet, I could only assume that Borya and the rest of his guys were handling him. I'd owe them big time for the trouble I was certain they were garnering just to deal with my impulse decision, but once I was out, I could make sure their commissary accounts were all well funded.

In front of me, the head Bonetti reached into his jumpsuit and pulled out a shank. He gave me an arrogant look like he clearly had the upper hand since he was armed. I'd long learned not to be afraid of someone with a mere knife, though. If I hadn't, Vladimir probably would have cut me loose a long time ago. I cracked my neck and watched him, waiting for him step forward.

"You're cocky," the guy said. "I'd like it if I didn't have to kill you."

Rather than responding, I just yawned. This seemed to piss him off and he came at me, being hesitant after seeing the way I'd dropped his compatri- ots. He was side-stepping, just outside of my range, but he could move as much as he wanted, it wouldn't matter. Eventually, he started to make his way behind me, but I didn't move, simply stared forward, keeping track of him easily by how loudly he was breathing. If I had to imagine, he probably wasn't used to this kind of task.

Finally, I heard him lunge. I didn't really need to avoid damage of any kind, just nothing fatal, so I slipped just enough to the side that his shank cut across my side. It stung, but I'd been through worse, and now his arm with the shank in it was right beside me. I grabbed his wrist and held him in place, then threw my head backwards, colliding with his. He groaned, and I kept a hold on his wrist and flipped around so I could start to slam it against the metal encasing around the telephones. In his defense, he took quite a few hits to the wrist before he dropped his weapon, but eventually, he'd taken so many hits that his hand opened of its own volition and the shank fell out.

He tried to drop to the ground and clamor for it, but when I turned around and saw his face, I could see his eye was covered in blood and already swelling. I'd caught him in a good spot and he was struggling to see and move. Before he could get to the shank at all, I kneed him in the face, sending him backwards onto his back. Cracking my neck once more, I bent down and picked up the shank and rolled it over in my hand. It wasn't the sturdiest weapon, but it would help me in a pinch.

I walked over to the man on the ground and kicked him in the ribs. He crumpled over to the side and I looked down at him and said, "Next time you decide to take on a task from your boss, you should be more confident that it's one you can handle."

"Maybe he couldn't..." I looked over my shoulder and Delta was standing there. He looked roughed up, but otherwise fine, leading me to wonder what had happened to Borya and his crew. "...but I think you'll find I'm a little bit better equipped."

Of course Delta worked for the Bonettis. That made a lot of sense, and connected the dots as to why the Bonettis never seemed to get any flack for hanging out around the phones, even though it clearly annoyed the guards. "I'm ready if you think you can handle it."

He pulled a gun out of his holster and pointed it at me. I frowned. "Don't bring a gun to a knife fight."

Without saying anything, he pulled the trigger. Once again, rather than avoiding all damage, I took some to get the advantage. I ducked to the side, but ran directly at Delta, and the bullet from his gun cut me across the shoulder. The bullet pierced right through the jumpsuit and burned into my flesh. I didn't feel it come out the other side and hissed, "Fuck," quietly to myself as I sensed it had gotten lodged.

I didn't have time to worry about that though, as I lurched at Delta, driving the shank in my hand into his stomach. He groaned but fought back, trying to get a good enough grip on me to wrestle me off. He caught hold of the shoulder where I'd been shot and I let out a howl of pain, responding by ripping the shank out and then stabbing it into a different spot. He tightened his clench on my shoulder while I stabbed repeatedly. He was clearly hoping the pain would eventually cause me to stop, but I'd dealt with more pain than that on a good day.

Eventually, I just wanted to bring it to an end and wrenched back. He was preparing to shoot at me again, but I stabbed the shank into the side of his neck. His eyes and mouth widened as blood began pouring from the wound and he gasped and choked for air. Once the pain had gotten unbearable enough, he fell backwards and the gun skidded out of his hand and across the room. It would have slid out from the phone nook, except Borya stepped around the corner just in time to stop it with his foot. He, too, looked like he'd been through it, but was okay apart from being a little bruised up.

We both stood in silence and watched as Delta clawed out towards us, but soon the light faded from his eyes, his arms fell flat, and his head fell to the side, splashing into the puddle of his own blood.

He was dead.

Borya surveyed my mess and sighed. "Bit much for a phone call, don't you think?"

"The Bonettis think I'm weak," I told him. "I chose to remind them that I'm not."

"Well, you better get the fuck outta here, otherwise you ain't never seeing the light of day again," he said.

I lowered my brow. "If I leave, when the knocked out Bonettis come to, they'll just tell the guards it was me."

"No, they won't," Borya said. "Because I'm going to tell them it was me."

CHAPTER SIX: CHLOE

Mitzy and I stood at the head of the room looking out at Cox and our co-workers. We'd gathered to discuss a different group that Mitzy and I had been looking into, but I was distracted taking in the way that Cox and the others were staring at me. It was pretty clear that someone had outed my relationship with Maks to Cox, and that relationship was making my coworkers view me like a traitor. It was incredibly frustrating because my job meant more to me than anything in the world. I actually really adored my crew, but it wasn't like I could address the issue, because I'd have to acknowledge it or call Cox a liar to his face to do so, and I was willing to bet whoever outed me did so with proof.

"So The Wreckers hail from Long Island, and aren't known to be associated with any other groups or organizations," Mitzy explained. "When Chloe and I did our recon there last week, we learned that this group appears to operate on an organized level and that there seems to be some sort of hierarchy, but from the scattered accounts of their crimes, it's somewhat difficult to determine exactly how the hierarchy works," Mitzy explained.

The room went silent after that, and everyone's eyes came to me all at once. I looked down at myself, with my heart beating a little faster. There was no way I was already showing or something. It would be impossible for these guys to know I was pregnant already.

"What?" I asked finally. I looked over at Mitzy, but he too was looking back at me, and then when I caught a glimpse of the projector behind us, I noticed it was one of the areas that I agreed to talk about when we presented this new group to the team. "Oh! Sorry!" My face burned and I nibbled on the inside of my cheek. "Uh... where were we?"

"Are you not taking this seriously?" Cox barked at me. "I already have my higher-ups looking at me like I'm stupid for not having a better wrangle on this group. They're all over the news and we barely know shit about them."

"No. I mean yes! Yes, I'm taking this seriously! This is important, I just zoned out a little. I'm sorry," I mumbled. I took a cue from the bullet points on the slide that was up and used them to help me find my place, and then I picked up from where Mitzy left off. "It's possible that this group has a tiered hierarchy, similar to the mafia, with a top boss, then a few smaller bosses under them, and then several more seconds under them, all the way down to the grunts at the bottom. We've heard a few terms used that seem interconnected, all related to the high suits in a deck of cards. King, queen, jack, and ace."

"We've also heard joker," Mitzy tacked on. "Though we're still unsure if the joker operates at the same level as the others, or if they are higher or lower ranking."

"Just based on the witness accounts we've gotten, it seems like those committing the crimes all report to one of these uppers, though no one has actually interacted with any of them personally. It's also hard to say if they're all equally ranked and co-running the group, or if they're actually something akin to underbosses or capos, working under one, larger boss. Joker could be the top dog, with the king, queen, jack and ace serving under them. It remains to be seen."

"What are their areas of crime at this point?" Sydney asked.

"That's the confusing and upsetting part," I said. "It doesn't seem they're focusing on any one or two things, but rather dipping their toes into everything. They've been associated with prostitution and trafficking, drugs, booze, exotic animals, and money laundering, and those are just the big ones."

"People in that area have also reported crimes like petty theft, carjacking, home invasions, and what appears to be the beginnings of racketeering, though we haven't seen anything large-scale yet, but people have been shaken down," Mitzy said. "That's part of the reason it took so long for their names to cross our desks, because they were at first believed to just be small-time criminals, nothing organized. It went to gangs before it came here even because they thought the high-card names were just nicknames for certain criminals and nothing more. It wasn't until the police out there started to realize that several of these small crimes were people *reporting* to them, that it became a case for OCU."

Gauge twisted his office chair to face Cox. "What do you want us to do?

At this point, no one has even been arrested from that group. All we have is circumstantial evidence tying them to anything."

"We've dealt with circumstantial evidence before," Cox said. "You and Lucas head out there. Street clothes, unmarked cars. I want to see if we can put enough of something together to start doing some deep sniffing around. We're supposed to be *cutting down* organized crime in NYC, not letting new ones pop up."

"You don't want us to go?" Mitzy said. "We've already begun the--"

"No," Cox cut us off. "You've both been playing a little loosey-goosey with your schedules as of late and I'm sure you have paperwork to catch up on. You'll spend your days doing that until you're all caught up."

"You're benching us?" I yelped. "Why?"

Cox looked at me as if I'd spat in his face by even *daring* to address him. "Don't question me. Do it or get out." I opened my mouth to speak, but Mitzy put a hand on my wrist and stopped me. Cox turned to Sydney and said, "I need you to follow up on what we discussed before. Head out as soon as we're done here."

Sydney nodded. "I'm on it."

That mysterious language didn't sit well with me at all. He had her doing something he clearly didn't want me to know about and that made me want to scream. After everything I'd poured into this job was one small thing, that at this point no one had checked with me, worth being completely turned on?

"Alright," Cox said. "If that's all you all have for the time being, then we'll get going. We all have a lot of work to do."

Mitzy held up a hand. "That's all we got."

Cox slammed his hands down on the table and stood up. "Let's go."

Both Mitzy and I just stood and waited while everyone else got up from the table and started to leave. Sydney was the last one lingering behind, especially given that Cox always made sure he was ahead of the pack, so I pulled away from Mitzy and went over to Sydney and grabbed her by the wrist. Immediately, she yanked her hand back from me and I frowned at her.

"What's wrong?" I asked her. "You guys have all been treating me like trash. Did Cox say something to you? Did I do something wrong?" She gave me a hesitant look, like she wasn't sure if she should answer or not. "Come on! It wasn't all that long ago that we were all ragging on Cox because he couldn't be trusted. All of a sudden you three are his flunkies or something?"

That evidently wasn't the right thing to say, because Sydney scoffed, barked, "You're one to talk," and walked away.

I looked back at Mitzy and he gave me a thumbs up. "You're nailing it, with the interpersonal relationships lately."

"What am I supposed to do?" I whimpered at him, falling defeated down into one of the chairs around the meeting table. "I love this job. I'm not going to be able to do it effectively if Cox has me benched and everyone is treating me like *I'm* the mafioso?"

Mitzy, who almost always had a whimsical, carefree expression on his face, gave me a saddened look. "Chlo..." My nose burned and I could feel tears coming up to my eyes.

"And I still have to figure out how to help Maks, which I'm never going to be able to do if no one will tell me anything." The tears slipped down my cheeks. "And it's sounding like I'm going to have to choose a side, so if I help Maks, who was definitely arrested illegally, then it's going to be the end of my career, and it'll be wrong, or I can ignore Maks and leave him in there and just let Cox's bad actions go unchecked, which is also wrong." Then I looked down and put my hand on my stomach and started to cry a little bit harder. "And I just want to be a good person who does good things so that I'm someone that my baby can look up to, and I don't want it to have to grow up without its mom like I did, or with a mom who can barely do anything for themselves like Maksim's mom and... and..."

I buried my face in my hands and started to sob. Showing this level of emotion was rare and difficult for me. I didn't like showing weakness, on top of the fact that I promised myself I would never allow myself to get into this sort of helpless, out of control place. I've strived to have a handle on my life at all times, but ever since Maksim showed up, it felt like all my beliefs were being disillusioned and everything was out of control. There were times when I was with him that I enjoyed that thrill of not knowing, but right now it was just leaving me feeling battered.

I felt a hand on my back and looked up to see Mitzy standing next to me and giving it a gentle rub.

"I'm sorry," I said.

"For what?"

"For dragging you into all my drama lately. I hate to be so misery-loves-company with you."

"Chloe." He smiled at me. "Remember what we said at the hospital? You're my best friend. Maybe we're slightly abnormal best friends, but I don't know, I think we'd make a pretty good buddy cop movie." Then the smile fell a little. "I'm not concerned about me. I'm more concerned about you and all this that you're going through. I know how much this job means to you, so I can't imagine it's very easy to learn that it's mostly a load of shit."

"You figured it out. I'm just stupid," I grumbled.

He scoffed. "You're not stupid. Please cut yourself some slack. You chose to have faith in people. I don't think that makes you a bad person. You chose to have faith that the criminal justice system was actually filled with people who weren't criminals and cared about justice. I fear you may be amongst the minority." He pulled a chair out and sat across from me. "You're one of the genuinely good people in this world. I'm sorry that the rest of us could never measure up."

I shook my head. "That's not true, though. I really do think that you're a genuinely good person and I really do think that Maksim is a genuinely good person. Even people like Katya and Vincent. It's just..." I wiped my eyes. "It's really difficult relearning everything I believed to be true. It doesn't feel like I quite know my place in this world anymore and..." I rubbed my stomach. "I'm going to have this little person who expects me to have it all together, but I feel like I've moved further away from having it together than I have moved closer since finding out I'm gonna be a mom. And that was only a couple of weeks ago."

"Well, it seems like you're at an impasse, so now you need to start changing your view. Figure out what you want to prioritize in your life. I mean... there's a pretty easy option, if you'd like to take it."

I looked up at him. "Easy option?"

"Mmhm." He poked my belly. "This is your new number one priority. Not a job. Not a man. Not even yourself. This is what all of your decisions have to point towards now. They have to be the best decisions for this one."

For some reason, the very thought brought a smile to my face. "Yeah. That's true."

"So don't give it too much thought, what's best for your baby?" Mitzy asked.

"To get its father out of prison," I replied quickly.

He nodded. "Uh huh. And what are the lengths you're willing to go to?"

"At this point?" I looked him straight in the eyes to say, "Just about any."

"Well, then I have a suggestion for you, but I don't think you're going to like it."

I lifted an eyebrow. "Okay...?"

"If we're doing things by the book, then yeah, it's going to be pretty difficult to get Maksim out. Even if we could expose Cox's tactics, I guarantee you he has more friends up the ladder than you do, and if he has proof that you and Maksim were involved, he'll be able to discredit you, or even me with the snap of a finger. There are ways to do it, but it's gonna be difficult as hell."

I lifted an eyebrow and said, "Okay, you're right, I don't like that. It's not really a suggestion though."

"No..." Mitzy grabbed a tissue from the box in the middle of the table and wiped my cheeks before crumpling up and just throwing it on the floor. "My suggestion is that we *don't* do things by the book."

"What does that mean?" I said.

"Cox may have more friends here, but we have a couple of friends in common that I think could probably get the job done, if not by the rules," he explained with a raised eyebrow of his own.

My eyes widened as I started to catch his drift. "The Costellos?"

"Katya's been looking for some girlfriends, and I'd be willing to bet good money that she could convince her fiance to help us out. Besides, I think as far as they know, they're still on good terms with Maksim. They'll probably want to help him, regardless."

Maksim wanted Vincent dead. I highly doubted that translated in any world to go ask him to help get Maksim out of prison. "Okay..." I took a deep breath. "That *is* a suggestion."

"You said so yourself, that you'd be willing to do it by any means necessary at this point. Between them knowing Maksim and the sympathy, we should be able to get the job done."

"The sympathy?" I said.

He nodded at me. "Yep. If we're going to do this, you're not just going to tell them that you know Maksim, you're going to have to tell them that you're pregnant with his child."

That thought scared me more than anything. "That sounds really risky."

"It will be," he said. "So what's it gonna be?"

CHAPTER SEVEN: MAKSIM

In the wake of Delta's death, the prison had been on total lockdown, as expected. Borya had been sent to solitary confinement for who knew how long for the death of a guard, and prisoners were only being let out in small, cell groups to use the bathrooms, phones, and eat. None of the guards could trust any of Borya's guys as far as they could throw them, so unless two of us shared a cell like Schmidt and I did, we were *not* being let out at the same time. That didn't really matter to me, as I'd managed to accomplish both my and Borya's missions simultaneously.

I'd taken care of the Bonettis and I'd gotten myself access to the phones.

Keeping in mind everything that had happened, and the fact that I probably needed to figure out a way to communicate with Alexei and update him about what was going on, I waited patiently for Schmidt's and mine turn to be released from our cell for one hour to use the phone and contact Brusch. Schmidt stood watch, but it wasn't necessary. The release schedule had been designed very specifically to keep any Russians associated with Borya and the Bonettis far, far away from one another.

"Boss," Brusch said in an exasperated tone. "I expected to hear from you so long before now. It's been weeks."

"I know, I apologize. It seems there were more than a few people in here who did *not* want me to have contact with the outside world, but thanks to some assistance from a few friends, those problems have sorted themselves out."

"Hey," Schmidt said. "Be careful what you say. They record and listen to all the lines."

I nodded a thanks to him and then made sure to be careful continuing forward. "Do you know Alexei Lachinov?" Given that Borya had specifically told me to tell Brusch to contact Alexei, I figured I was okay to mentioning him by name.

"Yes, of course," Brusch said. "Vladimir had extensive dealings with him. I know precisely where he and his group hail in Little Odessa."

"Good," I said. "I need you to contact him and tell him that I'm working with Borya and that, if he can help with getting me out of here, there are certain deals that Borya and I have discussed to benefit him and his group that can be further solidified when I'm out. Borya is pretty confident that Alexei should be able to give us the assistance we need."

"Okay. I'm working a couple of additional angles as well, so if he can help, maybe he can use some of the balls I have rolling already to get you out sooner."

I nodded, even though Brusch couldn't see me. "Good. Getting to the phones shouldn't be an issue anymore, so I'll be in contact again soon."

"Well, hopefully we'll have you out before you need to contact me again," Brusch said.

"Wishful thinking," I replied. "But I'll take it. Bye."

"Bye."

I hung up the phone and then walked over and tapped Schmidt on the shoulder. When I did, he jumped a little and then looked back at me and forced a smile. "Oh, sorry boss, er, bud. After Borya told us how you handled those other guys, I realized that I may have underestimated you. It sounded like a scary story when he said it."

My brow furrowed deeply between my eyes, almost of its own volition. "They were enemies. I wouldn't do that to friends."

He snickered. "Guess I need to make sure we're always friends then, huh?"

The way that sounded didn't sit right with me. I'd heard several people take that tone with Vladimir before. No one actually gave two shits about him, they were just all terrified of him. When I held his funeral, there wasn't a single person who shed a tear for him. Most of the attendees were there to honor Sasha's life, not his. That wasn't the kind of legacy I wanted to leave behind, yet I felt almost like I was being forced to walk in his goliath footsteps at every turn; it felt like I had no choice but to choose violence to succeed. With the Bonettis, with Chloe, even with Vincent--no matter how hard I'm trying, I just find myself defaulting to his ways.

Maybe that was why each victory only felt temporary. If I wanted lasting results, then I needed to do it my way.

"I feel bad for Borya," I told Schmidt. "I want him out."

"I know what you may be thinking," Schmidt said, "but turning yourself in doesn't help anyone. It just makes his sacrifice useless."

"No. I can't turn myself in. My guys are working on getting me out, I can't afford to misstep now, but maybe there's a way we can get Borya back out as well."

Schmidt tilted his head. "How?"

I remembered the guard that Borya had spoken with before, Patty, the one that he seemed to have charmed into his pocket. "What shift does Patty usually work?"

"Night shift, but she's not about to bend any rules. She likes Borya, but she abides by the law here. She would sooner die than become a guard like Delta or his minions."

"That's what I'm banking on," I said.

Patty did what she did for Borya to sleep at night, that was what he told me. There was certainly a way to use that to my advantage.

Killing most of the day in my cell due to the lockdown, I was glad to see that Patty was on staff when Schmidt and I were let out of our cell. The prisoners were being let out for an hour for bathroom and meals, once in the morning and once in the evening. She was keeping to herself, which was good, because it meant no one else would overhear what I had to say but her.

"Patty," I said, nodding to her. "I never got to thank you for getting Borya and I a moment to pray the other day."

She gave me a knowing nod. "Of course."

"Borya's a good man. Being a foreigner, it was quite terrifying getting locked up, but he's made it so much easier," I explained.

"Yeah," she replied. "I think he's a good man, too. It felt like it was only a matter of time before he flipped and ended Delta, though. The two have been at it like cats and dogs for years."

"That's what I keep hearing," I said. "It's so strange. If he was going to do it, why wouldn't he have done it sooner? It just doesn't make sense to get so comfortable here and *then* screw everything up."

She gave me a look. "You don't think he did it?"

"From what I hear, Borya Isn't a stabby kind of guy," I told her. "When they said he'd been caught with a shank, all his guys were bewildered. Just doesn't sound like his work. Even on the outs, he preferred to work with finesse."

Patty looked around like the conversation was starting to make her nervous, but she leaned in nonetheless, and said, "I had a really hard time believing he'd done something like that. Delta was in bad shape. Borya's not that messy of a guy. He can't even wear dirty clothes, and I have no idea how he'd get ahold of a shank like the one that had been used. He doesn't do any of the prison jobs because it's not like he needs a skill and his commissary is fine."

"It was a stolen screwdriver or something?" I asked, as though I hadn't used the device myself.

She pulled back from me and gave me a nervous look. "I'm sorry. I shouldn't be discussing this with an inmate. You're too easy to talk to. That's dangerous."

I smiled. "No, you're right. I'm sorry. I should have asked. Since you appear to be the only guard around here with some actual sense, I'd feel bad if I got you in trouble. I really just wanted to thank you for your kindness."

"You're very welcome," she replied. "Now go get something to eat before you lose your chance."

I nodded at her and walked off, eventually finding Schmidt in the cafeteria eating dinner. It was going to take some time for me to see if my planted seed was going to take root, so I got some food of my own and tried to push everything out of my mind for the night except for Borya's note, that someone obvious may have had something to do with my arrest other than Chloe. I'd been making mental notes for the last several hours, but it was still a short list, and no one that I would expect to turn on me.

"You all right there?" Schmidt asked. "You look about a thousand miles away."

I responded only, "I wish."

The next morning, all of the inmates in my cell block were awoken earlier than usual to the sounds of guards shouting, "Out of bed! There's a bunk search happening!"

"That's weird," Schmidt said. "They don't typically like to do this shit first thing in the morning, and we all got flipped after Delta died."

I didn't say anything, only climbed out of bed and went to stand by the cell door. Schmidt joined me, yawning as he did, and eventually the loud buzz echoed through the block that meant the doors had been unlocked. One by one, guards went to each of the cells in shifts, calling the inmates out to stand by the door while their room was flipped and searched. No one mentioned what they were looking for.

But I had a feeling I knew.

Schmidt's and mine room was turned over about ten minutes before one of the guards called, "Hey!" from the lower floor. "Over here! Cell seven, Bonetti and Carson!"

A smile crossed my face as I stood listening to the commotion.

"N-no!" a man yelled. "I don't know why that piece is missing."

The image of the shank the Bonetti had attempted to use to kill me popped into my brain. Thinking back now, it *did* sort of look like a piece of the metal from the bunkbeds broken off and sharpened.

"Gotta be Bonetti," I heard a different guard say. "They're notorious for shanks."

"We'll take 'em both," someone else said.

"It was him!" the original man screamed. "He used soda and water to rust it then broke it off!"

Bingo.

"I'm gonna fucking kill you!" a gravelly voice said, and I recognized it as one of the underlings of the man who tried to kill me and was killed instead.

The block was silent as the guards locked everyone down again, save for the Bonetti and his cellmate that they were leading out of the block.

"How?" Schmidt asked me quietly.

I just smiled. "A little bit of charm."

By the afternoon, the lockdown had eased in the block, just in time for Patty to come walking in with Borya in tow. He offered her humble thanks before she released him, and then she gave me a quick, warm smile before turning and walking away. The feeling of victory that was bleeding through me was almost addictive. For the first time, I'd done things *my* way, and it worked. It even had multiple positive outcomes, and no one but Patty knew I had anything to do with it.

That was the kind of legacy I wanted to leave behind.

Borya's crew had all found a table in the cell block atrium to sit around and hang out, so Schmidt and I joined them. When I approached the table, one of the guys stood up and offered his seat to me, and feeling proud of myself, I nodded and accepted it. The look on his face when he gave me his seat told me that he wasn't doing so out of fear. He was doing it because he respected me and knew what I'd done to help his boss, which was an amazing feeling. I'd garnered a bit of honest notoriety all on my own--this wasn't a moment from under Vladimir's shadow. This moment was all my own.

"Boys," Borya said as he approached the table. "Give me a sec with our new friend, will ya?" After each of the guys had a chance to greet Borya and welcome him back, they stood up and left, leaving he and I alone. Borya let out a long grunt as he lowered himself down onto one of the table's seats, then he folded his hands into one another and looked across at me. "Well now. Didn't you get a little creative while I was gone? Patty, huh?"

I shrugged. "I figured she'd still need to sleep at night."

He chuckled back at me. "When I saw all that damage you caused, I thought I might be looking at Vladimir reincarnated, but you're a different breed, I see." I couldn't help but beam a little at that. "He was a man who solved his problems with violence because he didn't know any other way, but you..." He tapped his temple with a finger. "You're smart. I like that."

"What'd you tell them when they asked why you took the fall for a Bonetti?" I said.

He lifted an eyebrow. "That they were planning on trying to frame one of my guys and I'd rather see myself go down than one of them because I'm a lifer. They bought it because they know I look out for mine."

I nodded, impressed. "I had a feeling you'd be able to pull something out from up your sleeve." I crossed my arms. "I managed to get some phone time."

Borya leaned his head back and a barking laugh came out of him. "Well, I should fucking hope so!" He looked at me overly amused. "Did he have good news?"

"Okay news," I replied. "He's working on it and I pointed him in Alexei's direction."

"Excellent. I imagine getting in touch with him will really start to speed things up." He stood up from the table after that. "Now, if you'll excuse me, I'm starving and exhausted." He lifted a hand and waved to his guys who were standing not too far away, and they drifted back over. "One o' you had gotta give me a bag of chips or something and I'll get you back come commissary day. I'm hungry."

"I got you boss," one of them said, and then they all walked away, save for Schmidt, who sat down where Borya had been sitting across from me.

"You're looking mighty pleased with yourself."

"Borya's too good a man to have taken that fall," I explained. "Let's just say that I wasn't confident in my ability to get him out, but I'm glad it worked."

"Not confident?" Schmidt said, snorting. "You sure seemed confident. A fake it til you make it kind of guy?"

For some odd reason, a large smile came to my face. I thought about my life up to that point, and how much of it had been based on just faking it until I made it. If Vladimir was the man who ruled by fear, then I was the man who could rule by the unknown.

"Yeah," I said. "That sounds good. Maksim Petrov, the bratva boss who faked it until he made it."

Schmidt crossed his arms. "So are you still faking it, or have you made it?"

I just shrugged. "That's for me to know, and you to find out."

CHAPTER EIGHT: CHLOE

My night was plagued with a variety of dreams about my mom and the man who stormed in our bodega and shot her in cold blood--Mitzy's deceased father-in-law. Maybe it was because I was about to go against the one rule I'd set for myself that day, but I simply couldn't shake the feeling that I was betraying her. That day, some young, upstart mafioso thought that he was entitled to rule over our bodega, even though he had no jurisdiction in Little Odessa, and killed my mom simply because she refused to comply with his bullying tactics.

When I first got my job, I saw that there were literally hundreds of organized crime goons all over the city of New York. Arrogant men and women who believed that they deserved to have more than the next person over for no reason other than that they wanted it, and in order to achieve this fortune that was apparently their birthright, they would steal, destroy and kill anything in their way. Ever since that day when I held my dying mother in my arms and sobbed as she took her last breaths, I *swore* that I would wipe these people from the planet however I had to do it. I didn't want another person suffering like I suffered.

Now I was about to work with one of them to help get another one out of prison.

The reflection of my face in the mirror when I got up that morning was a little darker. The bags under my eyes were deeper. The crows feet in the corners of my eyes were more defined. There was nothing that couldn't be covered up with makeup, and thankfully my mother had blessed me with her looks, but there was no denying the toll all of this was taking on me.

More terrifying than anything, though, was that I didn't know the path back to happiness.

There had been a time when I was delighted to wake up in the morning and the people in my life made me happy. I got along well with my coworkers and my boss trusted me as his right-hand. I felt like I was doing the work I'd set out to do, and that gave me a feeling of fulfillment that was hard to explain, but now...

One of my hands drifted to my belly.

...Now there was this new, life-altering thing that seemed to be at the crux of my whole world being restructured.

What was I supposed to be aiming for next?

Agreeing to meet with the Costellos was the path forward that I'd chosen to get Maksim out of prison, but what was I hoping for with this? Was I going to tell him I was pregnant? Was I hoping to try and make a family with him? Was I just trying to get him back to Russia and out of Cox's clutches? But then what? I'd take my baby and go start over somewhere else? I couldn't just leave my father and sister. The reason the bodega remained mostly safe from criminals was because they knew the place was owned by a cop's father ,and therefore meticulously secured. Could I convince them to come with me? To run off to some other part of the country, or world, because I'd managed to screw up the life I built here? They didn't even know I was pregnant yet, and I had no idea how they were going to react once they found out. Maksim terrified Chandler down to her core. Would she hate me because he was the father of my child? If I *did* choose to try and start a life with him, would she ever speak to me again?

The ratio of questions to answers was disheartening to say the least, but I wish I just had *one* answer. If I felt definitive about anything at all, I'd feel better about the decisions I was making, but for the first time in my life, I was only thinking of my next step and not the future at all. I couldn't look ahead, because I honestly didn't know what I was looking ahead to.

I was so scared.

By some miracle, I managed to bathe and feed myself without a total mental breakdown, and then I waited for Mitzy's call. We didn't have a set time with the Costellos, Mitzy only told me to be ready to go first thing in the morning, and once he knew when we were meeting with them, he'd come pick me up and we'd go. It was surprising to me how confident Mitzy was that he could get them to meet at all, given my job title, but then again, Mitzy was a detective too, and the Costellos could rely on him far more than the NYPD could.

After what felt like decades, but was actually about forty-five minutes, Mitzy called me to let me know he was downstairs. I left most of my items at home, but I did pack my gun just in case, and of course I brought my cell phone. I was asking for help, so I imagined that this wouldn't turn into anything volatile, but given that I was going to meet a man that I'd long hunted, but never captured, I figured I'd better be prepared for anything.

"You look nice," Mitzy said when I climbed in the car. "Did you think this was a business meeting or something?"

I looked down at my magenta, button-up blouse, black slacks, and black pointed toe pumps and frowned. "Is it too much?"

"No. I mean, Vince is likely to be in a suit himself, I just didn't expect to see you so dressed up."

This was coming from a man who exclusively wore sweatpants and t-shirts. I didn't think he knew the meaning of the words. "Well, I'm asking for help, so I wanted to look presentable."

"Presentable--check," Mitzy said. "You ready?"

I nodded. "As ready as I'll ever be."

The Costello's estate was outside of the city, off the beaten path, and surrounded by a lush forest. A fence separated the property from the main road, and stretched far beyond what I could see from the front gate. There was a small security station situated right where the gate and fence met, and there was a bored security guard sitting inside. When Mitzy pulled his car up, he sat slightly higher at attention, but deflated quickly when he saw who it was.

The security station was on my side, so when Mitzy pulled the car up to the gate, he rolled down my window and leaned over a bit. "Hey Dave," he greeted.

The man in the security box, a younger looking man with light brown hair and tired eyes, replied "Hey Mitzy. Vince is expecting you. Head on in. He's in building four, his office."

"Thanks."

"*Building* four?" I yelped. "There are multiple buildings?!"

"Yep. After he got into it with the Petrovs, one of his capos came up with the idea to make Vincent and Katya's main house for them and family only. Not even most of their staff are allowed there, only people they trust. There are additional, smaller buildings on the property that are used for Vincent's office, the offices of his capos, and Katya's mother."

My jaw fell slightly open. "Annika Petrov lives here?"

He nodded. "Yup. After Vladimir and Sacha died, Katya convinced her to move to NYC to be closer to her, Vincent and the baby. Annika didn't really have anyone else, so she agreed."

That made my heart burn with sadness for Maksim. The Petrovs were like his family, and he lost all four of them in the blink of an eye. I could see why that kind of thing would make him crazy. I still didn't agree with his need to kill Vincent or take back Katya, but I supposed I could see why he would want to try and regain the little bit of semblance of a family that he had. Just thinking of it made me lift a hand to my belly. My only options were to tell Maksim that I was pregnant or never allow him to find out. He'd want his family if he knew it was out there. I could never dangle one in front of him and then take it away.

"You okay?" Mitzy asked. "Feeling sick?"

I looked out the window at the trees rolling by as we drove down the winding path. "I feel like I'm always sick these days."

After about five minutes, we made it to the actual property and my eyes nearly popped out of my skull. There was indeed one massive mansion directly in front of the road, with a shrub outlined cobblestone path curling around a fountain as a grand entryway. On either side of this fountain were a smattering of buildings, some larger and some smaller. It looked like we'd just driven into a brand new kingdom, with the mansion as the castle in the heart of a small town at its feet.

"This is insane," I said, looking all around. "If I never spent money on anything, and saved up from the time I got my job until I retired, I still don't think I could afford this."

"Isn't it outrageous? Sometimes I leave this place and go home to my four bedroom house and it suddenly feels so small," Mitzy said.

He took a right in front of the cobblestone path, and entered into a small parking lot with about ten spots. Mitzy picked one and parked, then we climbed out and started up the cobblestone path towards the fountain.

Just before the fountain, Mitzy took a right and we followed the path down, under a beautiful terracotta awning with marble legs, and eventually reached one of the smaller buildings, though it was still at least twice as big as my entire apartment complex. Mitzy walked up to the front door and rang the doorbell, then he pointed up to where a small camera was hanging.

"Smile for the mob boss." He waved and laughed as if he was super proud of his joke, but I just continued to stand there nervously.

When the door buzzed, I actually jumped a little. This was an experience I never thought I'd get to have. Vincent Costello had been in my crosshairs more than once, but for how effective I'd been in roping him in, he may as well just be another man on the street. I couldn't believe I was at his home and about to sit down in his office, like we were old friends, and actually ask for help.

If my crew back at the precinct thought I was a traitor before, they should see me now.

Mitzy led the way, pushing the door open, and we entered into an adorable looking atrium with marble floors, tons of ferns hanging around, and a small, crystal chandelier hanging from the apex of the ceiling. There was a small receptionist's desk with a young woman behind it with massively curly red hair and thin glasses over her green eyes.

"Good morning, Mitzy," she said, then she motioned to her right, to a set of double, dark oak doors. "Mr. Costello is expecting you."

"Thanks, Anna. Is Katya here, too?" he asked.

She nodded. "Yep. Both waiting for you inside."

We walked over to the double doors and opened them, letting ourselves into one of the plushest, most comfortable-looking offices I'd ever seen. Directly across from the doors was a massive picture window that looked out over the garden behind the building, and in front of the window was an L-shaped desk with a computer on top. There was a small dry bar to the left of the room, nearby which was a round dining table with four chairs around it, sitting atop an expensive looking rug. It was here that the office's two occupants were sitting, working on a cup of tea.

Though I'd only met Katya before, both faces were familiar to me. I'd looked at Vincent Costello's mugshot maybe half a thousand times or more over the course of my time as a detective. To his credit, however, I could say that the mugshot didn't do him much justice. He was devilishly handsome with a perfectly diamond cut jaw, covered in short beard along with a goatee. He had a piercing, dark brown gaze and black hair that was cut short and gelled back. As Mitzy had warned, he was wearing a suit, though only the vest and button up, along with the navy pants and a crisp pair of shoes. He had on a watch that looked more expensive than my car, and was a piece of jewelry second only to Katya's incredible engagement ring.

Compared to her brooding betrothed, Katya looked fresh and light in a white sundress with cherry blossoms all over it. She had her hair up in a high bun and seemed to have skipped makeup for the day in the interest of letting her natural face shine through. Her round belly bulged the front of her dress, but she didn't seem to mind as she and Vincent sat enjoying a platter of meats, cheeses, fruits, and crackers that had been placed in the middle of the table.

They both stood up as we walked in and Vincent walked over to Mitzy with a smile. Seeing that cold exterior melt away behind his warm greeting was surprising and infectious. It made me smile just to look at it. "Mitzy," he greeted. "What's going on, man?"

"Another day, another dollar, boss," Mitzy replied. There was a new obedience about him that was curious to see. "This is my very dear friend--"

"Chloe Nikitina," Vincent cut him off. "New York City detective in the Organized Crime Unit. You've been there for five years since the unit's inception, and before then you focused on organized crime down in the gang unit in Manhattan. Graduated from NYU with your BA in law enforcement, and you have a father named Alton and a sister named Chandler, correct?" he ran off quickly.

I was smart enough to know that, despite the friendly way he read me my dossier, he meant it as a subtle threat. "You've got it," I replied.

"Vince," Katya said, walking over and standing a little in front of him, "I thought we agreed that we would *not* be creepy when we met up with her." She then looked at me and rolled her eyes quickly before reaching out for a hug. "It's good to see you again, Chloe."

I accepted the hug, still feeling that friendly pull towards Katya that I felt before. "You too." As we separated, I addressed both Vincent and Katya to say, "I appreciate you all meeting with me. I'm in a bit of a predicament, but Mitzy thinks you'll be able to help."

"Mitzy speaks very highly of you, otherwise I would never allow a detective in here," Vincent replied.

Mitzy held his hands in the air. "Hey. I'm a detective."

"Sure you are," Vincent replied quickly.

Katya motioned to the table. "We have some snacks and homemade lemonade. Let's sit down so we can chat."

The four of us sat down around the table and spent a few minutes enjoying a bit to eat and something to drink before I finally cleared my throat to get started. I didn't feel good sitting around and eating like everything was fine, when every extra moment that we spent was another moment Maks was locked up and needed our help.

"Um, so... It has come to my attention that we have a friend in common, and he's in some trouble right now," I started quietly. "Maksim."

"Maksim as in Maksim Petrov?" Katya said. "You know him?"

"Yes. He and I were friends as children, but then my father moved my family to the United States and we lost touch. It just so happened that when he came here, I was the detective assigned to suss him out in a raid. We realized that we were old friends, and well..." I looked at Mitzy and he nodded to encourage me, so I looked back at Vincent and Katya and said. "I'm now pregnant with his child."

Both Vincent and Katya's jaws dropped. "You're pregnant by Maks?!" Katya yelped. "Wow. I..." She looked over at Vincent. "I can't believe it."

"I know, especially because I thought he was obsessed with you," Vincent said begrudgingly.

"Not obsessed, you drama queen," Katya huffed. "I think he had a crush on me, but that was mostly because I was *the* only woman consistently in his life." Then she looked at me, "but you know what? He told me about you before. He said that his first crush ever was his childhood friend and that he always wondered what happened to you. I had no idea, when we met before, that it was you."

Of course I wasn't about to tell Vincent and Katya that Maksim still had a plan to kill Vincent, so I just said, "Yeah... I wasn't sure if he wanted you guys to know he was here, or what. I just kept it quiet. I wasn't entirely supposed to be... cavorting with him anyway, so I was mostly just keeping it quiet that I knew him altogether."

"He's in trouble?" Vincent said. "What happened?"

"He found himself caught in my boss' crossfire, Detective Cox," Mitzy explained.

Both Katya and Vincent hissed in unison, "Fucking prick."

I shook my head. "You're not wrong." I frowned. "He pulled something, probably something backhanded, to raid Maksim's club Dacha and arrest him on some bogus terrorism charges."

"Terrorism?" Katya said. "That's ridiculous." She pulled out her phone and dialed a number, then set it flat on the table.

"Who are you calling?" Vincent asked.

"Alexei," she responded.

My jaw fell slack. "Alexei, as in Alexei Lachinov?"

Katya held a hand up and a few seconds later, the phone answered and a man's incredibly deep voice said, "Katya?" It was Alexei Lachinov, a bratva who operated out of Little Odessa. Last I heard, the Lachinov group and the Costellos were *not* on good terms, which made it interesting that Katya seemed to be in touch with him. She was clearly functioning outside of Vincent's leadership as well as within his ranks, which was intriguing and inspiring.

Katya swapped to Russian to speak, "Alexei. It's Katya Petrova. A friend of mine has been targeted by Detective Cox and--"

"It wouldn't happen to be Maksim Petrov would it?" he asked.

My eyes widened. "How do you know that?"

Vincent, Katya, and Mitzy looked up at me with wide eyes, and Mitzy put his finger to his lips.

"Who was that?" Alexei asked.

"Just a friend of Maksim's," Katya replied. "Has word already gotten to you that he's in a tight spot?"

"More than that. He's already made contact with one of my lifers, Borya. Borya told his guy to get in contact with me, so we're working on pulling some strings to get him bail. Once he's out, we can deal with getting the charges dropped."

"Alexei," Vincent said in English, "it's Vincent Costello."

Alexei let out a long, angry sounding sigh. "Costello."

"Yeah, I know we're not the best of friends, but it's very important to me that Maksim is released from prison immediately. What do you need from me to help?" he asked.

"Someone will need to post his bail. Preferably in cash that can't be tracked. I've got a judge friend who won't want any of this falling back down on him," Alexei responded. "And I need you to pull your men out of Poda's."

The table went eerily silent as Vincent took in a deep breath. Poda's was a speakeasy that looked like a meat supplier from the front, but had premium liquor and musicians in the back. We'd tracked Vincent's drugs through this place before, but we'd never been able to make anything stick directly to him. I was unaware that the Lachinovs had an interest in Poda as it was far outside their territory, but I didn't inquire, mostly because the less I knew, the better.

Katya and Vincent locked eyes, and though neither of them were saying anything, it still felt like they were communicating. Katya's eyes were pleading, and though Vincent seemed annoyed, there was a much stronger emotion dominating his expression--love.

"Fine," Vincent said. "You can have Poda's, but I expect your guys to quit firing off on mine every time they see them in the street."

"I suppose I can tell them to focus their attention elsewhere for a while," he replied, then he switched to Russian again. "Katya, you know I don't like your dog making demands of me."

"I know, I'm sorry," Katya replied.

Vincent started to boil. "Stop speaking in Russian. You know I can't understand it."

"Aw, don't get so upset, Vince. I didn't bring my popcorn," Mitzy joked.

Vincent looked at him. "I'm gonna fucking smack you."

There was something very amusing about these interactions to me, it just felt... homier here.

"Thank you so much, Alexei," Katya finished. "When will we be free to post the bail?"

"I'll send you a text," he said. "Talk soon. Take care."

"You too. Bye," and then he hung up the phone.

"I'm not exactly sure how much bail will be, but with a charge like terrorist threats, it'll likely be substantial," Mitzy explained.

"I don't have much, but I swear, I can pay back whatever--"

"It's not a problem," Vincent cut me off. "Maksim is a friend. We'll take care of it."

I looked from him to Katya, who smiled and nodded, then I looked back at Vincent. "Thank you so much."

"Of course," he said. "My only request is that, once he's out, I'd love to talk to him."

I swallowed hard. "Really?"

My voice echoed and I looked over and saw that Katya had said the same thing as well.

"Yes," Vincent said. "I feel like he and I have some business to take care of. Some air to clear. The last thing I'd want was him trying to kill me or pull something like Vladimir did," he explained. "Is that going to be a problem?"

Yes. That was going to be an huge problem. He *did* want to kill Vincent and he was never, in a million years, going to agree to come and sit down for a chat. I was half hoping that I wasn't going to need to tell Maks that I came to the Costellos at all. "Nope," I lied. "Not going to be a problem at all."

CHAPTER NINE: MAKSIM

I couldn't say that I was getting comfortable behind bars, but at the very least I was beginning to get a hang of the schedule. When I wasn't lying in my bunk trying to figure out exactly how I was going to take care of the growing list of business that I had when I finally got out of prison, I was hanging out with Borya's crew. Both the Bonettis and the guards were leaving us alone in the wake of what happened with Delta and the Bonetti ringleader, which was making it much easier to just get through the day. It'd been two days since I'd spoken with Brusch, and though I was anxious to call him back and hear how the effort to get me out was going, Borya assured me that these things took time in America. and to just be patient.

Although if too many more days passed without me getting out, I'd be calling him back to light a fire under him.

Some good news finally came the morning of the fifth day since I'd spoken with Brusch. The guards normally opened all of the cells at the exact same time in the morning to let the inmates out for the day, but a guard visited my cell early in the morning, and all on its own.

"Petrov," the female guard that was normally hanging around Delta thundered. "Get up."

I sat up and looked over at haer, still half asleep. "What's wrong?"

"Nothing's wrong. You're outta here."

That made me jump up much quicker. "Really?"

"Yeah. Get your shit. Let's go." Due to the fact that I hadn't been there long enough to collect anything, I didn't have anything to bring with me. I signaled this by standing up out of the bed and just staring at the guard until she figured it out. Then she said, "Put out your wrists."

I did as I was told, lifting my wrists so that they could be cuffed, and then she wrapped a hand around my arm. "Thank you, Schmidt," I said as I was led off. "Extend my thanks to Borya as well, please. I'll be in touch."

"See ya," Schmidt said. "You know I like my chocolate bars! I'd love it if my commissary could support my addiction."

I smiled back over my shoulder at him. Little did he know I planned on making sure everyone's accounts were well supplied for the foreseeable future. They'd done me a great service and I was not the kind of man who didn't pay back debts.

My mind was already going a mile a minute as I was led out about all of the things that needed to be taken care of. Since Borya was likely the one picking me up, I could have him fill me in on everything that was going on with Dacha while I was away. I'd have to reach out to Alexei as well.

And I would, of course, have to figure out things with Chloe somehow. If it *wasn't* her that got me locked up, then I needed to figure out who did.

The last thing I was going to need to do before skipping town was kill Vincent Costello. I'd have to think about who Katya was going to be in my life if she wasn't going to be my wife as I had always planned, but I couldn't just let Vincent off for his crimes. Those pieces of it would need to be figured out, but I could think about that once Vincent was dead.

No use in planning around something that hadn't happened yet.

The guard led me into a room where the clothes I was arrested in were folded up and waiting for me. I'd been intentional about leaving my phone and wallet with Brusch, so there were no personal items to be returned to me apart from the cufflinks I had on the wrists of my suit, which had been placed in a small plastic bag that appeared as though it had been hot sealed shut.

"Get changed and leave the jumpsuit on the table and the sandals on the floor. You can take the bag with you, but do not open it until you're out the front doors," the guard explained. "Do you have any questions?"

I shook my head. "No. I'm good."

With a roll of her eyes, she stepped back towards the door and said, "Knock twice when you're ready to go," then she walked out, shutting the door behind her.

Exactly as she'd told me, I got dressed, more than happy to leave my regulation prison gear behind, and then grabbed the bag with my cufflinks and made my way towards the door. I knocked twice and the door opened up. Rather than cuffing me again, she motioned me to the right, to a door that, once we were standing at it, buzzed so that it could be opened. She pulled the door, but didn't walk though, and instead stood aside so I could walk through.

"Enjoy your freedom."

I didn't bother to respond because I knew she didn't mean it. I walked through the door out into the front entryway of the prison. There was a scattered group of people who were all likely waiting for their loved ones to be released, but I didn't see Brusch anywhere.

"Maks."

I turned my head to the left and saw Chloe standing amongst the empty seats for those waiting. She offered me a small smile, but didn't approach me, more likely than not because the terms we'd ended on when she visited weren't good. I'd done a lot of thinking about her though, especially since Borya had said what he said to me, and I was actually really happy to see her.

"Hey," I said, slowly walking towards her. I looked her up and down, loving the sight of her in a simple jeans and t-shirt ensemble, then I said, "Can I hug you?"

The smile on her face grew a little and she nodded. "Okay."

I went for something more than friendly and slid my arms down her sides and eventually around her back. As I dragged her into my hold, her arms came up to loop around my neck, and I was delighted to feel her set her head on my shoulder and let it rest there. For a long moment, we just stayed that way. I could feel her heart pounding as fast as my own, and it almost made me laugh how I'd gotten to this point. I adored Katya, but she never gave me *this* kind of feeling.

"I know you're probably not in a rush to get back to reality," Chloe muttered. "Wanna go get some food that I'm sure is way better than anything you've had in here?"

I nodded heavily. "You have no idea how badly I want to do that."

"I'm parked outside. Let's go."

Of course, part of me wanted to ask why it was Chloe here picking me up and not Brusch. Had the two of them been in contact? Did Chloe pull rank somehow? Was Alexei Lachinov involved, and did he know that Chloe was actually a detective?

Rather than firing off into asking all sorts of questions, I waited and just enjoyed breathing fresh air and having control over my own life and schedule once again. Riding in Chloe's car, temporarily not thinking about the slew of circumstances that existed between and around us was too precious for me to cut short just yet. I wanted to enjoy it just a little bit longer, especially because I had a feeling that once we did come back down to earth, things were going to be ruined again.

"There's this greasy burger place near here," Chloe said. "It's like a two hour drive back to the city, but I'm guessing you want to eat first."

"I'd love to eat first," I confirmed. "Greasy burgers sound great. It'll be nice to actually be able to discern the meat I'm consuming."

She wrinkled up her nose. "I can only imagine. I'm..." She quickly glanced at me and then back at the road ahead of her. "I'm sorry. I know that this has not been an enjoyable experience." At a stop light, she gave me a longer look. "I swear that I didn't--"

I held up my hand to stop her. "Let's not just yet. I know that we'll have to talk about it, but it's like you said; I'm not ready to get back to reality yet. I just want to enjoy this... you."

Her cheeks tinted a little and she nodded. "Yeah. Okay."

By my best approximations, I'd been locked up for about three weeks including the undefined amount of time that I was in isolation. That was nearly a third of the time that I'd been in the United States in general. Even though it was a short period of time by comparison to people like Borya who would never see the light of day again, for me, it was a long time.

The burger place that Chloe took me to would have been disgusting by my standards three weeks ago, but after the horrendous food inside the prison, the juicy, greasy burger and the obviously cheap cheese tasted incredible. Not only that, but the place had fresh cut, double fried french fries that were crisp and salted to perfection. I was even enjoying a soda, and I hated soda, but it was a nice, chilly cola that bubbled down my throat and I actually found myself letting out a cliche "Ahhhh," as I drank.

Chloe giggled. "The food in there was that awful, huh?"

"I don't really think that 'food' is a word one could use to describe that drivel," I explained. "Some of them eat it like it's gourmet, too."

"Well, when it's all you have access to," she replied.

I frowned. "I feel bad. The ones who helped me in there, I'm going to make sure to stock their commissaries so they can get some things that are at least marginally better tasting. Speaking of which, can I use your phone for a moment? I need to contact Brusch."

"Sure." To my surprise, Chloe quickly pulled out her phone and just handed it over to me.

I honestly expected her to be a little more reserved with me about it, but it was clear she trusted me, and my kinder demeanor with her has brought something nicer out in her as well. It seemed to be that this was our rapport. Whatever energy one of us put out, the other one wanted to match. It was almost like all we needed to do to be a successful couple was just meet one another honestly, and put in our best.

Who knew?

"Hello?" Brusch answered my phone with confusion.

"Brusch."

He let out a quiet gasp. "Boss! Are you out?"

"I am. Were you unaware?" I asked.

"Alexei told me he was working on it, but I didn't realize he'd already gotten you out. Are you with Chloe?" he asked.

"Yes. She picked me up when I was released about an hour ago. We should be back into the city in a few hours. I'll contact you once I'm there. Do you think you can start working on a meeting between myself and Alexei for tomorrow?"

"Sure boss. Just... be careful."

I looked across at Chloe, who was watching me with almost painful innocence. "I'll be fine."

After we finished eating, Chloe and I began the long trek back to the city. We maintained light conversation about my time behind bars until I started to feel tired, then Chloe stopped speaking, and I realized she was doing so in order for me to sleep if I wanted--an opportunity that I ended up taking. It wasn't my bed back home that I was excited to melt into tonight, but it was a hell of a lot better than a flat, uncomfortable prison bunk bed, and knowing that Chloe was nearby was comforting.

I woke up to the feeling of the car coming to a stop and was shocked to see that we were parking in the Dacha lot.

"I slept the whole time?" I said.

She smiled and nodded. "Yeah. You must have needed it."

"I didn't realize it."

After stepping out of the car, I stretched my arms high above my head and looked up at the club. After stepping into my own a little bit while I was locked up, it started to feel like a new opportunity rather than something that was bogging me down and stressing me out. I couldn't wait to see what I could potentially work out with the Lachinovs to bring the Petrov group new success.

When I looked back at the car, Chloe was still just sitting inside, staring off into space. I opened the door and peeked my head in. "Not ready to go back to reality?"

"The other shoe always drops," she said without even looking at me. "We get like this and it feels so nice, but inevitably something comes along that just..." She sighed. "I wish it could just be like this. I wish it wasn't so... complicated."

There was something odd about her that I couldn't quite put my finger on.

She'd always been an introspective kind of person, but right now she seemed like she was teetering right on the edge of something more cosmic. She never seemed this... serious before.

"Come on," I told her. "Let's go have that talk."

She took another long, deep breath and then turned off the car. Neither of us said anything as we approached the back door of the club, where the door was immediately opened as we approached and Brusch stepped out.

"Boss, welcome back," he said. "I'm working continuously on getting your charges dropped altogether."

I looked over at Chloe. "My charges haven't been dropped?"

"No. Only your bail has been posted for now, but like he said, the powers that be are working to get your charges dropped," she explained.

I furrowed my brow. "Are... Are you working with Alexei Lachinov?"

She shifted her gaze back and forth and then finally said, "We should talk."

"Right." I looked at Brusch and said, "We're going upstairs. Ensure that no one bothers us. Continue to work on the charges and the meeting with Alexei. We'll connect in the morning about everything else."

"Yes boss."

We walked past him and into the club, then boarded the elevator to ride up to my penthouse. It was unlocked and waiting for me to come back to it, perfectly clean, and thankfully with food and water already set up on the coffee table in the living room. I sat Chloe down and apologized for not getting right into the conversation right away, but a shower and change of clothes was necessary. She seemed to understand and started to nibble on the food that had been laid out while I washed myself up.

Thankfully, when I was showered and in a suit, I felt like a new man. I never wanted to go to prison again, but I was glad for the experience to help me determine how to best run my empire. It would only resort to violence when absolutely necessary, and when it was necessary, I didn't want to be near it with a ten foot pole.

"You look better," Chloe said with a smile when I walked into the room.

"Thank you," I replied. "I feel better."

I walked into the living room and struggled to decide how close I could sit to Chloe, but eventually I chose to just sit next to her. It turned out to be a good choice because when I sat, she immediately slid over and set her head on my shoulder. "I'm glad you're okay."

"This is a different tune from when you stormed out before," I told her.

She let a couple of her fingers dance across the palm of my hand. "A lot has changed since then."

"Like what?"

She sat up and looked me right in the eyes. "Maksim, I did not tell Cox anything about you or anything you told me. I had nothing to do with your arrest. I didn't know he was going to do that."

"I know," I told her. "I jumped to a conclusion, but a... friend behind bars helped me realize that I was wrong. I'm sorry."

"I'm sorry, still," she said. "Cox may have used me in a way I didn't know, or maybe there was a plan all along. He and my entire department know about you and me. I have no idea how, but clearly, Cox was keeping a better eye on me than I realized."

"I'm not sure who was responsible, but I intend to find out," I told her.

"To answer your question from before, in a roundabout way, I am working with Alexei Lachinov. We..." She hesitated. "We have a friend in common. I asked them for help and they asked me for help."

"You're doing things the not-so-legal way?" I asked.

She frowned. "There'a a judge that Alexei has some pull over. It was that judge who signed off on your bail. I'm going to work on proving that Cox's methods were unsavory in order to get the charges dropped."

"How do you feel about that?" I asked. "It has to interfere with your sense of justice."

She was quiet for an intense moment after that before she finally said, "I've found that my sense of justice has changed recently. Mostly..." She looked deep into my eyes, her beautiful blue ones sparkling with an emotion I hadn't seen from her yet. "Mostly I just want you to be safe."

"Honestly..." I said before sliding both my hands onto either side of Chloe's face and pulling her into a kiss. What was I ever going to do with someone who made me feel the way she did? Someone who made me feel so powerful and so powerless at the same time.

Chloe didn't fight me on the kiss, but rather let her hands find my sides and hung on. I pushed my tongue out and she welcomed it in, allowing it to twist along her own. I didn't realize how much I missed having Chloe in my arms until she was back there again.

She pulled back from me, her face splashed red and asked, "When I get your charges dropped, how quickly can you get out of here and get back to Russia? Cox won't stop until he gets you."

"I have a private plane waiting," I told her. "As soon as the charges are dropped and I deal with Vincent, I'll go."

"Maksim..." she whined.

"No," I told her. "I swear, it's not about Katya, but I still can't leave NYC until Vincent Costello is dead."

CHAPTER TEN: CHLOE

It felt like I was experiencing deja vu. It felt impossible that Maksim and I could keep going around and around about the exact same topic so many times. He claimed that it wasn't about Katya, and no one was expecting him to get any sort of vengeance for Vladimir and Sascha, so I didn't understand why he couldn't just see reason and let this go. When I went and sat down with Katya and Vincent, they both bent over backwards, without even a second thought, in order to get Maksim out of prison. Maks' bond ended up being five digits, and Vincent dropped that amount without blinking and not expecting anything in return.

These people actually cared about him, how could he want to hurt them so badly?

"I don't get it," I said. "Really, I don't."

"I don't want to have this argument again," Maksim said.

"Neither do I," I retorted. "So let's not argue. Let's just talk about it. Help me understand. There are so many reasons for you *not* to follow through with this. It would be so easy for you to just let it go and live a much happier life, not letting this bog you down. I just want to understand what it is that has latched you onto this so severely. I mean, didn't Vladimir's actions lead to the death of Vincent's father as well?"

"They did, but that was different," Maksim said. "Vincent's father had it out for him from the beginning. When Sascha killed Nick, it was because he was threatening Katya. He had no choice."

"But Vincent kidnapped Katya because Vladimir stole from the Costellos," I said.

I was very well versed in the story. It was all my unit focused on for *months*. The bloody battle between mafia and bratva. Shootings at a townhome in an affluent neighborhood, an entire mansion exploding, leveling the very ground it stood on. People lived in fear for weeks thinking the next battle would be too close to home. We were relieved when the showdown moved from NYC to St. Petersburg and effectively out of our jurisdiction.

Cox was unhappy to lose the notoriety that would have come with handling the issue on our soil, but the rest of us were happy that no more innocent people had to die.

"It's true," Maks said. "If Vladimir hadn't tried to pull the double sale on the Costellos and the Bonettis, Katya may not have been kidnapped. And if Vladimir hadn't left her there for as long as he did, then maybe Katya wouldn't have become fooled that--"

"She's not fooled," I cut him off. "I've spoken to Katya myself. I've seen her living her own life. She does her own job. She has her own contacts. Katya isn't a pushover who'll just let some man trick her. She is not that kind of woman, even if that means challenging Vincent Costello. Katya is very aware of who he is and she loves him legitimately." I saw the sting of pain on Maksim's face when I said it and it broke my heart. "You say this isn't about her, but it is, isn't it? You're in love with her. You just can't let her go. You can't accept defeat."

Maksim stood up suddenly and I thought he was about to flip. I could see that famous temper of his bubbling near the surface, and I was glad that I had my gun on me, just in case. I didn't want to hurt Maksim, not just because he was the father of my child, but because he *did* mean something to me, but I couldn't be a pushover with him anymore. He either needed to meet me on equal footing or I would come up to where he was.

Meaning I'd get just as nasty as he was getting, and feel just as little remorse.

But he didn't flip. He stood looming over me for a second before taking a deep breath and calming himself down. I was shocked, but it seemed like he was intentionally wrangling in his temper for me, and I didn't know what to say or do with that.

"I wasn't defeated," he said calmly, sitting down on the couch. "My relationship with Katya was borne out of a slurry of things, none of which were healthy. She was a person in my life that I guess you could say I was too attached to, much like I was attached to the rest of her family, but she was beautiful and smart, and she cared about me. I didn't get treatment like that from many people." Then he snickered. "Plus, I'd developed an affinity for brunettes because of *someone*, but I guess we don't have to talk about that."

A tiny smile came to my face. "No idea whose fault that was."

"But I need you to understand this. If you understand nothing else about me, it's that I'm a man who will fight endlessly for what he believes in."

"You've always been like that," I said.

"Maybe Katya's life went winding down an unexpected road because of the decisions her father made, but at the end of the day, I believe that Katya wanted to live a happy life in St. Petersburg. I saw her strive *endlessly* to be included in her father's ranks. Some of his greatest successes came from her efforts, but he refused to acknowledge her. When she and her brother Sascha and I talked about the future of the Petrov empire, it was always with the understanding that, when Sascha took over, Katya would get the rank she was due. She's not meant to be serving under someone, she's meant to be leading. I'm helming a throne that's half hers. And maybe she's not 'tricked' into being in love with Vincent, but I do think he's managed to convince her that she's happy where she is when she could have so much more. He's stifling her and holding her back."

"So it *is* about her," I replied. "That's why you have to kill him?"

"I have to kill Vincent for the entire Petrov family." He sat back down on the couch and looked directly into my eyes as he continued to explain. "Vladimir was a *terrible* man, but he took care of me when no one else would. Even my own father left me, but Vladimir didn't bat an eye. He spent millions of dollars over the course of our relationship making sure that I was happy and well cared for. He bought my family home so that I wouldn't lose it to foreclosure. He set my mom up in a private care facility and paid for her to be tended to around the clock. Those inroads are *still* what keep my mother living to this day. And Sascha? Sascha wasn't *like* a brother to me, he was my brother. If Vincent hadn't come to Russia, I never would have..."

His head drooped and I put my hand on the side of his face. "What Maks?"

To my extreme shock, when Maks looked back up, he had tears in his eyes. "I was trying to kill Vincent," he whimpered. "I thought if I could just get rid of him, then our lives would go back to what they were supposed to be. He'd convinced Katya to kill Vladimir, he'd turned Sascha against his own family. He's poison and I saw the opportunity to neutralize it."

"But Sascha didn't want you to?"

He had a deeply set frown and was now staring off into space like he was reliving it. "Vincent was in front of me when I pulled the trigger, but somehow the bullet sunk into Sascha's body."

I closed my eyes in anguish for Maksim. It wasn't that Vincent had killed Vladimir *or* Sascha, but rather his presence in the Petrov siblings' lives led them to turn against their father and ultimately ended in both Vladimir and Sascha's demise, and Sascha's at Maksim's own hand.

He'd killed his best friend--his brother.

"Maks," I said quietly. "You don't actually want to kill Vincent. You're in pain. You haven't mourned and you are afraid to blame yourself so you blame him instead. I can't imagine the pain you must--"

"I can't." Maksim pulled back from me and stood up suddenly. "I can't do this."

"Maksim," I called after him, but he was already rushing down the hallway away from me. "Please come back!"

"Just get out!" he yelled. "Leave!"

My stomach twisted up in sadness. I didn't want to leave. Everyone left Maksim. There wasn't a person in his life who'd ever stuck around. Whether by unfortunate circumstances or pure selfishness, everyone that Maksim ever held close to him had been taken from him. Killing Vincent wasn't about revenge, it was about the small possibility that he saw to get at least two of the people back that he'd lost--Katya and Annika Petrova.

What he was failing to realize was that forcing anyone to stay around was never going to result in true happiness.

He was also failing to see that there was at least one--I set my hand to my stomach--soon to be two people that would choose him over anything else. The thought of giving up everything terrified me, but when I imagined getting to be with Maksim and start a family with him there was a *sliver* of me that thought that might just be okay. But not if I had to constantly live in the shadow of the lost loved ones he was chasing.

Not if I had to be concerned he was going to try and kill Vincent and run off to the past at the first possible turn.

But I was thinking too far ahead. This was the first answer I'd been looking for. The first step towards a possible future that I might just be okay with. In a perfect world, where would I end up? With Maksim and our baby, somewhere safe and sound.

So, though Maksim had told me to leave, I wouldn't. There was a throw pillow on the couch, so I repositioned it against one of the arms and laid my head down on it. For the first time ever, I wanted Maksim to know that there was someone in his life who wasn't just going to cut and run. Maybe, once I'd fully earned his trust and he earned mine, we could see past the fog that still seemed to exist between us.

I was unsure of how much time had passed when I came to, but blinking my eyes open, I could see the sun was going down outside the window. My phone was still sitting on the coffee table where I'd left it, and looking at it proved that I had several missed calls from Mitzy.

After the last of these, he'd left a voicemail. "God dammit, Chloe. You're lucky that I was able to call Vincent, who was able to call Katya, who was able to call Alexei, who was able to call Brusch, who was able to tell us that you and Maksim had gone up to his penthouse and hadn't come down yet. I was worried sick about you, you know? I know you were probably looking forward to jumping his bones, but you at least could have let me know that you were safe first. I guess I'll go since I don't *matter enough*." Then the line went dead.

I probably should have called Mitzy after I picked up Maks, but I was so happy to see him and know that he was out and safe for the time being that I didn't think of much else. A quick glance around proved that Maksim wasn't in the immediate area, and I didn't want to bother him if he was getting sleep, so I took my phone over to the deck door and slid it open. I stepped out into the early evening air, taking a deep breath of it before dialing Mitzy's number.

"Oh hey," he said in a deeply sarcastic tone when he answered. "Thank you for climbing off Maksim long enough to let me know you're alive. I really appreciate it."

"Okay," I moaned at him. "Don't be such a brat. I'm sorry. I should have called you. And for your information, nothing happened, except for more arguing and not seeing eye to eye before Maksim stormed off."

"How'd he take the baby news?" Mitzy asked.

I looked over my shoulder to make sure he wasn't there before responding, "Pretty well considering I haven't told him let."

"Chlo!"

"I know. It just hasn't come up in a natural, appropriate way," I replied.

Mitzy snorted. "Uh, yeah. This isn't really a natural, appropriate situation. If you're waiting for it to come up organically over a cup of coffee, let me be the first to tell you it ain't gonna happen."

"I know, I just... I'm trying to deal with this whole Vincent vengeance thing, and I don't want to throw too much at him at once. I'm kind of thinking I need to get him *out* of the US first, and then I can tell him," I explained.

"Like back to Russia?" Mitzy asked. "You know he's just gonna come flying back once he hears you're pregnant."

"Not... unless I'm there," I said.

"There? Are you moving to Russia?"

"I don't really know what I'm doing, but I still have extended family there. I think I could convince my father and sister to go back." I looked over my shoulder again, but still no Maksim. "I don't know, I'm just considering all of my options, and I really think that the safest and healthiest thing for Maksim is to get him back home sooner rather than later. Once I get that done, I can deal with the rest."

"I think waiting is a bad idea, but you know him and yourself better than I do. If that's what you think is the best plan, then I trust you," Mitzy said. "What about Vincent and Katya? Have you told him they know he's here?"

I frowned. "No. I haven't gotten around to mentioning that yet either. I'm not really sure how to explain to him that it was my only choice."

"That what was your only choice?"

My stomach bottomed out and Mitzy huffed in my ear, "Ahh... He overheard you, didn't he?"

"I gotta go. Talk to you later."

"Good luck."

I hung up the phone and then turned around and Maksim was standing in the doorway leading out to the deck. "I didn't realize you'd woken up."

"Just a few minutes ago," I replied. "And Mitzy was being a drama queen about the fact that I didn't update him about where I was and wasn't answering his calls, so I was just telling him to calm down."

"What was your only choice?" Maks asked. "Did you do something bad to get me released?"

"No. Well, I mean aside from working with Alexei."

"But you already told me that," Maksim said. "Did you have to do something with him or something?"

"No, no, no," I said, shaking my head wildly. "Nothing like that, just..." I didn't want to lie to him, but I wasn't ready to piss him off again either. "Just, you know, giving up on my job in general. I had to pick between it and you and..."

"Oh..." He furrowed his brow and then said, "I'm sorry. I didn't mean for you to give anything up for me."

I shook my head. "No, it's more for me. I'm just realizing that maybe that wasn't what I wanted with my life after all."

"Did you quit?"

"Not yet, but with the way I'm being shunned and benched, I might as well," I replied, not having meant for this to bleed into the truth. "Anyway. I don't really want to think about that right now."

"You slept for a long time," Maksim noted.

I nodded. "I've been sleeping pretty poorly lately."

"My couch couldn't have been comfortable."

"It was fine."

"Why didn't you just leave?" he asked. "After I told you to?"

It wasn't an accusation, it was an honest question, like he legitimately didn't understand why I stayed.

"Because I didn't want to just walk out on you," I said honestly. "That's happened to you a lot. I don't want to be part of it."

"But you did walk out before."

"I know. And I've regretted it ever since."

He took a step towards me. "Really?"

I nodded. "Really."

He closed the distance between us and kissed me, wrapping a hand around my back to pull me against him. I was almost afraid to hold him back, terrified that the moment I chose to grip on, he'd slip from me again, but he squeezed around me tighter and soon my impulses acted for me and wrapped him up.

"Why have you been sleeping so poorly?" he asked randomly. "Something seems different." He'd said that to me before and it made me as nervous as it did now. I thought I was going to have to come clean about the baby before I was ready, but Maksim used a finger to loop my hair out of my face and said, "It must be all the stress I'm putting you through."

I grinned. "You *are* pretty stressful."

"I apologize," he said. "Can I make it up to you?" I tilted my head and he got a wicked grin on his face. "I happen to know your favorite way to relieve stress."

CHAPTER ELEVEN: MAKSIM

Something about waking up and seeing that Chloe was still there after I'd so rudely walked away from her and demanded that she leave, filled me with an emotion I didn't think I ever experienced before. It was so rare for me to find that someone was still there after I'd told them to leave me alone, or even if I hadn't told them that. She stayed because she didn't want to walk out on me? Because she regretted when she walked out on me before?

How could I not take that to mean that she felt something real for me and celebrate that a little bit? I didn't know how long it would last or even if there was a 'last' for us, but I wanted to enjoy Chloe as much as I could, while I could.

She did seem stressed, even though she still hadn't shared why, but I didn't have the right to ask her that right now. I knew I was a source of stress in her life, and if she was willing to stick around for me, then I could give her the space she needed to present me with everything on her own time.

For now, I'd do what I could to relieve her stress.

Taking her back to my bedroom, I sat her down on the edge of my bed for long enough for me to light some candles and dim the lights, then I took her hand and stood her up again.

"Would a massage help?" I asked, turning Chloe around so her back was to me.

She let her head fall back on my shoulder. "That sounds wonderful."

I ran my hands around her stomach and down until I was able to crawl my hands under the base of her shirt. She shivered a little under my touch, but in a good way, like the anticipation was almost too much. I moved slowly, letting my fingers caress her skin slowly upwards until I was able to squeeze my hands over the fabric of her bra and work her breasts over. Her hands came up to grip onto my arms, encouraging me to do more.

And I would, because she deserved it.

After flipping the cups of her bra back, I gave her nipples some direct attention, pinching them between two fingers each and pressing my lips against the cook of her neck. She let out quiet moans of pleasure and put her weight on me.

"That feels good," she whimpered.

"Good," I replied before nibbling her ear lobe.

Finally, I grabbed the base of her shirt and pulled it up over her head, then I popped the front clasp of her bra and let it fall to the ground. After that, I returned one hand to her breast to massage it while I used the other to undo the button of her pants and push them down. I kept my hand latched to her chest as long as I was able to until I had no choice but to let go to continue removing her pants. She didn't seem to mind, however, as I bent down to slowly roll her jeans off while sprinkling kisses all along her thighs and down her shins. I was delighted to see that she was wearing a cheeky set of magenta panties that matched her bra.

Clearly she'd come prepared for this possibility.

I didn't say anything, though. My arrogance had melted away behind gratitude and I only wanted Chloe to feel the absolute height of pleasure. Nothing else would do for me this time around.

As sexy as the panties were, I pulled them down as well, of course, taking a few moments to stop and take small bites out of her ass. She had absolutely perfect curves that made it difficult not to spend hours just appreciating them all individually. But Chloe was a package best enjoyed whole, so once she was totally bare, I stood back up and guided her down onto the bed on her stomach.

"No blindfold?" she asked.

A huge smile came to my face. I honestly wasn't planning on going for sensory deprivation given that was *my* kink and this was about her, but if she was asking for it, then perhaps all I'd done was help her discover something about herself instead. She felt so compatible with me in so many different ways that it was difficult to believe sometimes.

"Pardon me," I told her. "Let me grab it."

She continued to lay flat while I walked over to my closet and fished out a blindfold for her to wear. I'd recently purchased a new velvet one to ensure her comfort when she was bound for extended periods of time. It was also imbued with a very faint lavender smell, designed to promote relaxation. Sensory deprivation wasn't just about depriving the senses, it was about heightening them and changing their construct, and subtle scents could do just that.

I returned to Chloe and crouched over her to loop the blindfold around her face and secure it behind her head. I was intentional in making sure that my already stiffening cock was rubbing against her below, just to give her a preview. It was there, and it would be back, though without clothes when it returned, and ready for much more than a gentle feel.

Chloe had honestly earned herself a massage, however, so I resisted the urge to dive right in and pulled back from her. Along with the lightly scented blindfold, I also had some oils with a subtle scent of lemon which is known for arousing the senses. After heating it up slightly over one of the candles, I squeezed drips of it down over Chloe's back, legs, and ass. She jumped a little as the droplets hit her skin, but then hummed with satisfaction.

Now, I was no licensed masseur, but I knew my way around a good massage. I started by setting my fingers directly in the oils on Chloe's back and applied pressure before pushing forwards towards the edge of her torso. I kneaded the oils into her skin, making the natural tan hue shine, and slowly worked my way up and down her back. Where applicable, I would lean in and drop a kiss or a nibble, just to increase the anticipation of things to come, but never too many all at once. I wanted those spots to linger and wonder when they'd be visited again.

When I repositioned myself behind Chloe so I could massage her legs, I took a couple of minutes to remove my suit jacket, white button up, and undershirt until my torso was bare. I undid my heavy, expensive watch and dropped it on the table right near Chloe's face, once again causing her to jump a little, but then she relaxed.

"Are you okay?" I asked.

She nodded against the pillows. "Wonderful."

I landed a kiss on one of the plump cheeks of her backside and then gave it a quick, sharp bite. "Glad to hear it."

She gasped out a moan, so I did it again, getting a longer moan that time, but had to stop before I got myself too excited. I continued to slick the oil around as I moved the massage down to Chloe's ass and thighs. I made circles across her skin, massaging in a pattern designed to both loosen any knots, and skate my fingers close to her center to increase arousal. Each time my fingers slid just past her pussy, she sucked in air, which she let out as I moved away.

I dragged my thumbs in overlapping patterns down her thighs and over her shins, first her left leg, then the right. With each movement, I could feel her loosening underneath me, relaxing more and more.

"Turn over, beautiful," I requested.

Chloe did just that, rolling over to her back and giving me an enticing view of her perfect breasts, curvaceous hips, and of course that wet, pink center, beckoning me forward. The crotch of my pants tightened at the sight, and I desperately wanted to strip down and help myself. I opted for a compromise in pulling the rest of my clothes off, but that was more than enough to keep my hard length from straining anymore than it already was. I still had much more pleasuring of Chloe to do before I'd allow myself any relief.

After painting her body with even more of the oils, I set to massaging her front, of course, starting with her pert breasts. Her nipples were already hard from the attention they received earlier, so try though I did try to resist the urge, I eventually ended up ducking my head down to suck one while I massaged the other. Chloe's jaw parted and she let out breathy monas. Out of the corner of my eye, I could see her toes curling and I grinned.

She loved having her breasts played with as much as I loved playing with them.

Just as it seemed like she was reaching an apex of pleasure, I left her breasts alone and started to work my hands over the rest of her chest and down her arms. She legitimately did feel very tense and it made me sad to think that I played a part in that. I lost myself in the massage a little then, pinching my hands across her shoulders to try and work those knots out, and pushing my thumbs up her neck. She let out soft hums that let me know she needed this, so I took all the time that was necessary, and before I left this part of her behind, I set a kiss on her lips. She eagerly lifted to me, wanting more than just that, but I restrained myself and broke it.

"Patience," I told her. "There's much more in store."

Next was hitting the lower-half of the front side of her body. Kneads to her thighs and a long massage of her feet seemed to bring her nearly to the brink of falling asleep. I kept her at my attention, though, and climbed up onto the bed on my knees. I wrapped around her thighs and pulled her towards me until her legs were draped on either side of my body. She took in a breath of anticipation, but I could admit I wanted to tease her *just a little*.

With the head of my hard dick poking at her center, I leaned forward to start massaging her hips, and eventually over her stomach. When my hands slid up onto her belly, she took a rapid breath in and held it, releasing it only when I moved away.

"Did that hurt?" I asked.

She shook her head. "No. I'm sorry."

That was strange, but she relaxed moments later, so I figured it was maybe the combination of smells in the room starting to throw her senses out of whack. I helped calm her more by massaging up over her breasts again, giving them both a healthy wring, before finally trailing my hands down the center of her stomach and between her legs.

"Maks," she whined as my hand passed very quickly over her sensitive center.

"Yes?" I said.

She threaded her own hands between her legs and actually parted her lips for me. "Please. I need you."

I let out a low growl of frustration. There was more I had planned before getting to this point, but when such a perfect woman *begs* for you, what power did I have to say no?

"You're going to be the death of me one day," I told her.

She was a sight to behold in front of me. Holding herself open and begging me forward, her eyes covered by the blindfold, her skin glistening from the oils, her face splashed red. It was a the same time overly erotic and pristine in its beauty, like a painting. Thankfully, she wasn't a painting though, I could take my fill of this artwork.

And that was just what I planned to do.

It didn't take much repositioning with my hand for me to pop myself right into Chloe's hole. She was slightly elevated from the way she was sitting in my lap, and it allowed me to slide into her at an optimal angle. She pulled her hands back, tossing them behind her to grip the pillows as I pushed further and further in.

A breathy, "Yes," slipped out of her mouth, and I couldn't help but reach a hand down and hook my thumb into her parted lips. Immediately, she started to swirl her tongue around it, and her walls clenched tighter around me below.

It shouldn't continuously surprise me that someone like Chloe liked it rough, but it always caught me a little each time I was reminded.

As if this was merely an extension of the massage, I hung onto her hip with my free hand and started to work in and out of her in long, dragged out strokes. It was like I was trying to smooth the stress out of even her insides. She arched her back and moaned through the feeling of me working her inside and out.

"Maks," she whined. "It feels good."

"I'm happy, beautiful," I replied. "I want you to feel even better. What should I do?"

Even though her eyes were covered, she tilted her head up and said, "I want to ride you."

"As you wish."

As hard as it was, I pulled out of Chloe and climbed off the bed. I let her sit untouched for a few seconds to build anticipation, then I reached down and grabbed one of her hands. I yanked her up off of the bed and pulled her backwards towards a chair I had sitting in one corner.

I sat in the chair and then Chloe moved on impulse, sitting in my lap. She folded her legs into the space between my legs and the chair, and then I guided myself back into her. She set her arms on my shoulders and started to raise and lower herself on top of me. In this new position, I was able to continuously press against her best spot inside. Her moans got louder and her movements more hastened until she was bouncing up and down, like I was an inflatable house. I was far from complaining, though, as each time I hit her spot, she squeezed down on me tighter, threatening to push me over the edge.

"I'm coming, Maks," she whimpered at me. "It feels so good."

I wrapped my hands around her back and pulled her closer to me. "Then come," I told her, then to punctuate the moment, I closed my mouth around one of her breasts.

"Yes!" she yelped, picking up the pace until she finally settled against me and then I could feel her spasming. She shuddered and spasmed before finally coming to rest.

Right before I came.

I clenched my jaw and fought hard not to complain, but Chloe clearly had a plan in mind already. She lifted off of me and then wrapped her hands around my dick and started to stroke it. She was pressing the head against her soft skin and stroking it strongly and firmly.

"Don't stop, Chloe," I told her.

She continued to fist me until I started twitching in her hand. She aimed right at her breasts and pumped me faster and faster until I grunted and exploded, painting her chest in ribbons of white. I ripped the blind fold off of her so I could see her face, then I clawed her head down to me and slammed my lips against hers. We let our mutual moans of satisfaction fill our mouths before finally exhausting.

Chloe let her head fall on my shoulder and I rubbed her back gently. "Chloe..."

"Yeah?" she replied quietly in my ear.

"Thank you for not leaving," I said.

She lifted and looked down at me with a small smile. "I'll be here as long as you let me stay."

Her lips fell to mine again and I wondered how true that statement was. What if I told her I wanted her to stay forever, would she?

Somehow I doubted it, but I chose not to ask, mainly because I was terrified to hear the truth. With our history and the way Chloe made me feel, I really felt like I could see a future with her, but what did that mean for me, and more importantly, if I killed Vincnet, what did that mean for Katya?

CHAPTER TWELVE: CHLOE

I climbed out of bed and prepared to go to the bathroom to clean myself up, but Maksim grabbed my hand and kept me from leaving. He was still sitting naked in the chair, totally spent, and I giggled at him.

"Do you want me to just keep this mess on my chest all night?" I asked.

He shook his head. "No. I just don't think it's fair that you're the only one who gets to get cleaned up."

I furrowed my brow. "Huh?"

Maksim stood up out of the chair and lifted me off the floor, throwing me over his shoulder like a sack of potatoes. I laughed as he did so, pretending to fight but not hating the handling in general, and he walked us into his massive, attached bathroom. Inside, he had a huge sunken Roman bath, big enough for eight people, but fortunately, it was just the two of us. Maksim set me down on the countertop next to the sink, then he leaned over and started to run the bathtub.

"That's going to take a few minutes to fill, so..." Maks said, then he walked over to the tile shower and turned on the head, "Let's wash off before we get in."

I hopped off the counter and walked over to the shower, drifting inside and letting the warm water splash down over me. Maksim climbed in behind me and wrapped his arms around me, kissing me on the shoulder, neck and back. The sensory deprived massage-turned-sex had me feeling like melted butter, and the second Maksim's arms wrapped around me, I fell back into him. I turned my head to take a kiss that he willingly gave and I honestly felt like I could stay that way forever and be perfectly happy.

At one point, Maksim's hands drifted down to my stomach and rested there, and I started to get illogically paranoid that he knew about the baby. There was no way for him to know, so it was just coincidence, but it was likely the fact that I felt like I needed to tell him and was starting to feel guilty about the fact that I hadn't yet.

There were a couple of soap dispensers mounted to the wall in the shower and Maks and I took turns over the course of the next few minutes loading some into our hands and helping wash one another off. Maks was very intentional about making sure he got each bit of his own left behind essence off of me, and what was meant to be a cleaning may have turned into another quick hand job by me--but Maksim didn't seem to have an issue with it.

Finally, after about ten minutes, we'd cleaned ourselves pretty thoroughly and the bathtub was nearly filled to the brim and ready to be stepped into. We climbed out of the shower and settled ourselves down into the bathtub. Maksim looked even sexier with his blond hair dripping wet, and pushed back over his head. He sat against one edge of the tub, and parted his legs so that I could sit between them. I made myself comfortable, leaning back against his chest, and then Maksim turned on the jets before wrapping his arms under mine and cuddling me even tighter against him.

It was sinful how satisfied I was.

"Do you think your sister would accept an apology from me?" Maks asked suddenly.

I was flicking my fingers through the bubbling water and trying to keep myself from falling asleep. "Um. I'm not sure. Are you thinking about apologizing?"

"I know she deserves one," he responded. "I feel bad about what I did. I didn't mean to terrify her the way I did, and knowing what you two went through with your mom, that was a low blow. When I first got to New York I was in a really bad place. That's not an excuse but..." He squeezed me tighter. "I hate that I did that."

"Well, I couldn't say for sure that she would *accept* your apology, but I bet she'd be willing to listen," I told him. "I think for all of us, if the man that had killed my mother had simply shown some remorse or apologized, it wouldn't have made it totally okay, but it would have helped soften the blow."

"I'm sorry to you as well," Maks said. "You didn't deserve for me to treat you that way. I didn't see an alternative, and in all honesty I still don't know what I could have done, but I should have tried to figure it out, if for nothing else, than to protect you from further harm."

I shook my head. "Everything that's happened up to this point is a result of the fact that you were still trying to be bratva, and I was still trying to be NYPD, and we were both prioritizing that over one another. I think, if we'd chosen each other instead, things would have happened differently."

I wasn't sure how much I bought into what I was saying. A lot of my decision making came from being a 'cop' instead of being Chloe. As soon as I started making decisions as myself, I found that I wanted Maksim to be a more prominent presence in my life, but I felt stupid for forgiving him and developing feelings after all he'd done. But when I saw the man that he was when he stripped everything away, when he wasn't trying to be a 'Petrov' or 'Vladimir's Successor,' then he was a much different person--someone I was okay with breaking the rules for. Maybe if I'd realized all of that sooner, things might have transpired differently, but I often felt like Maks and I were on a train off the rails, that was going to go wherever it was going to go regardless of what either of us wanted.

Ultimately, I wasn't sure if wanting it was enough to twist fate.

"I suppose you're right," Maksim replied. "If I'd decided that you were more important than the goals I came here with, it certainly would have changed my course of action."

What was he saying? That I *was* more important than them now, or that I *still* wasn't more important?

"I didn't anticipate any of this," I told him. "Meeting you again, but finding that you were on the other side of a war I've been fighting for a long time. I knew that I shouldn't be developing feelings for you, but the more time we spent together, I couldn't deny it. I couldn't keep myself from..." I swallowed hard, not knowing if I was ready to say the words. Even if I felt like they were true at this point, there were still too many unknowns and it was terrifying just to think about. "I wanted to see you more and more, and my job started to mean less and less to me. Maybe I'm being stupid, but I found myself wondering if there was a way to make it real. Not just something forced, or a layover until you could..." My stomach knotted up. "Until you could go and be with the woman you really wanted."

I pulled my knees up in the water and dropped my head to sit on top of them. My face was burning, partly from embarrassment and partly from sadness. It was probably stupid of me to be admitting so much, but I'd kind of reached this point where it felt like if I didn't lay everything out on the table, everything would be misunderstood and confused again. If nothing else, I wanted Maksim to know my honest feelings, even if I was throwing myself on my sword to express them.

"Chloe." Maksim's voice resonated in my ear and reverberated down my spine.

Chills rose to my skin and I felt like an idiot for being so moved by something so simple. He'd only said my name, but the way it almost sang out like a hymn sunk well past my skin and wrapped around my very bones.

How dangerous it was that his voice alone had so much control over me.

Maksim's arms curled tighter around my torso, and I felt his nose poking at the back of my neck. "Look at me."

"No," I muffled into my lap.

"Chloe look at me."

My throat was tightening with emotions from my unexpected confession, but I was determined not to cry. I lifted my head and twisted it so that I could look at Maksim, but apparently that wasn't enough for him. He used the lighter gravity in the pool to fully twist my body around until I was facing him. He looked so handsome with the droplets of water dripping down his chiseled upper body, marred in places with the scars and scrapes that told a story of his past, but only managed to heighten his beauty.

"I don't have feelings for Katya," he said. "I thought that I did. I'd never really allowed myself to feel much of anything for anyone growing up. Katya was there. She was an option, she was the easy choice. I thought that she was special, and she is, but not in that way. When I came here, and I reconnected with you, I realized that I've only ever been trying to fill the void you left behind when you moved away. Even as a little boy, you were the one that my heart wanted."

"Really?" I asked.

He nodded with a warm, inviting smile on his face. "Really. By comparison to you, Katya is no contest."

Whether or not those words were true, just hearing them sent butterflies fluttering through my stomach. He had an earnest look on his face, and there was an honest confidence in his voice. It made me believe that might really be true.

I set my hands on either side of his face and pulled him into a kiss, almost desperate in that moment to just feel him and not think about anything else.

Thankfully, the same seemed to be true for Maksim, who didn't break the kiss, but rather let his hands begin to wander under the water. He pulled me up onto his lap and started to kiss his way down my neck, and I was fine with forgetting everything else for the time being. If Maksim just wanted to continue making love all night, that'd be perfectly fine with me.

Only after we were too tired to move much anymore, and our skin was starting to get pruny from the water, did we finally move from the bathtub back to the bed. I was so tired that, as soon as Maksim wrapped an arm around my back and laid my head against his shoulder, I felt like I might immediately pass out.

But Maksim lifted my hand with his other one and started to play with my fingers. "You remember when we used to play house as kids?"

I smiled a little into the darkness of the bedroom. "Vividly."

"There was one time we were playing like we got married. We did it because my mom said that--"

"In order for us to have a baby we had to be a mommy and daddy, and a mommy and daddy are married," I finished. "Yeah, I remember that." It made me think of my baby. This mommy and daddy were *not* married. "My mom cut a hole in the top of that pillow case and your dad put that tie on you that was *way* too big." I remembered the image of little Maksim in his regular, cartoon character t-shirt and shorts, but wearing a tie that went from his neck down to his knees. "You were so cute."

"We got to that one part where normally the bride and groom would kiss, but then all of the adults stopped us because we weren't supposed to kiss," he explained. "I never told you this, but I cried the whole way home."

"What?" I said laughing. "Why?"

"Because I wanted to kiss you!" he huffed, then started to laugh. "I was whining to my parents the entire walk home that I wanted to kiss you. My dad told me to wait until I was older. Maybe I had divine sight or something, I told him that I didn't think I'd get to when we were older."

I frowned at the last part and the sadness in Maksim's voice. I still remembered that awful day that my parents told us we were moving to the United States. My dad had a chance to open up a bodega that was apparently going to make us filthy rich. It was so obvious on my mom's face that she didn't want to leave Russia, and it broke my heart that I had to leave Maks behind. Our parents brought us together for one last playdate, but we barely said two words to each other. We were both too sad to do anything.

"I used to get bullied because I talked about you so much," I admitted. "I kept telling everyone about my friend Maksim and how amazing he was and everyone assumed you were just an imaginary friend. It didn't help when Chandler tried to help me convince people. I didn't really make many friends because no one really felt good enough." I snickered. "I guess I didn't entirely realize it, but I've missed you this whole time."

Maks tilted my head so that I was looking at him, then he very gently skated his lips across mine. "I missed you too. The whole time."

My heart was swelling more and more with each passing minute. Could I actually spend my life with this person? Could we be together and raise our child? When I thought about being like this, it was a no brainer, but what about when the outside world started to seep in. That wasn't a challenge we'd successfully stood up to yet.

"Maks," I asked quietly. "Would you do something for me?"

"I'd do anything for you," he replied genuinely.

I sat up a little bit so that I was looking down at him. "Will you get on a plane tomorrow and go back to Russia?"

He slowly sat up too, looking almost hurt. "What about us?"

"They aren't mutually exclusive," I said. "I would need to sort things out with my job, and figure out how to convince my sister and my dad, but... maybe I could come there too? We could pick up from here back in St. Petersburg without any of the background noise here to weigh us down."

"That sounds wonderful, Chloe, but you know I'm not finished here," he explained gently. "I have--"

"Don't," I said. "Don't say you have to kill Vincent."

"I told you it's not about Katya. It's about the pain he's caused the family that's done so much for me. I can't just let him slide for his crimes. I have to kill him no matter what."

I climbed out of bed, pulling some of the sheets with me to keep them wrapped around my body. "No. You can't!"

"I assure you, I'm capable of it," he responded.

But I shook my head violently. "No, you can't kill him. You're not allowed to."

"Not allowed to?" he said. "Why not?"

I wasn't thinking it through and before I could stop myself I just barked out. "Because he's the one who got you out of prison!"

CHAPTER THIRTEEN: MAKSIM

I was unsure how long I sat in total silence, but it was at least long enough for Chloe to start pacing back and forth across the room. The emotion I felt was a mix between anger, betrayal, confusion, frustration, and something akin to absurdity. Hearing Chloe say that Vincent got me out of prison made all of my blood boil under my skin. I didn't even want to hear Vincent's name coming out of Chloe's mouth, but to know that she *worked* with him and that I was now, in some way, *indebted* to him.

I'd never been so mad in my entire life.

"What...?" I stood up out of bed and rapidly grabbed the nearest pair of pants I could find to pull on. This didn't feel like a conversation I should have while naked. "I don't know what that means. What do you mean he got me out of prison?" It was shocking how low and reserved I was managing to keep my voice given how beside myself with fury I was. "What does that mean, Chloe?"

She was clearly nervous based on the way she was looking at me, but I didn't know if that was because she was afraid of me, or a silent acknowledgement that she'd done something wrong.

"Mitzy is the person who has been helping me through this whole process," she started to explain quietly. "He told me that if I wanted, he could help set up a meeting with the Costellos because, as far as they knew, you were on good terms, and they'd probably be willing to help."

"Did you tell them we know each other?" I asked.

She nodded gently. "Yes. I felt like I had to, for them to understand why I wanted to ask them for help. I'm a detective. If they didn't know that we had history, they might have thought that I was just trying to set them up or something."

I was angry beyond the point of being able to scream and yell. I was borderline bewildered. "So you actually went and met with them."

"Yes, and Maks, they care about you. They really do. Even Vin--"

"Don't say his name," I hissed.

"Katya wanted to help you as soon as she found out. She called Alexei Lachinov, who was already sort of working on getting you out, but he needed some additional assurances to be able to make it happen. Apparently, Vi... *He* had a property that Alexei wanted, so he gave it up in order to seal the deal with Alexei, and then your bail was five digits. I couldn't afford that, but they dropped that amount without even thinking twice, and they don't want anything in return. They just wanted you out. He said you were important to him. Katya stopped doing what she was doing to pull it off."

"So after *months* of me telling you how much I hated that man and how much pain he's caused me and the people who care about me, you decided the best way to deal with this problem was to ask him for help?"

I hated this recurring theme that Vincent was some big hero when he was anything but. He was doing it again, smoothing his way into the life of another person that I cared about and trying to steal them from me yet again. Why did it feel like nothing could happen in my life without involving Vincent Costello? How was he haunting me severely without me at least getting to enjoy the fact that he was dead?

"I didn't know what else to do," Chloe whined. "I was willing to do what-ever I had to in order to get you out. When the Costellos and the Lachinovs got involved, you were processed for bail and it was posted within a few hours. I left my meeting with Katya and... him, and got a call that evening telling me that I could pick you up this morning. I knew I was going to have to operate *outside* of the law to get you out because Cox worked outside of the law to get you in. It's not like I know that many criminals." She walked over and sat down on the edge of the bed, looking up at me. The fact that she was still naked under the blanket didn't help, but I was angry enough to ignore that for the most part. "What about all that stuff we were talking about before? Going back to Russia? Me maybe moving there as well? You said that sounded nice. Let's just do that."

There was so much I wanted to say, and yet I just remained silent for a moment. Of course that sounded nice. I'd love that, and I think if I *could* get Chloe back in St. Petersburg, away from the complications of New York and her job, then we could be happy and actually maybe build a life together, but I felt like I had to kill Vincent even more now. If I didn't, he was just going to continue to haunt my life until I had nothing left at all.

He had to die.

"Chloe, I've explained to you how important it is to me to wipe Vincent from this planet. If you don't understand why I need to do that, then I don't know what to say. If you plan to stand in my way, then I consider you an enemy."

The heartbroken look on Chloe's face made me regret my words instantly, but I didn't want to take them back because they were true. I couldn't leave Vincent alone now. Who knew what reason he actually had for wanting me to be indebted to him. It was probably only a matter of time before that came back to bite me and Vincent tried to use that to his advantage. I refused to let him control my life in any shape, form or fashion.

"Can you just talk to him first?" Chloe asked. "He said that there were things the two of you needed to hash out to clear the air. He wants to talk to you man-to-man."

"Don't insult me," I demanded. "I'm supposed to go and sit down with him and let him try and work me over like the rest of you? I have nothing to say to that man. I can't believe you indebted me to him. I trusted you to keep me out of his crosshairs, and now he has something that he can leverage against me. And not only that, but he now knows that you mean something to me ——he has a way to get to me now."

"Maks——"

"No!" I thundered, finally losing my patience. "I'm not *meeting* with him, and I'm not sparing his life. Not for all of the suffering he's caused me."

Chloe stood up off the bed, still looking heartbroken, but also now had a determined expression on her face.

"I thought that maybe we were learning how to prioritize each other over our own selfish needs, but clearly I was wrong," Chloe said. "Katya and Vincent aren't bad people, and if you are that hellbent on killing Vincent, then I consider you *my* enemy."

Hearing it put so bluntly like that only made me angrier. How did Vincent manage to take even Chloe away from me? That she would protect him so staunchly even though she knew how much it meant to me to end his miserable existence. I felt like such a chump. Here I was this entire time trying to fight my way out of Vladimir's shadow, I didn't even realize that I was standing in Vincent's much more looming one.

"If that's how it has to be," I said.

It seemed like Chloe was on the brink of tears, but she took a deep breath and held back. She collected her clothes from around the room, dropped the sheet, and gave me one last look at her bare back as she walked out of the room. My stomach churned with sadness in her wake, and I just felt defeated. When the only things involved were Chloe and I, we did fine, but as soon as anything from the world outside of these walls got involved, we disintegrated, and quickly at that. I sunk down onto the bed, fighting hard to resist the urge to run after Chloe and tell her I'd do whatever she wanted if she would just stay by my side.

But Vincent had to die. I would settle for nothing less.

It was already past midnight when Chloe left, but I still attempted to lie down and get some sleep before the sun came up. It was a relatively useless effort, as every time I closed my eyes, I felt like I could feel Chloe slipping into bed next to me. My eyes would slam open, hoping to see her in my arms, but there was nothing there but an empty bed.

When the sun finally came up, I just gave up trying to make it happen. I'd expected sleep to come easy after spending so much time in those uncomfortable prison beds, but I was finding a lack of Chloe in my life created more issues than one. She was upset with me now, but if she was willing to come to Russia just to be with me, then maybe once Vincent was dead, we could start fresh. I'd have to put my eggs in that basket, because letting VIncent live simply wasn't an option.

Not long after I got out of bed and got some coffee for the day, the doorbell from the elevator rang. I walked over and opened it, and Brusch was standing on the other side with food in hand.

"I figured you would probably need something good after the fare you've been subjected to for the past few weeks."

"That's excellent, thank you." He handed me a styrofoam box and a melody of spices wafted up from it. I brought it over to the dining table and set it down and opened it, to see a delectable looking scramble. It had a few different kinds of meats, cheese, veggies, fluffy eggs and potatoes and was topped with a kind of salsa. "This looks delicious."

"It's a place that some of Dacha's employees turned me onto. I think I've had breakfast there every day this week," Brusch said, sitting down with his own box. "Is everything okay with Chloe? I saw her rush out of here looking pretty upset this morning during club hours."

I frowned. The food had temporarily erased her from my brain, but just like that, she was back. "We don't see eye-to-eye on Vincent," I told him simply. "I suppose we've decided that if we can't see one another's point of view on it, then we are closer to being foes than friends."

"That's unfortunate," Brusch said.

I tilted my head at him. "Really?"

He nodded. "Yes. I know that she is, or was, a detective. But she feels like such a good fit for you. She helps you see the world more clearly, I've noticed. Gives you confidence."

"What are you, my dad now?" I growled.

He snickered. "I'll shut up about it, I suppose."

"I care about her, but she's sympathetic towards Vincent as well," I explained. "I need this man out of my life. I can't deal with anyone else I care about choosing him over me. You agree he needs to be punished for what he's done, right?"

"Of course," Brusch said. "As a member of the Petrov group, Vincent's crimes against us should not be ignored."

There was a hint of something lingering in Brusch's voice and I said, "Is there more you want to say?"

He shrugged. "I don't know. This vendetta against Vincent just seems like a lingering facet of Vladimir's old empire. I wonder how much killing Vincent would benefit *you* as opposed to hurt *you*. If it's already costing you someone that you admittedly care about, then is it worth it?"

I sat staring at him in silence for a long time. Even though he *just* admitted that he wanted Vincent punished, he was still saying that he wondered if there was a benefit to me backing off. "Would it not help me to not let him run all over us?"

"The beef with Vincent feels like Vladimir and maybe Sascha's, but they're both gone now. We can safely conclude that Vincent didn't steal Katya from you if she always would have preferred to be with him regardless. Maybe your new empire doesn't need to start with a fight with Vincent. Maybe it starts with finding someone to rule by your side, instead." I opened my mouth to respond, but Brusch kept speaking before I could get anything out. "In any event, Mr. Lachinov will be here in about an hour per the meeting you asked me to set up with him. Is there anything you'd like me to do to prepare?"

That seemed like a very sudden and random change of subject, but maybe that was his way of forcing me to think about what he'd said without replying. Borya had done something similar with me.

Was I someone who impulsively replied without thinking?

"Just make sure there is something to drink and eat in one of the VIP rooms," I told him. "I want him to be comfortable. Also make sure the entire club is in tip top shape. He'll likely want a tour at some point. I plan on offering him the Bonettis' vacant position."

Brusch nodded and a smile came across his face. "Yes boss."

Alexei Lachinov was a tall, well dressed man with short, feathery brown hair parted off-center to the left, with the left combed straight back behind his ear and the right swooped slightly in front of his face before flowing back. He was wearing an expensive looking Italian cut suit, and his fingers were encircled with tons of rings. He had a look of opulence about him, and it made me glad that I'd chosen to don the best suit I had on me for the meeting.

"Alexei," I greeted, holding out my hand to shake.

He grabbed my hand firmly. "Maksim. Vladimir's protege. He spoke of you many times when we met."

I furrowed my brow. "He did?"

"Oh yes. He often told me about how his son did not share his visions, but you did. He often told me that one day he would bring you along to start preparing you to rise to power in his wake. When he passed, I had a feeling I would be hearing from you soon, I just didn't think it would be from inside an American prison."

I motioned for Alexei to sit down at the table in the VIP room that I had Brusch set aside. "Yes, well, he always spoke very highly of you, so I was glad that you were available in a pinch. I made an enemy of the wrong detective, it seems."

"Yes. Cox is a deplorable man to say the least. He claims to be a detective committed to justice, but really, he's just looking for his own come up. You need to be careful around him. He's not above using any methods to bring someone down if he needs to."

"So I learned," I said. "Anyway, I didn't set up this meeting to discuss Cox, I wanted to discuss a possible opportunity for the two of us to work more closely together."

"Consider me very interested," Alexei said. "I always appreciated my working relationship with Vladimir and am excited to see what a partnership with you will garner."

"We've established a powerful and incredibly lucrative network of sales of a variety of products through VIP rooms such as this one," I explained. "In previous partnerships, we allowed those who kept new clientele coming through the doors and making sales to take seventy percent of the sales, while I maintained thirty percent, and then of course, the income from those parties spending money in the club. Would something like this work for you?"

"Would we have use of the club for other matters?" Alexei asked.

I bobbed my head back and forth. "I suppose. So long as none of it negatively affects me, my business, or the club."

"Quite the opposite. I think there are some expansion opportunities for you here. I'd be more than willing to share the fruits of my labor with you as well."

I smiled, knowing that this was one area where I was seeing success. "I'm looking forward to helping one another along the way," I lifted a glass to him, "and hopefully keeping one another out of Cox's clutches."

CHAPTER FOURTEEN: CHLOE

Unlike the last time Maksim and I parted ways, I felt more frustrated for the things I said and the circumstances in which I said them, than anything else. More than anything, I wish that I had just bit the bullet and brought up the baby, because that might have made him see things differently. There were moments when I felt like his desire to be with me was starting to overpower his need to kill Vincent, but he just needed that final push. Perhaps if he knew that he could have a family with me and be happy that way, his need for vengeance wouldn't be so strong.

Of course I didn't mean what I said to Maksim--he wasn't my enemy. If I had the ability to make him my enemy, I would have done it a long time ago so that I could have done my job effectively. The fact that I was struggling to make him my enemy was the whole issue.

I went and decided to develop feelings for him and get pregnant by him instead.

But until I figured out how to make Maksim let this need to kill Vincent go, we couldn't move forward. I didn't want the moment he found out we were going to be a family to be borne of an emergency situation where I needed to stop Maks from literally pulling the trigger. What I couldn't figure out was which one should come first. Should I tell Maksim about the baby first, or wait in the event that I couldn't get him to drop his vengeance and my baby and I needed to go on without him?

It terrified me that I was beginning to accept that this was Maksim's life. Dealing with people like the Costellos and the Lachinovs. After seeing how easy it was for the lines to get blurred, I'd been thinking that as long as we were people of standards like the Costellos, then maybe it wouldn't be so bad. At the rate I was going, I'd do a better job of protecting the innocent from the inside out.

That needed to be where Maksim was at, too. I was beginning to realize that I could look past many things, but I couldn't let him hurt Vincent and Katya who had been good to us and who saw Maksim as a friend. That wasn't right, and whether by legal means or illegal means, I had to stop him from doing that, plain and simple.

As the thought of Katya crossed my brain, I started to wonder what her opinions on the matter would be. She'd been in a similar situation, hadn't she? It was Vincent against her father and brother, but the concept was similar. I was unsure of how and when she came to tell Vincent about their child, but she knew she was pregnant when she went back to Russia because Maksim mentioned that it was why he was going to marry her, to help her raise her baby.

I needed some advice, and even though I would normally call Mitzy in this situation, I needed advice from someone who was more closely related to the situation.

So for the first time in my entire life, I contacted someone that I knew was technically a criminal, and I did it of my own free will.

"Hello?" Katya's voice said when she answered the phone.

"Katya?" I said. "Hi. It's Chloe."

"Oh my gosh! Hi!" she sounded elated to hear from me. "I've been hoping you would call!"

I crinkled up my nose. "Really?"

"Yeah! I mean, don't get me wrong, I love Vincent and really the whole Costello crew, but, I don't know, you seem really cool to me. I was hoping we could be friends." Then she chuckled. "So long as you don't try and arrest me or something."

I rolled my eyes. "I don't think I'll be arresting many people anymore."

"You sound sad," she said.

"A little. This has been my passion for a long time, but lately it feels like being a cop is doing more harm than good."

"What are you doing right now?" she said. "I know that two pregnant ladies can't drink alcohol *or* coffee..."

I whined. "I miss coffee."

"But there's this place that serves these really delicious smoothies with all sorts of fresh fruits--they even have one that's specifically made for pregnant women with all the best nutrients and stuff. Wanna meet me there? We can talk it out."

I never really made that many friends after moving away from Maksim, so the idea of suddenly having one was a little nerve wracking, but also really exciting. "Yeah. I'd like that a lot."

"Okay cool. I'll send you the address. Give me twenty minutes to ditch my man and I'll meet you there."

My smile got even bigger. "Okay. See you soon."

Exactly as she said she would, Katya sent me the address for the smoothie shop and met me about ten minutes after I got there. She was wearing an adorable maternity dress with ruffled layers and had her hair down, and she greeted me with a huge smile and hug. We each ordered a smoothie then we picked a table in the corner by the window to bask in the sun.

"Sorry if I seemed needy," she said. "I still haven't made many friends since moving here."

"It's okay. My closest friend, really my only friend, is Mitzy, so I think it's safe to say this branch out is good for me," I replied.

Katya nodded. "It's good too because it allows me a little space from Vince when I need it. It's not often, but I don't think anyone could survive being with their partner around the clock, you know?"

Maybe it was the nature of my job or just because I'd been spending too much time with Maksim, but I had to ask, "Do you struggle to get away from Vincent when you want to go out on your own?"

She shook her head wildly. "Oh no! It's nothing like that! Vince is actually really intentional about always giving me space and freedom. Given how we started, it's an area of communication we always need to be clear about. It's just that I almost died and then he almost died. I think our anxiety goes up a bit when we're apart, but him more than me, because..." She smoothed her hands over her belly. "Can't say I blame him."

"That makes sense," I responded.

"Maks has got to be the same way, right? He's always been overprotective."

I winced. "Yeah, um... He doesn't know."

Katya was halfway through sipping her smoothie when she froze. "What?"

I nodded sheepishly. "I haven't told him I'm pregnant yet."

"Why?"

"Honestly, I'm not really sure," I explained. "I mean, at first it was because we had *just* gotten into this huge fight and broke up, for lack of a better term, and then, I found out that night, that he'd just gotten arrested. Then I went to the prison to visit him with every intention of telling him, but he thought I had something to do with his arrest and he was livid. Then when I picked him up yesterday, we kind of got caught up in being happy to see each other, so I never brought it up. Before I could get to it we got into *another* fight and I left. I regret not saying anything, though."

Katya lifted an eyebrow. "Do you two fight a lot?"

"Just about the same one thing," I said. "He believes something from the bottom of his soul and I totally disagree. It's not really something that can be compromised about either. It has to be my way or his way, and whoever doesn't get their way may not be able to get past it for our relationship."

"What is it?" Katya asked.

Obviously, I couldn't come right out and tell her that the disagreement was that Maks wanted to kill her fiance. "Just, you know..."

"Maks wants Vince dead?" That time, it was me who froze mid-sip and Katya laughed. "Yeah, I know all about it. I won't bore you with the details, but someone from back home tipped me off. And I get why Maks is holding such a grudge."

"You do?"

She nodded. "We're all to blame. My parents, my brother. We were all totally unfair to him. We all defined him differently in our lives. To me, he was a romantic interest; to Sascha he was a sibling; to my mom he was a charity case; to my dad he was a protege. He had to have been confused about his role and we never really gave him the freedom to build meaningful relationships outside of us. We allowed him to become totally reliant. Normally when you lose people you lose a lover here, a parent there. For Maks, Vince showed up in Russia and everything fell apart. He lost his fiancee and the child he was going to raise. He lost his brother. He lost his surrogate mother and his mentor. All at once." She turned her face down, looking frustrated. "I feel more and more guilty about it every day. Not just because of the pain he must be suffering, but because he wants to take it all out on Vincent because he could never blame us."

Hearing it laid out that way made me even more sad that I'd let things end on the note they did before I left. It was so obvious how blown away Maksim was that I'd stuck around after that first argument. Now it was clear that part of Maksim's fury with Vincent was the correlation he was drawing between Vincent's presence and his misfortune. To have me defend Vincent and then walk out, it probably felt like more of the same and likely only made things worse.

"I need to talk to him," I told Katya. "The way things ended last night, er, technically this morning, he's more likely than not even angrier. I defended Vincent and then walked out."

"Yikes," Katya said. "Well, please do. He's such a good man. I just want him to be happy. He deserves someone who really loves him, and it seems like you do." Before I could mention that we hadn't confessed that level of feelings to one another yet, she continued, "And you should really tell him about the baby. I had a single conversation with Vince after I found out I was pregnant, and didn't take the opportunity to tell him. He nearly died after that. In fact, I believed he was dead for months. I regretted not telling him everyday. In this world, every single day is borrowed time, it feels like. Take nothing for granted."

"Yeah. Thanks. I should go call him." I started to stand up, but Katya grabbed my arm and stopped me.

"Happened just this morning, you said?"

I nodded. "Yeah. I checked the time in my car on the way home and it was like one-thirty in the morning."

She pulled me back down into my seat. "Trust me on this one. Give him a little more time to cool off. If I've learned anything about Maks, it's that he takes a *looong* time to process things. If he hasn't called you by this evening, then you can call him."

A little smile actually came to my face. "You know a lot about him, huh?"

She snorted. "Potentially more than I care to. He practically lived with us."

I balanced my head in my hands. "Can you tell me more about him?"

Katya gave me a sweet smile. "I'd love to."

Over the course of the next few hours, Katya told me everything she could think of about the father of my child. She talked about the top marks he got in school to avoid detention or a need for extra lessons outside of school hours, and about how both he and Sascha were on the track team in high school. She told me all about how she used to get bundled up to go watch them run and it actually made me a little jealous. Maybe if I'd never moved out of Russia, I might have been the one watching Maks run on chilly nights.

I would have loved that.

My favorite part of the story, oddly enough, was when Katya talked about what a wonderful partner he was when the two of them were briefly engaged. It made me feel a little jealous to hear of the two of them together, but Katya *fawned* over how supportive he was and everything he did for her and the baby. It sounded like Maks was just so excited to have a family.

I hoped that excitement would extend to a family with me instead of her. Katya believed he'd be even *more* excited.

The last thing she talked about was the unique relationship Maksim had with her father and how it always made her uneasy. Apparently her brother, Sascha, had more faith in their father, but Katya knew better than to trust him. It didn't surprise her at all to learn after her father's death that Vladimir had been grooming both Sascha *and* Maks for his throne.

By her best guess he probably didn't even know which one of them he'd honestly give it to, he just wanted options.

"I feel so bad for him that he feels even an ounce of remorse for my miserable father," Katya quipped. "I can assure you, Vladimir Petrov would have felt no such sadness if the roles were reversed."

"I wish I knew how to break him out of it," I said. "It's such a source of darkness in his life."

"Vincent had demons too," Katya said. "Trust me on this, once you've shown him enough light through your love, he'll get better."

At that exact moment, my phone rang. I looked down and then my heart jumped.

"It's Maks."

Katya perked up. "Oooh, told ya. Answer it."

I pressed the button then lifted the phone to my ear before nervously saying, "Hello?"

"Chloe," Maksim said. "Where are you right now?"

I glanced up at Katya and said, "Out with a friend."

"Well, call me when you're done."

"No!" I yelped, sounding too desperate. "I mean, I can talk now. What's going on?"

"I need to speak with you right away... In person."

I swallowed hard. "Okay. I can come to you."

He went quiet for a second before saying, "Good. I'll see you soon."

I hung up the phone and looked across at Katya. "You were right. He wants to see me."

She waved a hand. "Good. Go. Call me later and give me the deets."

It was like I had an actual girlfriend. "I will. And thank you for everything."

"Of course, just promise me something." She looked directly into my eyes. "Promise me you won't leave him again without telling him about the baby."

The thought made my stomach churn, but I knew she was right. "Yeah. I promise."

CHAPTER FIFTEEN: MAKSIM

In the wake of my success in meeting with Alexei and the things that Borya had said to me, I began to wonder if I was making a mistake letting things linger so nastily between Chloe and I. She *did* mean something to me, and Borya was right, I didn't want anything in my empire to prevent me from having her in my life. I knew that she didn't agree with me about Vincent, but there had to be a way to compromise, or at least help her understand why I had to do this. We always got so close to landing in happiness, but it felt like we were finding it impossible to part ways without getting into another fight.

For that reason, I was going to do something that I'd never done before--give someone else the power to dictate my life.

I was going to apologize to her and tell her earnestly that I'd be willing to do anything she wanted from me, so long as she would allow this one thing.

It was actually a pleasant surprise to hear that she didn't sound mad when she answered the phone, and then said that she would come over and see me right away.

Maybe that meant she was feeling regret from our earlier disagreement as well.

After demanding that I not be bothered at all for the rest of the night, I poured us a couple of glasses of wine and changed into something a little more relaxed. I didn't want Chloe to feel like she was business to me, so I went for a pair of ripped jeans and a dark blue zip-up jacket that I kept over a white t-shirt and unzipped. I did keep my watch on, but I tried not to look *too* pretentious. I was just hoping to have an honest, laid back conversation with her. There *had* to be a way to sort this out.

I was sitting with such anticipation of Chloe arriving that I actually jumped when I heard the elevator bell. But I jumped up as quickly as I could and ran over to the elevator so that I could unlock the elevator, and my heart actually leapt when I saw Chloe on the other side.

"Hey," I said quietly.

She smiled at me. "Hey."

"Come in."

She walked in, looking fresh and beautiful in a teal romper with her hair up in a ponytail. As she passed me, she looked me up and down and then smiled. "You look nice."

"I was just thinking the same thing about you."

What was this nervous energy all of a sudden? We'd dated, we'd slept together--just last night, even. Why was I all of a sudden nervous like it was the first time my crush was coming over?

Perhaps we both realized that this was the time we were trying to make it work for good.

We walked into the living room and I picked up one of the glasses of wine and handed it over to Chloe. She gave it a strange look for a second and I asked, "What's wrong?" I knew it was a kind she liked because we had it before.

"Oh, nothing." She took it, but didn't drink from the glass. "Thank you."

Maybe she was just nervous about the impending conversation.

"Um. Thanks for coming," I said, sitting down next to her. "I really didn't like the way things transpired between us earlier. I said things I didn't mean."

"Me too," she responded. "I don't see you as an enemy, Maks. I could never."

"I know. I feel the same way." I sighed a little and then laughed. "Why are we so bad at this?"

She just shook her head. "I've been trying to figure that out myself."

For some reason, the way that we were sitting and looking at each other transported me back in time to when we were kids. There were so many days when our parents expected us to be playing while they were inside doing adult things, but Chloe and I would just take whatever snack her mom had made us and sit under the big Larch trees in her backyard. We didn't really need to talk or play anything to enjoy one another's presence. Several times, I considered trying to hold her hand or give her a kiss on the cheek, but I was way too nervous, and I was still just a kid, I didn't really understand all of that back then.

I was kind of experiencing that same feeling now. Just errant nerves and being unsure of what to do or say next.

"Chloe," I said. "My life... This world, they aren't consistent with being a detective. I know that's what you've always dreamed of, and that you want to make the world a better place, but I can't always promise that my life won't involve some sort of violence or illegal activity. I know that will be hard for you to accept, but that's a part of what it means to be with me. Can you accept something like that?"

Chloe was quiet for a long moment before she looked at me, and surprisingly said. "I can."

I lifted my eyebrows. "You... you can?"

"Yeah." She looked at me. "I'm never going to be okay with just reckless violence, but if I've learned anything these past few months, it's that very few people in this world are actually following the rules of any place. I'll never be involved in that side of your life, but as long as I know you're not a monster--not like Vladimir--then I can just chalk it up to your job." I got a little closer to her face, almost like I was afraid I was looking at an imposter. She pulled her face back and chuckled. "What?"

"I just... I wasn't expecting that. What about justice?"

"Justice is always going to be situational," she said. "I trust that you won't intentionally do something to hurt me or that you know would make me see you differently. You don't want to kill just to kill, right?"

"No," he said. "I don't want to be that kind of leader. I want to lead with my brain, not with a gun."

She smiled. "I believe in you to do that."

That made me feel elated. It was unbelievable to hear say that. If Chloe understood, then that made everything easier. I could finish up in New York and head back to Russia, maybe even bring her with me, or I could send Brusch and the private jet back to get her at some point.

"I can't believe that--"

"But if I'm going to look past everything else, absolutely everything else, I need you to do something for me," Chloe said.

I grabbed Chloe's hand and kissed the back of it. "I'd do anything for you, if you're willing to do that for me," I told her.

"I need you to let Vincent go." Just like that, all of the euphoria I was feeling from learning that Chloe was actually willing to accept my lifestyle went away as she asked me, yet again, to give up the one thing that meant more to me than anything else I wanted to complete while I was in NYC. She slid closer to me and said, "You said you'd do anything for me."

"I will," I said confidently.

"Then I need you to decide. I need you to choose between killing Vincent or being with me," she said.

I did care about Chloe, and the thought of having her in my life without barriers made me incredibly happy. I wanted more than anything to just be with her--to start that new life in St. Petersburg that we were talking about. It felt like I'd never be able to escape his relentless interference in my life if I didn't kill him, but if Chloe was honestly telling me I needed to make a choice, I knew what I'd choose.

I'd choose her.

Finally, I just shook my head to snap out of my train of thought. "Okay."

Her eyes widened and she let out a little gasp. "Okay?"

"Okay," I said. "It kills me. I don't think I'll ever fully be happy knowing he's still out there, but I don't want to lose you."

Chloe deflated. "Do you really think that? That you'll never be fully happy. You don't think we could find a way to honestly be happy if you didn't get to kill Vincent?"

"I don't know what you want me to say," I told her. "I'm just being honest. That's something that I feel like I need to do. Not getting to do it feels like I'm not fighting for my name or the people who were like family to me. I'm trying to carry the legacy I inherited, and one man threatens it so severely and you won't let me deal with that problem. That's upsetting to me, but if the alternative is losing you, I won't do it."

Chloe frowned. "This makes me nervous ,that you'll flip one day and just try and do it behind my back."

I shrugged. "I can't promise you that I won't."

"Maks!" Chloe ripped her hands from me and stood up. "Why are you so hellbent on this? He didn't even do anything wrong to you!"

"Please stop yelling," I begged. "I didn't want this to turn into another argument."

"How can it not when you're being so unreasonable?" she barked.

"Me?" I stood up as well. "Don't *you* think it's unreasonable to claim that Vincent never did anything wrong to me."

"He didn't!" she screeched.

"What did he do to you? What did Vincent Costello do to you directly?" she asked. "Not a situation that you think he caused that led to something else. How did he hurt you? He didn't *take* Katya away. The first time, her father allowed her to be kidnapped and left her there, and the second time he went back for her because he knew she wanted to be with him. Katya told me about her father--she thought he was a horrible man. She killed him because she hated him, not because Vincent convinced her to. Even you told me that he left her with Vincent and that he started the fight between him and the Costellos. You said that Vladimir wouldn't give Katya the acknowledgement she was due."

I shook my head, gritting my teeth. "He didn't."

"And *you* were the one who killed Sascha, and you did it by accident. Because even though Katya and Sascha tried to tell you that Vincent wasn't the enemy, you panicked, and didn't believe them."

I thinned my gaze towards her. "How do you know that?"

"Because Katya told me!" Chloe whined. Tears started to fill her eyes and I was unsure where the sudden influx of emotion was coming from. "She was the friend I was with earlier. I like her, and I like Vincent, too! They're good people! I don't want you to ruin their lives!"

"Chloe."

She raked her hands across her eyes, pushing away the tears that were forming there. "They care about you, they told me! They see you as a friend, and even though they know they have some differences to work out with you, that's what they want to do, because they don't want you to be the enemy."

I took a step towards her. "Chloe."

"No!" she yelled. "I don't want to do this anymore. I don't want to keep telling you over and over that it will only make things worse! We have a chance at happiness here. I don't want you to constantly be preoccupied with trying to defeat someone who isn't a threat to you. You care about Katya, don't you?"

"Of course I do."

"She's having a baby with him! You want to kill the father of that child. You grew up without your dad. Do you want to do that to someone else? What if Katya never forgives you? What if that baby grows up and feels like it has to kill our baby because you killed its father? They could be friends!"

"Our baby?" I said. "How did you get all the way to our baby? Something like that would be way in the future!"

"It's not!" she yelled. "It's not in the future. It's now!"

"You want to have a baby right now?" I asked.

"No, but I'm going to!" Chloe sunk down onto the couch and took a deep breath. "Okay..."

"Chloe, what are you talking about?" I asked. "You're freaking out and you're freaking me out."

She looked up at me teary-eyed. "I'm pregnant."

It felt like my heart thudded to a halt. I stared at her trying to determine if I'd heard her incorrectly or if I was just hearing something I wanted to hear because I was still hurting from losing the family I thought I was going to have with Katya. Maybe all of this was actually just a dream, or a nightmare, or both?

To be certain I was really in this moment, I pinched my skin so hard that it started to bleed. Chloe jumped up and wrapped her hand around it. "What are you doing?"

"I needed to make sure this was real," I said quietly. "Are you really pregnant?"

She nodded, tears running down her cheeks. "Yes. I found out the same day you got arrested. After we broke up, I went home and I ended up getting so sick I passed out. I guess it's heightened stress from being pregnant during all of this... bullshit." She sniffled in. "Mitzy took me to the hospital and the doctor ended up asking me to take a pregnancy test and..." She sighed. "I've taken about ten additional tests since then because I still can't believe it."

I was beside myself and unsure of how to respond to this news. Chloe was pregnant? With *my* child? I was going to be a dad? Chloe was going to be the mother of my child?

"Maks..." Chloe said quietly after a few minutes of silence. "Please say something. I've been panicking trying to figure out how to tell you. In my little panic attack there, it just came out. You're not mad are you?"

"Mad...?" I said. "Am I mad?"

"Or anything?" Chloe said. "Please just tell me what you're thinking and feeling right now. I need to know."

"I'm going to tell you," I said, staring her in the eyes. "I'm going to tell you *exactly* how I feel."

CHAPTER SIXTEEN: CHLOE

Maksim's lips were on mine before I could even make heads or tails of what was going on. My heart was still pounding from the fit I'd accidentally thrown myself into, and just when I was beginning to fear that Maksim wasn't going to be happy to hear that I was pregnant, all of a sudden he was all over me. I probably shouldn't have gotten so swept up in the moment so we could actually legitimately discuss what Maksim's thoughts were.

But I guess the fact that he was pushing me down onto the couch was enough of an indicator.

"Maks," I said, when he finally came up for air, but only to start kissing his way down my neck. "We should probably figure out how to communicate without yelling at each other or having sex."

He lifted up so he could look down at me. "Can we figure that out later?"

There was such an intense look in his eyes that it rendered me temporarily speechless. The logical part of my brain was telling me to say, "No, we should figure it out right now. That's what adults do. We're going to be parents, and each day that passes is less time to get our acts together for that child," but instead I nodded slowly and said, "Okay."

Maksim pressed his lips back against the crook of my neck then, letting his hands push behind my back to pull down the zipper of the romper I had on. He massaged his hands over my shoulders to push down the straps of the romper, and I found myself helping speed the process along so that I could claw his jacket off of his torso. He looked so sexy in this more laid back look, but something told me I'd enjoy him just as much with nothing on.

Once he was able to pull the romper totally down my body and slide it off, he tossed it aside and then returned to my stomach. He kissed directly on top of my belly and then set his head there temporarily, almost like he was listening. It was so sweet and romantic, that it actually made me a little emotional. The wacky hormones related to being pregnant had me all over the place, but this was separate from that. This was me realizing that Maksim *was* happy that I was pregnant. He was just a man who struggled to express himself in any normal way.

We'd have to work on that.

In the very back of my mind, I still didn't know if I'd actually talked him out of killing Vincent, but I'd at least distracted him from the idea for now, which was something. And I was able to maintain my promise to Katya, so for the rest of whatever came next, I planned to push everything from my brain and just enjoy this man who had become such a big and important part of my life in such a short period of time.

Finally leaving my stomach behind, Maksim kissed and licked the rest of his way down my stomach until he was at my hip bone. He bit down on my left hip and I whimpered with pleasure. His teeth sinking into me always drove me wild, regardless of the situation, but my hips were particularly sensitive.

Something Maks had discovered throughout our time together.

While he continued to nibble on my skin, one of his hands caressed upwards again. It passed slowly over my stomach, lingering there again for a brief moment, before continuing upwards to slink under my bra. He squeezed down on one of my breasts and I let my head fall back as the different sensations washed over me.

"Maks," I hummed.

He kissed my hip before saying, "Shh. Just let me take care of you."

Not letting his hand leave my breast, Maksim ducked his head between my legs. My thong was still there, but it seemed that was an inconsequential obstacle for Maksim as he placed a firm lick over the top of the fabric. Even with the divide, my core tingled in reaction to the heat of his tongue and I let out a moan. He pressed a couple of fingers to my clit and massaged it back and forth gently while allowing his tongue to slide along the string of the g-string, pressing some of it directly on my skin.

My hands moved on their own, combing into Maksim's hair and massaging his scalp gently in reaction to the pleasure. He let out a groan of satisfaction, so I applied a little more pressure, pulling at his hair now, which worked like a machine making him lick me with more fervor below. He used his free hand to pull aside my underwear and finally allow his mouth to touch me fully. I shivered at the feeling and squeezed my hands through his hair even harder.

He responded by poking a couple of fingers into my hole.

The sounds of his lewd slurps filled the room and swirled into the sounds of my moaning. I was lifting my hips, bucking against his face, and squeezing around his fingers--anything I could do to increase the friction.

Finally, I looked up at him through lusty eyes and said, "I want to taste you too."

He lifted his head up to look at me, his eyes excited with that suggestion. "I think I can accommodate that request."

After placing a firm kiss on my pussy, he repositioned himself so he was on his back on the couch. He lifted his shirt over his head while I clamored forward to undo the button on his jeans. Hooking my fingers into the sides, I pulled his pants and boxers down in one swoop, only bothering for the time being to pull them down enough for his impressive length to spring forward. It seemed to bend towards me, twitching happily when I wrapped a hand around it, and then I gave it a stroke for its kind greeting.

Maks placed a gentle hand on the back of my head and I dove forward, setting a kiss on the tip of him before gliding a lick from the top of his balls to the head and back down again. I watched as he closed his eyes and started to take in shorter breaths.

A wrecked Maksim was a sexy Maksim.

I didn't consider myself an expert on blowjobs or anything, but I enjoyed giving them, especially to a man like Maksim who responded so delightfully. I cupped one hand under his sac and used the other to stroke as I licked him like the tastiest popsicle.

Eventually, the teasing got too much and he huffed out, "Don't tease me any longer, beautiful."

I hummed happily, responding, "I think I can accommodate that request," then I moved my mouth to the head and closed over.

The hottest grunt of ecstasy bubbled out of Maksim while I worked my way as far down on his shaft as I could get. He was... blessed, to say the least, so even the practice I'd had taking him in hadn't yet afforded me the ability to swallow him whole. That didn't stop me from trying, however, and I continued to take more and more of him down my throat until he was poking at the back. Even through a couple of gags, I continued to gulp him down, filling my mouth with as much of him as I could, until I couldn't handle it anymore and started to choke on him. He seemed to enjoy it, scratching the back of my head with each additional inch, and engorging inside of me.

In one long pull, I popped off of him before very rapidly taking him back in as far as I could go.

"Argh!" Maksim growled. "That feels so good." I repeated the process, maneuvering him in and out rapidly until he started to twitch in my mouth. "Chloe," he warned.

But I didn't stop. I was a little hypnotized by his taste, his smell, his sounds, and couldn't bring myself to cease. I buried him in and started to use my tongue to pincer him against my throat. His grunts got louder and his hold on my head got firmer until he pushed himself even deeper inside and then I could feel his hot, salty seed pouring down my throat. I hummed and swallowed every bead of it, until he was twitching, but releasing nothing else.

"That wasn't fair," Maksim groaned as I pulled off of him.

I just tilted my head. "I don't know what you mean."

He grabbed my arm and pulled me up until I was straddling his chest. He yanked my strapless bra up and over my head and kicked his pants and boxers the rest of the way off. Immediately, he latched onto one of my breasts and began to suck, sending electric pulses of euphoria skittering through my body. Even though he'd just orgasmed, I could feel Maks' dick fighting to re-harden against my backside. To help out, I reached behind me and started to give it light strokes.

Maksim's head fell back and he started to twitch. "Insatiable."

"I want more," I told him simply.

Wrapping a hand behind my head, he dragged me down to kiss him, leading with his tongue and lacing it between my lips. I accepted him and allowed my own to tumble with his, tasting the remnants of us both in the exchange.

And then it happened, the most unexpected thing at that moment.

Maksim looked up at me through green eyes laden with nothing but passion and hummed, "I love you."

For a moment, I just froze. We'd been dancing around the subject for a while, and I'd been unsure of how I felt. I knew that I had feelings for Maksim that were deeper and truer than anything I'd felt for anyone in the past, but I refused to let myself go to love just yet. There were so many unknowns and so much to fear that I didn't know if I'd be walking into a trap to admit I'd fallen for him.

But I knew a long time ago that I had.

Looking down at him now, I could see how earnest he was, and his hands were gripping onto me and there was even a slight shake. For someone who has lost everyone, admitting to having fallen in love must be terrifying. How could I ever convince him that he had nothing to fear with me--that I wasn't going anywhere? How could I make him secure enough to know that me and our baby were all that he needed? That there was so much happiness waiting for him if he'd let us be the thing that mattered most to him?

"I love you too," I sang to him. "So much."

We kissed again, but that time it was much less erotic and much more romantic. Maksim pressed his head against mine with all of his force, like he was trying to kiss *into* me somehow, and his arms entangled me so tight that it would have hurt if it didn't feel so wonderful to be nearly suffocated by this man.

If this was how I died, I'd take it.

But Maks was quick to regain naughty steam, and with his hands behind my back, he flipped us once more so that I was on my back and he was on top of me. Somewhere between my lazy strokes and the confession of love, he'd managed to get back to full length again. He used a hand to slowly guide himself into me, then he laid himself on top of me fully and pulled me back into a kiss.

There was something about the feeling of Maksim's huge length sliding into me, mixed with the feeling of his body weight on mine, and his lips desperately searching for a connection from me that set my heart on fire. I wrapped my arms around him and held on tight, breathing into the feeling of him thrusting in and out of me. This was the closest, most intimate we'd been, and though I loved our sensory deprivation sessions, this way was incredible too. Connected at every juncture, trying our damnedest to get ever closer to one another, even past the bounds of what was possible.

The feeling crept on me, starting in my toes and shivering its way all the way up to my head. All I could do was moan into Maksim with increasing volume to let him know I was close, but he seemed to understand in the way he picked up the pace. With a slight angle adjustment, he found that spot inside of me that he'd memorized by now and slammed after it, stabbing it repeatedly until my body started to shake against my will.

I had no choice but to release my lips from Maksim's as I fought to breathe through my orgasm, but he kept his arms wrapped around me, and dropped kisses on my chin and neck, as he stroked himself into me over and over. I whimpered with overstimulation, but he pressed on until he finally buried himself all the way inside of me and went stiff, apart from his twitching cock which was releasing into me.

Not that it mattered--it was a little too late to be worried about me getting knocked up.

Maks collapsed on top of me, and we both stayed that way in silence for a while, just trying to catch our breath. I rubbed Maksim's back gently and smiled at the ceiling. For that moment, I felt absolutely, one hundred percent content. If there was love between Maks and I, we could figure the rest out.

I believed that firmly.

After about ten minutes of blissful silence, Maksim lifted himself up again to place a gentle kiss on my stomach. He rubbed it and had the cutest smile on his face.

"So I guess you're excited about the baby?" I joked.

He snickered, kissing my stomach a few extra times. "I'm so happy. I can't believe it." He smiled up at me. "Are you excited?"

"I'm a little scared, but I'm coming around," I told him.

He gave me a concerned look after that and said, "Well, you have to come to Russia now right? We'll be together?"

He looked so scared, but I lifted up to place a hand on his face. "That's what I want."

"Good," he said with a sigh of relief.

"But I just need a little bit of time," I added on. "I have things I still need to take care of, and in all honesty, I'm still concerned about this vengeance you have. Let's just take it a day at a time for right now, okay?"

Though he seemed disappointed with that addition, he nodded nonetheless. "Whatever you want." He kissed my stomach once more. "Whatever you both need."

CHAPTER SEVENTEEN: MAKSIM

"Wait," Chloe said to me. "Do you realize what's about to happen?"

I tilted my head and gave her a strange look. "Apart from the fact that you woke me up way too early and so I'm going to go back to sleep as soon as you're gone?"

She finished pulling on her romper and sandals and then looked at me and giggled. "No. I mean, I believe that will happen too, but no. The fact that I'm about to leave and not because we got into some huge blowout fight that ended with us screaming at each other."

I sat up on the couch, the small throw blanket falling slightly off of me, but I didn't care. If Chloe got distracted and chose to stay instead of leave for work, that'd be fine with me. "Is this that communicating without screaming or having sex that you were talking about?"

She nodded with an amused smile on her face. "It just might be."

Not long after we'd finished up the night before, did we fall asleep and stay passed out on the couch until Chloe's alarm went off to wake her up for work. At that point, she quickly jumped up and started getting dressed so that she could head back home and shower and change before she had to go in. If I had my way, she wouldn't leave at all, but I understood that she still had her existing responsibilities to think about.

"I don't even know why you're so worried about getting to that place anyway," I said. "Didn't you say that it's not really going to work out for you there?"

A depressed look came over Chloe's face that actually made me really sad.

She slumped onto the edge of the couch and looked down at the floor. "My entire crew has disowned me at this point, except for Mitzy, and Cox is already grooming the next person in line to be his right hand. I think it's safe to say that my career there is probably over, at least as a legitimate detective. I'm more like Mitzy now, doing it for the money and resources while doing other things behind the law's back."

She seemed so frustrated as she talked about it and I couldn't help but feel guilty. I knew that being a cop, or at least being someone who had a positive impact on the world had been a dream of Chloe's, really ever since she was a kid, but definitely from the moment when her mom died. I imagined that was part of the reason she wasn't quite ready to go all in yet, because she'd be giving up such a huge part of herself.

Chloe was ready to make her identity that of our child's mother and my partner, but I was completely stumped on how to make it so that she could still be happy with the massive compromise she was making.

"I'm sorry," I told her finally. "If I weren't a criminal, this would be easier."

She looked up at me and a small smile crossed her face. "Just the fact that you would say that means the world to me." But then the smile faded. "I'd be lying if I said I didn't feel a little lost right now, but..." She rubbed her stomach. "I'm okay focusing on the baby for now. At this point, I'm being paid a fair amount of money to drive a desk. There are people with harder lives." She stood up and walked over to me and bent down to give me a kiss. "I'll call you later on?"

I nodded. "Okay."

Then she gave me another shallow grin and said, "I love you."

"I love you too," I replied.

After I gave her stomach a kiss, she collected her things and left. I should be feeling good about the way that this ended up going, but I somehow felt out maneuvered still. Here was this incredible woman whom I loved and who was going to give me a family, and I couldn't even make her happy. I couldn't promise her my undivided attention with me still feeling like Vincent needed to be dealt with, and she was going to have to give up, not only her passion, but some of her morals for me.

Was there no way I could give her everything she deserved?

I did have every intention of going back to sleep, but once Chloe was gone, I just felt unsettled and got up. I had to do something--anything--to feel like I was taking a step towards giving Chloe a life she could be satisfied with.

And of course, my mind came back to the same thing it felt like it'd been coming back to so frequently.

Vincent Costello.

I glanced over at the coffee table and my laptop was sitting there, and I knew that I still had the Costellos' estate under surveillance. Even though Chloe felt so strongly that Vincent should be left alive, the thought of bringing a baby into this world while he was still out there made me incredibly anxious. Maybe Chloe was worried about their future child having a vendetta against our future child, but I was worried about our future child suffering by Vincent's hand right now.

As I opened up my laptop and started to look at the feed viewing their home, I started to realize that it would be fairly easy for me to get in undetected, given how well I knew their schedule. It was early enough in the morning that a majority of Vincent's upper ranks hadn't arrived for the day. The guards who watched the front security guate swapped out in about an hour. If I was quick, I could take advantage of that temporary distraction.

Maybe it was reckless, and maybe Chloe would be upset with me for a while, but it felt worth it to me. If I could just snuff out this flame, then I would just beg for Chloe's forgiveness forever, if I had to. I could finally clear our air of this disagreement and we could get on to bigger and better things.

As rapidly as I could, I got dressed and quickly took to my rental car. I had a couple of guns on me, small ones that were easy to hide, and had a mission embroiled in my gut.

I wouldn't leave this estate until I had eliminated Vincent.

The sun was just barely coming up in the sky by the time I got to the Costellos' estate, which was a benefit to my plight. I parked my car a little up the road from the estate, and crept down the fence line until I was just around the corner from the security station. Based on the schedule I'd slowly been studying since first coming to New York, the guards were scheduled to switch out about ten minutes from when I arrived, and I'd long understood that this change happened like clockwork.

Thanks in part to Vladimir's tactics to blow up Vincent's old estate, he had this one ultra-fortified, including a strict guard schedule. Some guards walked the perimeter of the totally fenced in property, while one maintained the security station at the front of the property, and they swapped out on four-hour shifts, likely to prevent fatigue. The two to six in the morning shift was the one that was about to swap, and that was my window to sneak in.

Right on cue, the front gate buzzed and then slowly started to creak open. Because the exchange guard was coming from inside the property, they had to open the gate to get out, and given that it was wide enough for two cars to fit--hypothetically if one was coming and one was going simultane-ously, that made it very difficult for the guards to keep an eye on the opening in the hazy sunrise while also swapping posts. I kept an eye out for the guards to meet each other and begin communicating outside the security station, and it was at that moment that they both had their backs turned that I was able to slip around the corner of the fence and crouch behind the secu-rity box.

"Nothing to report," the outgoing guard said. "It's supposed to be hot today, though. Make sure you crank the AC up in about an hour or so. Vince is gonna be pissed if someone else passes out from heat exhaustion in here again."

The incoming guard snickered. "Jesse's a dumbass. Don't loop me in with her."

As the guards clocked in and out of the station's timeclock with their badges. I very carefully and very quietly crept along the ground, behind the security station, and slipped through the gate opening. The treeline was close, thankfully, so I slipped into it and waited for the outgoing guard to climb into the golf cart the incoming guard had traveled in and start making his way up the long road to the house.

Being extra careful to stay off the main road, or even close, I followed the dirt path within the trees, getting ever closer to the looming mansion in the distance. It was probably pretty stupid of me to bring the fight to Vincent's turf, but I knew that he didn't let anyone besides Katya and close friends in the main house. There had to be a moment where he felt totally secure and safe when I could get the jump on him, and when that moment arose, I'd be there to take advantage.

I was thankful for some of the long treks that Vladimir made Sascha and I take during training, because otherwise I might not have been able to make the jaunt to the house without exhausting myself. It was already starting to get hot, and by my guess, the road was between five and ten minutes long, and that was driving. It was an additional thirty minutes for me to walk from the fence to the property, but eventually I reached the edge of the woods where acres of clearing gave way to the impressive Costello estate--or small city depending on how one looked at it.

This was where my intel fell short. I'd only been able to surveil the prop-erty from the outside, and had no idea which of these buildings served which purpose. If I wasn't careful, I'd wander right into one of these buildings and--

My back split open with pain as something cracked me right across the spine. I let out a loud grunt and fell to the ground below, landing my face directly in a patch of dirt still wet from the morning dew. Pain shockwaved from the point of contact up and down my back, extending to the very reaches of my fingers and toes--even my head felt rocked.

I clamored, trying to get to one of my guns, but a pair of hands were on me a second later, pulling my guns out of their spots with precision, like the person reaching for them knew they were there.

"Fuck," turned into a grunt as a foot jabbed into my stomach, and I flipped over onto my back, writhing in pain.

Though they were blurry from the sudden assault, I blinked my eyes into the overhanging light, and was actually surprised at who was hovering over me. A shorter person, with a bat slung over her shoulder, and brown wavy hair in a side ponytail slung over her shoulder. She was wearing a pair of combat boots, dark gray leggings, and a light gray exercise maternity tank-top that was still struggling to cover her extremely round, pregnant belly.

"Katya," I grunted.

"This is not the way I wanted to start my morning, Maks," she hissed in Russian at me.

I sat up, and raked the mud off my face with the back of my hand. "Is a bat your weapon of choice?"

"No. A gun is my weapon of choice, but only when I want to kill someone. I only wanted to cause you a little bit of pain," she explained, then she held out her hand for me to take. Unsure of if I should trust this interaction or not, I took Katya's hand and let her pull me to my feet. I held out my hands for my guns, but she snorted, "Yeah right," then turned around and started walking towards the estate. "Follow me, you jackass."

I didn't know if I was more embarrassed or angry at this turn of events. Was this how low my skill level was? I couldn't even make it to Vincent, but was easily stopped by a seven-months pregnant Katya instead?

I followed her out of the trees and onto the main road, continuing up it and onto the property proper. She led me around this massive marble fountain and then turned to the left, and I kept in stride with her. As we passed one of the buildings, the security guard that I'd just seen leave the security station was standing there staring at me, and he seemed both unsurprised and unimpressed.

"Yeah, I saw you," he grumbled at me as I passed, and I just dropped my head in shame.

Was I stupid for thinking that I'd be better at this?

Eventually, Katya and I made it to the furthest building down this left path, which looked like a small two story house from the outside. She pulled out a key fob from her sports bra, then balanced the bat against the wall next to the door before flashing it in front of an LED monitor. The monitor blinged to life, and she set her thumb on the screen, allowing it to be scanned, and then the door opened.

She stood to the side and looked back at me, giving me an amused, if not slightly exhausted look. "Well? Come in." Any number of things could be inside this building, but I walked in nonetheless, doing the best I could to ignore the pain in my back. "Do you need an ice pack?" Katya asked behind me.

Embarrassed, I nodded. "That'd be good."

Inside the front door, I could see that the building was, in fact, a small house. It opened into a small living room with a fireplace against the wall to the right and a flat screen television hanging above it, and three sofas situated in a broken U-shape around an expensive looking rug. A doorway directly across from the front door looked like it led to a kitchen, as well as a staircase leading up stairs.

"Have a seat," Katya told me, motioning to the couch. "I'll get your ice pack. Do you want something to drink? There's lemonade, orange juice, water?"

I'd already made enough of a fool of myself, I didn't need to be served hospitality by someone who had foiled my plans mere minutes ago. "I'm okay."

Katya gave me a half-lidded gaze and then said, "I'll bring you lemonade." She wandered towards the kitchen, but stopped at the stairwell and craned her head up. "Mother! Come down for a second! There's a visitor!"

My heart lightened a little bit knowing Annika was there, and when I heard footsteps start to move above me, I smiled and stood up from the couch-- even though it hurt.

"Is it my son-in-law?" Annika's voice called out, irritating me a little bit, but then she rounded the corner and saw me and a massive smile came across her face. "Maksim!"

"Hello Annika."

She rushed forward and wrapped her arms around me, pulling me into a huge hug. I almost didn't know what to do at first because Annika had never greeted me *that* warmly before. Maybe a light hug, but mostly it was cheek-touches or nothing at all. But her squeeze was so inviting that I eventually gave in and closed my arms as well, hugging her close to me.

When she pulled back, she put her hands on either side of my face and frowned. "You look bruised and tired. Is work not going well?"

"He got arrested," Katya said, wandering back into the living room with an ice pack and a pitcher of lemonade. "I heard he got his ass kicked too."

"Oh," Annika hummed. "Well, I'm glad you're out." She looked at Katya and said, "Do you need me to get glasses?"

"You're gonna be late for your coffee date with Vince," Katya told her.

"Oh my gosh! You're right." Then she looked at me. "Oh. I wish I'd known you were coming, though. I would have rescheduled."

"His arrival was a surprise to us all," Katya said. "Don't worry. I'll make him stick around. Let Vince know he's here, will you?"

That twisted my stomach into a knot. Not only would I not be killing Vincent, but now he'd know I was there.

"Of course." Annika looked up at me and gave me a kiss on the cheek. "Don't go anywhere until I get back, okay?"

At this point, what else could I do? "Okay."

Annika collected a purse and keys from near the fireplace, then gave Katya a kiss on the cheek, rubbed her belly sweetly, and then left through the same door we'd come in through. Katya handed me the ice pack, set the pitcher down on one of the end tables, then turned around to head back into the kitchen, I assumed for glasses.

"They have coffee dates?" I called out.

Katya's snort filled the entire first floor. "Yeah, those two. Sometimes I think they're more in love than me and Vince are." She walked back in with the glasses in hand, and walked over to fill them from the pitcher. She then helped me situate the ice pack where she'd struck my back with her bat, before forcing the glass of lemonade into my hand. She was the same old, brash Katya. That made me happy, at least. "They have coffee dates, movie dates, and she actually convinced him to go with her to pottery class. You haven't lived until you've seen Vincent, tatts, guns and all, getting pissed off because he can't make a flower pot out of clay." She sat down on the adjacent couch and kicked one leg over the other. "So... Are you here to kill my fiancé?"

"That was the plan," I admitted.

She tilted her head to the side. "Maks, do you honestly think Vincent doesn't have cameras all over the place? That we didn't see you when you pretended to be someone in a car broken down on the side of the road, or when you planted that camera out front? Vincent has security cameras watching this place for two miles in every direction. My father *blew up* his last home."

"I suppose I may have underestimated him," I said.

"Not just him, but the rest of the Petrovs as well," she spat back.

"What do you mean?"

"Latva called me," Katya said. "He told me that rival groups are starting to move in without a Pakhan to man the station. He said he told you of this threat but you mostly blew him off. Not two minutes into the conversation did he let it slip that you'd come here to kill Vincent and bring me back to Russia. He was wondering if he'd been successful already. Wondering if I was safe."

There wasn't much I could say in response to that. I had not, at all, responded to Latva's concerns the way I needed to, and I was arrested shortly after he informed me of the problem. It had been the few weeks' time that he gave me at least once over, and was working on the second.

"I'll take care of that."

"I already did," Katya barked. "Luckily, I have more than a few friends in St. Petersburg who were willing to step up. Of course, I did so in the name of Maksim Petrov, the new Pakhan, to make it very clear that our family is not without a head. Latva has reported that they haven't had many issues as of late, but you need to get back to St. Petersburg and sort things out."

"I can't leave the country," I told her.

"You could if you really wanted to," she replied. "Besides, that's not the reason you're still here. You're here because of Vincent and because of Chloe."

I couldn't deny what she'd said. If not for those two people, I'd already be on my plane halfway home by now. "I have to take care of business."

"You need to start thinking more than one step ahead," Katya said. "Now that you're going to be a father, you need to do far more than just think about the immediate. You have to consider the future and all possible outcomes of your actions. You have a little person who is going to be relying on you."

"You know about the baby?" I asked.

She seemed to let out a sigh of relief at this. "Yes. And I'm glad to see that you know as well." Then she gave me a sweet smile. "You must be excited."

I couldn't stop a smile from coming to my face. "I'm so excited."

"We should be focusing on that, not this unjustified vengeance you hold against Vincent," Katya said. "Maks... I'm sorry. My family placed you in a really bad position, and then we all left you in some way or another. I know it probably feels like Vincent's arrival in our lives and us leaving were interconnected, but they weren't. Vincent didn't cause those problems. They existed long before he even kidnapped me." I didn't want to admit it, but hearing her lay it out that way almost made me feel like she was right. "I'm not asking you to be his best friend, but he's such a big part of my life, and I want you to continue being a part of it. You saw how happy my mom was to see you. I already lost one brother, I... I don't want to lose another one."

Brother.

Being referred to as Katya's brother made me feel equal parts happy and sad. There was a young man inside me who always pined after her who was crushed to be sibling-zoned, but the little boy and the man who loved Chloe and was so indebted to the Petrov family felt much better in this place. It shed any false pretenses and felt like I could wear the Petrov name with pride--like I actually belonged here.

"Chloe told me I have to choose between killing Vincent or being with her," I said.

Katya scoffed. "And you chose killing Vincent?"

"I was hoping for both," I admitted. "It was more of an 'ask forgiveness, not permission,' sort of situation."

"You're incorrigible," she barked. "Just go be the Pakhan of the most powerful bratva in all of Russia and raise your cute family. What's so hard about that? Why bother with us? Why risk all of that for a moment's satisfaction? It isn't going to bring my father or my mother back, but you can damn well bet it would cost you me and my mother--and it would cost you Chloe and your baby, too. You only have so many chances with someone, Maks. Eventually she'll give up."

"I feel haunted by Vincent," I told her.

She shook her head. "You're haunting yourself with him. He actually likes you.'

Maybe all I needed was a good whack to the back with a bat held by Katya, but it felt like the fog was shaking loose. Would I ever stop hating Vincent? Probably not. But I was beginning to see that there was more to lose than there was to gain from killing him.

As if the conversation summoned him, we heard the front door click, and Annika walked in with Vincent right on her heels. He looked down at me with a surprised, and oddly enough, not hostile expression.

"Hello Maksim," he greeted.

I looked him up and down before saying, in English, "Hello, Vincent."

It seemed we were on the precipice of a really awkward conversation when my phone started to buzz in my pocket. I expected that it might be Chloe, but it was actually Brusch. I answered it, knowing the man's tendency not to bother me for anything short of an emergency. "Hello?"

"Boss, I need you to come back immediately," he said.

I furrowed my brow. "Why? What's wrong?"

"It's the Bonettis," he replied. "They've got Dacha totally surrounded."

CHAPTER EIGHTEEN: CHLOE

After how well the baby conversation and subsequent night with Maksim had gone, it was difficult to drag myself away from him, but I knew that, even if my job was rapidly losing its value to me, I still needed the paycheck, at least. In the midst of dealing with Maksim and the news with the baby, I'd pretty much gone through my vacation days, so all that was left was to go to work and ride the desk until the wheels fell off. Once I knew more about if I was actually staying in New York or not, I could make a determination about what needed to happen with my job, but until that moment, I'd collect the paycheck, build up my pension, and bank my money for me and my baby's future.

"Well, look who decided to blow in," Mitzy said as I walked into the office with a couple of cups from the nearby coffee shop in each hand. When he noticed them, he furrowed his brow and hissed. "Hey! No coffee for you, missy. You certainly can't double fist."

I just shook my head at him, holding one out. "This one is for you." I set it down on the desk, "and this one is decaf," I added on, taking a sip of the swill. "Although, I don't understand the point of decaf coffee. It's like there's caffeinated coffee, and then there's murky water." He snickered at me as he lifted his cup, but then his gaze narrowed on me. "What?" I asked.

"Nothing. You just seem to be in a good mood."

I sat down at my desk, which was in front of Mitzy's, but turned around so I could continue talking to him. "Well, I finally told Maks yesterday."

He lifted his brows. "About the baby?"

I nodded. "Yep. It went really well. He was excited."

Mitzy rolled his eyes. "Well I could have guessed that from the massive hickey on your neck." My hand flew directly to my neck and he laughed. "Not that one, but thanks for pointing it out."

I'd noticed the marks while I was getting ready for work that morning and did the best I could to cover them with makeup, but I'd had them all night, so I didn't quite get to them in time to hide them without using about fifteen layers more makeup than I usually used, and somehow it felt like showing up looking like an oompa loompa would be at least as suspicious as just rocking the hickeys, if not more so.

"And then this morning we actually managed to part ways on a high note and..." I smiled, remembering the confession. "He might have used the l-word."

Mitzy's jaw dropped. "Wait... I thought this was a drama. When did it turn into a sappy romance?"

"Shut up," I hissed at him.

"No, no, no, I'm serious. You were all, 'What am I going to do? Where's my sense of justice? Can I even trust him? He's so dangerous.' Now you're all hickeys and the 'l-word.'" He mocked me in a frilly tone.

"Well, for the record, I am still reasonably anxious about my purpose in life now, if you were wondering," I told him. "I think I'm honestly just trying to ignore that with the hopes that I won't completely meltdown and implode."

"Ahhh." He wagged a finger at me. "Avoidance. The best solution to any problem."

"Okay, but seriously, though, can you help me? I could really use some of that sage, Mitzy advice," I told him. "Maks obviously wants me to go to Russia and be with him, and I kind of told him that I might like to do that, but..." I frowned. "Can I seriously do that? I feel like my mom is rolling over in her grave."

"Can I give you a *really* fucked up way to think about it?" Mitzy said.

"*Please.*"

"In his line of work, Maksim will likely end up eliminating a lot of bad men." I glared at him. "You know? You'd still be getting rid of them, apart from the one in your bedroom. There would always be at least one you'd miss here anyway. So the one who got away is the one who knocks you up, and you'll probably have a way higher success rate with him than you would here."

"That is an *incredibly* fucked up way to think about it," I said.

He shrugged at me. "I told you it would be."

"I want to be with him, I do, I'm just having a really tough time justifying making the leap from organized crime detective to..."

"Organized crime baby mama?" Mitzy finished.

I stared flatly at him. "I'm regretting bringing you coffee, you ass."

"Look, Chloe, I..." Mitzy's voice faded away and his eyes focused on something behind me. None of the rest of the crew was in for the morning yet, so I didn't think it was that, but when I followed his gaze behind me, I saw that it was much worse.

For some reason, strolling into the precinct as if he belonged there, was none other than Stavio Bonetti. He had an arrogant smile on his face and even dared to look at Mitzy and I and give us a head nod. After that, he walked up to Captain Cox's door and knocked a couple of times, before actually grabbing the door handle and letting himself in.

"Um," I whispered, as the door closed. "What the hell is Stavio Bonetti doing meeting with Cox?"

Mitzy jumped up quickly. "Come with me."

He was already rushing out of the precinct before I had a chance to respond, so I quickly jumped up and ran after him. Rather than going for the elevator, he pushed into the stairwell, holding the door open until I was in, then he let it go and rushed down a couple of flights of stairs. Eventually, he sat down on one of the stairs and motioned for me to sit down next to him. He yanked his wireless earbuds from his pocket and handed one to me and I popped it in.

After flipping through a few apps on his phone, he opened one and then all of a sudden I heard a couple of voices through the headphone in my ear.

"About ten minutes ago," Stavio Bonetti answered a question we hadn't been quick enough to hear.

"Good," Cox said. "He wasn't there, right?"

"No. Your tip was correct, he'd left about an hour earlier," Stavio said.

I looked over at Mitzy. "Do you have his office bugged?"

"Yeah. After he started keeping shit from us, I figured it was necessary, now shh."

"We're planning to just wreck the shit up," Stavio said. "After Maksim embarrassed me and then killed my cousin behind bars, I'm done with his shit." Maksim had killed someone behind bars? Somehow that never came up. "I want him to suffer for what he's done to me."

"Do what you want so long as you don't touch him. He's mine," Cox said. "He may have weasels his way out of prison somehow, but it's inconsequential. I'm planning to have his charges dropped in the interest of extradition anyway. I've already got a detective from the Investigative Committee lined up to take him and all of the credit for catching him in exchange for a hefty sum of money. You'll get your ten percent of course, and whatever you can get out of the club."

"Ten percent is nice, but I really wish I could take his head clean off," Stavio responded.

I lifted my hand to my mouth. Cox was planning on extraditing Maksim back to Russia and handing him directly to the authorities there. He would end up bearing the entire weight of all of the Petrovs crimes as far back as the statute of limitations would go, and in Russia, things like this bore so much more weight.

Maksim was in real trouble.

"If it's about making him suffer, you'll have your opportunity," Cox said. "For now, cause your ruckus and walk him into that trap, and let me take it from there."

I ripped the earbud out of my ear and started to run back up the stairs.

"Chloe, wait," Mitzy said, but I wasn't listening to him.

I needed to get to Maksim as soon as possible. If Cox got his hands on him, he was going to have a much larger issue on his hands than being stuck in an American prison for a few weeks.

Though I wanted to move as fast as I could, I didn't want to attract any unnecessary attention to myself and made sure to move as casually as possible into the precinct and over to my desk. Cox's office didn't have any windows because he was a paranoid who liked to keep shit to himself, thank God, so I was able to grab my keys, phone, and wallet, and head back out without being noticed.

Mitzy caught me halfway to the elevator though and snatched me into the break room. "I need you to wait a minute."

"I can't! He's setting Maks up. You heard Stavio, he said the Bonettis arrived at Dacha to wreck the place and draw Maksim into a trap. I have to get in touch with him or stop him somehow."

My heart was thundering in my chest at the thought of something bad happening to Maks. It wasn't just that he was the father of my child, it was that I was helplessly in love with him and couldn't imagine never being able to see him again. If the police in Russia got their hands on him, if he wasn't killed, he'd be locked up for life. He'd never even get to meet our child.

Suddenly, my throat started to tighten and it was getting harder to breathe. Water was blurring the corners of my eyes and I could hear my blood pumping in loud thumps in my ears.

"Chlo?" Mitzy's voice sounded a thousand miles from me. "Chloe."

It was like it was muffled in a tube, and when I tried to look up at him, it was like there were four of him standing in front of me and nothing I tried helped me to focus on the real one. "Mitzy," I whimpered.

"Hey." He put his hands on my arms. "You're having a panic attack. Just try and breathe. Can you hear me?"

"Barely," I said. "I'm scared."

"Shh. It's okay. Sit here." He led me over to a chair and guided me down into it, then he crouched in front of me and looked up. "Look at me. I'm right here, okay? I'm not gonna leave you." My vision was wavering like my world was turning over on its axis and I felt like I was going to fall out of the chair. Mitzy set his arms on either side of me though, trapping me in firmly. "Chloe. Look at me."

"I'm trying!" I sobbed. "I can't!"

"You can. What color are my eyes?"

My whole body was shaking. I couldn't really look at Mitzy properly, so I searched my brain for that information and remembered that Mitzy had a pair of dark gray eyes that seemed to change to brown in some lights, and closer to a deep blue in others. He claimed it was his ancestry.

"Gray," I said.

When I said it, I suddenly found myself able to focus on his eyes, seeing the concern seated deep behind the gray. Then his face came into focus and my chest started to open up a little more.

"Good girl," Mitzy said. "Breathe in." I pulled air in to my full lung capacity, and then Mitzy said, "Breathe out," and I let it go. He sounded normal again, and I swallowed hard. My stomach was twisting and I closed my eyes, forcing it to settle. Now wasn't the time for me to completely lose myself. "We need to not go running out there," Mitzy said. "He's not the only one in danger."

"What do you mean?" I said.

"Did you hear what Cox said?" He looked at me with the deepest look of worry I'd ever seen on the man. "He told Stavio if he was looking for a chance to make Maksim suffer, then he'd get the opportunity. He means you. He knows that you'll end up going out there once you hear about the chaos, and he's planning to sacrifice you to Stavio to satiate his need for vengeance. You can't go there."

Tears filled my eyes. "I have to. I have to save Maks."

"If you go there, you could die," Mitzy said.

"If I don't go, Maks could die," I told him, then I stood up from the chair.

He stood up and tried to keep his body between me and the way out. "Chloe, think of the baby."

"I am," I demanded. "I'm thinking of the baby. Right now its father is in trouble and if I don't do anything, then neither of us could see him ever again. I didn't come through all of the bullshit I came through just to lose Maksim to Cox's bullshit." Mitzy gave me a defeated look, almost appearing on the verge of tears himself. "I understand if you don't want to come, but I can't not go. He needs me."

"Don't insult me, Chloe," Mitzy growled. "I'm not going to let you go alone."

"Then we need to go," I said. "This little plan of theirs is already underway. For all we know, we could already be too late."

CHAPTER NINETEEN: MAKSIM

It was safe to say that I didn't want to cut my conversation with Katya and Vincent short in order to rush back to Dacha and deal with an issue with the Bonettis, but that was the situation I'd found myself in. I should have expected that, after everything happened with the Bonettis behind bars, that they wouldn't just let me get away with it. Not only did I actually kill one of the Bonettis, but I ended Delta as well, who had to be a pretty important resource for them.

With Katya and Vincent assuring me that they'd have my back if I needed them, but of course, I was quick to tell Vincent to go fuck himself. Katya told me to quit being a brat, and I left before that could devolve into the most unnecessary and ill-timed fight ever.

It seemed a little strange to me that the Bonettis would arrive so early in the morning, and specifically when I happened to leave. It just seemed a little too coincidental to me, and I couldn't help but wonder if the Bonettis had been keeping Dacha under surveillance ever since I got back, or maybe even before. Things obviously didn't end on the best of terms between the Bonettis and I even before I went to prison, and of course, that trickled into my time behind bars. Then that of course led to what happened behind bars, which was now spilling back out into the real world again.

Clearly, I just needed to deal with the Bonettis once and for all. I could afford to have them figure out that Chloe was pregnant, or even that we were together in general, because who knew what they would do with that information.

It frustrated me that I wasn't a quick skip from the city because it meant that the Bonettis could be doing any amount of damage while they were waiting for me to arrive. Instead, I figured it was in my best interest to call for some help that I was okay accepting, and from someone that was a little bit closer to the scene than I was.

Using the bluetooth feature on my car, I dialed up Alexei with the hopes that we could put our new partnership to use. I wasn't expecting to have to ask him to run into battle for me this early in our relationship, but desperate times called for desperate measures.

"Ah, Maksim," Alexei said when he answered. "I hope you are well. I was just talking over our new plans with my group."

"I wish I were better, Alexei. It seems there's a bit of a disturbance at my club, and I'm about thirty minutes away," I said. "I hate to call on our partnership so quickly, but--"

"It's not an issue," Alexei said. "What seems to be the problem?"

"As it turns out, my issue that began with the Bonettis outside of prison and followed me in has now followed me back out again. I just received a call from my sovietnik about five minutes ago saying that the Bonettis have the club surrounded and are starting to swarm. It seems they specifically waited for me to leave and then showed up knowing I wasn't there. I'm on my way back now, but like I said, I'm far away and can only move so quickly."

"Do not worry, my friend, I will go and assess the situation. Be sure to take extra care yourself. If I didn't know any better, I would say this almost sounds like a trap to me. Perhaps they waited for you to leave so they could lure you back into a precarious situation. When you return, you would do well not to be seen."

That thought hadn't even occurred to me, but made sense once Alexei laid it out like that.

"I understand. Thank you. I will see you soon."

"See you soon."

As frustrating as it was, I made extra sure to obey all the rules of the road because I had a feeling Cox had his feelers out for me from the second I left prison. Knowing him, he was probably waiting for an opportunity such as this to catch me doing something really stupid, like speeding or running a red light. The entire drive home, I wondered if there was any way that I could have avoided this backlash with the Bonettis, but frustratingly realized that it came as a result of my bad temper. I allowed my anger issues to make me run the beginning of my new empire like Vladimir ran his, and as a result, I was catching reverb the way that he did.

The way that ultimately led to his death.

This was just another reminder of the fact that I needed to do things *my* way. If I'd talked the Bonettis out of my life, I wouldn't be in the situation I was in. And Stavio Bonetti wasn't an intelligent man, I probably could have done it easily. Katya called my need for vengeance against Vincent momentary satisfaction to solve no problems, and that was precisely what my temper was in general.

Chloe helped me manage my temper, which would help me in the future, but didn't do much for me when dealing with the fallout of the issues my temper had already caused.

For as slow as it was, I felt like I made good time getting back to Dacha, and was terrified to see that Brusch had not accurately communicated the situation when he simply told me that the Bonettis had the place surrounded. On paper, that was a good way to describe the situation, but the actuality was much worse. "Surrounded" ended about fifty cars before the Bonettis stopped loading in. The street looked like it was made of cars from the way they had it blocked in with vehicles.

I could only imagine the *entire* Bonetti clan had come out for this extravaganza.

What was weird to me was how much of a scene they were making in broad daylight. Men very obviously holding assault rifles, representatives of the Bonetti gang that had to be wanted just standing around like they didn't have a care in the world.

It was like they didn't fear the repercussions of their actions at all.

I didn't see Alexei or any of his cohorts, but knowing him, he was staying out of sight. He said he'd be around to help, and I believed him, so I just had to hope that he was managing this issue from somewhere other than what I was looking at--which was an absolute army of Bonetti soldiers.

Alexei's advice hung right on the edge of my mind as I arrived, so I decided to park in front of Nikitina's convenience store, which was within walking distance of the club. The downside to the massive amount of people that the Bonettis brought for this excursion was that one man who excelled at stealth--my earlier run-in with Katya the *Pantera* aside--could make use of the crowd. Tons of black-tinted trucks and people with their heads on swivels were actually pretty easy to get around.

The front of Dacha was a no-go. The Bonettis had the place so blocked off that I would never be able to get in without being seen. Luckily for me, however, the back door wasn't watched, but not nearly as well.

Or rather, this seemed to be where Alexei had shown himself.

There were more cars than people, and those people who were left seemed a little spooked. I'd always heard that Alexei could be a phantom in business, but I didn't take it literally. These people, however, looked as if they had been haunted by an actual phantom, which given that there weren't even the bodies of the missing Bonettis left behind, was probably more accurate than I cared to admit.

Pulling out my blade as the obviously quieter weapon that I had, I slid up behind the closest Bonetti to me, one of about six left, and wrapped my hand around their mouth. I slashed my blade across their shins, immediately causing them to drop, then I stabbed into their stomach repeatedly until I saw the life fade from their eyes.

I was hoping that I had gone unnoticed, but then one of them looked over and said, "Tanner? Shit! They're back!"

Those who were around went into full panic mode, ducking behind whatever car they were nearest and becoming twice as alert.

I'd never get to the backdoor without being noticed this way.

In the midst of me trying to figure out what my next best course of action was, my ears perked up and I heard police sirens in the distance. It was a quiet wail at first, but it rapidly got louder, and it was obvious that those police were en route to Dacha. I looked around, fully expecting the Bonettis to get spooked by the sirens and take off.

But they didn't move at all.

My eyes widened and I watched in confused horror as the Bonettis continued to stand confidently as if there was nothing the police could do to them even if they *did* show up.

Or rather, nothing they would do to them.

All of a sudden, I closed my eyes in frustration and realized how big of an idiot I really was. Borya tried to warn me that I wasn't seeing the situation clearly and that I was likely missing the obvious, but the moment of clarity that was washing over me now was so angering I could scream. It was exactly as he'd said--someone close to me, who knew my plans while I was in New York, and would work with the police to their own benefit.

Cox was tipped off and supplied evidence by the Bonettis.

Delta was working with the Bonettis, and Borya was confident that some of the guards had to be working with Cox based on the way things always went inside. It was painfully obvious and yet it flew right over my head.

Either Cox was in the Bonettis' pocket or they were in his, and neither of those was good for me based on what the Bonettis knew.

Cox likely had Dacha under surveillance, which was not only how he knew to come and arrest me as soon as Chloe left, but also how the Bonettis knew to show up today as soon as I left for the Costello's estate. I wondered how long that relationship had existed, was it just since I fired the Bonettis, or was it long before that?

That meant a couple of things that were truly terrifying for me. The first, was that the *inside* of Dacha could easily be bugged. If the Bonettis had Cox in their back pocket all along, they could have laid listening devices any number of places inside, which meant they could have heard tons of sensitive information, even more than what I shared with them willingly as partners.

It also meant that the sound of sirens racing towards my current location were not a good thing, but a bad thing.

Those sirens were the Bonettis' *backup*.

Just as the fear that perhaps they'd overheard that Chloe was pregnant was starting to settle in my gut, a police car came screeching up to the back of Dacha with its sirens blaring. I was trying to curl myself up in a ball behind the engine block, hoping that I could find a way to back out and reassess what I needed to do, when the car doors opened and a pair of people climbed out.

Thankfully friends, not foes.

Chloe rapidly jumped out of the driver's seat with her gun already at the ready, and Mitzy climbed out of the passenger's seat. The Bonettis seemed shocked when Chloe and Mitzy turned their guns on them and immediately started demanding them to drop their weapons and get down on the ground.

"What are you doing?" one of them called. "You're not supposed to interfere with us."

"You heard the woman," Mitzy said. "Drop your weapons and get down on the ground, now!"

More police sirens blared into the silence and I was wondering if these sirens were a good thing or a bad thing. I had to pick the right moment to reveal myself, hopefully in a way that wouldn't result in either Chloe's or mine deaths, but this didn't feel like that moment. I quietly pulled my gun and waited, making sure not to jump the gun, but ready to jump in and save Chloe if I needed to.

The additional police car pulled in next to Chloe's and when the two occupants climbed out, my heart sank.

These two were foes, not friends.

Cox slowly climbed out of the driver's seat and pulled a gun out. Chloe and Mitzy stood defensively, but seemed apprehensive to assume just yet.

However, they were certain he was the enemy when Stavio Bonetti left the passenger's seat with a disgusting smile on his face.

Cox pointed his gun at Mitzy and huffed, "I wouldn't move," then he nodded in Chloe's direction, and Stavio walked around the car and started over towards where she was standing. She was just about to pull the trigger when Cox warned, "Do it, and I'll kill your little friend here."

Chloe looked worriedly at Mitzy and he seemed to be trying to tell her with his eyes to just take the shot, but I knew how much Mitzy meant to her. I knew she wouldn't do it.

With no other choice, I climbed out from my hiding spot and revealed myself to Cox and Stavio. All of the Bonettis guns turned to me, and I knew that, even if I got one shot off, I'd be riddled with bullets before my own hit its mark. Besides, this wasn't about turning the tables.

This was about saving my baby and the woman I loved.

"I'm the one you want, right?" I said, dropping my gun and kicking it across the tar. "I'm here. Just let them go."

Cox gave me an evil smile. "Thanks for making things easy for me." Then he looked at Stavio again, who finished crossing the distance between himself and Chloe, and wrapped an arm around her and set a gun to her head.

"Chloe!" Mitzy and I screamed in unison.

"Unfortunately, it's not going to be so easy for you," Cox said. "The Bonettis want you to suffer and I'm sick of this little traitor." He looked back over his shoulder at her. "You've betrayed me for the last time, Nikitina."

CHAPTER TWENTY: MAKSIM

Why did it always take life-altering moments to bring clarity? Why couldn't people like me see sooner than the moment that it might be too late that there were things more important in the world than arrogance and vengeance?

Even before I knew Chloe was pregnant, it had become obvious to me that she was someone important to me. From that first moment she was dragged up to my penthouse during her department's first raid, I'd been intrigued by her presence in my life. As we started sleeping together and eventually dating, I started to develop feelings for her. Every threat I made against her was empty because I never would have been able to hurt her even if it made sense for my life to do so.

She told me to leave and go back to Russia, both before I went to prison and after. She begged me to let my petty vengeance against Vincent go and consider the relationship we could have instead. Nothing she asked of me was unreasonable or unacceptable, yet I let my own arrogance get in the way.

And now I was being forced to watch as Stavio Bonetti dragged her out of my control with a gun pressed to her head. She was crying and silently begging for me to save her, but there was nothing I could do. The only true love of my life was moments away from who knew what level of torture and anguish before the end of her life, and I was powerless to stop it.

"Cox!" Mitzy thundered. "Stop him or I swear to god, I'll end your miserable *fucking* life!"

In response, Cox just fired the gun he had pointed at Mitzy, striking him straight in the chest and sending him backwards.

"No!" Chloe screamed, sobbing harder. "Max!" She fought to try and get free of Stavio's hold as he pulled her backwards towards Dacha. "Let me go! Mitzy!" she screamed. "No! Please!"

It was hard to tell from the distance I was from Mitzy if the shot had killed him or not, but he hit the floor and a pool of blood quickly started to surround him. I didn't know Mitzy enough to have a strong opinion of the man, but I knew he was important to Chloe. I knew that he took care of her when she was sick and was by her side when she found out she was pregnant with our child.

I at least knew enough to know I didn't want him dead.

I took a step towards him, but Cox quickly turned his gun on me. "Ah, ah, ah."

"Stop it!" Chloe screeched.

"I've got plans for you, Petrov, but don't think I won't hesitate to bring you within an inch of your own life just for the hell of it. You've pissed me off and turned my own crew against me. I won't stand for it any longer."

"Cox!" Chloe barked. "You don't know what you're talking about. This is a mistake. Please!"

"Get her inside!" Cox barked. "I don't want to hear that bitch's voice anymore."

Stavio was nearly at the back door to Dacha, and if he felt safe bringing her inside, that probably meant that the entire inside was totally compromised. I had no idea if Brusch was alive, or any of my other lower-ranks that were there. Thankfully, because it was so early in the morning, a majority of the club employees weren't in for the day yet, but there was likely at least one manager, including my new go-to person, after Dino, Tonia. There could be casualties inside, but I felt guilty for being way less concerned about them than I was about Chloe.

Was there seriously nothing I could do?

All of a sudden, a gunshot split the tense silence and Stavio Bonetti fell to his knees. Chloe yanked away from him just as another bullet sliced right through his torso. He hit the floor face-first and there was no denying that *he* was dead. I followed the angle of the shots to where Katya was perched on a building across the street with a sniper rifle. If I wasn't in the midst of panicking, I'd be able to appreciate how badass she looked up there.

Chloe ran over to where Mitzy was crouched on the ground, still sobbing as she went, and Cox turned his gun to her. I rushed Cox, but he quickly shifted and tried to turn on me instead.

"Maks!" Chloe yelped, but before Cox could fire on me, a car came screeching into the clearing, bowling over a handful of the Bonettis and distracting Cox.

As much as I wanted to deal with Cox, getting Chloe and Mitzy out of the line of fire was much more important. I ran over to her and was relieved to see that Mitzy was still breathing at least, even if he was bleeding profusely and fighting to catch his breath.

"Help me get him inside," I said to her.

Cox wanted to try and stop us, but the driver of the car that had toppled a bunch of the Bonettis like a house of cards stepped out. A fair amount of rage filled my body as Vincent appeared in the sunlight with a gun in his hand. Out of the passenger's side of the car stepped a man that I'd last seen fighting for his life in St. Petersburg, Vincent's underboss, Mario.

"Come on now, *Clayton*," Mario barked. "We wouldn't want things to get any worse here, huh? You've already shot a cop and tried to sacrifice another. I'm far from a defender of the police, but in this situation, I'd hate to see any more boys in blue hit the ground. All we got here are a couple of yahoos that no one is gonna believe. You can claim a pickup gone wrong and walk away before anyone else gets hurt." He looked at Vincent and then snickered. "And by anyone else, I mean him."

Almost on cue, a few more black trucks with tinted windows pulled up, and what I imagined was the entire Costello gang started to unload. A man that I'd seen before from Nick Costello's reign, Devrick, was there, along with a younger looking man who seemed to be high ranking, as well. There was also a severe-looking woman with her hair pulled back into a tight bun that seemed like she would be trouble to cross. Between them and Katya, these were Vincent's caporegimes and his consigliere.

He'd managed to rally his entire upper ranks.

Vincent didn't look as humored as his friend, but also didn't look concerned. For as much as I didn't care for the man, this moment was humbling, to say the least. The Costellos were rallied and put together. I assumed I was ready to pick up directly from where Vladimir left off, but it was clear I had a long way to go as a leader. I could take my cues from people who were used to steering a ship, like Vincent, Katya or Chloe, but only if we all got out of this sticky situation alive.

Though I hated to leave things up to Vincent, I allowed him to handle things outside and finished helping Chloe get Mitzy inside Dacha's back door. There was no one in the immediate vicinity, so I nodded towards the elevator and instructed her to drag him on, which she did. If we could get him up to my penthouse, he'd be safe from any additional damage at least. Although it wouldn't make much difference, he was living on borrowed time.

Just as Chloe was finishing pulling a groaning Mitzy onto the elevator, a couple of the Bonetti's men came flying around the corner. I looked between them and Chloe, weaponless, and not wanting her to get hurt.

Mitzy pointed a weak hand down at his waist, and Chloe yanked out his gun, and threw it to me. I flipped on my heel and fired at the Bonettis, sending them retreating around the corner. I reached around and slammed my hand on the penthouse button, then pulled back so that the elevator could go on without me.

"Maks!" Chloe screeched.

"I'm right behind you. Get Mitzy to safety!"

Right as the door was closing, I pulled my keys from my pocket and tossed them through the opening. The doors closed, separating the two of us from one another. But I knew she was safe. My penthouse was fortified, so no one could get in or out without the keys. I had to figure out how to get this war under control before anyone else got hurt, and in enough time to hopefully save Mitzy's life.

The two Bonettis that I was facing off against poked their heads around the corner to fire at me, and I was just barely able to back up into a nook near the elevators to keep myself safe, and we were at a standoff. It was the two of them versus the one of me, and if I wasn't careful, being outmanned would cost me my life.

Seeing that the Bonettis clearly had free reign of Dacha didn't bring me any comfort that Brusch or Tonia or anyone else who was in Dacha at the time of the Bonettis descent was still living. The Costellos were outside handing things with the Bonettis and Cox, and I had to imagine Alexei and his crew were nearby helping out as well. Everyone was pulling their fair share of the weight but me.

If I could get Dacha's insides cleared out, then I didn't have the right to call myself a Pakahn.

So I stopped hiding and came out to face the Bonettis outright. I'd taken gunshots before, I'd taken blades before. Vladimir's training made what I'd experienced in NYC so far feel like a tropical vacation. There was a reason Katya could silently make her way through the woods or to the top of a building, seven months pregnant, and pull off military grade executions as if she'd been doing it her whole life.

Vladimir Petrov didn't raise children. He raised killers.

Assuming I was letting my arrogance do the decision-making, both Bonettis peeked out and tried to fire on me. One of them did manage to cut across my leg, but for his efforts, he got a bullet to the face. Brain matter splattered against his partner, who immediately started to regret his position in life and tried to run. Giving chase wasn't necessary, as I rounded the corner and saw him hustling down the long hallway. He wasn't smart enough to duck into the bathrooms or storage rooms, so I made short work of him, sending him to the ground with one shot, and then finishing him off with another when I caught up to him, stepping over his deceased body.

Dacha proper was *crawling* with more Bonettis, and not one of my people was in sight. It actually gave me a little bit of relief to see that the dead bodies of my crew weren't scattered about, but I wouldn't be satisfied until I knew where they were.

Outside, I could hear a full-scale battle starting to erupt as a cacophony of voices and bullets started to surmount. I knew I was running out of time and had to act fast. Fortunately, I had an advantage that the Bonettis lacked--a lay of the land. The breaker box was right at the entrance to the hallway, so I wrenched open the lid and flipped all the power inside this main part of the club off.

A murmur of voices bubbled up as those trapped inside peered through the darkness in confusion. These circumstances called for finesse, so I pulled out my blade again and quickly became the bogeyman. Those who caught a glimpse of me did so only moments before they lost their lives, and weren't able to get the word out before I rendered them speechless. The club's blueprint was flashing in my brain as I crept around, leaving two or three bodies in my wake everywhere I went.

Before long, I'd decimated the Bonettis' numbers, save for a few runners. One of them had nearly made it to the front door when Brusch stepped out of into the front doorway and punched a guy unconscious. "

I was so relieved to see that he was okay.

"Casualties?" I asked.

He shook his head. "None. I evacuated everyone."

"Well done." I returned to the breaker box to turn the lights back on, illuminating the litter of bodies. "Did you get it from here?"

He nodded. "I've got it."

"Good," I told him, because Chloe is in trouble and I need to get back to her before it's too late.

CHAPTER TWENTY-ONE: CHLOE

Every bone that I had was shaking as I held Mitzy's dying body in my arms. I was covered in his blood from putting pressure on the spot where he'd been shot, but the wound was so bad that the crimson ichor was bubbling up around my hand.

"Chloe," Mitzy groaned at me.

"Shh," I demanded, trying to control my sobs as the elevator carried us upstairs. It felt like it was going at a snail's pace up to the penthouse. I'd ridden it dozens of times before and I never remembered it going that slow.

"Chloe," Mitzy said again.

I let out a choked sob before saying, "Shut up! Don't talk. You need to save your energy." He opened his mouth again, but I shook my head again before he could say anything. "Stop it. Stop talking. Whatever you're going to say doesn't matter to me. I'm not leaving you. I'm not letting you die. I can't lose you. So just shut up, please."

"You're not..." He gurgled a little bit. "You're not safe here."

"I'm not safe anywhere," I whimpered to him. "For a really long time, the only place I've ever been truly safe is with you by my side." Tears were rushing down my cheeks. "Please just stop talking. Maks has some supplies at his place, I can patch you up and then start figuring out how to get you to a hospital."

It was clear from the strained look on Mitzy's face that he wanted to say more, but thankfully he didn't, because I didn't think I could handle it. There were very few people in my life that meant the world to me and he was one of them. If it wasn't for me, he never would have been here, to begin with. He took a bullet because of me and I refused to let him die. He had a wife that he loved. He had children. I couldn't just let him go.

My baby deserved to meet its godfather.

Finally, after what felt like an eternity, the elevator reached the top floor and stopped. I used the fob on Maks' keys to authorize the doors to open, and then they slowly parted. As carefully as I could, I dragged Mitzy off the elevator, not taking him too far, only until he was just inside the entryway and the elevator doors could close. No one could come in now without me answering the doorbell, so we should be safe from additional problems up here.

"Okay," I said, fully panicking but trying my hardest to hold it together. "Okay. You're going to stay right here. I'm gonna get... I need..." I lifted Mitzy's hands and set them on the wound, but they limply fell down to Mitzy's sides. I looked up at Mitzy's face and his eyes were closed and his face was covered in sweat. "No!" I yelped. "No. Mitzy!" I set my head on his chest and his heart was still beating, albeit very slowly, so I tapped his face a few times until his eyes slowly peeled open. "Don't do this, okay? Here, you need to put pressure on the wound so I can go get stuff, okay?"

"Chloe."

"No," I cried. "No. Keep [pressure on the wound." I lifted his hands again and set them on the spot where he'd been shot, and thankfully, he kept them there. "I'll be right back, okay?" He didn't respond to me and started to close his eyes again, so I shouted. "Okay?!"

"Okay."

"Okay."

As quickly as I could, I started running around the penthouse trying to collect anything that I thought would help. I got a pillow for Mitzy's head, but then chucked it because he probably had blood coming up and I didn't want him to choke on it. I grabbed a bottle of water from Maksim's fridge, and then I bolted into the bathroom and started tearing through the supplies in there. I found gauze, medical tape, and pain relievers, all of which I snatched up, then I ran to the utility closet and grabbed a pair of scissors and a bucket which I filled with water. I carried everything back to Mitzy's side and set it all out, preparing myself to patch him up.

His hands were shaking, but it was clear he was trying to keep pressure on the gunshot wound, which was good, because it meant he had at least *some* will to keep living.

"I need to wash the spot so I can wrap it," I told him. "Once we stop the bleeding I have some pain relievers."

He gave me a weak nod, so I took the scissors I'd found and started to cut his shirt off so I could get to the wound. Terrifyingly, there was so much blood that when I tried to pull it away from the point of entry, the shirt wouldn't lift away. Trying, even a little bit, made Mitzy groan with pain.

"I'm sorry!" I whimpered. "I'm so sorry. I have to get it off."

"It's okay," he choked out. "Do it."

I didn't want Mitzy to suffer any more than he already was, so I ripped the shirt from the spot as fast as I could. Mitzy let out a roar of pain and it made new tears fall from my eyes. "I'm sorry," I cried. "I'm done. I'm done with that part."

His body fell slack again and his chest was lifting and falling heavily. Though the spot was covered in blood, I could see that the wound was bad and already starting to fester. By my best guess, the bullet didn't pass through, but rather was lodged inside, probably near an organ that would threaten his life if I tried to pull it out. I'd been considering that, but I knew I'd probably kill him for sure if I tried, so I just chose to wrap him up and hope we could get him to an *actual* doctor sooner rather than later.

Because I couldn't get my emotions under control, my eyes were filled with tears and it was blurring my vision. I dragged my palms against my eyes, just trying to get them clear enough to see, but every time I looked down at Mitzy dying in front of me, it made me emotional all over again. I just shook my head through it and tried to blink the tears away.

I needed to focus, or my best friend was going to die.

"Okay," I warned. "I'm gonna wipe the spot down a little bit. It may hurt. I'll be fast."

"Yeah."

I realized I didn't have a cloth, but I didn't want to leave his side again, so I took a piece of his shirt that wasn't tarnished with blood and cut a square out of it. I dunked it in the bowl of cool water, swished it around, wrung it out, and then gently set it on the spot. Mitzy still winced, but he was gritting through it, and I knew I wouldn't do him any good by starting and stopping, so even though I knew it was hurting him, I pressed on, trying to wash away as much of the blood as I could.

The wound was still actively bleeding, and in no time, my makeshift rag was nothing but a dark red blob. I set it in the water again and wrang it out, and it turned my previously clear water a murky maroon. Still, I ignored that and continued wiping at the spot until it was at least clean enough to see the actual spot where he'd been shot. It was right at the base of his sternum and slightly to the left, probably threatening one of his lungs.

I unraveled a fair amount of the gauze and pressed it down on the spot and Mitzy let out another grumble of pain. I took his hand and set it on top, begging him to "Hold this," then I cut that patch free and pulled a long piece of gauze out that was, at least, the full width of Mitzy's body.

This was going to be the difficult part.

I brought this swath to his head and then slowly maneuvered it under him, holding the gauze on both sides, and slowly sliding it further and further down because I knew that Mitzy had no energy to lift up. The cut end, I secured to the patch directly over the wound with tape, moving Mitzy's hand to do so, and then I pulled the roll over, wrapping the spot up, and pulled as tightly as I could. I was standing over him with my legs on either side, and using my full weight to pull the bandage as tight as it would go. Mitzy reared his head back and was howling in pain, but I chose to take that as a win because it was the loudest he'd been in a bit.

With the wrap pulled tight, I set my foot down on top of it to hold it firm, then I had to twist, almost at an impossible angle, to drag the roll under Mitzy's head again the way I'd done the first time, and drag it back down to wrap it over once more. I repeated this process a few times until it didn't seem like Mitzy could handle the pain anymore-and neither could my back or arms--and then I cut the roll, and taped the end off along Mitzy's side.

I was covered in sweat and collapsed onto the floor next to him, sitting and watching him for signs of getting better or getting worse.

"I'm sorry," I said. "I'm done now."

Although it seemed like he was struggling to do so, Mitzy turned his head towards me and looked at me. "You did good, kid."

New tears filled my eyes and my nose burned. "I'm so sorry. You got hurt because of me."

He just shook his head. "I told you, I'd never let you come here alone."

I looked towards the elevator doors, praying for help to come, but with each minute that passed silently, I lost a little more hope. Maybe I'd wrapped Mitzy up pretty good, but he didn't have a ton of time. We had to get him to a doctor quickly.

"Chlo," Mitzy said. "I need you to tell my wife and kids--"

"Don't," I begged him, sobbing again. "Please don't."

"Chloe please," he said. "Just in case."

I looked down at him and he was watching me wearily with those gray eyes that had seen me through many hard times. "Okay," I whimpered.

"I have a safety deposit box at Midtown City Bank on 18th. It's not under my real name, it's under Mitzy, just Mitzy. I gave my wife a necklace for her birthday a few years ago, it's the key. She'll know which one."

I nodded. "Okay."

"There's bearer bonds inside. It's for my kids' college and to make sure the house is paid for and stuff. Make sure they get it."

"I will," I told him. "But I'm not doing it right now, because you're gonna make it through this, okay?"

He let his head fall flat again, just staring at the ceiling. "You always had so much more faith in me than I had in myself. Thank you for being a real friend to me, Chloe."

I sniffled in. "Thank you for being a real friend to me."

The elevator's doorbell went off, and I stood up and ran over to it. There was a security panel that would allow me to see who was standing inside before I allowed the person in. I pressed the button to show me the feed, but my heart fell into my stomach when I saw that it was Cox. He looked rough, bleeding all over, scratched up and bruised. I had no idea how he managed to escape the fray outside, but he could die on that elevator for all I cared.

I refused to let him in.

Looking back at Mitzy, I didn't dare move him, so I had to just defend. My gun had been pulled off of me and we'd given Mitzy's to Maksim.

But a bratva boss had to have guns everywhere right?

I ran through the penthouse, opening up every single drawer, door, and box until I finally found a gun. It was loaded, thankfully, so I turned off the safety and returned to the elevator doors. Cox still shouldn't have been able to get in without me letting him in, but after I didn't answer the door, he pulled a key fob out of his pocket and held it up to the monitor.

"No," I whispered.

Somehow, he'd gotten a copy of the key.

The doors started to slide open, so I lifted the gun and trained it in Cox's direction. When they'd parted fully and Cox saw me standing there with my gun in his direction, he lifted his hands to the air.

"Whoa, Chloe. Let's just take it easy now," he said.

"Shut up," I barked. "Give me your fob and go back downstairs."

"You know I can't do that," he said. "This has to end, and it only ends when I get what I want. Being a detective is a farce--I want to run my own empire, and it starts with selling Maksim back to mother Russia."

"I won't let you," I demanded.

"You don't really have a choice," he said.

"I could kill you right now," I told him.

He perked an evil grin at me. "You won't though." Slowly, he started to step off the elevator towards me.

"Chloe, fucking kill him," Mitzy groaned. "Give me the gun, I'll kill him."

"He looks rough," Cox said. "If you don't kill me right now, I could finish him off easily."

"Shut up!" I screamed. "Stop moving!"

"It doesn't matter," Cox said. "You're not a murderer. You don't have what it takes to kill a man in cold blood."

"I don't want to kill you," I said. "That's letting you off too easily. I want you to suffer."

"Then kill me." He walked up until the gun in my hand was pressed against his chest. "All you have to do is pull that trigger and I'm dead. You'll never have to worry about me again."

"Chloe!" Mitzy barked. "Take the shot! He's a threat!"

"Go on," Cox mocked. "Do it."

"Chloe!" Mitzy shouted from behind me. "Fucking, *kill him!*"

CHAPTER TWENTY-TWO: MAKSIM

After taking a few minutes to make sure that the Bonetti threat inside of Dacha was truly neutralized, I rushed back to the elevator and pressed the button to call it down. It took longer than I was expecting to come down, and I wondered if Chloe and Mitzy were still just laying on the elevator--hopefully not, because that would make me assume the worst.

Eventually, however, the elevator came and I climbed on, my heart pounding. There wasn't really any reason for me to think that Chloe and Mitzy wouldn't be safe in my penthouse, especially having the only keys that would actually get someone into the unit without being let in from the inside, but I had a bad feeling in my gut.

Just before the door closed, the back door opened and I lifted the gun I'd collected while I was sifting through the Bonettis, but it was Alexei that came walking in the door and I lowered my gun.

"I'm headed up to find Chloe," I told him. "The Bonettis have been neutralized, but another sweep couldn't hurt."

"I'll do it," he replied. "I also heard your cop friend got hurt. I've got a medic waiting outside if we can get him out there."

"Is Cox gone?" I asked.

Alexei lowered his brow. "He came in here. Have you not crossed paths with him?"

My heart started to beat even faster and I immediately started to rapidly press the button to close the doors to the elevator. I cocked my gun and prepared for a battle as the elevator climbed up to the penthouse floor. When

I got to the floor, I rang the doorbell and waited, but after about thirty seconds, there was no response.

I pounded my fist against the elevator doors. "Chloe!" Again, there was no response, so I continued to bang. "Chloe! It's Maks! Let me in."

Again, no response.

At this moment, I was beginning to lament the fact that I'd prioritized fortification in the penthouse's design. It was made so that no one could get in or out without the key or being authorized from the inside, and I'd made sure to get the strongest material possible for the elevator doors. Even though I knew it wouldn't work, I still threw my body weight into the elevator doors, begging them to give and let me in. Chloe wouldn't have willingly let Cox in, but I guess when I first arrived that the entire inside of Dacha was compromised.

That, of course, included the penthouse, which may have had spare keys made without my knowledge.

Feeling helpless and trying to decide if I needed to go outside the building and figure out how to scale my way up to the windows, I kicked my legs against the door. They rocked, and I felt a shivering all along my spine. After all of this, I refused to let this be how it ended, I had to get in to help Chloe somehow.

"Chloe!" I screamed. "Cox! If you can hear me, I swear to god, you better not touch her!"

Suddenly, the elevator clicked, indicating that someone inside that unlocked the doors, and then they parted. I stepped in and looked down at Mitzy, on the edge of his life, slumped against the wall with his hand on the panel. He opened his mouth like he wanted to say something, but there was blood sputtering from his mouth and his eyes were about as hollow as I'd ever seen on any dead man.

It wasn't looking good for Mitzy.

I had to get to Chloe, but knowing there was a medic just downstairs, I wondered if there was a way I could get Mitzy down, at least to Alexei. I reached down for him, and he tried to shake his head, likely wanting me to go after Chloe, but she'd never forgive me if I didn't at least make an attempt to save her friend. He wasn't going to survive if he was left up here anyway, even if I did save Chloe, by the time we got back, he'd be dead no question.

So it was worth the risk to put him on the elevator, send him down, and hope for the best.

It seemed like Chloe managed to get him wrapped up, which was probably the *only* reason he was still alive right now, so I dragged him backwards onto the elevator and hit the button for the final floor.

"If you have *anything* left in you, there's a medic outside," I said to him, stepping off of the elevator. I stared down at him as the doors slowly closed. "Thank you for protecting her," I said. "Good luck."

The doors slowly closed to Mitzy's face, and I said a silent prayer to any god who was listening, then I flipped around and ran into the penthouse. I didn't know where Chloe was, but the fact that Mitzy used the last of his strength to get me inside, meant she had to be inside and hopefully alive.

"Chloe!" I didn't bother keeping quiet, because I knew that Cox was inside and that he was probably going to kill her. I wanted to bank on the fact that he wanted me to suffer and wouldn't do it until he knew I would see it.

If I could just get to her, I could save her.

The kitchen and the living room were both empty, so I bolted down the hallway towards the bedrooms, but stopped in front of the metal door that led into my kill room. The instant I stood in front of it, I knew that they were in there, and given that there was nothing inside to hide behind or in, I knew as soon as I opened the door, I was taking a bullet, whether or not Chloe was still alive.

I'd be no use to her if I walked in and immediately got shot to the point that I couldn't move. I looked around, searching my brain for anything that could help me, when I finally ran into the bedroom. I lifted one of the long, king sized pillows from the bed and then snatched a shirt from the dresser and wrestled it over. It felt ridiculous, but I had to imagine Cox wasn't at the top of this game, for how quickly the tables turned against him.

All I needed was for him to temporarily think I'd entered the room and fire. In that lapse, I could gain the upper hand that I needed.

I walked back up to the kill room door and cracked the door ever so slightly. I slid my gun just inside, making very sure that, if Cox was inside, he'd see it. After that, I threw the door back and chucked the pillow inside.

And success.

Cox whipped around and shot at the pillow, and in that moment of confusion, I was able to shoot at Cox's leg. He dropped to his knee, and I quickly shot him in his other foot to make sure he couldn't move. His gun had fallen out of his hand, so I kicked it out of the door and far from his reach. The fact that he wasn't reaching for any additional weapons made me confident that he was probably unarmed and had just taken a gun from Chloe.

Chloe.

I scanned the room and eventually my eyes found a different mass in the corner. The clothes were ripped and there was blood everywhere.

"No," I said quietly. "Chloe."

With my gun trained on Cox, I walked over and reached down to touch her. She jumped under my touch and the relief almost made me throw up. She rolled over and looked up at me, and I could see that she had been beaten within an inch of her life.

"I tried to keep him alive," she said. "I wanted to arrest him instead." A rage the likes of which I'd never experienced before filled my body from my feet upwards. It was almost shocking at first, and I just stood there staring down at my poor lover. She looked down at her stomach and her hand was covering a particularly bloody spot. "He knows. He tried... to kill it."

I looked back at Cox and he was looking up at me with fear in his eyes. "N-now, just wait a minute."

I handed Chloe the gun that I had, and then pulled my suit jacket off and draped it over her. She was shaking and crying, even weakly murmured, "Mitzy...?"

"I did what I could," I told her, though I still had my eyes on Cox. "It's up to him now." My body was shaking with anger. "I'm sorry, Chloe. I decided to let Vincent go for you, but I can't let him go. Not after the way he hurt you."

Chloe was fighting to speak from how injured she was, but she managed to squeeze out a handful of words for my benefit.

"He tried to kill my baby," she said. "Make him suffer."

I rolled up my shirt sleeves and started closing in on him. He looked terrified and I cracked my neck to the side.

"Make him suffer, huh?" I said through gritted teeth, glaring down at him. "That, I can do."

I lifted my foot and slammed it into Cox's face, smashing his head between my foot and the wall behind him. It ricocheted bouncing between my foot and the wall, and he let out a yelp of pain.

"Just kill me," he demanded.

"Just kill you?" I repeated. "After what you did to her? After what you did to my child?" I bent down and socked him right across the face, waiting for him to recover, and then I did it again, and again, and again. Blood was splattering across the walls but there was nothing that was going to deter me at this point. "What was it that you said? You wouldn't kill me but that wouldn't stop you from making me suffer?" I cracked my knuckles. "Let's see how far we can take that concept, huh?"

CHAPTER TWENTY-THREE: CHLOE

I sat on the couch in Maksim's living room, fighting for air, and still hearing the sound of smashing flesh and crushing bones in the back of my mind, even though Maksim had stopped "dealing with" Captain Cox close to twenty minutes prior. Even though I loved Maksim, and he was only doing what I asked him to do when I told him that I wanted him to make Cox suffer, I didn't expect the monster that he would turn into. Cox hurt me and our baby, and it seemed that was the switch that turned Maksim into a demon.

I think I heard the paramedics that wheeled Cox out of the room say that both his arms were broken, both of his legs were broken, his left eye-socket was caved in, he had three gunshot wounds, and he'd taken a hit to the back of his spine, which might render him paralyzed for the rest of his life. As they read off each injury, I remembered Maksim causing it. I never thought the father of my child would be capable of such violence, but after what I witnessed...

I could remember it all--the way he smashed Cox's arms against the wall until they both snapped. The way he threw his entire body weight on his legs, specifically focusing on the areas where he'd been shot, until he could no longer move either of them. He had to have punched him a hundred times or more, so it wasn't shocking at all to know he'd caved in his eye socket.

And the worst...

Just when I thought Maksim was done torturing Cox, he drove his face into the wall, grabbed his arms, pulled them both behind him, and then kicked into his spine, further damaging his already broken arms, and causing severe and intense damage to his spine.

Cox fell to the ground as nothing more than a shell after that, not dead, but could hardly be considered alive, and to my surprise, that was when Maks stopped.

"You said you wanted to keep him alive and have him arrested instead," Maksim said to me after he finished. "If that's what you want, that's what I want."

I looked at Cox's mangled body. "He'll have no quality of life that way. He'd be better off dead."

"I don't want him to have quality of life," Maksim replied. "I want him to suffer for the rest of his days. To always regret crossing me and hurting you."

"Boss." Brusch came flying into the room and looked at the mess in front of him. "We have to get out of here. The real police are showing up."

Maksim looked at me and I nodded him off. "Go. If you get caught here after already having gone to prison, you'll get locked up again. I'll deal with the police and catch up with you later."

He kissed me and said, "What about the baby?"

I looked down at my stomach. "I honestly don't know. I'll need to go to the hospital to be sure."

"We'll go as soon as this is done," he said. "I'm never letting you do any of this on your own again. I love you."

"I love you too," I replied.

"Boss," Brusch demanded.

"Go," I said. "Hurry."

And then Brusch took Maksim and the two of them fled the scene before the cops could arrive.

My hand came up to my stomach on its own and tears filled my eyes. I wondered if my baby was okay. I felt like such a failure of a mom to have let it get hurt already. It helped assure one thing firmly within my spirit, I needed to *never* let anything happen to my baby again. With men like Cox out there, or even men like Maksim that *weren't* on our side, I had a lot of work to do if I was going to protect my baby from the evil of this world.

I knew I couldn't give up on being a cop. This was what I was meant to do. To rid this world of horrible men who would hurt the innocent, like my baby, or a young Chloe and Chandler so long ago. I'd come full circle and knew that, even if I was going to be in Maksim's life, I was going to need to find a way to continue walking this path.

"Detective." I looked up and, shockingly enough, Ace, my friend from narcotics, was walking towards me. "You look rough."

"Hey," I said weakly. "I need to go to the doctor."

"Don't worry. We're going to get you medical attention right now. I'll question you down at the ambulance."

"No, you don't understand," I told him. "I'm pregnant." I showed him the bruises over my stomach and his eyes widened. "I need to get to the hospital right away."

"Oh my god, okay... Uh..." He pulled the walkie talkie out of his waistband and said, "I need to get Detective Nikitina to the hospital. I'm leaving. I need someone else to come up and finish scanning the scene."

"Why are you here?" I asked. "This isn't your jurisdiction."

"When I heard you were involved, I came right away. Besides, I've been hoping to switch departments for a while. Figured this was a good way to dip a toe. Can you stand?" I nodded and dragged myself up off the couch and Ace slipped an arm around me to help me, which was good, because I was wobblier than I was expecting. "Petrov did this to you?" he asked as I got on the elevator.

I gave Ace a wide-eyed expression. "No. This was Cox. All of this was Cox."

"Cox?" he said. "What do you mean?"

"Cox was working with the Bonettis to try and illegally take down Maksim Petrov," I explained.

"But Petrov fled."

"He left because he knew what would happen if he was caught here with two bloodied police detectives."

"If Cox did this to you, who did that to Cox?" Ace asked.

I looked at him and answered his question without answering it. "Maksim is the father of my child."

He took a deep breath in and nodded. "Got it. Don't say anything else. In fact, don't say anything to anyone else unless you have a lawyer present."

I nodded my head. "I know. I know the drill."

Ace delivered me to the hospital and helped me get in and situated with a doctor, and then thankfully looked the other way when I told him I needed to call Maksim so he could be here. Ace was a good cop, and admitted honestly that if he laid eyes on Maksim he would have no choice but to arrest him, so after helping me get in touch with Maks, he turned to leave so that he wouldn't feel obligated to take Maks away from me when we just wanted to make sure that our child was okay.

"Wait!" I called as he started to leave. "What about Mitzy?" Ace gave me a downtrodden look and my heart sank. "No."

"It's not confirmed," Ace said, "but he was in really bad shape when we got here. When they loaded him onto the ambulance, I overheard them saying they'd be surprised if he made it to the hospital."

Tears filled my eyes, my throat clenched up, and my nose started to burn. The thought that Mitzy wasn't going to make it out of this after everything was too much to bear. When I thought back, I knew that the only way Maksim could have gotten inside the penthouse was if Mitzy had managed to get up and get the door open. He was on death's door already when Cox dragged me away, so he must have used the final fumes of his vitality to get Maksim in.

That made three times that Mitzy had saved my life, and I couldn't even protect him once.

"Will you let me know as soon as you know more?" I whimpered.

He nodded at me. "Of course. Just worry about you and your baby for now."

Ace left, and about five minutes later, Maksim entered the room I was in. He came over to me immediately and put his hands on either side of my face and gave me a kiss. "Are you okay?"

I shook my head. "No. I don't know if the baby's okay, and Mitzy..." I sniffled. "They said they don't think he's going to make it."

"I'm so sorry, Chloe," he said. "I did everything I could. I put him on the elevator, but I had to get to you." He set a hand on my stomach. "I had to get to both of you."

"I understand why you did what you did," I said. "I just... He's my best friend. I don't want to lose him."

Maksim wrapped his arms around me and held me close. "I know."

We had to wait close to twenty minutes for a doctor to come in. While we were waiting, Maksim filled me in on everything that I missed in the midst of being taken by Stavio Bonetti, all the way through to being captured by Cox in the penthouse. He told me about the Costellos showing up to help, and how Alexei managed to get things under control.

"The Costellos?" I asked. "How did they know?"

He winced at me. "I was at their home when Brusch called me to tell me that the Bonettis had the place surrounded."

"You went to see them?" I said. "You decided to hash things out with Vincent?"

"Please don't be mad at me," he said. "I went to kill Vincent."

"Maksim!"

"I know!" He held up his hands defensively. "I know, I promised you that I wouldn't, but I thought if I could just get rid of that issue, then we wouldn't have to discuss it again. I wanted that gone from our relationship, but..." He rolled his eyes. "I didn't even make it that far. Katya caught me sneaking in and hit the hell out of me with this bat, then she invited me in for an ice pack and lemonade."

A smile came to my face. "That sounds about right."

She helped me start to see that you were right, I was being ridiculous, and then when I saw you being dragged away by Stavio and I couldn't get to you, it finally just clicked how stupid I was being. Nothing was worth risking you, but I was being so arrogant." He lifted my hands and kissed them gently. "I'm so sorry."

"As long as you've realized it, that's what matters," I said. "So you're done with vendetta against Vincent?"

He looked annoyed, but nodded nonetheless. "At the end of the day, more people's choices than just his led to what happened to Vladimir and Sascha, I see that now. I'm sorry that I didn't listen to you when you tried to explain it to me. Plus, he did play a role in saving your life, and I can never repay him for that."

I gave him a kiss on the cheek. "Yeah. I feel the same way." Finally, the doctor came in, stopping short when she saw how destroyed I looked. Immediately, she gave Maksim a side-eye, but I was quick to jump in before she could assume the worst. "I know how it looks, but I'm a cop and I just had a *really* bad day on the job. This is the father. He's here for support."

It was clear she didn't entirely believe me, but thankfully she moved on to taking some tests, running my bloodwork, and ending with an ultrasound. Maksim seemed a bit nervous. Though he'd experienced some of this before when he was standing in for Katya, he'd never done it with his own child, and those nerves were apparent all over his face. I took his hand and held it in my own.

"Don't worry," I said. "We're doing this together, remember?"

He nodded and smiled, letting some of the tension fall out of his shoulders. "Yeah."

The doctor felt around my stomach, causing me a little bit of discomfort when she moved the scanner over the bruises, but eventually she hit a spot and we heard a rhythmic thrum. "Ah," she said. "Hear that? That is your baby's heartbeat."

"Oh my god," Maksim said. "Really?"

"Yep. Now let's just see if we can find it," the doctor said.

She continued to move the scanner around, until finally she stopped at a small collection of gray matter on the screen. She pointed with a smile. "Here we go. Looking healthy as ever."

Both Maks and I let out sighs of relief. I reached out and touched the screen and a smile came to my face. "Hi little one. I'm sorry I put you in harm's way today."

Maksim set his hand on top of mine. "We both are."

The doctor flipped open our paperwork and made some notes before smiling at me. "From what I can tell, she's happy and healthy."

Both Maks and I looked at the doctor and in unison we said, "She?"

The doctor's jaw dropped. "Oh my god. Yes. I'm so sorry. The paperwork has the gender notated so I assumed you already knew!"

"We're having a girl?" Maks said, then he looked down at me. "We're having a girl."

I nodded. "We're having a girl!"

He bent down and wrapped his arms around me and held me in a huge hug. Some of my bruises hurt, but I was too over-the-moon to care.

After getting some pain relief from the doctor, along with a clean bill of health for the rest of me, save for the bruises of course, Maksim and I left the hospital both floating a little on cloud nine. He held my hand as we walked out and I shielded my face from the sun. It seemed so insane that the day wasn't even half over. That entire extravaganza felt like it took a week.

"Chloe," Maks said, turning me around to face him. "I know that you have a certain dedication to fighting crime, and I don't want to take that from you."

I nodded. "I've been thinking about that, too. I realized today that I can't just stop. This world is full of people like Cox, with only people like Cox in positions to do anything about it. I don't want to move *out* of this role, I want to move up. I want to continue to exact more change. I don't think that goal and us have to be mutually exclusive, I just don't know how I would go about balancing the two yet."

Maks frowned. "I'm not sure either. It feels like they'd have to be mutually exclusive."

"I'm sorry to ask this of you, but... Can you wait just twenty-four hours more for me to think it over? I think that this was scary and that our gut reaction is to just be together and screw the rest of it, but I just need a *little* more time to figure it out. I'm sure there's a solution out there, I just have to find it."

"I understand. What do you want to do for right now?" he asked.

"I wanna go see Mitzy," I said. "Ace texted me where he is. He's still unconscious, but I want to be by his side."

Maksim nodded at me. "Okay. I'll take you there."

We drove in total silence away from the hospital to the trauma center where Mitzy was. They'd performed emergency surgery on him to remove the bullet, and he was in ICU. His wife and kids were there just waiting to hear more.

"I'm... I'm so sorry," I told them.

None of them had much to say, they were too anguished, and I couldn't blame them. With their grace, I was allowed some time to take the one visitor Mitzy was allowed in his ICU recovery room to spend some time with him.

"Hi," I said weakly to him, knowing he wouldn't respond. "I'm sorry. I'm so, so sorry. You've done nothing but save my life and I've done nothing but put yours in danger. I'm a shitty partner and a shitty friend." He was all strung up to several machines like a marionette doll and it broke my heart. "I don't know if you can hear me, but the baby's okay. The doctor accidentally slipped and told us the gender. It's a girl. I didn't even know I could know this early, but then again, none of what's happened to me the past four months had made much sense. Sometimes I think I'm just losing my mind."

After that, I sat in silence at his side for a few minutes, just listening to the beeping of the machines, the hollow sound of his breathing, and the murmur of voices from outside. I hated that Mitzy was here, but at least he hung on long enough to get here.

Now I just had to pray he'd hang on long enough to get out.

"I don't get you," I told him. "I don't get why you do this job. Knowing you care for the Costellos and who your wife is. Wouldn't it just be easier not to do this? How do you find the balance?" I sighed. "I really wish I could hear your voice right now."

I reached out and grabbed his hand, squeezing it gently.

"You once asked me what I would do if I couldn't do this. If this job ended tomorrow, what would I do? My answer is, I'd spend a lot of time trying to figure out how to be just like you."

Saying those words crashed over me like a tidal wave.

That *is* what I would do. If I couldn't be NYPD anymore, I'd want to figure out how to tow the line the way Mitzy does. How to do both. How to be a little bit of a cop and be a little bit of a criminal. Maybe he hadn't intended to be my role model, but unbeknownst to us both, he illuminated a path forward for me a long time ago.

"I figured it out, Mitz," I said with a huge smile on my face. "Thanks to you, I know what I want to do."

CHAPTER TWENTY-FOUR: MAKSIM

The thought of not knowing which way Chloe was going to fall kept me up all night. I knew that there was an impasse we'd struggle to get around with her still having her commitment to justice. I supposed, to her, being a cop was like how transfixed I was with killing Vincent. There was a version of our lives in which we let both of these things go, but it wouldn't stop us from wondering if we'd made the right choice or not.

For me, I knew now that Vincent wasn't meant to hold me back from my future--not from the woman I loved, nor the baby girl that she was carrying. Chloe still had a decision to make, but I'd already made mine.

It was time to officially bury the hatchet with Vincent and make nice with the Costellos once and for all.

If Chloe *did* choose me and a life in Russia, I wanted nothing to stand in our way, and because she had asked for some space to make a decision, I didn't want to bother her. Instead I decided to button up my work, so I could leave for Russia as soon as I got her answer. I knew that I had to meet with Alexei at some point as well, but I figured hashing things out with the Costellos took top priority and decided to do that first thing in the morning.

So this time when I went to the Costellos' estate, I did so in pure daylight, and with them knowing full well that I was coming. I saw the same security guard that I'd failed to sneak past when I came before. He was at the security station, and he gave me a vastly annoyed, half-lidded gaze when I drove my car up.

"Doing things the right way this time," I joked.

He seemed highly unamused. "Name?"

"Maksim Petrov," I told him.

With that same disgruntled expression, he typed a few things on his computer, and then pressed a button to open the gate. It buzzed as it sprang to life, the loudly creaked to the side so that I could drive through.

"Don't make me come find you and kick your ass," the security guard warned. "I nearly lost my job last time"

I held up a hand. "I'll be on my best behavior."

Then he waved me past and I drove onto the road that twisted and wound its way towards the Costello's huge estate. When I got up to the front--a much easier trek driving than walking--I saw a small parking lot inside which there were a few cars parked along with a couple of the golf carts that I'd noticed the staff using to get around the massive property. I pulled my car in there and parked, then sent Katya a text to let her know that I had arrived.

"Come on down to my mom's," Katya texted back. "There's more lemonade."

Snickering, I powered off my car and followed the directive, walking the same path that Katya had taken me down the day before to visit her mom's small house on the land. The door was already open and Katya was propped up in the doorway, and she smiled when she saw me coming.

"Now, see? Isn't this a much more delightful way to arrive than a bat to the back?"

I arched my back, remembering the sting. "I can confirm that it is."

This time when I entered the quaint living room, Vincent and Annika were already inside, each sitting on their own couch and working on a glass of lemonade. They were staring down at a scrabble board with the concentration of two people trying to disarm a bomb.

"What's happened?" I whispered to Katya.

"They play scrabble on Tuesdays," she replied. "They get into these really funny fights whenever one of them uses a word from their home language that the other doesn't know. You're supposed to be using an English dictionary only, but they go at it like cats and dogs over Italian and Russian words that would be allowed under no circumstances if it wasn't the two of them playing."

I just shook my head at the scene. "It's too wholesome. I feel uncomfortable being near it."

Katya snickered. "I know."

Suddenly, Annika yelped, and then started swapping around the tiles on her easel like she was solving a complex equation. When she was done, she lifted all seven tiles between her two hands and laid them down on the board, spelling out the word, "Penises." She then proceeded to giggle like a twelve year old at the word she'd used.

"She couldn't really be herself with you dad," I said.

Katya nodded and then looked at me. "None of us really could be."

"Fine, you win," Vincent growled. "I'm not coming back from a sixty point deficit with only four tiles left in the bag."

"Well, there's always next week," Annika said. She jumped up from the couch, walked over and gave me a kiss on the cheek and said, "Hi, honey."

"Hey Annika," I replied.

"I'd love to stay and chat, but it's a perfect day for a dip in the pool." She handed her half-drunk glass of lemonade to Katya and scuttled off.

Vincent leaned back on the couch and laughed. "I don't know about the rest of us, but that woman really is living her best life."

At the exact same time, Katya and I said, "She deserves it," then we exchanged a look and smiled.

"Should we go to your office, Vince?" Katya asked.

"No need." He motioned for me to sit. "We can talk here. This isn't going to get ugly, is it?"

I shook my head. "I don't think I can handle much more ugly."

"Agreed," Katya replied.

I sat down across from Vincent and just watched him in silence for a minute. Nothing reasonable to say came easily to me, especially considering I still wasn't the guy's number one fan. But I thought of the way he helped me yesterday and finally mustered up the gumption to say, "Thank you for yesterday. Chloe is safe and the baby is safe, and that's because you guys showed up when you did. You brought out the cavalry for us, and I really appreciate it."

"We love Chloe," Katya said. "I know we're still getting to know her, but Mitzy speaks so highly of her, and she clearly loves you so much. It already kind of feels like she's part of the family."

"Speaking of Mitzy," Vincent said.

I just shook my head. "So far, he's still out. No word. Doctors keep warning his family they may have to pull the plug." Both Katya and Vincent stared down sadly at that. "I'm sorry," I told them.

"Chloe means the world to Mitzy," Vincent said. "I'd heard him talk about her before, his younger partner, who was like a little sister to him. He's crazy about her. If he died protecting her, I know that he will have died with honor."

"Still, all of this was precipitated by my bad manners with the Bonettis," I said. "I caused everyone around me so much pain."

"We've all been there," Katya said. "It's learning from it that's key."

I looked across at Vincent and said, "You need to take care of this woman with everything in your body. *I'm* crazy about *her*. If you make even one hour of her life unhappy, I will renew my path to end your life, and this time, I won't stop."

Vincent nodded at me. "Fair enough."

I looked sideways at Katya. "I want to repay you guys for the bail."

"No." Her voice was firm and steady. "We did that because we love you and because we didn't want you locked up for foolishness. We won't accept your money. I just expect you to go back home and lead the group we left to you with pride, and in your own way. No offense, but fuck my dad. He was terrible. You're going to create something way better than he ever did."

"And my market has been missing the Petrov supply," Vincent said. "Maybe we aren't best friends, but I think we could be good business partners."

The thought of being able to regain the income that Vladimir lost when he burned the Costellos was incredibly intriguing. "I'm interested," I responded. "Let's continue to explore that."

"When are you heading home?" Katya asked.

"As soon as I hear from Chloe," I admitted. "She's still trying to decide what she's going to do."

Katya frowned. "Like there's a chance you won't be together?"

My stomach knotted up at the thought. "She's committed to justice, almost as much as she is to me and our child. She's trying to reconcile how to do both, or if it's even possible. She asked me for twenty-four more hours to talk it over, and that was yesterday, so I should be hearing from her soon."

Vincent crossed his arms. "If she chooses to stay, what will you do? What about the baby?"

"I've been trying not to give that much thought because I'm hoping it's a nightmare I won't see," I explained. "I suppose there would be a lot of traveling back and forth. Honestly, I don't know how that would work."

"Well, it's like you said, let's hope that's not the outcome." Katya reached out and put a hand on my leg. "She's so in love with you. I bet she'll choose to be with you."

"I sincerely hope so."

From the Costellos, I drove right back into Little Odessa and met Alexei at one of his warehouses. Thank god for work, because otherwise I would have driven myself mad wondering what Chloe was going to decide. Thankfully, it was pretty easy to give Alexei and his warehouse my undivided attention.

The man had a full-scale, industrial sized, OSHA regulated factory printing and distributing counterfeit money. If anyone walked in, it would look like just a regular old production plant. It was the most streamlined and efficient form of thievery I'd ever seen.

"Alexei," I said, shaking his hand. "I wanted to thank you again for your assistance yesterday. I don't know if word found you, but Chloe, that detective that Cox was trying to kill, she's carrying my baby. The two of them probably would have died were it not for your help. I'm extremely appreciative."

"Of course," Alexei said. "If I can't help keep my partners out of hot water, I'm good for nothing. I assume our deal hasn't changed?"

"Not at all. It just may take a little longer to get off the ground. I'm having Dacha completely combed out, making sure there's no remnants of the Bonettis or Cox behind, then I'm having a brand new security system installed to protect our assets and interests." I crossed my arms. "Also, I know you aren't his biggest fan, but I just left a meeting with Vincent Costello and it seems we're going to be opening our professional relationship once more. I believe the three of us could potentially be a superpower. If you all were willing to look the other way on your differences, there's a massive opportunity for growth and lots of money."

Alexei's nostrils flared a little bit. I knew he hated Vincent almost as much as I did, but he also had a look of piqued interest. "Keep me in the loop about this. If the risk is low dealing with that reckless cowboy of a mafioso, I'll consider it."

I nodded. "Of course."

"Since you're here. There's another matter I wanted to discuss with you."

I furrowed my brow. "Okay?"

"It's something of a targeted attack, I suppose you could say. It's nothing I'm too concerned about, but every now and again these upstart groups begin kicking up dust and cause problems for us vets. Usually, they have to be dealt with swiftly and violently, but this new group I'm battling with seems to be a hair more intelligent than others I've dealt with."

"Who are they?" I asked.

"They call themselves The Wreckers," Alexei responded. "I've got several in-roads throughout Long Island, mainly in the bar and club scene, but I've got a couple of specific people who deal through the high-brow society out there. Celebrities, politicians, designers, and other artists. It's a lucrative cash flow for me, but recently, they've begun hitting my upper crust clientele specifically, and running them out of my pocket. I'd like to circulate a bad batch of drugs in their name--really just dismantle them from the inside out. The Petrovs make the best drugs in the world, so I imagine you could make the worst ones as well."

"There's not even a question," I responded. "In fact, allow me to have a batch made for you free of charge for the incredible amount of aid you've given me."

He smiled. "Well, I won't turn down that generosity. That would be great. Thank you."

The Wreckers. I was pretty sure I'd heard Chloe mention that same group before. She was working on them, too. I wondered what their deal was. "Anyway. I believe I'll be heading back to Russia as early as tomorrow, so if you need anything else from me between now and then, let me know."

"Of course." Alexei held out his hand once more and I gave it a firm shake. "I'm looking forward to doing business with you, Mr. Petrov."

"You and me both," I replied. "But Maks is fine."

I left Alexei's warehouse feeling good about the way that I'd tied up my loose ends. It felt like I'd successfully sorted things out with the Costellos, Alexei's and mine relationship was cemented, and I had taken time that morning to completely stock the commissary accounts of Borya, Schmidt, and the others behind bars who helped me while I was there. There wasn't much left for me to do except wait to hear from Chloe.

But as the day started to tick towards the evening, I was becoming less and less hopeful.

It was just around sundown when I got a text from Chloe that was nothing more than an address. I was going over plans for the renovations at Dacha with Brusch when I received it, and dropped everything I was doing to head to the address she'd sent me. It was a place far outside the city, technically in New Jersey, if the sign I passed was any indicator, where we could sit on a grassy hill in the sunset and look at the city in the distance.

She was already sitting there looking out when I arrived, and I just quietly walked up and sat down next to her.

"Sorry," she said quietly. "I went a little beyond my 24-hours."

I shook my head. "I would have given you 24 more if you needed them."

"I did a lot of thinking," she said. "I went and sat with Mitzy, who somehow managed to give me sage advice even from his coma, and I came to a conclusion about who I am and what I want to do. It was terrifying, because for the first time in my life it feels like I'm stepping out of this shadow of my mom's death and actually fighting for something I want for *me*, but it's also so exhilarating. I'm learning so much about who I am and who I want to become."

I looked at her face, painfully beautiful against the sunset sky. "Does that mean that you've made a choice about whether you will stay or go?"

She nodded, looking up into the sky where the faintest hints of stars were starting to poke out. She had a look of pride on her face as a blinding smile crossed from cheek to cheek. For a few moments, she stayed that way, just smiling and staring up, and then she turned and looked at me, with beauty in her green eyes.

"Yeah," she said quietly. "I've made my choice."

TWENTY-FIVE
EPILOGUE: CHLOE

One Month Later

When my alarm started to blare next to my head, I leaned into one of Maksim's bad habits and just reached over to smack it off. I looked over to where he would normally be laying next to me if he was in my bed, and I frowned. It was weird not having him by my side. He'd be griping about how early in the morning it was if he were, but it was what my job called for. I'd gotten used to it a long time ago.

After stretching my arms above my head and twisting the kinks out of my body, I climbed out of bed and started my morning routine. Ever since what happened at Dacha, it started to include daily visits to my family's bodega to check on my father and sister, spend a little bit of time with them, and make sure they were okay--just generally not taking life for granted, and stuff.

It did mean that I had to move a little bit quicker through my morning, so I grabbed the outfit I'd chosen for the day and quickly went into the bathroom. I preferred cooler showers to warmer ones ever since I found out I was pregnant. From Russia to New York, the cold weather was in my blood, and the baby would be coming along right at the end of winter--maybe it was already a little snow person.

My hair, which I'd cut short in your cliche, identity crisis fashion, now fell to just above my shoulders and was much easier to wash and style than it used to be. I didn't really wear it up anymore, but preferred to wear it down. It was much easier to work this way anyway. As always, the makeup I applied was subtle and then I put on my outfit, collected my keys, phone, and wallet, and left for my family's bodega.

"Hey!" Chandler said as I walked in. "Look what *I* did." I walked up to the counter where she was standing holding out a tupperware bowl. "A breakfast sandwich. It's really good, too, plus, I did a *bunch* of research on the best stuff for you to eat when you're pregnant and it's got a ton of that. I've got lunch versions too for later on."

"Wow," I said. "It looks great, Chan."

"Thanks. You'd be surprised what you can do when you're not high."

I snickered at her. "Who would have thought it?" Then I looked around the bodega. "Where's dad?"

She pointed a thumb over her shoulder. "In the back meeting with Abella."

"Ah, did he choose her then?" I said. "Finally, someone takes my advice."

Chandler rolled her eyes. "*I* still think we should have gone with Dante."

"You think we should have gone with Dante because he's hot," I told her. "And it doesn't even make sense, because it's not like you'd be able to do anything with the fact that he's hot."

She sneered at me. "I could make it work if I really wanted to!"

"I'm gonna just poke my head in and say hi. I'll be right back."

I left my tupperware with Chandler and walked towards the back office where my dad was sitting on either side of a table with a tall, stocky woman, with thin graying brown hair, some of which hung down into her face. Despite having that 'sweet old lady' look, she had cuts and scars all over her face and arms, and one of her eyes was sewn shut.

"Hey," I said. "Sorry to interrupt. I just wanted to say hi."

"Hello Chloe," Abella said in her *thick* Russian accent.

"Congrats on landing the gig," I told her. "Gonna be a difficult job, are you up to the task?"

She gave me a look like I'd just slapped her in the face. "Do I look like a woman who isn't up to any task?"

I shook my head. "You do not." Then I smiled over at my dad. "Hey daddy."

"Hi." He stood up and came over to me, and after giving me a huge hug, he set a hand on my belly. "Hello there. It's me, your grandpa. Your favorite person. Don't forget okay."

"How could they, when you tell them every single day?" I said. "I'm headed to work, but I'll call you around two. Will you be ready to go?"

He nodded. "Yep. Chandler wouldn't let me breathe for a moment last night."

"Good, that's what I told her to do." I gave Abella a final smile. "I'll make sure Alexei connects with you sometime later in the week."

She gave me a crooked grin. "Good. Tell him to bring a bottle of wine and we can... toast."

I snickered. "I will warn him you're still trying to seduce him."

I winked at my dad and then ducked back out of the office. Chandler was helping a customer at the counter, so I slipped behind the counter to quickly snag my breakfast sandwich and then started to walk away.

"There's two in there! Make sure you share!" Chandler called after me.

I lifted my hand into the air and waved. "You got it!"

Though I would always be grateful for New York City's incredible public transportation system, I'd been feeling a need to control my life a little more since the battle at Dacha, and had been driving myself around more frequently. It did mean that I had to battle with NYC traffic, but at least I felt like there weren't so many things in my life that were totally out of my sphere of influence. It also meant that I didn't have to walk from the subway station to the precinct, which was good, because my future child was already giving me a whole host of problems.

My pregnancy was not shaping up to be an easy one.

Riding the elevator up, I took a deep breath and just sort of took it in. I could damn near hear Mitzy's dopey laugh echoing off the elevator walls. It was kind of surreal to think about how much my life changed in the span of just four months. It felt like I'd lived an entire lifetime since Maksim first showed up.

The elevator dinged on my floor and the doors slid open and I walked into the precinct. There were a couple of uppers hanging around, as they had been since everything went down with Cox.

One of them noticed me walking in and nodded at me, "Captain."

I nodded back. "Good morning."

Not breaking my stride because I didn't have time for it today, I walked into my office and sat down at my desk. There was a pile of paperwork stacked to the ceiling that was going to make my morning a little difficult, but I was just keeping the end of the day in mind.

"Knock, knock." I looked up and a huge smile came across my face as Mitzy limped his way into my office. "Hey boss."

I shook my head at him. "You're supposed to be resting."

He rolled his eyes. "Was I *not* going to be here today? Come on, you know me better than that."

"I do, which is why..." I lifted up the tupperware bowl. "I came with breakfast."

"Hell yeah." He lowered himself down into one of the chairs facing my desk, wincing as he did it. He looked around and laughed. "This place looks so much nicer as your office than it did as Cox's."

"Well, that's not a high bar, is it?" I said. I popped open the tupperware bowl and then held it out to him. "This is a pregnancy special breakfast sandwich, made fresh by Chandler."

"Oh good!" Mitzy rubbed his belly. "Gotta do right by the baby." I snorted as he lifted one out of the container then I pulled it back so that I could grab mine. There was silence between us as we each took a bite out, and then both of our eyes widened. "Whoa! This is delicious!"

"It really is!" I quickly took another bite. "She's been getting into cooking while she's getting sober. She loves it."

"That's awesome," Mitzy replied. "I wish I'd known that sooner. I would have loved to be her crash test dummy."

Just as we were finishing our sandwiches, there was another knock at my door, and Ace, my good friend from narcotics, was standing in the doorway. He had a huge box in his hand and held it out towards me. "Is this classless?"

I shook my head. "No, it's helpful!"

He set the box down on top of a pile of others in the corner of my office then walked over, sniffing at the air like a dog. "Ooh, what are we eating?"

Mitzy rapidly scarfed down the rest of his sandwich. "Nothing."

"Brat," I snapped at him. "My sister made breakfast sandwiches." I had only gotten through half of mine and held out the other half. "Wanna try it?"

He held up a hand. "Thanks, but the two of you," he pointed at my belly, "need it more than I do. Especially for a day like today."

Mitzy looked up at him. "Big day for you too, though. Are you ready?"

Ace nodded his head. "Yeah. I think I am. Chloe's been doing a good job of preparing me, and I think I'm gonna fit in really nicely around here. We'll do good work, *actual* work, not like Cox." Mitzy, Ace and I all hummed in sounds of approval with that statement. "Speaking of which, I'm sure you heard they ended up throwing the book at him. Conspiracy, kidnapping, attempted murder, attempted murder of a police officer--about a dozen other charges. He's not getting out of prison until he's in his 90s."

I lifted an eyebrow. "If he makes it that long." I thought of Borya and the others from the Lachinov group that Maksim met when he was inside. "There's more than one person with an axe to grind at that prison--and I made sure that he went to the one where he had the..." I smiled evilly. "Most friends."

Mitzy clapped his hands eagerly. "I *love* evil Chloe. She's *so* cool."

"Both of you should stop talking. I have half a mind to arrest you both," Ace joked.

"You won't," Mitzy replied. "Coward."

"That sounds like desk duty to me," Ace said and Mitzy's expression neutralized.

"That's a joke, right?"

One of the higher ups that had been sticking around, poked his head into the office. "Captain?"

Both Ace and I looked at the door. "Yes?"

"Oh, sorry," he said. "Incoming Captain. We'd love to chat with you if that's alright."

He nodded. "Yeah, of course." Ace gave Mitzy and I a final smile and then walked out, leaving us alone once again.

"Is it strange hearing someone else called captain?" Mitzy asked.

I just shook my head. "No. I was only intramural, and only for a month. If anything it's strange hearing myself called captain."

Mitzy stood up from the chair and said, "Well, should I help you get the rest of your stuff packed up?"

"Uh, no. You should sit down because you're still recovering. That's an order."

He rolled his eyes and held up his hands. "Yes ma'am."

With Mitzy keeping me company, I filled out the last of my paperwork for this job, and then finished packing what was left of my personal items in the office into the box that Ace had brought. It wasn't my office for very long, so I hadn't really moved in a whole lot, but there was at least a few boxes worth of stuff, between the office and my old desk outside.

As we got closer to lunch, Mitzy started to get really fidgety and then eventually started to demand that we go to the break room for a coffee. Between packing and paperwork, I was planning to skip lunch or a break of any kind until it was time to go, but he was insistent. I finally gave in and walked with him to the breakroom...

...where my entire squad and several of my acquaintances from the building were all huddled around a cake and presents.

"You guys," I said. "This was *so* unnecessary."

"Are you kidding?" Sydney said. "We weren't going to *not* throw you a goodbye party, and besides, after what you put up with, you deserve it."

Lucas fought with a popper for about thirty seconds before accidentally blasting it in his own face, and Gauge just shook his head in irritation. "I can't believe you're leaving me with them."

"You'll be fine. Plus, Ace is awesome, and he's really dedicated to this, like I am. Trust him and he won't steer you wrong," I said.

Ace smiled. "Thanks Chlo."

Though there was so much left to be done, I did spare about forty-five minutes to enjoy a piece of cake and chat with my old squad mates. We'd managed to clear the air after Cox was gone, and I didn't blame them for feeling betrayed to know that I was sleeping with the enemy. If the roles had been reversed, I would have felt the same way.

"So, are you seriously gonna hunt him?" Sydney asked, popping a bit of cake into her mouth. "That's insane."

"He's a criminal," I said. "I'm not just going to let him do what he pleases." Everyone laughed as I rubbed my belly. "Well... not anymore."

Eventually, I had to get back what I was doing, so I bid my squad a farewell, promising to give final hugs before I set out for the day, and returned to my office. It was just about two o'clock, so before I got back to packing, specifically figuring out how to fit all of my new going away presents in my box, I picked up my phone to call my dad.

"We're all ready to go, Chloe," my dad said when he answered. "I told you we would be."

I smiled. "Glad to hear it. The car should be there to get you in about thirty minutes. Don't worry about your stuff, the movers will take care of all of that when the ship arrives next week, so just make sure to leave your keys with Abella."

"Already done," he said. "What about you?"

"The car is coming to me after it picks up you guys, so I'll see you around three then we'll head to the airport."

"Okay. We'll see you soon then," he said.

"I've got our sandwiches!" I heard Chandler screech in the background.

Laughing I said, "See you soon. I love you."

"Love you too. Bye."

We hung up the call just in time for Mitzy to appear in my doorway again, but this time he looked really sad. I lowered my gaze at him and frowned. "Come on. You promised you wouldn't."

"I can't help it. You're my best friend. What am I gonna do without you?" he replied.

I fought back the tears that desperately wanted to rise to my eyes. "You're going to realize that the United States isn't for you either and move to St. Petersburg. I can get you a job."

"I could never do that to my family. Everything they know is here." He frowned. "I'm worried about you, kid."

"I'll be okay. For the first time in a really long time, maybe ever, I'm totally confident that I will be." I stood up and walked over to him, carefully wrapping my arms around him. "I sure am gonna miss you, though." The tears came even though I tried so hard to hold them back. "I don't know what I'm going to do, not seeing you every day."

"Oh you'll see me every day. You're gonna get so sick of me facetiming you." He laughed, but there was a shake in his voice.

It had gotten to both of us.

"Okay," I said, pulling back and wiping my eyes. "I have to finish. The car is gonna be here in an hour."

"You can be angry at me if you want to. I'm helping."

We spent the hour playing tetris to get the rest of my stuff into the boxes and then managed, by some miracle, to get the boxes taped shut. Just as we were finishing up, I got a call from Chandler that the car was downstairs, and it was time to go.

Mitzy walked me down to the car and then gave me another huge hug. "Promise me you'll call when you land."

"I promise," I said.

It was hard to wrench ourselves apart, but we did so eventually so that I could get into the car with my dad and sister. I watched Mitzy as the car drove away, all up until I couldn't see him anymore.

And it officially felt like my old life was behind me.

"Onto the new?" my dad said.

I nodded. "Onto the new."

We arrived at the private tarmac where the jet was waiting and Chandler started to bounce up and down excitedly. "I can't believe we get to ride in a *private jet*. That's so epic."

I snorted at her. "You sound like a thirteen year old."

As we approached the jet, the door to the plane folded out, and my heart jumped up into my throat as I saw Maksim step out onto the stairs. I hadn't seen him in a little under a month, which was *way* too long. Not even bothering to wait for my father or sister, I leapt out of the car and went running up the tarmac. Maks quickly climbed down the stairs and opened up his arms so that I could leap into them. It felt overly cheesy, but I didn't care.

I'd missed him so much.

"Hi," I said with a huge smile.

He gave me a long kiss before responding, "Hi."

Looking out at my father and sister, he raised his eyebrows. "This is going to be an adventure."

"It sure will be," I said.

"Oh, this was delivered for you yesterday." He handed me a manilla envelope and I opened it to find my Investigative Committee of Russia welcome information. "You're gonna be able to make Russia a better place, one criminal at a time."

I laughed. "I plan on taking down the Petrovs first."

A massive smile crossed his face. "I'd like to see you try."

"You guys are insane with this Mr. and Mrs. Smith shit," Chandler barked as she passed us to climb on the plane. "You'll never last. They'll figure you guys out in a second."

"Well, that's the deal," Maks said. "Whoever loses has to change careers."

"Like they'll let you be a cop," my dad said, passing us by as well.

Maksim frowned. "Is that your way of assuming I'm going to lose?"

My dad shrugged. "My Chlocumber isn't a loser," then he and Chandler climbed onto the plane.

"Looks like I have a few things to prove to your family," Maksim said.

I nodded. "Looks like it."

Who knew that the most important thing Maksim and I would have learned in these past four months was that our relationship was most successful when we kept our jobs out of it. Neither of us needed to stop doing what we were doing--we proved that. He'd stay bratva and I'd still be a cop.

"I love you," I said to Maks."

He set a hand on my belly and used the other to pull me close to him. "I love you too."

One of us would lose eventually, and I couldn't wait to see who it was.